To my nephew Ryan Connor Byrne,
the newest member of the clan and
excellent at being Giant Attack Baby during playtime.
You're more effective than Godzilla.
I love you, Ryan!

"So where were you last night?" Rick asked quietly, watching her.

"Sightseeing," she answered.

"Tell me you didn't just go walking around Manhattan at two o'clock in the morning, Sam."

"Okay, I took a cab. A couple of cabs. With enough walking in between that they don't make much of an alibi." She eyed him. "You don't think I had anything to do with this, do you?"

"Of course not. But my insurance company isn't going to pay out twelve million dollars without conducting an investigation. Apparently I'm as much a suspect as you are."

"No," she gasped, horrified. "That's stupid! You're worth like twenty billion dollars. Why would you—"

"Rumors could be as destructive as a conviction," he cut in.

"I didn't do it, but maybe I can help figure out who did." Except that she already had a good idea about that.

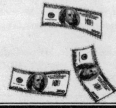

By Suzanne Enoch

Contemporary Titles

BILLIONAIRES PREFER BLONDES
DON'T LOOK DOWN
FLIRTING WITH DANGER

Historical Titles

SOMETHING SINFUL
AN INVITATION TO SIN
SIN AND SENSIBILITY
ENGLAND'S PERFECT HERO
LONDON'S PERFECT SCOUNDREL
THE RAKE
A MATTER OF SCANDAL
MEET ME AT MIDNIGHT
REFORMING A RAKE
TAMING RAFE
BY LOVE UNDONE
STOLEN KISSES
LADY ROGUE

SUZANNE ENOCH

Billionaires *Prefer* Blondes

AVON BOOKS
An Imprint of HarperCollins*Publishers*

AVON BOOKS
An Imprint of HarperCollins*Publishers*
10 East 53rd Street
New York, New York 10022-5299

ISBN-13: 978-0-06-087522-0
ISBN-10: 0-06-087522-4
www.avonromance.com

First Avon Books paperback printing: November 2006

Printed in the U.S.A.

10 9 8 7 6 5 4 3 2 1

Chapter 1

Tuesday, 2:17 p.m.

Samantha Jellicoe liked New York City. Hell, her vagabond shoes were longing to stray, just like the song said. The rest of her verses would go a little differently than Sinatra's, though. She would croon about how the wealthy citizens lived in basic insecurity amid the huddled masses, how all the taxis handily looked the same for timely escapes, and how everyone was so involved in their own crap that they couldn't be bothered to notice anyone else's.

And for people like her, who made their livelihood by slipping their vagabond shoes in and out of places they shouldn't, that made it very close to heaven.

Or rather, she used to make her living by slipping through the shadows and snatching up other people's very expensive belongings. Not any longer. She was now retired from that business. R-E-T-I-R-E-D. Retired. Which didn't explain why she was currently standing on the doorstep of one of the influential elite. All right, she hadn't entirely retired. She'd just gone legit. She had a day job. Yay, her.

With a slight, professionally considered tilt of her head, she smiled and shook the hand of Mr. Boyden Locke. "Glad I could be of help, Boyden," she said, still not entirely certain his name hadn't been designed by some MIT think tank for the purpose of encouraging investors. She would choose something like Samantha Safehouse for herself. "And thank you for the coffee."

He held on to her hand for a moment too long, undoubtedly his way of letting her know that he was interested in more than her advice. As if she couldn't have told that from the way he'd chatted with her boobs for the past forty minutes. Mr. Locke probably had no idea what color her eyes were. His were brown, and they shifted toward his valuables when he talked about them.

"No, thank *you*," he returned. "In my position, it's impossible to be too cautious. I know the house is badly in need of a security upgrade, but I wanted to make sure I found the right person to handle the job."

Somehow he made the comment seem vaguely obscene, but Samantha smiled anyway. She had a hunch that her being the right person for the job had more to do with the man with whom she was currently living than with her credentials. But if being associated with Rick Addison brought her business, then so be it. "I'll write up my recommendations and get them over to you."

"And I'll have my people look them over. And you're welcome to come by for coffee anytime."

Samantha forced her lips to curve further. "I'll keep that in mind. You should have my invoice in the next week or so."

She retrieved her hand and sidled out his door. Once in the clear, Samantha dug into her purse for a tin of Altoids mints. "Coffee. Blech," she muttered, popping a pair of the wintergreen-flavored tabs into her mouth.

Apparently she'd do anything in the name of expanding her business, if she had lowered herself to drinking—okay, barely sipping—coffee. At the corner she turned around and surveyed Locke's house again. Old, elegant, and perfectly located in the old-moneyed East Side, she could see why he'd called to meet with her about his security situation practically the second her flight had landed at La Guardia.

A few years ago she'd hit the house three doors down from him. The Monet inside had netted her a quarter million, and Locke had a Picasso in his drawing room. If the buyer she'd contracted with had preferred modern to Impressionist art, it might very well have been his house she'd hit that night.

His security system was pretty standard, alarms on the doors and windows and sensors on the artwork. For a moment she was tempted to break in through the back door just for old times' sake before she advised Locke on his upgrade. She could have his Picasso in her hands before he had time to pour himself another cup of coffee. With her luck, though, he'd probably think she was coming on to him.

The phone in her purse rang, interrupting her reverie over the semi-good old days. At the familiar sound of the James Bond theme, she grinned. "Hey, studmuffin," she said, with her free hand waving down a taxi.

"Your meeting went well, then," a cool masculine voice replied in a slightly faded British accent.

"You could tell that from three words?"

"Yes. Good is those three words. Bad is five words."

She chuckled, stepping forward as a yellow cab stopped at the curb. Pulling open the door, she slid in. "Madison and Sixtieth," she said, shutting the door. "Which five words?"

"Usually it's 'Get off my back, bub,' as I recall."

"Yeah, but that's not always about business."

He gave an unaccustomed snort. "Samantha Jellicoe, I dare you to come over here and say that to me."

Her mouth went dry. All he had to do was hint about sex, apparently, and she practically had an orgasm. "Randy much?" she joked.

"You have no idea. I actually called, though, to see whether we were still on for dinner tonight."

"I wouldn't want to wreck your surprise."

"I do appreciate that. You're going shopping?"

Samantha resisted the urge to check the cab for hidden cameras. "Which word gave it away?"

"Madison Avenue, darling. Buy something sexy. And red."

"I wouldn't have to keep buying red if you'd stop ripping them off me. And, I have to say, red and sexy would hardly be appropriate for Pauly's Pizza."

"We're not going to Pauly's Pizza."

"If you say so. Since you won't tell me where we *are* going, I'll just see you tonight," she said, and clicked the phone closed.

The taxi stopped and she stepped out onto Madison Avenue before she realized that she'd forgotten to ask Rick how *his* meeting was going. "Shit," she muttered, reaching for her phone again. She dialed his cell.

"Addison," his voice came, cool and professional.

Oops. "You're back in your meeting, aren't you?" she asked, swearing at herself. Of course he would have called her at his only spare moment.

"I am."

"Sorry. I just wanted to find out how it was going. How about saying 'merger' for great, and 'stock options' for fucked?"

For a moment the line was silent. "Merger," he finally said, humor lacing his deep voice.

"Good. I'll see you tonight."

"Certainly. We'll be talking about our stock optioning then."

This time he hung up first. She was getting a little better at the couples thing, anyway, though after five months of living with Rick Addison she probably shouldn't have to remind herself that when he called her, he would be interrupting his own business to ask about hers. Well, there was one way to make up for her slip. "Sexy and red," she murmured, walking up the street and heading into Valentino.

Two hours later she stood in an alley behind an elegant East Side Manhattan townhouse, her shoes and a very slinky red dress tucked up into a ball beneath her tasteful yellow blouse.

Hm. Four o'clock in the afternoon trying to get into a house that opened onto Central Park wasn't exactly something for a rookie, but then she hadn't been a rookie since she'd turned seven and her father had started taking her out for pickpocketing excursions to the park or piazza in whichever city they happened to be.

The butler and two maids and the chef were inside the house, but Samantha had learned their schedule over the last couple of days. At the moment *Dr. Phil* was on, and they'd be in the kitchen, watching. As for the townhouse's owner, he was in his Manhattan office a mile away, meeting about buying something or other. With a slight smile she pulled from her purse the pair of leather gloves she always carried, slung the handbag across her neck and under one shoulder, and Spider-Manned her way up the old, rough brick wall to the fire escape, jamming her fingers and toes into the minute gouges in the mortar. Breaking into Locke's house might be out of the question, but sometimes an itch just needed to be scratched. And she was fairly humming with tension after a day of bored frustration.

Hiking herself over the railing, Samantha trotted up the metal stairs to the third floor. The window at the end of the hallway was shut and locked, of course. Because it was off the fire escape, it was alarmed, as well. The trick, then, was to keep the circuit from being broken. Pulling a metal nail file from her purse, she dug out the silicon seal from around the bottom center panel of glass in the window.

Before she loosened the last bit, she took the small roll of duct tape she always carried and wrapped a length of it backward around her hand. Laying her gloved palm flat on the glass, she made sure she had a good contact, and then gouged out the last bit of sealing with her free hand. The glass panel came free, attached to her glove palm by the tape. She set it aside, picked up the nail file again, and reached inside the window. Pushing the metal file in under the frame to keep the circuits connected, she secured it with another piece of tape, then leaned up and in to unlatch the window. Two seconds later she was inside the house.

Samantha took a moment to frown. That had been way too easy. Somebody was definitely due for a security upgrade.

Easy or not, at least the adrenaline surge took a little of the edge off of nerves that had spent the past two days being polite to people who kept snapping her picture and staring at her chest. Humming to herself, she pulled off her gloves and strolled to the upstairs office to help herself to a Diet Coke from the fridge inside. Halfway through the office door, though, she stopped dead.

A dozen men and women in typical high-class business attire sat around the room, facing the man who stood at the center. In almost cartoon unison everybody turned to look at her.

Crap, crap, crap. "Hi," she said. "Excuse me. Wrong door." Backing out, she closed the door behind her.

She was halfway down the stairs when the door opened again. "Samantha, stop right there."

"I'm sorry." Sam turned on the landing to face the house's owner. "You said you were at your damn office."

Richard Addison. British billionaire, businessman, collector, philanthropist, body like a professional soccer player, and eyes bluer than sapphires. And after five months he still apparently had an incurable woody for one former thief. Hot damn.

"And you said you were shopping." He descended the stairs after her, stopping to lay a palm on her stomach—or where it was under all the padding. "You look good plump."

Yep, he still thought she was cute, bulges and all. "I had a burger for lunch."

"And apparently several large buildings, Godzilla."

"Ha, ha. It's my dress and shoes." She lifted her blouse to pull the bundle out from under her clothes. "I told you I went shopping."

Those deep blue eyes lowered to the bag. "You did buy red."

"You suggested it. But that was when I thought you were at your office, which you apparently weren't."

"I was," he countered, taking the bag from her and draping it over the banister. "We were on *Extra* last night."

Samantha scowled at him. "You see? And you said we'd just slip out of the airport, 'quiet as church mice,' and spend a couple of low-key days in New York." She imitated his British accent as she spoke, noting the responding twitch of his sensuous lips.

"Yes, well, apologies. Anyway, half of New York decided to give me a call today to welcome me back. There's only so much screening a secretary can do when it's everybody from Trump to Giuliani to Bloomberg to George Steinbrenner ringing me. I got tired of it, so we relocated here."

"That's your fault, for being so handsome and rich and famous." She grinned at him. "Just don't try to cancel on me for dinner or the auction tonight."

"How do you know where we're going?"

She flashed him a grin. "Ben asked me what time we wanted the limo. I wheedled it out of him."

"Sneak."

"That's me, all right."

"So are you wearing that dress, then?"

"That's why I bought it."

Rick edged closer, sliding a hand around her waist and drawing her up against him. "All the better for me. No one will be able to take their eyes off you long enough to bid on any of the artwork."

"Everybody dresses up for Sotheby's evening auctions."

"Not the way you do." He kissed her, soft and slow. It made her knees weak. "Tell me how you know about Sotheby's evening auctions."

"I haven't hit Sotheby's in three years, if that's what you're implying." Well, two, anyway, if she counted their London establishment.

"Mm-hm. I'll be finished in the office by six." He leaned down and kissed her again, bending her spine back just to let her know that he meant it. His hand crept up beneath her blouse, sliding along the bare skin of her stomach.

Her toes practically curled. "Okay," she returned, forcing her mind back to matters at hand. "I'm going to grab a snack, then fax Stoney and take a shower." She brushed his hand away, slipped out of his arms, retrieved her dress, and continued down the stairs.

Deep satisfaction swirled down her spine to mingle with heady arousal as he headed back up to his office. *Ha*. She'd done it. This was the third time now she'd broken into one of his houses, and this time he hadn't caught her. He hadn't suspected a thing.

"Samantha?"

Damn. She looked back up to the head of the stairs to see him gazing toward the far window with its missing pane. He had good vision, but hell, not that good. "Yes, Rick?" she said, echoing his tone again. *Never give anything away*. That was one of the thieves' rules as quoted to her by her dad on a regular basis until Martin Jellicoe had ended up in prison and then dead just over three years ago.

"There are a dozen coats and two briefcases in the entryway," Rick was saying. "How did you pass them by without realizing I was here with company?"

"I was distracted. Have fun with your minions."

"And why would you walk through the front door and up the stairs with a dress wadded up under your blouse?"

"My hands were full."

"With that missing windowpane up here, by any chance?" He descended the stairs again. "You broke into the house."

"Maybe," she hedged, backing down to the first floor. "What if I just forgot my key?"

Rick joined her at the foot of the stairs. "You might have knocked at the front door. Wilder is here, and so is Vilseau," he said, tilting his head at her, his eyes growing cool. "And the daytime staff."

He hated having her try to pull one on him, whatever the circumstances. Samantha blew out her breath. At least she knew when to give up. "Okay, okay. Boyden Locke talked to my boobs for forty minutes while I sold him on some security upgrades for his townhouse. And then I went shopping for the dress, and I just kept noticing . . . things."

"What things?"

"Cameras, alarm systems. Everything. It was making me crazy. Plus we're going to an art auction tonight at Sotheby's, of all places. I was just feeling a little . . . tense. So I decided to subvert my bad self by busting in somewhere. I picked a safe place."

"And I caught you again." He reached out, curling a strand of her auburn hair around his fingers. "The last time I did that, we broke a chair afterward, as I recall."

Technically this time he'd caught her well after the fact and only because of a huge mistake on her part, but as the raw, hungry shiver traveled down her backbone, she wasn't about to contradict him. She drew her free hand around the back of his neck and leaned in to give him a deep, soft kiss. "So you want another reward, I suppose?"

He nuzzled against her ear. "Definitely," he whispered.

She was going to explode. "Why don't you get rid of your minions, and I'll reward you right now?"

Rick's muscles shuddered against her. "Stop tempting me."

"But I broke into your big old house. Don't you—"

He pushed her back against the mahogany banister, nearly sending them both over it as he took her mouth in a hard, hot kiss.

Ah, this was more like it. There had to be something wrong with her, with the way that even after five months she couldn't get enough of him. Thank God he had the same problem where she was concerned.

Still, the sooner he finished his meeting, the submerging logical part of her brain said, the sooner they could get to

Sotheby's. Deep as her hunger for Rick ran, that place was like a thief's Mecca. Knowing the special auction was taking place was the reason she'd agreed to abandon her new security business in Palm Beach and join him in New York, though she'd never admit it aloud.

His mouth crept down to her jawline, and her legs turned to spaghetti. "Stop, stop, stop," she muttered, probably so quietly he couldn't hear her.

He could. Rick backed off an inch. "I'm supposed to be the responsible one. Not you, sweetheart."

"I know, but I'm getting hungry."

Rick narrowed his eyes. "For me, for dinner, or for the auction?"

"All three, Brit. Get back to your office and get rid of those guys."

"Give me an hour, Yank."

"You got it. Any more, and I'm going to dinner with the butler."

"No, you're not."

With that he vanished back upstairs, quietly closing the door behind him. For a long moment Samantha frowned up the staircase. Man, she'd screwed up. No, Rick hadn't exactly caught her, but he wouldn't have known anything about her window entry at all if not for her own bumbling. Not that there was any real harm in interrupting one of Rick's meetings except for the embarrassment factor, but she'd just waltzed into a room full of people without having a clue that they were there. If she'd done that in her previous life, she'd probably be lying on her back with a chalk outline around her right now.

She grabbed an apple from the kitchen, probably offending Vilseau the chef, then returned upstairs to the room beside the office. In the large brown and black bedroom suite that she and Rick shared, Samantha flopped backward onto the bed. No doubt about it, she was getting soft. The question was, did it matter?

Obviously as long as she stayed with Rick she couldn't go back to her old way of life. He was too high-profile, and there was that sticky issue of morality, plus the fact that he was chummy with far too many of the people from whom she'd stolen.

It was only the rush that she missed, the intense sensation of being alive that came from sneaking into places she wasn't supposed to be in order to acquire things she wasn't supposed to have. She didn't keep those things, but she had damned well enjoyed the money she got for them.

Right on cue her cell phone rang, to the tune of "Raindrops Keep Falling on My Head." "I told you never to call me here," she said once she dug the phone out of her purse and flipped it open.

"Where are you, then?" came the familiar voice of her ex-fence, surrogate father, and current business partner Walter "Stoney" Barstone. "'Cause unless it's the john, baby, I don't remember you telling me any such thing."

"I meant while I'm on vacation."

"You've never taken a real vacation in your life. And I just wanted to find out how the thing with Locke went."

She blew out her lips. "It went fine. The guy's a perv, but he's loaded. I'll fax you in half an hour or so with the details so we can send him a bill."

Stoney stayed quiet for a beat. "You sound real excited about it."

"Yeah, well, I kind of broke into the house here, and stumbled right into the middle of Rick's meeting."

"What the hell did you do that for?"

"Because I tried to go shopping earlier, and I cased every

store I walked into on Madison Avenue. It was giving me a fucking panic attack."

He had the bad manners to laugh at her. "Then stop shopping on Madison Avenue, honey. There's better stuff at the Metropolitan Museum of Art, anyway. In fact, I know two guys who have open requests for anything you can pick up by Renoir or Degas. We're talking a cool half million for each."

"Shut up. I don't want to know about those people." Frowning at the phone, Samantha rolled onto her stomach. "Besides, I don't do museums, if you'll recall."

"I recall. What about Sotheby's? Did you talk the billionaire into going with you tonight?"

"It was his idea," she returned defensively. "And I'm keeping my hands in my pockets. I'm just going to take in the view, and maybe to advise Rick on artwork."

"Uh-huh. Whatever you say."

"That *is* what I say."

"Fine, honey. I was just trying to help distract you from your crisis."

Samantha blew him a raspberry. "With friends like you, yadda yadda yadda."

"I love you, too, Sam. And hey, as long as I'm already interrupting your vacation, those business cards we've been spreading around Palm Beach are paying off. Aubrey took three calls for appointments over the weekend. One mansion, one art studio, and an attorney's office."

Oh, good, more joy and excitement for her. "Blech. Go talk to 'em, then."

"They don't want to take security advice from me, Sam. They want Rick Addison's girlfriend. The one who has fistfights with murdering heiresses and lays the smackdown on guys who steal paintings from Rick."

"Christ, Stoney, you make me sound like the Masked Mangler or something. I used my brainpower, thank you very much." Of course on various occasions she'd also ended up with a concussion and a bullet graze and a series of other cuts and bruises, but hey, she'd won.

"Then that's what they want. Your brainpower. And you in person."

Three calls on a March weekend in Palm Beach, Florida, wasn't bad at all, when she considered it. Most of the wealthiest part-time residents had left for their summer homes, and the number of year-round residents was tiny compared to the winter influx. "Did Aubrey tell them I was on a business trip?"

"Is that what you're calling it now?" She heard his sigh. "Yes, he told them."

"Then we'll schedule something when I get back. It'll be another ten days or so."

"Whatever you say. Just keep in mind that I'm not running this shit all by myself. We're partners, remember? And besides, I think Aubrey's getting kind of interested in me."

Samantha snorted. "You are pretty cute. Ten days. I promise. I'm trying to be a good significant other."

"Then you'd better quit casing stores. Addison probably wouldn't like that."

He actually hadn't seemed too upset, or even surprised. And she'd told him, which had to count for something. "I'm hanging up now. 'Bye, sweetie."

Groaning, she sat up again and strolled into the bathroom to turn on the shower. As if she needed Stoney to tell her that thievery wouldn't mix with her new life. Hell, she'd been straight for five months now—and it was for her as much as it was for Rick. It was still so odd, to think of a life where she could settle in one place and not have to wipe her fingerprints off every doorknob in case the police or Interpol were following her, looking for evidence.

She was in that new life now. Why, then, did she feel like she both wanted to keep on her toes, and that she needed to? Old habits and all that shit, she supposed. But to stop looking over her shoulder—that would be harder than remembering to smile for the paparazzi.

Chapter 2

Tuesday, 6:08 p.m.

By the time Richard Addison ushered his minions—as Samantha called them—out the front door, he was ready to forgo both dinner out and the Sotheby's auction in favor of spending a quiet evening with Samantha. If he knew her, though, she wouldn't want to do any such thing.

He'd half suspected, in fact, that her enthusiasm to accompany him to New York had a great deal to do with the Sotheby's invitation he'd received—whether she pretended ignorance about it or not. "The Great Masters Auction" sounded right up her alley, so to speak. And if she'd ever attended one before, it hadn't been to bid.

"Samantha?" he said, pushing open the door to the master bedroom suite.

Considering how little time he had to put on his tuxedo and get her to dinner if they were to make the auction, part of him was relieved that she wasn't in the room. On the other hand, having to sit behind his desk for the past hour in order to maintain his dignity hadn't been easy. Forced to concentrate on images of the old Queen Mum while trying to hammer out a reasonable offer for the new Manhattan Hotel, he'd ended up with both a headache and a fair concentration of sexual frustration. Wilder had laid out his tuxedo for him, and after a quick, cold shower that didn't help either affliction, he dressed and headed back downstairs to find his obsession.

She was sitting in the front room, gazing across the street at Central Park. "I hope you took the tag off that dress," he murmured, his throat constricting at the sight of her, "because I'm thinking you should wear it to bed every night."

Samantha faced him, grinning. "We'd get sparklies all over the sheets."

"Yes, we would."

The red of the dress brought out the copper color of her shoulder-length hair, which she'd pinned into some sort of upswept tangle. Richard wanted to run his hands through it. He walked over to offer his hand. "Shall we?"

"Such the gentleman, you are," she drawled in a very good Southern accent, dipping her fingers across his and rising.

The gesture was more because he wanted to touch her than because of his deep-seated gentlemanly qualities. "If you had any idea what I'd like to be doing with you right now, I doubt you'd call me a gentleman," he returned, drawing her up against him to kiss her soft red-colored lips.

"Don't smudge me," she stated, sweeping her arms around his shoulders.

"Later, then," he whispered, taking a step backward and

not trying to hide his reluctance to let her go. Every time he did so, he had the whisper of a thought in the back of his mind that he'd never be able to catch her again. "We have reservations at Bid."

"I've been wanting to see what it looks like now," she said, following him to the foyer where Wilder waited for them, her black shawl in his hands.

"Now? It's only been open a few months."

Samantha flashed him a smile as she allowed the butler to put the shawl over her shoulders. "As a restaurant, yes."

Wonderful. So she'd been in the Sotheby's basement *before* it had been converted to a restaurant. Did he want to know more than that? Yes, but he damned well wasn't going to ask her in front of Wilder.

The limousine pulled up in front just as they reached the bottom of the steps. The driver jumped out and hurried around to open the door for them. "Ben," Samantha said, smiling at the driver. "Did you find that . . . thing I mentioned?"

"What 'thing'?" Richard broke in.

Ben grinned, pulling a candy bar from his pocket. "Chocolate and caramel," he said, handing it to Samantha.

"You rock, man." Favoring the limo driver with a kiss on the cheek that made him blush bright red, Samantha dove into the back of the limo. For a moment Richard second-guessed his decision to fly Ben up from Palm Beach with them. Acquiring a driver in New York would have been a simple matter, but Ben knew things about them, about their . . . habits, that he would never discuss. And therefore having him about provided both of them with an extra layer of security. Or so Richard had thought. The bloody driver was supposed to work for *him*.

Richard followed her. "Don't you dare eat that now."

She was already unwrapping it. "I'll share."

"You'll spoil your dinner."

Samantha scowled at him, and deliberately took a huge bite of the chocolate bar. "We are *not* having this conversation," she mumbled, chewing.

Dammit, she was doing it deliberately, annoying him about the candy so he wouldn't ask her what she knew about the basement at Sotheby's. And he'd very nearly fallen for the distraction. Again. "So tell me about your experiences at Sotheby's."

"Nope." She swallowed, folded the wrapper back over the bar, and tucked it into her purse. Fleetingly he wondered what else she had in the small, red-spangled Gucci bag—probably paperclips, electrical tape, a magnet, and some string. It would all pass security anywhere, and with those tools at her disposal she could lift a Picasso in thirty seconds flat with nothing else needed.

"You said you've hit them before. Three years ago, wasn't it?"

She faced him, her green eyes as cool as her dress was hot. "First of all, do you really want to know the details of my lawlessness? And second, would my answer one way or the other change our plans for tonight?"

Holding her gaze, Richard blew out his breath. "Yes, and no."

Quicksilver humor crossed her face. "I'll assume you're not being wishy-washy."

"Not where you're concerned, my love." He took her hand in his, fiddling with her long fingers. "You know your secrets are safe with me."

"I know." For a moment she gazed past him out the window. "We play at things a lot, but I have to admit that it still makes me . . . squirmy to realize how much you know about me. And how much damage you could do with what you know about me."

"If I may make an observation, I could say the same thing about you where I'm concerned."

"Right. I could tell the world that you're a Great White in the world of business sharks, that you don't like American-style baked potatoes, and that you're hell on wheels in bed. Your reputation would be forever destroyed."

God, he wanted to kiss her right now. Everywhere. "You're changing the subject again."

"Am not."

He tugged her closer, carefully tucking a straying strand of her auburn hair behind one bare ear. She hated earrings; apparently they could fall off at very inopportune moments during cat burglaries. "You asked me if I wanted to know, and I said yes. Now it's up to you. Tell me or not, Samantha, but don't pretend you're not dodging the issue."

"Smart ass." She drew a deep breath, which did some nice things for her breasts beneath the low front of the spaghetti-strapped gown. "I've hit Sotheby's six times."

Six times? That made it the Jellicoe equivalent of a supermarket. "And why are you so set on going there again, and tonight specifically?"

"Do you think I'm setting up another job or something?"

"I think someone might recognize you, and you might end up in prison for a very long time, you nitwit." He shifted his grip from her hand to her elbows, barely restraining himself from shaking her. "And you'd better not give me some flip answer to that."

She actually opened and closed her mouth, as though she'd been considering that very thing. "I always wore a disguise. Wig, colored contact lenses. The last time I was a really hot, booby blonde. This is the first time I'll be attending as me."

Whoever that was. Sometimes he thought that he really had no clue at all. "You think after six times that there's still no chance of anyone coming up with a composite that looks like you?"

"Are you going to let go of my arms?" she asked, her voice dropping. "Because you may remember that I really don't like being grabbed."

No, she didn't. Clamping down on his concern, he released her. All he needed was a knee to the groin to spoil any possibility for fun later in the evening. "Six times. How frequently were you here?" he returned in a more even tone.

"I made it like a yearly thing, starting when I turned sixteen. For some reason I won't be doing it this year." She sent him a sardonic look. "But yes, I probably should have warned you earlier that they might be looking for a girl who's about my build."

The chill in his chest turned into an iceberg large enough to sink the *Titanic.* "Then why are we going, again?" he asked very quietly.

"Truthfully? Because it's a rush." She put a hand over his mouth before he could comment on that tripe. "But nobody's going to do a thing about me being there, firstly because you have an engraved invitation that says 'Richard Addison and Guest,' and secondly because I'm with you. Like they'd try to take down Rick Addison's significant other."

For a moment he ignored the fact that she'd voluntarily referred to herself as his significant anything. Despite his serious reservations, her argument made sense. "So I'm your stay-out-of-jail-free card," he finally muttered.

"You betcha, studmuffin."

"So how booby was this blonde you became last year?"

"*Baywatch.* I think I still have the stuffing somewhere."

"And the wig?"

She sent him an amused glare. "If you prefer booby blondes, you should have stayed married to Patricia."

"I was just curious."

"Hm-hm." To his surprise, she turned her back to settle against his chest. "So how was your meeting, dear? Any hostile takeovers or venture capital thingies?"

Richard lowered his face to her hair, careful not to disturb the arrangement of her 'do. "I love you, Samantha Jellicoe," he breathed, settling an arm around her waist.

"I love you, too, Rick."

She still hesitated, but at least she could say it. And whenever she chose to do so, however rarely it happened, he felt like King Kong climbing the Empire State Building, swatting down all comers. "Hoshido wants to sell the Manhattan," he said. "He can't appear to want to sell it, though, or he'll put himself in the weaker position."

"That whole Japanese honor thing," she returned, nodding against his chest. "They're hard to work with in my biz, too. My old biz, I mean."

The little tangle of worry touched him again, and he forced it away. "Most of the work today was about crafting an approach that both sides can live with. We haven't even gotten close to price or conditions yet."

"Ah. You're still at the dangerous 'howdy' stage of negotiations."

He chuckled, kissing her hair. "Exactly."

"Well, you'll take him down, Brit. You always do."

"That's my plan." Unable to resist, he shifted his hand to glide it down her leg along the slit of her dress. "Are you certain you wouldn't rather do something else tonight?"

"I'm planning on fitting in dinner, Sotheby's, *and* copulation, thank you very much. And in that order, I might—"

The intercom buzzed. With a sigh, Richard reached back to tap it. "Yes, Ben?"

"We're about to pull up, sir. Shall I stop, or go around?"

Ben knew his business routine alarmingly well—Richard preferred a drive around the block to emerging before he was completely prepared for a meeting. Now the driver had grown accustomed to his and Samantha's social routine, as well—he knew he needed to check whether the passengers in the rear seats were clothed or not. "Here is good, Ben."

They pulled to the curb. Samantha straightened as Ben trotted around to pull open the door. "Oh, great," she grumbled, plowing into her purse for a mirror to check her hair and lipstick. Rick hadn't smashed anything too badly, thankfully.

"What?" Rick asked, from his expression clearly not seeing anything wrong with her. Her heart did one of those happy flip-flops. "You look great."

"Not me. The paparazzi."

He followed her jabbing finger toward the monolithic building beside them. "You had to expect it. This is a big night for Sotheby's."

"I know, I know." She took Ben's waiting hand and stepped onto the curb. "But don't you think it would be nice if we auction-going people could enjoy it in privacy for once?"

"Snob," he murmured with a grin. Rick followed her out of the limo and took her hand. Immediately the annoying flashes of mini-lightning began, and she pasted on the bland smile she'd been working on since her first terrifying public outing with Addison. Tomorrow everybody who read either the *Post* or the *Enquirer* would see her name and her photo and know exactly where she was, with whom she spent her time, and what she was doing. But hell, she and Rick had been on nationally syndicated TV last night, so what did it matter, anymore?

"Are you all right?" Rick asked, leaning closer to her. More flashbulbs went off.

Get it together, Sam, she ordered herself. Whatever she'd told him about being in his company at Sotheby's, something could still go wrong. And as Martin Jellicoe used to say, if something could go to hell, it would. The key was to have a contingency plan. "I'm good. Just wondering how badly I'll get flamed on your fan website for this."

He nodded, his gaze on the doorway in front of them. "If you'd quit going on the message board as 'Sally from Springfield,' you'd never know."

"Hey, somebody has to defend my honor, even if it's just me." She dug her fingers into his arm. "And I *knew* you were going there to read the messages."

"You're the one who told me I had a fan website, my love."

Samantha had always thought of herself as the master of distraction and deception, but Rick had turned out to be a fair hand at it, as well. At least she'd stopped grinding her teeth about the press ranged outside Sotheby's.

Obviously they weren't the only auction-attendees who'd decided to dine at Bid before the event, but she—and Rick, especially—definitely didn't just blend into the crowd. Not even when the crowd consisted of the wealthy American upper crust. As they walked inside she recognized them mostly from the magazines Rick had in his office—*CEO*, *BusinessWeek*, and the like. A couple of actors, though most of those in New York tended to be working on Broadway at this time of the evening. Critics and producers, though, who apparently didn't bother to show up to the theater when they didn't have to, were all over the place. She doubted the critics would be bidding.

As soon as they hit the interior of the restaurant Samantha went into her blending routine. She'd learned the rules a long time ago—the key to not being remembered was to be exactly like everyone else. She'd done it for what seemed like forever, and it would take a lot more than Rick Addison to convince her to change that.

"This is great," she murmured, taking the seat the waiter held for her.

"I thought you'd like it," Rick answered, asking for a bottle of wine.

"I didn't expect the color scheme to be beige," she said, half her attention not on the beige walls, but on what covered them and stood tastefully in every nook and cranny. "That's an actual Renoir."

He followed her gaze. "They decorate with pieces going up for auction." Reaching across the table to take her fingers in his, he used the gesture to indicate the alcove in the south corner. "See that one?"

She looked. "The Rodin?"

Rick chuckled under his breath. "You're better than a book."

Samantha grinned at him. "And I can do so many more things than a book can do."

"Don't I know it. What do you think of the piece? The Rodin, to avoid any unnecessary innuendo."

Yep, he knew her pretty well. Taking a sip of wine, she looked again. From his manner he wanted her to be discreet about showing interest, but she practically had a doctorate in that kind of thing. "I've never seen it before. It's definitely his, though. Bold lines, the unfinished stone at the bottom. The mood's very similar to *The Thinker*, isn't it?"

"There's been some speculation that it's a companion piece. It's been in the hands of a single family in Paris since 1883. Their story is that Rodin wanted to put both sculptures on public display, but the city of Paris would only pay for the one."

She continued gazing at it. A nude woman in mid-step, her body slightly twisted as she looked back over her shoulder, her back-facing hand closed and downturned, and the forward-reaching one palm up, fingers stretched out. Her rear foot looked as though it were rising out of the stone, her front one as though it were sinking back into it. "What's it called?" she murmured.

"Fleeting Time."

Before he or anyone else could accuse her of staring, she faced forward again. "I like it."

"I'm going to buy it." He spoke in a whisper, obviously concerned that at least one of their fellow diners might pass that word along and encourage interest in other buyers. "It reminds me of you."

Her cheeks heated. *Great.* A little flattery, and she went all gooey. "I have a better tan."

"And your skin's warmer," Rick agreed, tapping his wine glass against the rim of hers before he took a drink. "Could you find a place for it in the gallery back in Devonshire?"

"Definitely. I designed the sculpture gallery at Rawley House to be oversized. We'll just squish in the Michelangelo closer to the Donatello, and I'll realign some of the lighting."

" 'Squish'?" he repeated, managing not to wince. "Don't tell me any more. You'll spoil my appetite."

"Hm. We wouldn't want that." Samantha glanced at the statue again. "Does it really remind you of me?"

"It does, in ways I can't quite describe."

"And that's why you want to buy it?"

He gazed straight at her. "That's why I intend to own it."

In Rick's presence she'd learned that it was possible to feel safe and uncomfortable all at the same time. At his words, that same whisper of satisfaction and uneasiness twisted up her spine. Of course, he was being metaphorical—he didn't want to precisely *own* her, but he did want a little more control. But hell, she was having a hard enough time handling herself without letting somebody else into that arena.

The waiter appeared, and she was grateful enough for the interruption that she probably smiled a little too hard at him as she ordered the guinea fowl. Rick went for the sea bass.

As soon as the waiter left, Samantha blew out her breath. "Look, I don't—"

"You never gave me any details about your meeting with Boyden Locke," he interrupted, buttering a piece of table bread. "Anything interesting?"

"So now *you're* changing the subject?" she asked, lifting an eyebrow.

A smile touched the corners of his mouth. "You're bloody fearless, my dear," he returned, "but I know when I've blundered into your panic button. Did Locke show you his Picasso?"

"Yep. And he showed me the wiring circuitry and the alarm panel. If I were still in the business, I'd have a field day with his shit."

"Samantha."

"I know, I know. But people are so damned trusting." She leaned forward, tapping his knuckles with her butter knife.

"If I walked into your house, would you show me your security system just because I said I knew Donald Trump and I had nice tits?"

He laughed. "No, but then I'm fairly suspicious. One time a female thief did try to break into my—"

" 'Try?' " she repeated.

"The point being, if you could *prove* that you knew Trump—as in you both appeared in several magazines together and were known to be living with him—then I might be more inclined to trust you. Locke knows your history. The part that's for public consumption, anyway."

"And that's all he went by. Poof, she's in New York. Poof, she knows Rick Addison."

"So I'm a passport and a calling card. If that brings your business more attention, then what's the difficulty?"

"There isn't one." She frowned at him. "I'm just cynical."

"I've noticed that about you. Some of your clients do call me first to check up on you, if that makes you feel any better."

"Who's called you?"

"Some of them. Obviously I say nice things about you."

"Gee, thanks. Did Locke call you?"

"No. Apparently he did use the 'poof' method, as you suspected."

She could have spent the next forty minutes speculating about why Rick had decided not to tell her that some of her potential clients were checking up on her until that moment, or she could enjoy some very tasty pancetta-coated guinea hen. She took the second option, mainly because it also allowed her to gaze about the room. Rick had been right about the decor: plain walls, but covered with representatives of the pieces going up for auction. Christ. She hoped nobody slopped spaghetti sauce on the English landscape painting by Constable.

They had to be alarmed, didn't they? Or did Sotheby's rely on the number of witnesses, the crowded gauntlet of booths and tables, and the scattered security to ensure the safety of what amounted to millions of very tantalizing dollars?

"What is it?" Rick asked, interrupting her thoughts.

Samantha blinked. "What is what?"

"You're practically drooling."

"I am not. I'm just wondering at the level of security. The last time I was at Sotheby's, this was the storage basement. I mean, forget thieves, but what if somebody sneezed on a Rembrandt?"

"I don't know what precautions they take. Would you like me to put in a request to see the director?"

She wasn't entirely certain whether he was teasing her or not, but she was not going to have a sit-down with a guy whose business she'd robbed a half dozen times over as many years. "I'm not that curious. When do we go upstairs?"

"The auction starts in an hour. I figure we'll have time to take a walk around the gallery before it begins."

"Good. I like that part."

"I imagine you would."

For a moment Samantha concentrated on her dinner. "You really are acting like you think I'm going to pull a job or something."

"You're the one who agreed to join me in New York only after I received the invitation to come here tonight."

Okay, so he'd noticed. "This isn't the only reason I'm in New York. But I admit, I *am* curious to be here in a legitimate capacity—even if it's just as Rick Addison's arm candy."

"You're a very sour type of arm candy tonight," he noted mildly. "I wish you would tell me what's truly troubling you.

It has something to do with your shopping today, I know, but you're a bit of a tough nut to crack, as they say."

"I'll take that as a compliment." Inhaling a deep breath, Samantha set down her knife and fork. "Okay. I don't know what's bugging me. I'm just all keyed up for something when I damn well *know* nothing's going to happen."

Deep blue eyes gazed at her. "It makes sense. You've spent most of your life walking into trouble and then avoiding the consequences of it. So now—"

"Hey," she cut in, scowling. "That does not sound very flattering."

"It's a fact. You steal a Monet, and then do your damnedest not to get caught. So now that your life has calmed down a little, I think you're waiting for the proverbial other shoe to drop."

"I really hate being analyzed."

"I'm just attempting to help."

"Well, stop it. Whatever's bugging me, I'll deal. And not by grabbing a Picasso and running for it, so don't worry."

"I always worry, but not about that."

After that it seemed a better idea to just keep her thoughts to herself and finish dinner. Rick evidently realized he was about one word away from getting a three-inch heel stuck in his calf, because he desisted as well. Yes, perhaps she was overly aware of her surroundings—like that was a bad thing. Maybe it wasn't entirely necessary any longer, but considering that in the five months since she'd met Rick she'd been nearly blown up, had her head broken, been in two car crashes, been shot, and had ended up on a first-name basis with at least one Palm Beach police detective, being aware seemed a pretty bright reaction.

"Dessert, or gallery?" Rick finally asked, touching his

napkin to his mouth in that very macho yet sensual and sophisticated way he had.

"Gallery," she decided, despite the sight of the decadent chocolates rolling by on the dessert tray.

Rick stood, making his way around the table to hold her chair and assist her to her feet. "Then let's get this show on the road."

"Amen to that."

Chapter 3

Tuesday, 8:21 p.m.

"I suppose we have you to thank for this?" Richard murmured as he retrieved his keys and watch from the far side of the metal detection kiosk.

Just behind him Samantha picked up her beaded red purse from the neighboring table. "Probably," she returned in the same low tone, hooking her arm around his. "The security seems to get a little tougher every year. It was kind of fun, trying to figure out what they'd come up with next, and what I'd need to do to get around it."

The most recent Sotheby's auction Richard had attended had been two years ago in London, and security had been adequate if low-key in deference to the clientele. Here in New York, he supposed the next step up would be a body cavity search. "And you're absolutely certain no one here will recognize you from those 'fun' little encounters?"

She leaned the curve of her body against his side, and his

heart accelerated in response. "They probably recognize me from being with you, or they think they recognize me from somewhere, but nobody's going to make me for lifting paintings here."

God, she was so confident—but from what he'd seen of and learned about her, she had every right to be. "I'll take your word for it, then—but I'm keeping my guard up, anyway."

Samantha shot him her quicksilver grin. "I have to admit, it'd be kind of cool to see you running interference for me while I make an escape."

"Just remember that you're not going anywhere without me."

They passed what seemed like an absurd number of both uniformed and plainclothes security officers, though if Samantha Elizabeth Jellicoe had actually been on the prowl, he doubted all of Sotheby's personnel would have been enough to prevent her from doing exactly what she intended.

And anyone who didn't know her would think Samantha was completely at ease and enjoying the evening. While he personally didn't doubt the latter, he could see her alert gaze, the way she noted every camera, every exit, and everyone who stood between her and the street.

Keeping in mind that Samantha's self-confidence could on very rare occasions be exaggerated or misplaced, he seated them toward the back of the room and right on the center aisle. Unnecessary as it probably was, Richard had made it his primary job to keep her safe. And however much that task might distract him from some of his substantial business interests, it was also quite possibly the most exciting, arousing thing he'd ever done. For someone of his experience and background, that was saying a great deal.

"Ladies and gentlemen, I am Ian Smythe," the thin,

black-clothed man said from the podium at the front of the room, "and I will be your auctioneer tonight. Please be aware that in addition to the bidders on the floor, we have twenty phone lines and five Internet accounts set up for interested parties unable to attend in person this evening."

Samantha leaned up to Richard's ear, the caress of her breath warm and intoxicating. "Or for those unwilling to reveal their identities to the IRS or to any cat burglars who might be seated in the audience," she finished.

Yes, she was definitely enjoying herself. "Shh."

"And one further announcement," Ian continued. "We are very excited to report that while our experts were evaluating the Hogarth painting listed in the sales catalog as number 32501, a second Hogarth was discovered stretched on the same frame beneath the first one. After consulting with the owners, Sotheby's is pleased to announce that they have decided to place the second Hogarth up for sale, as well. The piece will be available for viewing at intermission, and will be designated as item number 32501A."

From the sudden chattering and excited murmurings of the crowd, Richard wasn't the only one surprised by the news. Samantha snatched the sale catalog from his lap and flipped to the appropriate page.

"The Fishing Fleet," she said, gazing at the photo of the known Hogarth. "This one's pretty famous. Do you know who the owner is?"

Richard shook his head. "Obviously it hasn't changed hands recently, or someone would have realized there was a second painting tucked behind the first one well before now. The theme of *The Fishing Fleet* is unusual in itself—William Hogarth's usual focus was on satirical social commentary. This one's just . . . lovely."

"That is so cool," she breathed, handing him back the

glossy catalog. "While I was working at the Norton Museum doing restoration, we—"

"Your legitimate job," he broke in with a slow smile.

"Yes, one of the few. Anyway, we discovered a second canvas behind a Magritte, but it was just an unsigned mess, like his kid had been doodling with the paints and he just didn't bother to take it off the frame before he put up a new canvas."

"It does happen, rarely. If I kept the Hogarth under wraps until our gallery at Rawley House opens, it would get us a great deal of free publicity. He is an English artist, after all."

Samantha lifted an eyebrow. "Jump the gun much? You kind of have to own it before you can exploit it."

Taking her hand, Richard lifted it to kiss her knuckles. "If I like it, I'll own it."

"Mm-hm." She pulled her hand free none too gently. "Watch that bragging, Brit. I'm here due to a coincidence of mutual insanity. Not ownership."

Dammit. Eventually he'd remember that she didn't need to be impressed by his power and wealth. In fact, their frequent mention was probably the surest way to drive her away. "Apologies, Samantha," he murmured. "I just meant that you shouldn't doubt my resolve."

She snorted. "Oh, I don't doubt that. You're one resolved guy. Bid away. I'm just here for the view."

Thankfully Ian Smythe banged his gavel and opened the auction before Rick could start protesting that he'd never tried to influence her with his money. Samantha sat back a little and blew out her breath. Rick made life easy and safe and comfortable, and the part of her that had been looking over her shoulder for most of her life just wanted to fall into the goose-down pillows and pull the satin sheets over her head.

Thankfully the other part of her—the one that could count to seven (the number of years before a statute of limitations for a nonlethal crime expired)—knew that she still had about six years to go before she could truly begin to relax. And that same part of her remained deathly afraid that "comfortable" might equal "boring." It certainly had when she'd talked with Boyden Locke today. And when she'd consulted with the other dozen clients she'd advised over the past two months. The money was good, but compared with the way she used to earn a living, it just felt too . . . easy.

Of course, the excitement of her old life had its own drawbacks, too. She'd gotten a couple of hard looks from the more senior of Sotheby's security staff, but she'd been right that Rick Addison provided a hell of a security blanket. Pressing a little closer against his side, she settled into the exciting rhythm of bids and nodding and the outbursts of applause and commentary. Funny, the last time she'd done this, her heart had been going a million miles an hour while she waited for somebody to make the winning bid on a particularly valuable Degas so the staff would return it to its secure location in the basement. And then she'd gone to work.

With a slight smile at the memory, she returned to gazing at New York's uppermost upper crust. Some of them were definitely old money, but even if they weren't regular newsmakers, she knew who they were. She'd relieved at least a dozen of them of some valuable or other in the course of her career. Halfway back on the far side of the room her eyes found a figure standing in the shadow of one of the modern sculptures up for bid. Medium height, thin, wiry build, light brown hair running to gray, and an expensive-looking, tasteful suit, he fit the room as well as anyone else did—except for his hands.

Long fingers twiddled, tapping his thighs in a rhythm

that had more to do with nerves than with Ian Smythe's melodious, cajoling voice or the bang of the auctioneer's gavel. As though sensing her gaze, he turned and looked straight at her, brown eyes into her green ones, then faced forward again.

She'd known those eyes for all but the last six years of her life. Martin Reese Jellicoe.

Samantha lurched forward, gasping forcefully enough that she could hear the ragged shake of her own breath. Her heart just stopped. Her fingers abruptly went ice-cold, and her purse clattered to the floor at her feet. Even in the drone of noise from the large room, it seemed loud.

"Samantha?" Richard murmured, glancing sideways at her before he bent down to collect her handbag and return it to her lap. "Sam? What is it?"

Get it together, get it together. Just because a ghost stood thirty feet from her and she'd lost her mind and she needed to scream and throw up and run away to somewhere quiet where she could *think*, didn't mean she had to let anyone else know. "Sorry," she drawled back. "All these dollar figures are making me giddy."

He chuckled softly. "Wait till you hear *me* get going."

Samantha barely noted what he said. She took a slower breath. Waiting long enough so no one would notice that her attention was focused on a particular someone in the audience rather than on the auction, she looked back into the shadow again. She'd more than half thought she'd be gazing at empty space, but he was still standing there.

Holy fucking shit. Her father—her *father*—was at Sotheby's. Her dead father. The one who'd died in a Florida prison three years ago, and whose cheap prison-grounds burial she'd watched through binoculars from a half mile away. Martin Jellicoe might have been a hell of a cat burglar at one time, but even at his peak he couldn't have faked his own death. Escape, sure—that was how he'd ended up at the Okeechobee Correctional Institution, the third and highest-security prison that had attempted to hold him.

Trying to keep her breathing steady and her heart from pounding right through her rib cage, Samantha reached into her purse and fingered her cell phone. Who was she supposed to call, though? The Florida State Board of Corrections? The Ghostbusters? Stoney? If Stoney had known about this . . . She couldn't imagine that he could know and not tell her. Not after all that they'd been through together. But then her father knew, obviously, and he'd been somewhere other than six feet under for the past three years. And for the past five months she'd had a very public address. If he'd bothered to contact her, she probably would have remembered.

"Here we go," Rick said beside her.

She jumped. "What?"

"The Rodin." He sent her a half-annoyed look. "Do try to stay awake. I, at the least, find this to be rather exciting."

"So do I," she countered, shaking herself again. It would be so damned much simpler if she could just walk over and ask Martin where he'd been and what he was up to, but every instinct she possessed screamed that it'd be a very bad idea. "I was just thinking about the Hogarth," she lied. "I wonder when they actually discovered the second painting."

"I'll ask at intermission." He lifted the catalog in his hand, easy and casual, and Ian Smythe added another ten thousand dollars to the going price of the statue. A minute later, the price started jumping in fifty-, then hundred-thousand-dollar increments.

Intermission. Maybe she could arrange to talk with Martin then. As she sat and tried to match her expression to Rick's calm, mildly amused and interested one, yet another thought joined the others crashing through her brain: the *why* of Martin Jellicoe—the why here and why now.

If *she'd* been the reason, he could have made his appearance anytime before now. Even not counting the past three years, there had been shopping for two hours earlier today, and the morning run she'd taken through Central Park several hours before that. Sotheby's wasn't a logical place to spring his non-death on his daughter, which meant he wasn't there tonight for her. Which left the other option—theft. But of what?

"The bid on the phone is twelve million four hundred thousand. Do I have twelve-five?" Ian Smythe's voice interrupted her thoughts again.

Rick raised the catalog.

"Twelve-five. Twelve-six anywhere?"

"Rick," Samantha whispered, "can I see the catalog?"

"Now?" he mouthed.

"Yes."

"I'm using it."

"I need to look at something." For a clue about what might have enticed her father to suddenly reappear after three years.

He signaled with it again. "Look in a minute."

Samantha drew in a breath. "Fine." Wrestling him for it wouldn't do her much good. Anxious, nervous as she was for answers, another five minutes would hardly change anything.

"The bid is now thirteen million dollars with Mr. Addison," Smythe said, twirling the gavel in his hand. "Do I hear thirteen two-fifty?"

The room around them buzzed, but no one blinked, nodded, scratched, or lifted a hand. Samantha held her breath, too. Rick wanted the Rodin, but he was also a keen businessman who wouldn't pay more than something was worth.

Whatever his limit was, they had to be close to it. His expression, though, remained calm and unconcerned. Despite her nerves, anticipation coursed through her. And she was only a damned interested bystander. He was amazing. No wonder he owned a good portion of the world.

"No one? Thirteen-two, perhaps? Mrs. Quay? No? All right, then, going, going, gone"—and the mallet struck the desk—"to Richard Addison for thirteen million dollars." Smythe smiled. "Congratulations, sir. Or should I say, my lord?"

The room burst into applause, which Samantha belatedly echoed, as Rick waved away the question. He was so low-key about his blue blood that most people—unless they were a part of his fan club—probably had no idea that he was the Marquis of Rawley, a real, genuine aristocrat. "You're so cool," she breathed at Rick, sliding over to give him a kiss on the lips.

"Thank you, my love." He had the good manners to pretend that she made such gestures of affection in public all the time, and broke the kiss before she could do so. Then he handed her the catalog. "Now, what did you want to look at?"

"Just some—"

"Rick, congratulations." Thankfully one of the other bidders interrupted before Samantha had to make up something that would hopefully sound less confused than she felt.

While Rick chatted with well-wishers and handlers brought in the next piece, Samantha flipped through the catalog. If Martin was here to make off with something, it would have to be a painting—none of the sculptures tonight were small or light enough for a snatch-and-run. But which painting?

She paused at the photo of the Hogarth again. The second

Hogarth, the one nobody here had set eyes on yet, wouldn't be the most expensive sale of the night, but it would probably be the most noteworthy. If her dad had learned about it at the same moment the rest of the room had, though, it probably wasn't what he was after.

"Did you find what you were looking for?" Rick asked, bending sideways to look down at the page with her. "The Hogarth again? You do hate mysteries, don't you?"

"I like them when they're solved," she returned. "When's intermission?"

"After the Manet." He gazed full at her, dark blue eyes curious. "What's going on?"

"Nothing." She shrugged, refusing to let her eyes stray toward the figure in the shadows. "Okay, maybe I'm used to being more occupied at events like this."

"Do you want to bid on the new Hogarth for me?"

Samantha blinked. "Christ, no. But are you sure *you* want to bid on it, sight unseen? What if you hate the look? Or what if it's a scam?"

"I generally like Hogarth's works. And don't worry, I'm going to get a verified provenance for the other painting before I do anything." He took her fingers in his. "Would you look at it, too? You're faster and more accurate at spotting fakes than anyone else I've ever met."

"Thanks, I think. Sure, I'll take a look at it." Crap. So much for spending the intermission talking with her dead father.

Rick brushed his thumb along the inside of her wrist. "Relax, Samantha. The only thing you have to worry about tonight is me. Have I mentioned that I find auctions rather arousing?" He kissed her earlobe.

Despite her distraction, she shivered. No matter what else might be on her mind, Rick Addison had the ability to make her hot and horny every time she set eyes on him. When he was actually trying to turn her on, Jesus, everybody just get out of the way. "You made me wet," she whispered, arching her neck to his mouth.

"Christ," he muttered back. "Let's forget the Hogarths and get out of here. I want to be inside you."

Oh, God, she wanted to. But if they left now, she might never catch up to Martin again. And she needed some damned answers. "Keep your pants on, Brit," she ordered in a barely audible tone. "You can have me later."

"I intend to. Now give me the booklet back so I can cover my lap and keep some dignity."

Samantha snorted. No, he wasn't distracting at all. She handed him the catalog. "You're so easy."

"Only where you're concerned."

The Manet went for seven million and change, and as Ian Smythe called for a twenty-minute break, half the audience rose and headed for the covered display to one side of the room. Rick wasn't the only one interested in a newly discovered Hogarth. As he took her hand and led her over to join the crowd, Samantha couldn't help glancing in Martin's direction once more. Her father hadn't moved.

If not for the tapping of his fingers, he might have been another piece of modern art. It was an old, effective trick, though. Stand still in an inconspicuous place, and people tended not to notice you. And then if you suddenly weren't there any longer, those same people thought they'd probably been mistaken about seeing you in the first place. Or at least they thought so until the alarms started going off and the cops showed up. You were long gone by then, of course.

Shock and disbelief still pushed at the back of her mind, but she shoved them out of the way. The how's and what's could wait until she had time to consider them. The why's were what mattered at the moment.

"Yes," one of the Sotheby's painting experts was saying, obvious excitement running just beneath the smooth saleswoman pitch in her voice, "it was about two weeks ago. Before auction we verify the authenticity and ownership of every item, and it was during that inspection that we discovered a second canvas tacked beneath the first. The first Hogarth had been passed down as an inheritance, and likely hadn't been closely examined for better than fifty years."

With a flamboyant twitch, she pulled off the sheet that covered the canvas. Samantha looked at it with the same interest as everyone else—with one exception. In addition to admiring the sure strokes and the pastels of an ocean at sunrise, a fishing fleet frothing across its surface, she also noted size and framing and deduced probable weight. Sotheby's had known for two weeks. It would have been discovered after the sales catalog went out, which explained the lack of publicity, but she doubted everyone involved had kept quiet about it. The auction house could use some positive publicity, and hell, they made a percentage on every sale.

Two weeks. In her experience that was more than enough time for someone to learn about it, decide he or she wanted to own what almost no one else even knew about, and make an arrangement for a delivery. Dammit. Martin had to be here for the Hogarth.

"It's magnificent, isn't it?" Rick murmured from her shoulder. "Better than the one that covered it."

"I like the rendering," she admitted. "They had to be companion pieces."

He nodded. "I agree. Looks as though I'll be acquiring both of them. They shouldn't be separated."

The expert started to cover the painting again. Samantha knew where it would go from there—back into a safe holding area until its turn for bidding. And she knew just how safe it was likely to be there. "Excuse me," she said, using her naive, breathy voice, "would it be all right to leave it in view? I'd like a few more minutes to look at it."

The crowd agreed with her, and after a quick conversation two employees carried the painting and stand over to one corner of the auction podium. When Samantha turned with Rick to take her seat again, she found Martin gazing at her. That answered that. He *was* after the Hogarth. And so was Rick. *Fuck.*

This was one nightmare she'd never expected to have. And she only had the space of three paintings to figure it out. After that the first Hogarth would go up for bids.

Okay. She was used to figuring things out quickly. Important things. Life-or-death things. What did she have, then, three options? One, tell Rick that Martin was not dead, that he was in New York, and that he was apparently looking to steal one or both of the paintings Rick had his eye on. Two, approach Martin, tell him hello and to lay off the Hogarths because her boyfriend wanted to buy them. Or three, get Rick to pass on the paintings, go home, and have sex with him until they both passed out and she could wake up and realize she'd just been dreaming about Martin.

Definitely option number three. He'd already suggested leaving early, anyway.

"Rick?" she said, edging up against his side.

"Mm-hm?" His gaze and his attention remained on the auction.

"I was just thinking about what you said earlier. Before intermission. You know, it was a pretty good idea." She stretched, brushing her fingers along his thigh.

He glanced at her. "Beg pardon?"

"How direct do you want me to be, sweetie?" she breathed. "All these paintings, all this money—I'm getting a little hot and b—"

"No, you're not," he countered, a brief frown crossing his lean face. "What are you up to?"

"Nothing. I'm not up to anything, except trying to tell you that I want to be hot and sweaty and naked with you."

He faced her. "Why do you want to leave right now, Samantha?"

Apparently she'd lost all of her mojo tonight, if Rick wanted an explanation for why she wanted to have sex with him. So was she supposed to be offended, then, or keep trying? "If you're going to interrogate me, I'm not going to put out, bub."

His expression eased a little. "Then you just lie there and watch, and I'll go to work on myself while you decide whether you want to join in or not."

Her mouth went dry. "Christ, Rick. Let's get out of here."

"Give me fifteen minutes, and we'll have two Hogarths if you want to bring them home with us. They can watch."

Okay. Option one had been telling Rick that Martin had reappeared. Crap. Rick hated that she stayed close to Stoney, and the fence had retired when she did. If he found out that an apparently escaped and not deceased felon who happened to be her dad was in the room and wanted the Hogarth, he'd go ballistic. He'd questioned her motives for being in New York as it was—and he was more than half right. Aside from that, she hated giving explanations when she didn't know all the answers yet herself. She needed to talk to Martin. There was kind of a thieves' honor code anyway, once they reached the level of skill that she and Martin had. When Rick began bidding, her father would acknowledge that the paintings were her grab, legit or not, and he'd back off. At least until she could talk to him.

That made sense. And since there was nothing else she could do at the moment short of setting off the alarms and yelling, "Fire!," it would have to do. She sank back against Rick's side, and he slung an arm around her bare shoulders.

"Are you back to putting out again now?"

"Hoo yeah. Just hurry this up."

"Your wish is my command, my love."

Damn, he was stubborn, but on the upside he was the smartest guy she'd ever met and sexy as hell, to boot. If she couldn't talk him out of bidding, she would have to hope Martin would remember—and would abide by—the honor thing. But she needed to be certain, and she still needed to talk to him.

She dug into her purse for a scrap of paper and a pen as bidding began on the first Hogarth. Only for a second did she consider that her first—well, second—reaction to seeing her supposedly dead father was concern that he might make trouble for Rick and for her. She'd never claimed, though, to come from the Brady Bunch or the Cunninghams or whatever passed for a normal family these days.

"M," she scratched out, while Rick's attention was on the rising price of Hogarth number one, "Meet me at the Balto statue at tee-2/devil." She had a great deal more she wanted to say, but time, space, and a well-honed paranoia made her keep it short and to the point. No names, no dates—even the "M" was pushing things a little. She had no doubt that he would remember the code for two a.m. Night was safer, though she badly wanted to see him in daylight.

The gavel pounded at the front of the room, making her jump. For a second she had no idea who'd won the painting, until the man seated behind them patted Rick on the shoulder. "Well done, Addison."

"Thanks."

As Rick faced her, Samantha leaned in to give him a soft kiss on the mouth. "You buy things better than anybody I know," she breathed.

He chuckled against her mouth. "Five million is a bit low. The fight'll be for the second one. What are you writing?"

"I thought of something I need to tell Stoney," she lied smoothly.

"Did y—"

"Our next lot," Ian Smythe announced right on cue, "is 32501A. I have an opening commission bid of . . . two million seven hundred thousand. Do we have eight anywhere?"

A dozen hands, fingers, catalogs, eyebrows, and chins went up. Obviously Rick and Martin weren't the only ones after the Hogarth. As she spied one of the CEOs of Mobil Oil waggling his fingers, Samantha hoped for a moment that someone besides Rick would end up with the painting. Then Martin could do whatever he wanted with it—which didn't answer the question of how the hell he was still alive, but it did mean he and Rick , and he and she, wouldn't be in direct conflict.

"Ah, I can see we could just skip ahead a little," Smythe said, to a murmur of laughter. "Let's go with five million, then, shall we? Anyone care to join me here?"

The same dozen bidders answered, plus another four or five. "You've got about fifteen competitors," Samantha murmured, surreptitiously looking around.

To her surprise, Rick lowered the catalog. "I'll wait, then," he returned in the same tone. "I hate to be just one of the crowd."

"That's one of the things I'm best at."

"Not from where I'm sitting." He took her hand, squeezing her fingers gently. "Who's that sitting about two rows straight behind us? Smythe keeps glancing that way, but I have no intention of turning around."

"Bill Crawford," she answered without looking.

"Great. The Getty buyer."

"Yep. Does he have more money to play with than you do?" she asked, as the bidding went up to seven million, with about a quarter of the bidders falling out.

"I suppose we'll find out, won't we?" He grinned; not the soft, sexy one he had for her, but the dark, predatory one where he practically bared his fangs. Sam was glad she wasn't Bill Crawford. Her Great White was about to glide into the feeding frenzy.

At nine million eight hundred thousand, only three others remained in the game, and Rick joined in again. Somebody behind them swore in response, the sound nearly buried beneath the excited murmurs and louder speculations of the onlookers. Samantha couldn't be certain that the guy cursing had been Crawford, but she wouldn't bet against her hunch, either.

She glanced in Martin's direction. He wasn't looking at the podium any longer, but rather half faced the audience, no doubt trying to assess who would walk off with the win and what that person would do with the painting. Most bidders, even the ones present, would probably have it shipped by Sotheby's, which meant it would still be vulnerable in the depths of the building for a few hours after the auction. Or during it.

Rick wanted the paintings to go to his estate in England, as well. That could be a problem. They were up to ten million six now, just Rick against one phone bidder and Crawford. If he was frustrated at not being able to see either of his opponents face to face, he didn't show it. In fact, for a guy who was probably going to spend something in the neighborhood of thirty million dollars in one night, he looked as cool as a proverbial cucumber. He might have been playing nickel slots in Vegas, for all the concern he showed. Oh, yeah, he'd come to play.

She pulled out her lipstick and mirror, glancing at Rick as she did so. If he didn't want her to take a look behind her, he would let her know. Instead, though, he glanced over at her, his eyes dancing. "How does Crawford look?" he breathed.

Taking a peek, she touched her lip with her pinky and then lowered the mirror again. "I'd give him another quarter million, and then he's going to either barf or pass out. You've got him."

"Don't you know it, sweetheart."

Even as she chuckled, she added an addendum to her note—"Hands off Mike." "Mike" was short for Michelangelo, their code for artwork in general. Paintings specifically were Vince—for Van Gogh—but Rick had just purchased a Rodin, too, after all. The thieves' code said Martin should pass on Addison's take just because she had the closer connection, but her dad had never exactly played by the rules when he could avoid it. And Martin was definitely out hunting.

Whether Rick ended up with the second Hogarth or not, she wanted to be able to talk to Martin without either of them risking arrest. She had a big basketful of questions for him—and for herself, when she had a few minutes to think in private. Hell, her father was *alive*. And that was huge. Huge, and very worrying. Forcibly she pushed those thoughts away to be stewed over later.

"Ten million eight. Do I hear ten million nine?"

Samantha shifted a little, for a moment wishing she was

one of those girls whose only concern in life was not messing up a fresh manicure. It would be boring as hell, but safe except for the worry over hangnails.

"Getting impatient?" Rick murmured at her. "Or bored?"

"Just anticipating the victory celebration," she whispered back, brushing her thigh against his.

"So am I. Let's test your theory about Crawford, shall we?" He lifted the catalog again. "Eleven million," he said in a carrying voice.

The audience muttered admiringly. Yes, her fella would spend an extra half million just to get a little more fuck time with her.

"We have eleven million from Mr. Addison."

She lifted her mirror again. "Crawford just shook his head. Wuss."

"Shut up," Rick murmured. "Don't rile the potential competition."

"Mr. Crawford," Smythe said, "I can take fifty thousand, if you don't wish to go by hundreds. No? Very well, then. Our phone bidder, Jenny?"

"Eleven million two," came from the short woman holding the phone.

Smythe gestured from her to Rick. "We have eleven m—"

"Twelve million," Rick interrupted, gazing at Jenny rather than the auctioneer.

The poor thing looked rattled as she repeated the amount into the handset. Samantha couldn't blame her. Rick could be pretty formidable, even toward the messenger. After a moment her expression eased into relief, and she shook her head. Game over.

"No further bids? Then"—The gavel slammed down—"sold to Mr. Addison for twelve million dollars. Congratulations again, sir."

The room burst into applause. Samantha joined in—until Rick stood, pulled her to her feet, and smacked a kiss on her mouth in classic Victory Day style. Little as she liked both being confined and public displays, she swept her arms around his shoulders and hung on as he bent her farther backward.

"Was that the victory celebration?" she asked, as he sat her upright and she could breathe again.

"Hardly," he replied, taking her hand in his as he kissed her again. "Let's get out of here, shall we?"

Not until she'd made sure all of his purchases were safe. "What about our art?" she asked, resisting his pull.

"I'll have it shipped to England."

Every fiber told her what a bad idea that was. "Can't we bring them to the townhouse? You suggested it, anyway."

He lowered his eyebrows. "Not the Rodin. It weighs half a ton."

"The Hogarths, though?" she pursued, wishing for a moment that her past would stop biting her in the ass. "Come on, Rick. I used to steal paintings that were set aside for shipping. Leaving 'em here makes me jumpy."

"Really?"

"Really."

Okay," he said after a moment. "I'll go have a word with Talmadge."

"Thanks." Ron Talmadge was Sotheby's director of sales, though she wondered how he'd managed to keep his job for the last nine years when she'd personally taken about eighty million dollars' worth of paintings from the premises. For a second she wondered whether Rick had any idea that her visits here had netted her nearly fifteen million bucks. Of course, *netted* wasn't exactly the right word; thieves had a lot of people to pay off if they wanted to keep out of jail.

Staying in the shadows could be damn expensive. Still, she was a member of the millionaire club, even if he'd surpassed that level.

As soon as Rick walked to the side of the room and signaled Talmadge, Samantha folded her note deep into her palm and headed toward the restroom. As she passed her father she took a shaky breath and slipped the note into his pocket.

Her fingers brushed the wool of his coat and she shivered, speeding up her retreat. Jesus, she'd touched him, and he hadn't vanished into smoke. He was real. Martin Jellicoe was actually alive. And she'd just made an appointment to see him in four hours. Life was very strange.

Chapter 4

Tuesday, 10:53 p.m.

Deep satisfaction ran through Richard as he waited near the Sotheby's entrance for Samantha. He had the Rodin, a classic painting, and one never-before-seen Hogarth, which left the rest of the evening with nothing to do but indulge his passion, his obsession, for Samantha Jellicoe.

She appeared a moment later, all mesmerizing green eyes, silky auburn hair, and very fine red dress. Whatever had been eating at her during the auction she seemed to have resolved, because her smile on seeing him could melt granite. It made his knees weak, and at the same time made him want to do great deeds worthy of someone as unique and exceptional as she was.

He took her hand as she reached him. Even after five months, he needed to touch her as frequently as possible, to assure himself that she hadn't vanished into the night.

"I called Ben," he said, drawing her up close to him. "He's waiting out front."

"And the Hogarths?"

"Wrapped and ready to join us."

She nodded. "Good."

They reached the doorway, and Richard held the door open as Samantha and a handful of Sotheby's employees, two toting paintings and the rest providing security, exited to the sidewalk. Ben already had the limousine doors open, and they stowed the Hogarths behind the driver's seat. Putting them in the trunk seemed . . . insulting.

"Thank you, gentlemen," Richard said, accepting another round of congratulations and ignoring the swarming paparazzi as he helped Samantha into the back seat. She could do it herself without any trouble, but as she liked to point out, he enjoyed playing the knight in shining armor. It ran in his blood, apparently.

"Satisfied?" Samantha asked, as Ben closed their door and hurried around to the driver's seat.

"I got what I wanted. Mostly." Reaching over to cup her cheek in one hand, he leaned in to kiss her, slow and deep. She was more intoxicating than champagne.

She kissed him back, reaching behind her with one hand to hit the button raising the privacy panel between the passengers and the driver. "So a fortune in art isn't enough for you?"

Slowly he slipped one of the red spaghetti straps down her shoulder, kissing her skin as he did so. "Not when you're here."

"Smooth," she breathed, the edges of her voice a bit unsteady. "Are you sure you don't want to wait until we get back to the townhouse?"

"I can't," he replied, sliding a hand up her thigh beneath the silky red skirts. Reaching back to the console on his door panel, he pushed the intercom button. "Ben, take the long way," he said.

"Yes, s—"

He flipped it off again.

"Great. Now Ben knows what we're doing."

"You think he didn't know before?" With a tug, Richard lowered the front of her gown to her waist. She hadn't worn a bra, so he didn't have to waste any time with that. He lowered his head, tasting her soft breasts, feeling her nipples bud beneath his tongue. She gave a shivery gasp that nearly had him splitting the zipper of his trousers.

"What if some photographer's following us with an infrared camera or something?" she squeaked, arching against him.

"There is a point where you're taking paranoia too far, Sam," he said, nudging her onto her back along the leather seat.

"Would this be the point?" she asked, sliding a hand down to gently cup his crotch, her green gaze holding his with an innocence that could still fool him on occasion. "Mm, somebody's happy."

"That is precisely the point, my love." He pushed her skirts up, bunching the dress at her waist. "Christ," he murmured, looking down at her. "Red thongs."

She grinned breathlessly. "I thought you'd like those. I'm trying a new style."

"I like them better off." While she lifted her hips, he slid the thongs down her thighs and her knees and off over her red high-heeled shoes. No hose for Samantha, unless it was a dress requirement. And thank God for that. "Are you going to tell me what was bothering you in the auction room?" he asked, tossing the underwear over his shoulder in the direction of the Hogarths.

"Nothing. It was just . . . weird, being on the legit side of things. Now, are you just going to kneel there, or are you going to do something?"

"Oh, I'll do something." Straightening, he unzipped his trousers, shoved them and his boxers down to his thighs, and moved in over her. As she wrapped her ankles around his hips, he slowly pushed inside her. Tight and hot and his. "How's this?" he grunted, elbows on either side of her face.

She shuddered, and he felt it to his roots. Wordlessly Samantha pulled his face down to kiss him openmouthed. Tangling her hands in his hair, she kept him against her as he pumped his hips into her, hard and fast. Finesse and taking his shoes off could wait until they were out of the damn car.

He felt her come, felt her thighs and her body tighten convulsively around him. It didn't make sense, that that sensation could make him feel more powerful than closing a multimillion-dollar business merger, but it did. He slowed, drawing the sensation out for both of them even though every muscle wanted to hurry and thrust and claim the territory for himself. It was already his, reluctant as she was to admit it aloud, and loath as he was to force her to do so.

"Rick," she moaned, shifting her hands to his arse. Lowering his head beside hers, he let loose, shoving in and out until, with a hard shudder and a groan, he came.

"Your tie clip's digging into my stomach," Samantha said after a moment, her voice deeper with amusement and her breathing still hard.

"Apologies." He shifted, his knee lowering onto air. "Da—"

They thudded onto the wide floor of the limousine, him

on the bottom. Samantha, curled catlike across his chest, shook with laughter. "You are so smooth," she chortled.

"Shut up."

The intercom buzzed. "Sir? Uh, Miss Sam? Is everything all right?"

Richard lifted his foot, smashing his heel onto the arm console. "We're fine. Carry on."

"I'm glad you didn't unroll the window or open the door, doing that," Samantha said, shifting upright to pull up her dress.

"And I'm glad nobody put an elbow through one of the Hogarths," he returned, chuckling as he lifted his hips to pull his trousers up.

"Where's my damn underwear?" Samantha, shoving the skirt of her dress back down to her thighs, crawled to the front of the passenger compartment.

He finished zipping. "I didn't see where it landed." A moment later he spied the red scrap, hung over the wrapped corner of one of the paintings. Richard leaned over and snagged it for her. "Here you go."

"Thanks. Now I'll only have to buy six replacements this week."

"You haven't misplaced a pair since we came to New York."

"That was yesterday, Brit."

Richard watched as she sat down and pulled up the thong, smoothing her dress down again. "Samantha?"

"Yes?"

"I love you."

She crawled back over to sit next to him, kissing the corner of his mouth. "I love you, too."

He smiled. He couldn't help it. She'd said it a handful of times over the past two months, but rarely enough that it still felt fragile and precious and new. He would have liked it more if she had said it first, but one thing at a time. "And you're certain nothing's troubling you? You didn't see an old partner casing the joint or something, did you?"

Samantha snorted. " 'Casing the joint'? Sometimes I think you speak thieves' lingo better than you speak American."

"Yes, sometimes I push my own boat out."

"You do what?"

"Outdo myself. I certainly speak better English than you."

"That's debatable." She sat back on the seat again, taking his hand to pull him up beside her. "Nothing's troubling me. But I am curious—what did you tell your minions about me walking into your office in my maternity getup earlier? Did they freak?"

He had gotten a few looks when he'd returned to his office, but he'd be damned if he was going to explain Samantha away. It had been rather amusing, actually. "You nearly gave *me* a heart attack, but I don't think anyone else was affected."

"Did I scare you?" she asked, digging into her tiny purse for a mirror to check her hair. "Me, or me having kids with you? Or you having kids?"

For a long moment Richard gazed at her. Generally he could at least read her mood, but tonight she was being difficult. "I refuse to answer that question on the grounds that any answer might prevent me from having more sex with you tonight."

"Oh, come on. You've never once mentioned it, and I know you have to have thought about it. Doesn't the Marquis of Rawley need an heir or something?"

"Of course I've thought about it." He pulled her across his

lap and kissed her. "And I'm not answering tonight," he said, then resumed kissing her before she could say anything else. It was a cheap ploy, but he had absolutely no intention of telling her tonight that yes, he did want children, and yes, he did want her to be their mother. She'd be gone without a trace before dawn.

"Chicken."

"Call me anything you wish, Samantha," he said, keeping an arm about her waist, "but don't think I don't know exactly what you're doing."

"Wiggling on your lap and trying to give you a woody again?"

"At best you're trying to distract me from asking you more about your very odd behavior at the auction, and at worst you're trying to pick a fight so you can vanish somewhere tonight without having to provide an excuse."

She stilled for a bare second, but it was enough. Enough to send a shaft of ice through his chest. *Bloody hell.*

"Okay," she finally said, sagging back against him. "I thought I saw somebody I recognized."

"Who?"

"You don't need to know that. But I thought maybe he could be after the Hogarth, which is why I wanted it to come home with us. So problem solved, nobody had to get shot or blown up for once, and here we are, shagging in the back of a limo. A pretty good end for the evening, if you ask me."

"You might have told me, you know," he said quietly, twining his fingers with hers, pleased that she'd finally spoken, and finally able to concede that he did feel some triumph at having figured her out. It didn't happen often. "I've already promised not to go about reporting your old comrades to the police—as long as nothing of mine goes missing."

He included her in his collection as well, but telling her

that would only get him an elbow in the gut. The high value she placed on her independence was something else he'd been able to decipher about her, though that *had* been at the expense of several bruises.

"Hence my telling you about it now," she said. "I'm working on being good. It's not as easy as you might think."

"I'm still not commenting on anything."

"Okay, Switzerland."

Richard grinned. "Let's go back to the house, then, shall we?"

Samantha reached across him to press the intercom button. "Home please, Ben," she said.

"We'll be there in two minutes, Miss Sam."

Richard mock-scowled. "Does he have us timed that well, or is he circling the block?"

With a snort Samantha kissed him again. "He was probably circling the gas station, hoping he wouldn't run out of fuel before you did."

At the responding tug low in his gut, Richard slipped his palm beneath the front of her dress to cup her right tit. "I'm not out of fuel yet, love."

She laughed a little breathlessly, pressing against his hand. "I'm beginning to think you're solar-powered."

"In this case, I think it's the moonlight." Actually all it took to excite and arouse him was the sight, the scent, or the touch of Samantha Elizabeth Jellicoe. He would trade a couple of Hogarths for that, anytime.

There had to be something wrong with the two of them. After five months together, and with less than a week apart in all that time, they should have been past the arousal-at-sight stage. Samantha had read several of the relationship articles in the magazines she'd subscribed to for her office, and "Getting Over the Same-Old, Same-Old Slump" and "Passing the

Ninety-Day Hurdle" made it pretty clear that she and Rick should have some intimacy issues to work through.

She shifted a little on the bed, Rick's breath soft against her cheek. Issues—she and Rick definitely had some, but sex wasn't one of them. Until now she'd never had a relationship that lasted more than a few weeks, but even so she was certain this couldn't be typical. Every time she caught sight of Rick she wanted to throw herself on him, wrap her arms and legs around him, crawl inside him where she felt warm and wanted and safe.

Therefore lying to him and sneaking out of the house in the middle of the night couldn't be a good thing at all. But until she found out what was going on with Martin—if that *had* been Martin and not some doppelgänger who'd by now be very confused about the note in his pocket—she wasn't telling anyone anything.

Moving slowly and silently, Samantha extricated herself from beneath Rick's right arm and slid from the bed. Out of habit she always kept a pair of jeans, a shirt, and good running shoes under the nightstand or the edge of the bed, and she carried them into the bathroom and pulled them on in the dark. In the old days a sneak began when she reached the location; now it began in the bedroom at home. *Great improvement there, Sam.*

Once she'd made her way downstairs, she shut off the alarm and set it again, which gave her thirty seconds to get out the front door—a lifetime in thief world. She trotted down the townhouse's short, narrow front steps and turned to walk north up Fifth Avenue. Even at nearly two o'clock in the morning cabs cruised, looking for passengers too drunk to drive home or too uneasy to take the subway at this hour.

At her first wave one of them dodged across the street and pulled to the curb. "Central Park at East Sixty-seventh

Street," she said, avoiding a tear in the black seat cushion as she sat back. It was only a couple of blocks; she could have walked it. But that would expose her to casual view longer, and leave her more open than she liked. There were some instincts she didn't think she'd ever put behind her.

The cabdriver craned his neck around to face her through the Plexiglas barrier. "I hope you tip big for a trip that short, lady," he rumbled in a heavy Ukrainian accent.

"That'll depend on how polite you are," Samantha returned smoothly, putting a touch of Manhattan in her accent. She knew the drill: not too nice, not too cranky—just enough conversation to not be remembered.

"Okay. My pleasure, Your Highness," he said, sending her another annoyed glance in his mirror as he faced front again.

"That's better."

Traffic was as light as it ever got in Manhattan, and the creepy-crawlies who hid from daylight had come out to roam the sidewalks. She liked New York City at night even better than she did during the day. Decent people out at this hour were few and far between, and if they weren't drunk or high, they were too worried about their own skins to look at anything outside their own very small circle of safety. And the rest of the midnight population had their own problems, real or imaginary, and couldn't be bothered with anyone else's unless they saw a benefit for themselves. She made certain it wasn't profitable to mess with her.

Three minutes later the cab pulled over across from the Central Park side of the street. "How is this, Your Highness?"

The meter read $3.50, so she handed him a five and a one. "It's perfect."

He chuckled, pleased at the tip. "You want me to wait?"

"No. I'll be a while."

With a salute he pulled out into the light traffic. Samantha stood where she was for a minute. Even with a few light posts along the main walking paths, Central Park was one big, dark glob. One big, dark glob with her father in the middle of it.

For the first time since she'd climbed out of bed, Samantha allowed herself to think about why she was about to take a stroll through the east side of Central Park in the middle of the night. She shivered, not with fear, but with nerves. It was a damned good place for a ghost sighting; maybe under the circumstances a more populated rendezvous point would have been a better idea, after all. She waited for the traffic light, then crossed Fifth Avenue.

Get it together, Sam, she repeated to herself—her new mantra. With a last look up and down the avenue, she squared her shoulders and walked into the park.

She'd seen the bronze statue of Balto the famous sled dog once or twice over the years, his flanks rubbed smooth by countless little kids' hands. Even in the dark it took her less than fifteen minutes to circle around the dog and pick her spot in the undergrowth on the south side of the clearing. Without checking her watch she knew she was about ten minutes early, and she leaned sideways against the nearest tree trunk to wait.

If not for the faint sounds of traffic she might have been in the wilds of New England. *No thanks.* She preferred her jungles urban, where even on the run you could get a burger without having to hunt it down and kill it first.

A pair of men crossed the path in front of her, close enough that she could have reached out and picked the nearer one's pocket. From the bulge in the back of his waistband she could have liberated a pistol, too, but that wasn't her style.

Briefly she wondered whether he could be an undercover cop, patrolling the park. Either way, she wasn't going to risk attracting his attention.

Her dad had used to call her a snob because she would only take the jobs in which the object to be stolen interested her—a rare painting, an antique, an ancient stone tablet. Even Martin, though, had his standards, and she'd never known him to carry a gun, either. Guns were for thugs who couldn't get in and out of a place without being seen, he'd always said.

A couple of church bells chimed, not quite in unison, but clearly enough that she could make out two separate rings. Two o'clock. Go time.

A pair of rabbits meandered past, noses and ears twitching as they alternated between dumping rabbit pellets and checking the sky for owls. A speeding cyclist sent them hopping into the shrubbery. Samantha stayed in the deep shadows of the tree, unmoving.

Forty minutes later she'd waited for too long, seen another half dozen people, a scrawny-looking dog, and either a cat or a large rat pass by Balto, but no Martin Jellicoe. In the old days she would have waited ten minutes past the designated meeting time and then bolted, figuring the rendezvous had been compromised. But she hadn't seen him in six years. And even when he didn't show on time, she couldn't make herself leave. Maybe he was as hesitant about this as she was.

She blew out her breath, and it fogged a little in the cool damp. "Where the hell are you, Martin?" she murmured, shifting. For Christ's sake, he hadn't seen her in six years, either, and she was his only kid.

Samantha frowned. If he hadn't died three years ago, he'd certainly been in a position to track her down well before now. So why hadn't he? Where the hell had he been, and what had he been up to? While she'd still traveled on the dark side she'd heard about nearly every cat burglary pulled, and nothing had sounded like the work of Martin Jellicoe. Again, though, she'd never expected to hear any such thing, and she'd never tried to match anything to his familiar fingerprints.

She heard footsteps down the path, and stilled again. Her heart pounded, though by now she wasn't certain whether she was more nervous or angry. But the guy who came down the path had about half a foot on her dad. He wore a ragged coat that sagged on his thin frame, and even from the far side of the clearing she could smell the stale booze on him. He crossed past her, mumbling something about Batman.

When she finally gave in and checked her watch, it was nearly three. "Fuck," she muttered, slipping out of the undergrowth and back onto the path. Either that hadn't been Martin after all, or something was up. And in her experience, "somethings" were never good news.

Chapter 5

Wednesday, 3:01 a.m.

A horn blared down on the street. Richard blinked, rousing reluctantly from a deep-sea-fishing dream which featured Samantha as a bare-breasted mermaid. The horn sounded again, and he turned over. "Bloody Yanks," he mumbled.

No response.

He opened one eye again, looking across the wide bed to the nightstand beyond. Across the wide, empty bed. "Samantha?" he called, sitting up and squinting in the direction of the dark master bathroom. Wide awake now, he rolled naked out of bed and shrugged into his blue dressing robe.

Samantha had been semi-nocturnal for as long as he'd known her, but her late-night wanderings seemed to increase when something troubled her. Whatever she'd said during and after the auction, and whatever he'd pretended not to notice, something troubled his former cat burglar.

Tying the robe closed, he left the bedroom to make a quick check of his office and then the sitting room opposite. Hm. His next guess was a midnight snack, and he padded barefoot down the stairs to the ground floor. The kitchen was as dark and silent as the rest of the house.

Unless she had a reason for sneaking, Samantha didn't make much of an effort to remain hidden in her own house. Frowning, his heart beating a little faster despite his resolve not to jump to any conclusions, he headed into the downstairs sitting room. Nothing but the new Hogarths, propped against the back of the . . .

One package leaned against the couch. Ice swept down his spine. A quick turn about the room verified it—only one painting. Abruptly Samantha's disappearance wasn't just mildly exasperating. Missing Sam, missing painting. For a split second, he doubted her. Just as swiftly, though, he pushed the thought out of his mind. The two things might be connected, but she hadn't taken the Hogarth. Heart and mind, he *knew* that about her.

Cursing, Richard charged back upstairs to pull on some clothes. As he dug into the wardrobe, he glanced into the mirror beside it. Reflected beneath the disheveled sheets was the bottom of Samantha's side of the bed—sans the neat little pile of emergency clothing she always kept there.

Yanking on a pair of jeans, he half hopped into the bathroom. No sign, but since she hadn't been wearing any jammies he didn't quite know what he expected to find, other than perhaps one of her rare sticky notes on the mirror. Nothing marred the ceiling-high reflective surface.

"Fuck, fuck, fuck."

For once in his life, he wasn't sure what the devil he was supposed to do next. Someone had stolen from him. He needed to call the police. But until he knew where Samantha was and what her involvement might be, he *couldn't* call the police.

Then he realized that he already had. As he strode past his nightstand, he noticed the small red light blinking on his phone. The silent alarm had been tripped. Since he resided there so infrequently, the security company would call Wilder downstairs to confirm a breach. *Bloody hell.*

Halfway down the stairs, the wail of sirens and the reflection of red and blue lights through the front windows began and grew louder and brighter. "Shit."

"Sir!" Wilder met him in the foyer, the butler disheveled and wearing a plaid bathrobe over black pajama bottoms and matching slippers. "The alarm's gone off. It showed a perimeter breach, so I confirmed on the phone that the police needed to be dispatched."

As he thought about it, for a bare second he felt relief. Sam had probably never set off an alarm in her life. Unless she did it on purpose. So much for relief. "Where was the breach?"

"The upstairs window at the back of the hall."

Fuck. "Answer the door," he ordered, taking the stairs two at a time. *Dammit, where was she?*

As his butler greeted the four policemen at the door, Richard threw aside his clothes and shrugged back into his dressing robe. All the while he undressed, he was running calculations through his mind—how much did he know, how much did they need to know, did he report the painting missing, or risk being caught in a lie later. Mainly, what would he say when they asked who else was in residence, and where the hell she might be at three o'clock in the morning?

At the sound of feet clumping up his stairs, he shoved open the bedroom door. "What the bloody hell is going on?" he asked.

"Your alarm went off, Mr. Addison," one of the officers said helpfully as they topped the stairs. "Stand aside and we'll make sure your residence is clear."

Weapons drawn, they made a show of checking behind each door and clearing each room on their way to the window at the back of the hallway. If they didn't find anything, he supposed he could send them on their way and make the discovery of the missing painting once he'd tracked down Samantha. The damned rub was, if someone *else* had stolen from him, he didn't want to lose any time recovering his property.

"Look at that," one of them said. "The pane's pushed out, and there are scratches on the glass."

It was the same pane Samantha had removed earlier in the day. She'd also repaired it, though, because he'd seen the results. He sent a glance at Wilder. The butler knew not to volunteer any information, but from the look on his face, he was clearly concerned.

"You didn't hear anything?" the officer with the name Spanolli pinned on his shirt asked, hauling a notepad out of his pocket.

"Not until the sirens," Richard answered.

"I'll need you to make a quick check of valuables, to see if anything's missing," Spanolli said, nodding.

"From the look of this place, that ain't gonna be easy," one of the others said, muttered agreement following that comment.

"Certainly I'll take a look." Richard started to his office. The longer he could delay discovering the missing painting, the more time he would have to decide on a strategy.

"Is anybody else staying here with you?"

He drew a slow breath. If they watched the entertainment news, they would already know the answer to that. "Yes."

"Who might that be?"

Abruptly he had another problem, though insignificant in comparison to the first. How did he describe Samantha? *Girlfriend* seemed a very juvenile term for someone in his mid-thirties to use; *lover* sounded vacuous. *My precious* was closer, but decidedly odd and too *Lord of the Rings*. "Samantha Jellicoe," he said reluctantly, deciding on what was simultaneously the most vague and the most precise description. "She lives with me."

The muttering started up again. Either they knew her current business was security, or they knew her father's had been thievery.

"Where is she now, Mr. Addison?"

The more information he gave, the more he would have to substantiate later. "Taking a drive, I would imagine," he settled for.

"At three a.m."

"She wanted to see Manhattan at night. I have an early meeting." He shrugged, offering a half smile. "She gets impatient." Taking a quick visual inventory of his office, he faced Officer Spanolli again. "No valuables missing in here that I can tell."

"You were in the bedroom, right?"

"Yes."

"Let's move on to the next room, then. And take your time, Mr. Addison. Your window's definitely been jimmied. We've got some robbery guys on the way."

Splendid. More questions that he didn't want to answer, and more questions that he couldn't answer. He needed to call Tom Donner, his attorney. At after three a.m. and several states away, though, and given Tom's reservations about Samantha, he needed something more substantial than "I can't find her" accompanied by "a painting's gone missing."

Tom would take less than a second to connect the two; if this had been three or four months ago, Richard might have come to the same conclusion himself.

Aside from the basic fact that he trusted her, if Samantha *had* finally decided to take him for all he was worth and make a run for it, she wouldn't have taken the Hogarth. In Palm Beach he had a Picasso, two Rembrandts, and a Gainsborough, among more than two dozen others. And the bulk of the collection was in his house in Devonshire, England. The Hogarth was a new find, of course, but it wasn't the most valuable thing in his collection. Besides, he would have given it to her.

"Mr. Addison?"

He started. "The sitting room is next."

It wasn't often that he didn't know how to proceed. Purposely stalling wasn't his style, either, and yet at the moment he was faced with both. When they got downstairs, he would *have* to notice that the painting was missing.

Another man, this one in a dark, surprisingly tasteful suit and tie, topped the stairs. With fashionably cut dark hair and nice shoes, he could have been a cop from one of those *Law and Order* shows. "You Addison?" he asked, from around a well-chewed toothpick.

"I am. And you are?"

"Detective Gorstein. Robbery. You were asleep when this happened?" The detective gave Richard's dressing robe an appraising look.

"Until I heard the sirens," Richard lied smoothly.

Gorstein nodded. "Anything missing so far?"

Spanolli stepped forward. "Not so far. We've cleared the office and one of the dens."

Dens. Americans.

"They came in that way," the officer continued, pointing

his pen toward the back window. "One of the panes is missing, and it's jimmied."

With a nod, Gorstein moved past them and stuck his head into the bedroom. "Where's your girlfriend?"

Richard stifled his annoyed frown. He was still in charge, but he would have to lead from the rear. And cautiously. This Gorstein apparently read the rag sheets. "Out. Sightseeing."

"Okay." The detective leaned sideways to mutter something to one of the officers, who then trotted back downstairs. "My forensics guys are downstairs. Spanolli, get Gina and tell her to dust the sill for prints. Send Taylor to the fire escape to dust out there. Whoever broke in wasn't Spider-Man."

"Yes, sir." With everything but a click of his heels, Spanolli vanished downstairs.

"You have an entire forensics team?" Richard asked. "This isn't a murder."

"No, it's a robbery. Maybe. But you're Rick Addison, and you pay a lot of taxes." Gorstein shifted the toothpick to the other side of his mouth. "You were at the Sotheby's auction tonight, weren't you?"

"How did you know that?" Not asking would probably have been more prudent, but he needed to know who this fellow was, and how much trouble he could cause for Samantha—and for himself.

"You were a news bit, right after sports. You bought a couple of paintings and a big statue."

Fuck. "Yes, I did."

"They here?"

"The paintings are downstairs, in the front room."

"Did you check them after we got here?"

"No. We started our search up here."

"That was kind of stupid, wasn't it?" Gorstein pursued, heading back for the stairs. "I mean, if I'd just spent a couple of million, I'd want to know it was safe."

Richard narrowed his eyes. "I wouldn't call someone who pays a lot of taxes 'stupid,' detective," he returned deliberately. Gorstein needed to remember where he was, and with whom he was dealing. And equally importantly, who was actually in charge.

"Right. Sorry." The detective paused on the landing to glance up at him. "Let's go check your paintings, then, shall we, Mr. Addison?"

"Certainly."

Obviously Gorstein was of a different caliber than the officers who'd been respectfully following Richard about. And the detective was already suspicious. To what degree, Rick didn't know yet. He needed to find out. Fast.

Richard took a slow breath as he descended the stairs behind Gorstein. Back in Florida, Samantha had managed to earn the respect and even the trust of at least one member of the Palm Beach Police Department. Here in Manhattan, all the police had was her father's name and reputation.

And perhaps some unsolved high-class cat burglaries. Martin Jellicoe, however, was the one who'd been caught and found guilty of stealing a myriad of expensive pieces of art and history, and he was the one who'd died in prison. They could speculate about Samantha, but she'd never left a clue that he'd ever heard of. And he'd spent untold hours checking, just to be certain no one could ambush her with an arrest warrant. She'd exposed herself in a high-profile public life because of him, and he wasn't about to forget that.

"Try not to touch anything, Mr. Addison," the detective cautioned, as they entered the downstairs sitting room.

"I live here," Richard returned flatly. "I would expect to

find my fingerprints, and Samantha's and Wilder's and the two maids', everywhere in here."

"I just don't want you smudging over somebody's else's prints. Okay, where are the paintings?"

"Over there."

The two of them made their way to the back of the couch, where one crated, cushioned, and brown-paper-wrapped painting leaned. The sight surprised him for a second time, though he wasn't certain why. Perhaps he'd thought Sam would have reappeared and replaced the painting.

"How many paintings did you bring home?" Gorstein asked, as he motioned at one of the officers in the doorway.

"Two."

"I see one."

Richard glanced at him. "I can see why you made detective."

"Yeah. I'm real observant. How much was it worth?"

"That depends on which one was taken. Between five and twelve million dollars."

"American dollars."

"Yes, American dollars."

Gorstein cleared his throat. "Okay. I want some photos of the room, and I want everything dusted for prints. Then we'll take a look and see which painting they got." He motioned Richard to leave the room ahead of him. "And I need another couple of words with you."

"I'd like to keep this low-profile," Richard said, leading the way down the hall and into the quiet kitchen. "The last thing I want is the press reporting that I've been robbed."

The detective leaned on the back of one of the kitchen chairs. "Excuse me, but you didn't seem all that surprised, Mr. Addison."

"Should I have fainted?" Richard asked coolly. "My house

was broken into, and a dozen policemen are wandering the halls. Something was stolen. No, I'm not surprised. And I doubt you were the only one to learn on the news tonight that I made several purchases from Sotheby's."

"Mm-hm. So all of Manhattan's a suspect. What about your girlfriend?"

That hadn't taken long. "Don't be ridiculous."

"She's not here, your painting's not here, and she's a Jellicoe."

"She'll be back, she had nothing to do with who her father was, and I would have given her the painting if she wanted it."

Gorstein took out the toothpick, looked at the ragged end, and then stuck it back between his teeth again. "I'm glad you're satisfied, but your opinion doesn't help me fill out my paperwork. And we have this contest at the station where we get points for finding perps."

"I appreciate sarcasm," Richard said, "but I'd rather you find the actual 'perp,' as you call it, than waste time looking at someone whom I know to be innocent."

"Look at it from my point of view," the detective countered. "I see on the news that you just spent almost thirty million bucks. Then I get a call that you've had a break-in. Then I find out your girlfriend, the daughter of a notorious cat burglar, is missing. I think, '*Uh-oh, she vanishes on the night that those Hobart paintings c—*'"

"Hogarth," Richard corrected, clenching his jaw.

"'—Ho*garth* paintings come home. That can't be good.' But you, not an idiot, haven't even bothered to check the whereabouts of the paintings until I practically force you to do it. It doesn't look good, Mr. Addison. Like maybe you knew it was missing, and you knew why. And I bet it was insured."

"I see. Then let's stop this conversation right now, and I'll call my attorney. I'd hate for you to have to go through your scenario more than twice."

"That's probably a good idea." Gorstein pushed upright. "Use the phone in here. And don't go anywhere else in the house until we finish with it."

Richard watched the detective out the kitchen door. Before he could summon relief at having a moment alone to think, another officer came in and took a seat at the table. Obviously he was there to observe and to listen. If not for Samantha, Richard would have flicked him away like a bug.

That was the bloody crux of the problem. Until he knew where Samantha was and what her involvement might be, his hands were tied. And if he wasn't very careful, they might very well end up handcuffed. *Fuck.*

Samantha checked her watch as the taxi dropped her off around the corner from the townhouse. Three-twenty. Great. Rick was early-riser guy, so he'd be up in an hour or two. She didn't mind losing sleep, but she preferred that it be because of sex or a good burglary. All she had was an hour in Central Park shrubbery.

Not that she'd be able to close her eyes if she *did* get the chance. She knew she hadn't just imagined Martin. He'd been there, and even though he *knew* she'd seen him, he'd declined a meeting. She needed to call Stoney. And she needed to figure out how much—if anything—she wanted to tell Rick.

It would help if she knew something, herself. An unexplainable sighting and a bad feeling hardly made for anything a sane person would believe. Still, if—

"Stop right there!"

For a bare second she froze. One man did a half trot toward

her on the sidewalk. She could handle one guy, even if the dark thing he held in one hand was a gun. What the fuck had she been doing, though, letting herself get so distracted that she hadn't noticed anything until he was practically on top of her?

Her heart began to pound, much-missed adrenaline flooding into her system. Samantha gave a half shrug, letting her purse slide off her shoulder and down to her wrist, where she clutched the strap. It wasn't much of a weapon, but he probably wouldn't expect her to be proactive.

"Why don't you slow down there, honey?" she drawled in a soft Southern accent. "You'll scare a girl half to death, charging up like that."

"Get down on your knees, hands behind your head."

She'd heard that lingo on every episode of *COPS* she'd ever watched. Her heart bottomed out and began thumping harder as she spied the glint of his badge.

"I live right around the corner," she said, edging toward the street and Central Park beyond. "At number twelve. With Rick Addison."

"Down on your knees!"

Shit. Every muscle, every instinct, screamed at her to run. Swallowing it back, Samantha knelt. She hadn't done anything wrong, she reminded herself. Spending an hour hiding in Central Park in the middle of the night might be crazy, but it wasn't illegal. Probably.

"Hands on your head. Interlace your fingers," he repeated.

"Okay. Just calm down. It's late, and I'm tired."

The cop tapped the mike attached to one shoulder and said something that sounded like, "I've got her," before he moved behind her and grabbed her hands.

Whoever was receiving that call obviously knew who

"her" was, which meant they were looking for her specifically. This was very, very bad.

A cuff clicked shut around her left wrist, cold, hard, and way too confining. "Jeez," she muttered, fighting back panic at the thought that she'd actually been caught, "will you at least tell me what's going on? Is Rick okay?"

The cop pulled her right arm around behind her back, yanking the left one down by hauling on the handcuffs. In a second, both wrists were caught.

"On your feet, miss."

At least he was still being relatively polite. Samantha rocked back onto her toes and then straightened her legs, standing. One hand holding the joint of the cuffs, the cop ran the other up and down her legs and arms, neck, and around her waist. He missed the paperclip in her front left pants pocket, which put her considerably closer to being at ease. With the 'clip she could be out of the cuffs faster than the cop could say "MacGyver."

More troubling at the moment was the fact that the cop hadn't answered her question. "Please tell me what's happened," she pleaded, moving forward as he gave her a light push between the shoulder blades. "Is Rick all right?"

"You can talk to Detective Gorstein about that."

"Homicide?" she asked, willing this Gorstein not to be.

"Robbery."

Thank God. Rick wasn't dead. Nobody was dead, which was an improvement over the way surprises usually went where she was concerned. The cop nudged her forward again. Obviously the guy was used to arresting thugs and drunks; if she'd wanted to, she could have knocked a heel into his groin and been gone into the night by now.

The flash of red and blue lights reflecting on the trees and buildings greeted her as they neared the corner. That figured. Another few feet and she would have realized that something was wrong and either made herself scarce or gone in through the alley.

She counted five police cars, a van, and an unmarked car with a light in the rear window. No ambulances and no fire trucks, but something had definitely happened—and it had happened in her—Rick's—house.

A good-looking guy in a dark suit met them at the foot of the front steps. "You must be Gorstein," she said.

"And you're Miss Jellicoe, I presume," he returned, his lips curled around a bent toothpick. Ex-smoker, probably—still not comfortable unless he had something stuck in his mouth. Well dressed for a cop, though.

For a heartbeat she weighed going friendly against being belligerent. With the handcuffs on and now outnumbered, friendly made more sense.

"I'm Sam Jellicoe. I'd offer my hand, but it's otherwise occupied."

He cracked a half grin. "I tracked one of your dad's burglaries about eight years ago. An Andy Warhol we never recovered. I'll bet you're even slicker than he was."

Christ. The Andy Warhol job hadn't been Martin's work; it had been hers. The thought shook her a little. "I'm not my dad," she said. "And I'd really like to know what's going on."

"I have a couple of questions for you, first."

"No." Samantha shook her head. "Not until you tell me whether Rick is okay."

"Addison's okay. He's sitting in the kitchen, probably on the phone with his lawyer."

Great. As if she wanted Tom Donner, Boy Scout, tangled in the middle of whatever this was. Then what Gorstein had said dawned on her. "Why does Rick need a lawyer?"

"You'd have to ask him. Now, where were you between about midnight and now?"

"This doesn't look like it's going anywhere good," she returned. "Am I under arrest?"

He looked at her for a minute. "Yeah."

"Then I'd like you to read me my rights. And I'd like to see Rick Addison."

"No. Ruiz, read the lady her rights."

The cop who'd handcuffed her pulled a small card out of his breast pocket. As he did so, Samantha glanced up at the windows of the surrounding townhouses. Half their neighbors looked back at her. Two of them even had cameras. *Wonderfuckenful.*

She drew a deep breath.

"You have the right to remain silent. If you give up that r—"

"RICK!"

Gorstein chomped through his toothpick. "Put her in a car. We'll do this at the station."

Samantha set her feet as Ruiz tried to steer her to the nearest patrol car. "At least tell me what I'm under arrest for."

With a mournful look at the two halves of toothpick in his hand, the detective dropped them to the sidewalk. "Grand larceny."

"Of what?"

The cop standing in the open townhouse doorway stumbled sideways. Rick, in his blue dressing robe and barefooted, charged down the steps toward her. "Samantha!"

"Get her in the damn car," Gorstein grunted, taking her free elbow and half lifting her in the air as another cop pulled the rear passenger door open. "I do not want them talking to each other."

Rick was a suspect in something, too? "What the hell's going on?" she yelled.

"A Hogarth's missing," Rick returned as Gorstein left her and charged him, herding him backward—or trying to. "I told them you'd gone sightseeing," he called, "but they obviously don't realize what a mistake they're making!"

Ruiz pushed her, and she fell into the back seat. Her expression must have mirrored some of what she felt, because Rick said something very quietly to Gorstein, and the detective abruptly moved aside.

"One minute," he said.

"Samantha," Rick murmured, coming forward to lean into the open car door, "don't do anything rash. I'll follow you to the station, and you'll be out by breakfast."

"Promise?" She gulped air, knowing how juvenile she sounded, and still needing to hear the reassurance.

His gaze met hers squarely. "I promise. Don't run, Sam."

Obviously he knew more about her skills than the cops did. "Okay," she grumbled.

She could have run; she would have run—except for one thing. Running would mean never seeing Rick again. To prevent that, she would even let herself be fingerprinted. Her father would be spinning in his grave—except that Martin wasn't dead. She, on the other hand, might very well be headed in that direction.

Chapter 6

Wednesday, 3:32 a.m.

Once the police closed Samantha in the back of a car and drove her away, the gloves came off.

"I haven't reported a bloody crime," Rick snapped, blocking Gorstein's way back to the townhouse. "I want your people out of my home, and I want Samantha Jellicoe unhandcuffed, apologized to, and returned here immediately. At that point I'll decide whether I should sue your department for wrongful arrest and harassment."

"Look, Mr. Addison, your butler confirmed a break-in, and your security company dispatched us. You've already admitted that a painting is missing."

"I was in error. Get out."

"Can't. Once we note that something is missing, we have to investigate. And if these paintings are insured, it's not your best interests I'm concerned about. It's getting to the truth."

"Very noble. I hope when you find your next employment

as a dishwasher or cabdriver, you feel the same way."

"How about we just get this over with as fast and painlessly as possible?" the detective returned, pulling a new toothpick from his pocket and jamming it between his teeth. "If you'll go back to the kitchen, we should be finished here fairly soon."

"*Fairly* soon isn't good enough. We're finished now."

"Okay. I guess I'll have to get my answers from Miss Jellicoe, then."

That was the wrong damned threat to make. "I suggest you get to it," Richard said in a low, barely controlled voice. "Good luck."

Gorstein grimaced. "This would go better if you'd cooperate."

"This would have gone better if you hadn't arrested Samantha."

"I could have arrested you. Don't make me change my mind."

Richard smiled, though he didn't feel anything close to amused. "I do wish you would."

Silence.

"No? Good day, then. You have two minutes to get your people off my property. Come back with a warrant. If someone wants to know why I've kicked you out, tell them it's because you arrested Samantha on sight." Turning his back, Rick strode inside. Grabbing his cell phone off its cradle, he hit speed-dial number three.

The phone rang three times and then scraped off the receiver. "Hello?" came raspily.

"Tom. Apologies for waking you, but I need your help," Richard said, climbing the stairs for the bedroom.

"Rick?" The voice became immediately more alert. "What's wrong?"

"We had a break-in, and one of my new paintings was stolen." Slamming the bedroom door, he shed his robe and dug for his clothes again.

"You okay?"

"I slept through it, apparently." He shrugged into his jeans.

"A stolen painting, huh? Where's Jellicoe?"

"On her way to the police station, in handcuffs." Richard couldn't keep the deep anger from his voice. Whatever her ultimate involvement might be, Samantha was his. Nobody got to take her away against her own bloody wishes.

"And did she do—"

"Don't you bloody dare ask me that. I'm going down to the station. I need you to call Phil Ripton and get him to roust his associates and every judge in Manhattan, if that's what it takes to have her out by sunrise."

"Rick, it's four o'cl—"

"Can you handle that?" Richard interrupted. "I'm asking you to do this because you know Samantha's history, and because I trust you with it."

Tom audibly blew out his breath. "I'm on it."

"Thank you. Call me on my mobile when you have some information."

Richard snapped the phone closed and tossed it on the bed to pull on a shirt and light jacket. For a second he debated calling for Ben and the limousine, but a limo at a police station would draw attention that he didn't want, and that Samantha didn't need.

He pocketed his wallet and the phone and went back downstairs. "Wilder," he said, spying his butler handing out cups of coffee to the police out standing on the public sidewalk, "I'm going out. I have my phone, if you need to reach me. Do not let them back in without a warrant." He wanted to stop the coffee bit, but he supposed Wilder had a point. Making enemies of the entire NYPD wouldn't be a good idea, especially with Samantha in their custody. His argument at the moment was with Detective Gorstein.

"I'll keep an eye on things, sir."

Spanolli stood outside drinking coffee and talking with a pair of other officers. "I assume Detective Gorstein has gone?" Richard said.

"He went back to the station. Do you need—"

"I'll see him there, then."

"Mr. Addison, you're not supposed to go anywhere until we wrap things up here."

"I'm going to the police station," Richard returned, half wishing the police *would* try to stop him. "If you have a problem with that, please tell me."

"Uh, no, sir."

Despite his dislike of assaults on his privacy, Richard supposed the gathered crowd of curious onlookers and paparazzi did have its benefits. The police were not going to do anything dicey with spectators about. Ignoring the flash of cameras, he hailed one of the taxis having to slow for the mess.

"Where to?"

He read out the address of the police station from Gorstein's card and sat back. The cab smelled faintly of something he didn't care to define. He noted that only in passing, though. Most of his attention was on what he was going to say to Samantha after she went free. It would have to be good to keep her from disappearing somewhere she felt safe—which would be somewhere no one, including him, could find her.

If she'd taken the painting, she wouldn't have called for him. He knew that as well as he knew anything. So therefore someone else had broken into his house and stolen something that belonged to him. A twelve-million-dollar something.

Odds were, though, that she wasn't completely ignorant. She'd vanished somewhere, and then reappeared just as the police were swarming over the premises. Under the circumstances, he wanted some damned answers from her. And he felt entitled to them, as well.

Richard cursed under his breath. Five months ago and with Samantha's help he'd discovered that someone he'd trusted had been removing his paintings and replacing them with forgeries. Three people had ended up in jail, and three more had died because of it. This hadn't begun much more auspiciously.

Yes, his collection was insured, and yes, he knew what Gorstein was suggesting—that he could fairly easily take a twelve-million-dollar insurance payout *and* still have a painting he could hide away for his private enjoyment.

What the detective didn't realize was that he would never tolerate the public reputation that he was a mark, even if he'd secretly arranged for and profited from the dealings. It wasn't the money that mattered; it was the fact that someone had stolen from him. And once he'd extricated Samantha from this mess, he had every intention of finding out who was responsible.

His cell phone rang. "Addison," he answered.

"Rick," Tom's voice came, "I woke up Phil, and he's working on getting Jellicoe released. He asked if you would give him a call so the firm can start on damage control."

"Damage control?"

"The morning news just started, and you're a teaser. They've already got cameras at the police station."

Richard cursed. "*I'm* not even at the bloody police station yet."

"Call Phil before you get there, okay? He's got a couple of ideas. It's not just about Jellicoe, Rick. This could damage your reputation, too."

"I know that."

"Okay. I know you're mad. I'm just trying to be the voice of reason."

He probably needed to listen to one this morning. As a plan, storming the jail and rescuing Samantha seemed a bit light on the details, and he hadn't exactly made a friend of Gorstein. "Give me Ripton's number," he said, remembering that he'd left his Palm Pilot on the dressing table.

He hung up on Tom and dialed the attorney's number. "Phil? It's Rick."

"Rick. Hell of a way to wake up, isn't it? Only in New York."

"What did Tom tell you?"

"That your girl got arrested, and that her dad has a record for this kind of burglary. It's pretty weak."

"Weak or not, she's at the police station being interrogated. That is not acceptable."

"Where are you right now?"

"In a taxi, about five minutes from the station."

For a moment he heard muffled voices on the other end of the line. "Rick, there's a Starbucks about a block south of the station. Wait for me there."

"I'm going in to get Samantha."

"If you go in there alone, they'll run you around and try to rile you up. They love it when rich guys make threats against the NYPD, especially when he's standing there empty-handed and the press is milling around outside. Makes the cops really want to put together a case."

"I'm not a fool," Richard retorted. And he had to admit that he was already riled up, and had already made some threats. "And I won't leave Samantha in there for a second longer than I have to."

"Look, I'm on my way to see Judge Penoza. Give me thirty minutes, and I'll meet you at Starbucks. We go in together with a court order, and then we get her out of there, no runaround, no delays."

It was a good plan, and the stronger they entered the fight, the better they would look later. For a long second Richard weighed the logic of Phil Ripton's approach against what Samantha referred to as his white-knight tendencies. "Thirty minutes, Phil. After that, I will call the governor and go in there with the National Guard, if necessary."

"Okay. I understand your feelings on this, Rick. Just wait for me."

He would wait. For thirty minutes. And not a bloody second more.

Detective Gorstein circled the gray metal table, then without warning slammed the flat of his hand down on the scratched surface.

Stifling a fake yawn, Samantha looked up at him. "Are you the bad cop, or the good cop?"

"I'm just the guy who wants to give you a break, if you'd tell me where you were last night."

Now that she had the handcuffs off and had gotten over her initial panic at being arrested and dragged into a police station, this was becoming . . . well, not enjoyable, but she definitely knew how to play people, and she meant to have fun with this guy. She didn't even have to be nice, because he'd already put the cuffs on—and because they both knew that Rick would raise the *Titanic* if that was what it took to get her out of there. In fact, the worst part of this was turning out to be the fact that she'd been fingerprinted and photographed.

Figuring out how to get herself out of the system—she'd worry about that later.

"I'd be more inclined to believe your sincerity," she drawled, "if you'd get me a Diet Coke and let me make a phone call."

He grabbed the phone from the far end of the table and thunked it down in front of her. "I'm not stopping you."

"And you're not leaving, either, I presume?"

"I'll leave."

"And you'll go stand on the other side of the mirror, right?"

His toothpick twitched. "Yep."

She blew out her breath. "Fine." If he'd given her a minute of privacy she would have called Stoney; she *knew* Rick was working to get her released, and she needed someone to help her with the Martin problem—especially now that she knew the Hogarth had gone missing at the very same time she'd told her father she would be elsewhere.

Noting that Gorstein watched, she dialed Rick's cell. It only rang once before he picked up. "Addison."

For the moment she pretended that a weight hadn't lifted from her shoulders just at the sound of his voice. "Hi, stud-muffin."

"Samantha. Are you all right?"

"They are totally shining lights in my face and making me listen to Manilow," she offered.

Silence. "I'm glad you're enjoying yourself," he finally said, "considering that I'm bordering on a stroke."

"Don't tell Mom about that," she returned smoothly.

"They're listening?" he asked immediately, his voice sharpening.

"You bet."

"Give me ten more minutes, love. Try to behave."

"Easy breezy. How—"

"Okay," Gorstein interrupted. "Time's up."

Samantha blew him a raspberry as she hung up the phone. She'd known Rick was on the way, but hearing him say it made her feel nearly giddy with relief.

"You may think this is pretty funny," the detective continued, leaning a haunch on the table, "but *I'm* trying to find a twelve-million-dollar painting."

"Then you shouldn't be wasting your time leaning on me, pal. Because if this is how you investigate, *I'll* find that painting way before you do."

"Why don't you tell me where to start looking, then?"

She had a good idea, actually—if not where, then who. "Hey, my business is protecting people's valuables, not stealing them."

"Then you weren't doing your job, either, were you?"

"Bite me." No, she hadn't been doing her job. In fact, her absence had probably made it possible for the cat—okay, for Martin—to break in. Dammit, she hated being played. Especially when she should have known better.

"Touched a nerve, did I?"

She looked up at him. "And what does that tell you?"

"That you're either telling the truth, or you're as slick as I thought you were. In other words, it doesn't tell me anything."

"Well, since I'm still waiting for a lawyer and for my soda, you'll just have to make do."

Gorstein chewed on his toothpick. He probably carried extras with him. "If I hadn't arrested you, would we be having a different conversation?"

Samantha was almost tempted to give him a straight answer. This guy was pretty slick himself, and she needed to remember that. "Probably not," she mused, "unless you gave me some information and brought me a soda so we could go through the facts together."

"So you would help me."

She smiled, not amused. "If you hadn't arrested me. That kind of thing can put a real damper on a relationship."

"You're a Jellicoe. In my book, that's reason enough for a lot of things."

"Well, your book is stupid. And where's my damned soda?"

Gorstein looked toward the wall-sized mirror. "Get her a soda, will you?"

"A cold one. A Diet Coke," she put in, facing the same direction.

"You may think you're cute," he grunted, standing to pace around her again, "but I'm running your prints. If you have as much as an unpaid traffic ticket, I'm holding you."

She'd only had a driver's license for three weeks, so the odds of her having a ticket were pretty slim. As for the rest, she didn't think she'd ever left a clue behind. This would be the test, though. "While you're at it, why don't you call Detective Frank Castillo in Palm Beach? He's Homicide, but don't be jealous. I help him out sometimes."

He bristled, actually looking physically larger. "Listen, Jellicoe, I am not—"

"Touched a nerve, did I?"

Gorstein narrowed his eyes. "You don't talk like somebody who lives in a townhouse on the East Side."

"I can get snooty if you want me to, but I still didn't take the painting."

"How about an alibi? Can you at least give me that?"

She probably could, actually, if she wanted to confirm that she'd been riding in a taxi at 1:35 and then at 3:10. Balto was too close to the townhouse to make it worth bringing in the cabbies, though; she could have ridden out, walked back, stolen the Hogarth, walked back to the park again, and gotten a ride home. "How about you start looking at people who might want to steal a painting instead of somebody who practically lives in an art gallery?"

Growling, he slammed a chair back into the table. "If you'd be straight with me and actually answer a damned question, maybe I could."

Samantha tilted her head at him. "I'm sorry, Detective, are you saying that you don't think I really did it? I'm getting confused now. Am I helping you find the thief, or am *I* the thief?"

"What you are is—"

The door to the interrogation room opened, and an older guy with crazy white tufts of hair sticking out over his ears walked in. "Let her go, Detective."

Gorstein straightened. "What?"

"This little chat is finished," a tall, balding man in an Armani suit snapped, pushing past Mr. Crazy Hair. "That's what. Unless you'd like to face a lawsuit for wrongful imprisonment."

Samantha didn't even try to hide her grin as Rick moved past the other two. "Sir Galahad," she murmured, standing.

He wore jeans and a black T-shirt with a flannel gray shirt over that, and still looked like the most powerful guy in the room. "Are you well?" Slowly he pulled her into his arms.

I am now. "Well enough," she said, beginning to realize just how tense she'd been over the past hour or so. Still, she wasn't going to admit any such thing in front of the cops, and they both knew it. "You made it by breakfast."

"I said I would."

"Come on, Captain," Gorstein was growling, "this is ridiculous. She's got no alibi, and her dad was—"

"Before you come after her again," Expensive Suit Guy said, "you'd best have more than her father's occupation as a reason. Good day."

With Rick keeping an arm over her shoulder, they trooped out of the interrogation room. As they left, Samantha couldn't resist a parting shot. She turned to face the glowering detective. "You still owe me a Diet Coke, Gorstein."

The hallway was lined with cops, none of them looking very happy to see her walking. So be it. She wasn't trying to make friends with any of them. And now that they were leaving, she *really* wanted to get out of there.

Armani stopped in front of them, handing over a paper bag that held her purse and phone. "Make sure your limo's here, Rick," he said, adjusting his glasses. "We don't want to have to wait around out there."

With a nod Rick pulled his phone from his pocket. "Samantha, this is Phil Ripton," he indicated as he dialed. "Phil, my Samantha."

When Ripton stuck out his hand, Samantha shook it. Warm, firm grip—no sweat, no hesitation, no over-masculine power play. Great. Another good-guy attorney. Until Tom Donner, she'd thought no such animal existed. "Under the circumstances," she said, smiling, "I'm very happy to meet you."

He nodded. "We're not quite finished untangling all this yet, but getting you out of here was Rick's first priority."

Rick snapped the phone closed. "He's waiting for us. Let's get the bloody hell out of this place."

"Amen," Samantha said feelingly, accepting his hand when he offered it for her to hold.

With a frown he twisted her wrist around, palm up. "They fingerprinted you," he said, his Caribbean-blue eyes lifting to meet hers.

He knew what that could mean, just as well as she did. "Yes," she whispered, starting to shake as reaction finally began to seep in.

"Can we get her fingerprints expunged?" Rick asked, taking the lead at Ripton's motion.

Shit. Rick was taking his cues from somebody else. By being a Jellicoe she'd brought this to his doorstep, and whether she deserved to be in jail or not, he was relinquishing his precious control because of her. Dammit, everything was going to hell, and she needed some fucking answers.

"I'll put together a motion as soon as I get to the office."

When Samantha had entered the police station, she'd done so from the back where only the crooks and cops had access. Now they were leaving out the front; and as Rick shouldered open the door, she realized why they'd wanted Ben there, waiting.

"Christ," she muttered, moving closer to him. "They're all here because of me?"

"We made the morning news," he murmured back, donning his steel-plated expression.

There must have been a hundred TV and news reporters, cameramen, sound guys, paparazzi, and groupies jammed onto the sidewalk in front of the station. As she and Rick emerged, they rushed forward.

"Mr. Addison, can you give us details about what was stolen from your home?"

"Have you been charged in the theft, Miss Jellicoe?"

"How many . . ."

"What are the . . ."

She spied Ben and the limousine parked on the street, and headed in that direction. If Rick wasn't going to answer any questions, she damned well wasn't. Whatever he'd had to tell Ripton about her past, the attorney wasn't talking, either.

Not even a "no comment" crossed anybody's lips. Ha. Let the reporters show *that* on the news.

The quiet inside the limo seemed almost deafening. Samantha reached into the refrigerator under the seat and pulled out a Diet Coke. "Apparently you can't get these in the slam," she said, popping the tab and taking a long swallow.

"So where were you last night?" Rick asked quietly, watching her.

Crap. "Sightseeing," she answered.

"Don't you bloody lie to me, Sam. When I woke—"

"Can anyone confirm that?" Ripton broke in from his seat opposite them. "A witness, or an alibi?"

With difficulty she turned her gaze from Rick. Problem numero uno was to get herself out of trouble with the cops. "Nope. Not anybody who could help."

"Tell me you didn't just go walking around Manhattan at two o'clock in the morning, Sam."

"Okay, I took a cab. A couple of cabs. With enough walking in between that they don't make much of an alibi." She eyed him. "You don't think I had anything to do with this, do you?"

"Of course not. But my insurance company isn't going to pay out twelve million dollars without conducting an investigation. Apparently I'm as much a suspect as you are."

"No," she gasped, horrified. "That's stupid! You're worth like twenty billion dollars. Why would you—"

"Rumors could be as destructive as a conviction," he cut in. "I want to know who did this." He faced Ripton. "Considering the way they bungled with Samantha, do you think you could get your hands on a copy of any evidence reports?"

Ripton pushed up his glasses again. "I think you should

refrain from interfering in a police investigation. They aren't your fans right now as it is."

"I want Samantha to look at what they've got. She's a security expert, and she knows more than most professionals do about breaking and entering. She might see something they'll miss."

Because she used to be one of those professionals. "If possible, I'd like to take a look," she seconded. "I didn't do it, but maybe I can help figure out who did." Except that she already had a good idea about that.

If it did turn out to be Martin, Rick would never trust her again. He would never believe that she hadn't known her father to be alive. And he would never believe that she hadn't somehow helped, consciously or not, to set up the burglary. He wouldn't be wrong, either. Yes, she was definitely up shit's creek, whatever happened next.

Chapter 7

Wednesday, 11:15 a.m.

Richard closed himself in the drawing room with Samantha. She looked over her shoulder at him as she clicked on the television. "What did you do with Phil?"

"He's making some calls in the office."

"You're letting him take charge?"

He clenched his jaw. "This is still a legal matter. I want that dealt with first."

"What about the hotel? Don't you have a meeting this morning?"

"That doesn't matter at the moment. I've rescheduled." Shifting a pillow onto the floor, he sank onto the couch beside her. "I'm starting to think I could use an assistant."

"You have one."

"Sarah's in London. I'm not spending as much time there as I used to."

Samantha curled a foot beneath her, graceful as a feline,

so she could face him. "You are so pissed off you can barely see straight, aren't you?"

Usually he would have commented about the different meanings of *pissed* in Britain and the U.S., but today he wasn't in the mood. "Someone stole from me. Again. Yes, I'm very angry."

"But you're madder at me."

"Don't assume you know what I'm thinking."

She gazed at him for a long moment, while the television in front of them blared the theme of one of her ubiquitous *Godzilla* movies. She had a bloody radar for them; if one was on, she knew it.

"Come on, Rick. You may as well say it. I went out, you don't know where, and you're pissed about it."

"Last night," he began slowly, keeping as tight a rein on his temper as he could—not because he was worried that he would injure her, but because he didn't know what her reaction would be—"at Sotheby's, you were jumpy. Something was bothering you, and you tried to talk me out of buying the paintings. And then five hours later, one of them goes missing."

"I'm not going to tell you again that I didn't do it," she retorted.

"You said you recognized someone there. Who was it?"

"So now I'm an accomplice? Why don't you decide whether I'm guilty or not, and we'll take it from there?" She folded her arms over her pert breasts. "Well?"

Richard ground his jaw. "I am not having this conversation right now," he growled, standing. "Watch your bloody movie and stay in the house until we get all the paperwork filed and put out a press release."

Halfway to the door, a pillow hit him squarely between the shoulder blades. Richard froze.

"You didn't just do that," he said, still unmoving.

"The next thing I throw is going to hurt."

He turned around. "What are you, five?"

"Maybe. You're the one who just sent me to my room." Samantha stood up. "You think you're mad? I used to be able to go wherever I wanted, do anything, be anybody. And cops were never fucking waiting for me at my front door, because nobody knew where I lived! Now they all know who I am and where I am."

Christ. Usually he loved her unpredictability. "They know because of me, you mean."

Her jaw snapped closed. "I didn't say that."

"Yes, you did."

Samantha turned her back on him and stalked to the television, punching the power button and turning it off. "Shut up, will you?" she grumbled. "I'm having a good yell. They put me in damn handcuffs, Rick."

"I know."

"At first when I saw all the cops, I thought maybe something had happened to you. I was worried. For you. I was in cuffs, and I was worried about you. What kind of fucking professional does that make me?"

"It makes you a retired professional," he said, moving back toward her. "And you weren't the only worried one. Of course I knew you didn't take the painting, but I didn't know where you were. The alarm tripped and the police appeared, and I didn't even know what to say to them. And as you may have noticed, I always know what to say."

Samantha blew out her breath. "I'm going to take a shower." She edged around him and pulled open the door.

"We're not finished yet."

"I am."

When she continued down the hall to their bedroom, he

followed her, only stopping for a moment at the office door. "We'll be ready in fifteen minutes, Phil."

The attorney looked up from his phone call and nodded.

She'd already stripped by the time he pushed open the bathroom door. "You're not invited," she shot, stepping into the shower.

"I'm not exactly in the mood," he retorted, folding his arms. "Why won't you tell me where the fuck you were? I thought you trusted me."

"And I thought you trusted me."

"*I* didn't vanish during the middle of a robbery."

The shower door clicked open, and she stuck her head out. "You're a jerk," she said, and closed the door again.

"And you're still retreating. First your movie, and now the shower. I'm going to stand here until you tell me what you know. Or at least explain to me why you won't say anything."

For a long moment he heard no sound but the water running in the shower. He supposed she could outlast him in a standoff, particularly since they needed to go to Ripton's office for the press statement. Dammit. He would *not* apologize or back down. He'd certainly done nothing wrong.

"I'm sorry that my being here has caused trouble for you," she finally said.

"I'm not," he shot back. "All I want is an explanation. Not an apology." He turned his wrist to look at his watch. "We have to leave for Ripton's office in ten minutes so he can read our statement to the press."

The water shut off, and the shower door opened again. "I'm not doing a Q and A with the press," she stated, stepping out and grabbing a towel.

"Neither of us is. We're showing a united front. Whether we have one in private, or not."

"A united front against what, then?"

" 'Against what'?" he repeated incredulously. "You were arrested, Samantha. And if the police can't come up with a viable lead elsewhere, I may well be charged with insurance fraud."

She ran the towel over her hair. "Like you'd risk prison over twelve mil."

"People do stupid things for stupid reasons."

"Maybe the reasons aren't stupid. Maybe you just don't understand them."

Torn between astonishment and anger, Richard grabbed the towel away from her. "Are you trying to tell me something? Just say it, for God's sake!"

Samantha put her hands on her bare hips. "Okay, yes. I did it. I took the Hogarth and stashed it in a bus locker in Union Station. Patricia's in on it with me. That's right, your ex-wife and I have joined forces."

"You—"

"What do you think I'm saying? Whoever did it, I used to be one of them. And a year ago, it could have been me. So excuse me if I'm not all 'stupid this and stupid that.' Obviously somebody wanted the Hogarth, and somebody stole it for that reason. If you think I had fun spending my morning being handcuffed and stuffed in the back of a police car, then fuck you." She grabbed the towel back and stomped past him into the bedroom.

Richard watched her swaying bare bottom for a moment, then followed her. The first day of their odd alliance, Detective Castillo had tried to handcuff her. He still remembered the sheer terror in her eyes as she thought she'd been caught. This morning she'd sat in that police car and gone into the interrogation room because he'd told her that he would get her out. They both knew that she could have escaped if she'd wanted to. But she'd stayed.

"Samantha," he said, turning her to face him and lifting her chin in his fingers, "I apologize. I think it's fair to say that we're both out of our comfort zone at the moment. Come with me to Ripton's office, and then we can stop and pick up some Chinese food." Very aware that she was naked and that he wanted to put his hands all over her, Richard kept his gaze on her face. "Truce?"

"Do you think I would let you take the blame for this even if I was the one who stole the painting?" she asked, green eyes narrowed.

She probably would find a way to prove him innocent even if *he'd* been the one to steal that painting. "No, I don't."

"Then stop with the 'I'm madder than you' shit. Because trust me, I'm way madder than you are, Rick. Whoever knew you had the Hogarth knew that I live here with you. This was a slap, and I'm slapping back."

"The first step you make that could be the least bit incriminating will have Gorstein all over you, Samantha."

She slipped her chin free of his fingers and pulled on her panties. "Only if he knows about it. You buy your hotel, and I'll take care of the painting."

"Forgive me if that doesn't make me feel any better," he grumbled. With a breath he walked to the closet to find a clean shirt and a power tie. "Whatever you said to the detective didn't seem to sit too well with him. He'll be looking for you to make a move, my love."

"He can look all he wants. I'll be standing outside a lawyer's office listening to how innocent I am, and then I'm having Chinese."

Since they seemed to have made up, he let it go at that. In the back of his mind, though, he couldn't help noting that she still hadn't answered his question of where the hell she'd been last night.

"Boy, we're a sorry pair of losers, aren't we?" she noted after a moment, as she slipped into a pretty sleeveless Luca Luca silk dress with orange and brown diagonal stripes.

"Mm-hm. I doubt we'll ever amount to anything."

He reached out one hand and took her wrist. When she didn't pull away, he tugged her against him. Samantha wrapped her arms around his waist and hugged him hard.

"We'll find out what's going on," he said, lowering his face to her hair. "And we'll find out who took my damn painting. When we do, I am going to demand a personal apology from Detective Gorstein, and I'm going to make a bloody example of the thief. Because maybe you used to be one of those, but you aren't now."

And that still occurred to him every time someone was arrested for a crime. That thief had once been Samantha. That might have been Samantha.

Abruptly she pulled away. "Okay. Let's get out of here and do this before I change my mind."

He gave a brief smile. "You won't." Because he couldn't help himself, he put his hands on her cheeks, tilted her face up, and kissed her.

As her arms slipped around his shoulders, the mobile phone in his pocket rang. Reluctantly he broke the kiss and flipped it open. "Fuck," he muttered.

She tilted his hand to look at the screen. "Great. Patricia. I should never have said her name out loud."

He pushed the talk button. "Addison."

"Richard, I just heard what happened," Patricia Addison-Wallis's refined London voice came. "If there's anything at all I can do for you, please—"

"We're fine, Patricia. I'm a bit busy at the moment, however. So goodb—"

"You might at least have told me you were coming to New York. I live here now, you know."

"I know. I found the apartment for you. And I paid for it."

"At the least you should have called me so we could go out to dinner, then. Really, Richard."

His ex-wife sounded pouty and triumphant at the same time. Of course she would, though, since he'd ignored her and Samantha had been dragged off to jail. "I'm here on business. I'll talk to you later."

"You brought Jellicoe here for business? Yours, or hers?"

"Are you doing reporting for the *Enquirer* now, Patricia?"

"Oh, please. It's a perfectly logical question."

"Hey, Patty," Sam called in a carrying voice, "can you call back? We're right in the middle of having sex."

Patricia gasped. "That woman is the most—"

Richard hung up the phone. "You really shouldn't antagonize her like that," he said mildly, leaning down to finish their kiss.

"She started it. And I still don't know why she hates me so much. You divorced her nearly two years before we met."

"She hates you because I love you."

Samantha pursed her soft lips. "Well, aren't you just the grand Poobah?"

"Apparently. Five minutes."

"I'll be ready."

With that he headed back to the office next door. If Patricia had one positive quality it was that her presence immediately shifted Samantha over to being on his side. On the negative end, Patricia Addison-Wallis knew that he and Samantha were in Manhattan. With her apartment only two miles from the townhouse, he had to anticipate that nothing good would come of any of this.

Rick's kiss left Samantha breathless; possessive, aroused, still angry—a little bit of everything. He might be all up in arms, but he wasn't the only one.

As for the rest, she knew what Martin would say—that she was playing Rick like a mark, getting his considerable wealth and power to back her up while she went about doing exactly as she pleased. If only it were that simple.

As soon as Rick closed the door behind him, Samantha dove over the bed for the phone. She tried her Palm Beach office first, and rolled her shoulders as she waited.

After three rings, the phone picked up. "Jellicoe Security," a warm, masculine voice drawled. "We're here to help."

"Hey, Aubrey," she returned, stepping into her tan sandals. "You should add that we're here to help for the right price."

"Miss Samantha, first we reel them in, and *then* we tell them the price."

"Right. Is Stoney there, by any chance?"

"He is. Hold on, sugar."

The on-hold music was soft Dixieland; obviously Aubrey had won some sort of contest over Stoney, who preferred the collective works of Enya. A minute later, the man himself answered.

"Did you get my e-mail, honey?" he asked. "I wanted you to check the figures before I send it to Locke. The—"

"Can you talk?" she interrupted.

She could almost see his eyebrows lift. "Hold on. I'll close the door." Silence. "Okay. What's up?"

"I need you to get on a plane and get your butt to Manhattan," she said, lowering her voice even with the bedroom door closed; the office was right next door.

"Why? If you and Rick are fighting or something, then it's none of my—"

"I think—I know—I saw Martin last night."

That shut him up. In fact, the silence on the other end of the line was almost deafening. "Honey," he finally said, in a voice usually reserved for invalids or insane people, "Martin is dead. You know that as well as I d—"

"He was at Sotheby's casing the place," she pushed, verifying reality for herself as much as for him. "Really interested in a newly discovered Hogarth that Rick ended up buying. I slipped him a note to meet me, and while I was out last night for the rendezvous somebody broke in and swiped the damned thing."

"But—"

"I know, Stoney! It's absolutely friggin' nuts. But he's here. And I think he played me to get that painting." Samantha cupped the phone. "You're the only one who can help me with this. I can't go to anybody else, and you know it."

More silence. "Does Rick know about any of this?"

"No. All he knows is that I went out last night, his alarm went off, and then the cops busted me—*me*—for the robbery. I spent a fucking hour in handcuffs. And I am not—" Her voice broke, and she took a moment to regain her balance. She was not going to fall apart over this. Not, not, not. "I am not going to let that happen again. And I'm not going to screw my life or Rick's life up any more until I know what's going on."

"I'll be on the next flight," he said.

"I really don't want Rick to know anything about this. Not yet."

"Okay. I'll phone Delroy. He'll set me up with a place to stay. I'll call you when I get in."

"Thanks, Stoney. I didn't know what else to do."

"Hey, honey, that's what family's for. Busting ghosts and shit."

She wiped a grateful tear from her face, surprised to see it there. "What are you going to tell Aubrey?"

"Twinkle toes? I'll just tell him I'm taking a long weekend, and that he can catch me on my phone."

Samantha smiled into the receiver. "Rick says Aubrey's not gay, you know."

"The billionaire's just jealous 'cause Aubrey hasn't hit on him. I'm running home to pack, and then I'm on my way. Hang in there."

"Okay. Thanks again."

Thanks didn't seem adequate, considering that Walter Barstone was the only person in the world she could count on to both be able to verify that the man she'd seen was actually Martin Jellicoe, and to not call the cops on him. And whoever *had* taken the Hogarth, whether it was Martin or not, she needed to take steps to get it back.

As soon as she hung up the phone she began feeling like a dirty rotten traitor. Rick was in the other room reading over a press release stating their innocence in all of this. And there she was, sitting around with a pretty good idea about who'd pulled the job, and bringing in secret help to investigate behind Rick's back.

She told herself that once she knew something for sure she would let him in on it, but that wasn't necessarily true. If her father came into the picture, she didn't know how she could possibly tell Rick without risking losing him.

Whether he trusted her or not, putting Martin back into the equation changed everything. She might have retired, but it was looking like Martin hadn't. And rich as he was, Rick Addison couldn't afford to have a thief in the family.

The phone in her hand rang. Startled, she nearly hurled it across the room before she got enough control over her nerves to hit the talk button. "Hello," she said.

"Hello," a crisp male voice returned in a British accent. "John Stillwell calling for Richard, Lord Rawley."

"Hold on." Carrying the phone, she went next door to the office and rapped.

"Come in."

She pushed open the door and bowed. "Lord Rawley, a John Stillwell is on the phone for you, Your Royal Immenseness."

Rick grimaced at her. "Damned Brits," he grumbled, taking the phone as she tossed it to him. "I must have left the house number for him by mistake. Apologies."

If Rick was giving out his private number for the house instead of the office one, he *was* frazzled. And that was her fault. "No problem," she said aloud, swallowing her annoyance at him, at least for the moment. "He sounds very well pressed."

She left again, closing the door behind her. With finally a minute alone in the hallway, she walked to the rear window. Rick probably found it suspicious that the burglar had gone in the same way she had earlier in the day, but any cat worth his or her salt would have evaluated the location and made the same decision.

Thank God she'd at least had enough sense left to wear gloves when she'd broken in. If not, she would probably still be in that interrogation room with Detective Gorstein.

Samantha scooted the low hall table out of the way and crouched in front of the window, being careful not to wrinkle her dress. The fresh silicone she and Wilder had used to repair the casing she'd broken was in still-damp blobs on the floor. Fresh scratch marks marred the sill where the alarm wires had been rerouted.

Hm. Whatever implement the cat had used was longer than the nail file she'd carried—from the shape of the scratches it was probably one of those old rolled copper measuring tapes. Those things were great. The actual tool, however, wasn't as significant as the fact that the cat had bypassed the alarm on the way in. Therefore, the alarm had been triggered on the way out. Which left her with the question of whether it had been on purpose or not.

If, as she suspected, her father was the cat, then there was no way in hell that he would set off an alarm that simple and straightforward by accident. And if he'd done it intentionally, she had a whole new set of problems.

"Be careful about fingerprints," Rick said from behind her, as he crossed into the bedroom to replace the phone. "The police have already dusted for them, or whatever the devil they call it, but they might be back."

"I'm not touching anything," she said, not moving from her squatting position. "I'm just looking."

"See anything interesting?"

"Lots. Whoever it was came in exactly the same way I did. Exactly."

"But you didn't set off the alarm."

"Not on the way in."

He stopped in the middle of the hallway. "Then it tripped on the way out. On purpose?"

Samantha stood, dusting off her hands more to stall than

because she'd touched anything. "He, she, they, came in, bypassed the alarm, walked down the hall and down the stairs, found the right painting—since I assume they would want the new Hogarth—went back upstairs and out. I'd bet that the alarm wasn't an accident."

"Which means I probably missed whoever it was by a minute, at most."

A cold sweat started beneath her hair. Martin and Rick—what would they make of one another if they ever met? Not much, she suspected. She hoped it would never happen. "I'm making some calls to get this place rewired," she said, moving past him.

Rick put a hand on her shoulder. "Why wouldn't they take both paintings?"

She shrugged. "I would have. I mean, jeez, it's all wrapped up already. Maybe they only had a buyer lined up for one of them and didn't want to store the other. Or didn't have a *place* to store it."

"I would think for a cut of five million dollars you could rent a storage locker somewhere."

Samantha looked sideways at him. "I thought you were turning me straight, not that I was making you into a cat burglar."

With a brief smile he tightened his grip on her shoulder and drew her around to face him. "As you've said, our worlds at times aren't all that different."

They held where they were for a long moment, standing a foot apart, his hand the only connection between them. Any other day in the past five months, Rick would have kissed her. Today, though, he let her go as Ripton emerged from the office.

"Ready?" the attorney asked.

With a deep breath she took Rick's hand, and they headed downstairs to the front door. And she would stand there while Phil read a statement she knew to be a lie, because she did know something about the robbery, and they weren't doing everything they could to cooperate with the police.

In the old days, that would have been a good thing. She knew her dad's rules, the ones that Martin had drummed into her head all through her childhood. Protect yourself, only give up information when someone else had already figured it out, look after yourself first. Here, with Rick, she'd begun to think that not only could she set aside some of the rules, but that a number of them were just stupid and selfish and didn't have a place outside the shadows. The shadows seemed to be closing in around her again, but at the moment she could deal with that. And the reason she could was holding her hand despite the fact that she wasn't being honest with him, either.

Not only did Rick already know enough about her to put her away for a very long time, but if she was forced to flee into the night, thanks to him she wasn't certain she would be able to go back to her old way of life. He'd made her see what she liked about herself. Before Rick, she'd only been able to be the real, actual Samantha Elizabeth Jellicoe on the most fleeting and rarest of occasions. She still thought like a cat burglar; she knew that. But not all the time, now. Her life felt . . . expanded. She spent less time looking over her shoulder, and more looking in front of her. That was still new enough that it felt precious and fragile.

Had Martin's plan been to force her back into his life? Considering that she'd thought him dead until last night, his methods didn't seem very fair. Martin had always been a Machiavellian kind of guy, though. His profits always justified his methods.

Samantha drew a deep breath. At the moment, however this turned out, she didn't see that it would be anything other than bad. Bad for her freedom, bad for her health, and bad for her heart.

Chapter 8

Wednesday, 9:18 p.m.

"That sucked," Samantha said, scooping a chopstick's worth of Chinese noodles into her mouth and pointing at the television. "They didn't even show the part where Ripton said we want the painting back."

Beside her on the couch, Rick filched another piece of her mushroom chicken. Any other time she would have questioned why he'd bothered to order broccoli beef if he was only going to eat her dinner, but at the moment it was kind of nice that he—they—felt easy enough to share.

"They're a celebrity newsmagazine," he commented, gesturing with one of his own chopsticks. "They don't care who did it, as long as we keep talking about it."

"But we didn't talk about it."

"We did show up, however. That's the only requirement, sometimes."

"Then why did we show up?"

"Because the newsmagazine is secondary. We're trying to impress the police."

"This is a new low."

"An unavoidable one."

She glanced at the grandfather clock in the corner. After nine o'clock. Stoney should already be in New York and staked out on Delroy's couch by now. Sneaking out for the second night in a row didn't seem the smartest thing to do, but she needed a face-to-face with him.

"I'm surprised Walter hasn't called you," Rick said abruptly, making her wonder if he could read minds. "This had to air in Palm Beach."

"He watches *Jeopardy!* and *Wheel*."

"You haven't called him, then?"

"I did. While you were in with Ripton. He thinks I'm an idiot and should run off to Paris."

"Oh, really?" Rick sat forward and scooped another mound of chow mein onto his plate. "And your reply was . . . ?"

"Springtime in Paris is no fun alone." She grinned briefly. "Is all this going to hurt your hotel deal?"

He shrugged. "Someone stole from me. That affects how I'm perceived. It gives the impression that I can be taken advantage of. At the moment I would imagine that Matsuo Hoshido is probably having a good laugh, adding a million or two to his price, and putting in a few more conditions that will not be favorable to me."

Samantha blew out her breath. "I know some people here in the city," she said slowly. "I could ask around." Sitting there wouldn't get her anything but insane, and she needed an excuse to get out of the house. And it wouldn't even be a lie.

"Right. That's a fine idea. You go and let yourself be seen with known art thieves or fences."

"Who says I would let myself be seen, smart ass?" She set her plate on the coffee table. "The way I see it, you need the painting back. I need the painting back. How it gets back is secondary."

"I don't know how many ways I can say it, Samantha, but Gorstein wasn't impressed by you or charmed by you. That—"

"I don't know about that."

"That makes him dangerous," Rick continued, as though she hadn't interrupted. "He will not look the other way like Frank Castillo does. And I'd rather risk a trial based on nothing but speculation and rumor than on photos or recordings of you chatting with felons."

Even the word *trial* made her break out in a cold sweat. For a long moment she gazed at Rick's profile as he ate, half his attention apparently on *Law & Order.* He knew how to push her buttons, and she had no doubt that he was trying to scare her into staying put.

"Frank does not look the other way. He gets that I have my own way of doing things."

"He gets that you helped him solve two murders," Rick countered.

"I could charm Gorstein if I wanted to. Under the circumstances, I didn't see the point."

"Mm-hm."

"What does that mean?"

Rick looked at her as he slurped in a chow mein noodle. "What does what mean?"

"'Mm-hm.' I charmed you, buddy. I can charm anybody."

So there. Samantha stacked the empty rice box into the chicken. Wilder would clean up the mess, but she still felt uncomfortable about having people sweeping up after her.

Housekeepers and butlers were well and good, but she disliked leaving a trail of evidence about her comings and goings for someone else to wipe away.

When she'd straightened up as much as she could considering that Rick was still eating, she stood. "I'm going to bed. And tomorrow, when you have your hotel meeting at the office, I'm going shopping again. Your social schedule's been wearing my wardrobe pretty thin." Because she couldn't seem to let an argument go without knowing exactly where he stood, she stopped in the doorway. "If we're still going to be socially active. Together, I mean."

Rick's plate clattered to the table. With that athlete quickness of his, he stood and crossed the room to stand in front of her. Before she could take a breath to respond to whatever he was about to say, he grabbed her arms and jerked her up against him. His mouth closed over hers, hot and insistent and tasting faintly of cream cheese wontons.

He overwhelmed her senses; he always did, no matter how jaded she was and how much she knew about need and greed and what steps people took to protect their own interests. Apparently—no, obviously—he considered her one of his interests.

She moaned, tangling her fingers into his black, wavy hair as he planted his palms on her ass and pulled her hard against his hips. God, how could she give this up?

"We're not finished," he murmured in between kisses. "And whatever I might think is best, I know you want to get some answers. Just promise me that you'll be low-key about it, and that you won't do anything to give Gorstein's suspicions teeth."

With luck, Gorstein wouldn't have a clue what she was up to. "I promise, Rick."

He ran his hands up under her T-shirt. "Then let's take this upstairs, shall we?"

"Heck, yeah."

She hoped that eventually he would understand why she couldn't just sit back and do nothing. It felt as though her old life was rising up to drown her, and she couldn't just let it go—not for either of their sakes. Rick trusted her, but he didn't trust her old life. And at the moment, neither did she.

When she woke up the next morning, it was nearly nine o'clock. Jeez. A little time in the slam clearly exhausted her. Rick was nowhere to be seen, but he nearly always got up before she did. It made sense; his business tended to start early, while her old life rarely began until well after nightfall.

With a stretch she got up and went into the bathroom. He'd left a sticky note on the mirror, and she smiled as she read it. "Out buying hotel. Call me for lunch? Love you, Rick."

Yep, that was her guy, and she did love him back. So much it scared her sometimes. Not for anybody else would she risk her freedom and her future the way she did just by spending each day with him. Other times, though, she wanted to knock him in the head and tell him to stop trying to be her conscience. She wasn't the only one who'd played with the law in this house, after all—even if her games had been of the easier-to-spot and simpler-to-prosecute kind.

Okay, she might do lunch with him, especially if it would help keep his level of suspicion down. The first phone call of the day, though, was for somebody else.

Once she'd dressed and thrown on some high-end shopping-appropriate makeup, she grabbed her cell phone and dialed Stoney's mobile number. Thank goodness she'd been able to talk him into getting a cell phone; since no one had arrested her after Rick got her one, he'd probably decided it was pretty safe.

"*Hola*," his voice came.

"*Hola*, big guy. *Cómo estás?*"

"I think I have Chee·tos wedged in my butt after spending the night on Delroy's damn couch," he retorted. "I'm moving to a hotel."

"Don't make it the Manhattan," she returned. That would be great. Stoney staying at the hotel Rick was trying to buy.

"Deal. When are we meeting?"

She glanced at the nearest clock. "How about half an hour at the Amsterdam Avenue entrance of Trump Tower?"

"Gotcha. Am I a tourist, or a businessman?"

She thought about it for a second. "I'm dressed to shop Madison Avenue, so you be a tourist. And we're using the old signals."

"Martin knows the signals," he said after a moment, his voice more serious.

"But the cops don't. Since they weren't too happy about letting me go, they might try to keep an eye on me. The head detective once tried to bust Martin. I don't want this getting any more tangled than it already is."

He snorted. "Yeah, because your usual amount of trouble is enough."

She blew him a raspberry.

"Hey, I didn't even point out that before you went straight, you never used to have this kind of trouble."

"Except for that last job. You know, the one where the security guard got blown up and I had to save the homeowner's life."

"Speaking of whom, how is Addison these days?"

"He still doesn't know anything. And I'm going to keep it

that way for as long as I can. It'll be a big deal to him, Stoney, if Martin's alive."

"*If.* And it wouldn't be your fault."

"It's not about fault. It's about having me around with Martin on the loose. If."

"I mean it, Sam—crime is simpler."

"Yes, but I like these sleeping arrangements better."

"Uh-huh. See you at ten, then, honey."

All of her things—keys, mirror, small roll of duct tape, paperclips, lipstick, cash, the credit cards she'd been slowly accumulating—were in the black purse she'd used last night. She pulled another purse out of the closet, looking at each of the items before she transferred them, and dumped the black purse into the trash. Maybe she was paranoid, but after last night she didn't want it anywhere around her, just in case somebody could use it to track her.

She'd never thought that living the straight life would be more expensive than staying on the fringes, but then she hadn't counted on living with a guy who bought hotels for fun. The black bag had been a $440 Louis Vuitton, which she'd bought for a charity luncheon in Palm Beach two months ago. "Crap," she muttered.

As soon as the cab Wilder had called for her rolled away from the curb, Samantha pulled the mirror from her new purse and began fiddling with her hair. Or pretending to. A couple of seconds after they turned the corner, a brown Ford Taurus made the same turn. Probably a coincidence, but she kept an eye on it, anyway.

By the time they reached 59th Street, the Taurus was still one car behind the cab. *Shit.* She leaned forward, rapping on the plastic dividing the driver from the passenger compartment. "Make a left up the next one-way street you can, and drop me off halfway down," she instructed. "Don't pull over. Just stop."

"*Qué*?" he said, looking half around.

She repeated the request in Spanish, and the driver nodded.

"Okay, *señorita*."

"*Bueno*." Pulling twenty bucks from a pocket, she fed it through the divider.

He did as she asked, and two minutes later she jumped out of the cab and headed back up the street against traffic. Tempting as it was to wave, she ignored the Taurus as it drove past her and then accelerated. They would be calling for backup, so as soon as they turned the corner she stopped and hailed another cab heading in the same direction as the cop car.

"Trump Tower," she said to the driver in the turban.

"Trump Tower. No problem."

Let the cops try to tail a cab in New York once they'd lost sight of it. *Ha*. But her hunch had been right; Gorstein was having her followed. That wasn't going to make things any easier.

Before she'd moved to Palm Beach, Florida, three years earlier and limited her thefts to the occasional interesting grab, she'd pulled maybe a dozen high-class thefts in New York alone, not counting the grabs at Sotheby's and Christie's. She wasn't sure she would call them happy memories, but they'd definitely been exhilarating ones.

And she'd given it up for Rick—well, not just for him, but also for herself, for a future where she wouldn't have to spend every moment looking over her shoulder, waiting to be caught—though with the way crimes kept happening around her, nothing much seemed to have changed. Nothing, that was, except for the fact that she didn't get to profit from the lawbreaking, any longer.

Stoney had a map, a camera, and a pair of sunglasses, topped by a Detroit Tigers baseball cap which covered his bald, black head. "Excuse me," he said, edging up to her as she drew even with him, "I'm looking for Trump Tower. Can you give me a hand?"

"No, I need both of mine," she returned, looping her arm around his and heading him toward the curb.

"Hey, I thought we were using the codes," he grumbled, lowering his sunglasses to glare at her over the rims.

"And you did. I happen to know that I was being followed, and that I lost them. Let's get going."

"Going where?" Stoney replied, holding out his map hand to hail another cab.

"Where would you start if you were trying to track down Martin?" she countered, slipping onto the worn black cab seat and sliding over so he could join her.

"He always found me. Assuming that you didn't eat some bad seafood or something and that he really is alive, I don't think he'd be inclined to answer any of the code ads we could place in the newspaper."

"I'm hoping I did eat something funny, but that wouldn't explain who took the Hogarth. And I agree; under the circumstances, I doubt he would be happy to be found. We used to spend a lot of time in New York, though, before we split company. He took me to some of his hangouts, but not all of them."

Stoney sighed. "He would have taken you to all of them, if I'd let him. A ten-year-old girl at Hannigan's, hustling tips."

"Hannigan's Bar," Samantha told the driver. "On the waterfront."

The disgust in Stoney's voice surprised her a little. She knew that she'd probably spent more time living with Stoney than with Martin, but it had never really occurred to her that the arrangement had been anything but for convenience' sake. "I used to make pretty good money toting drinks at Hannigan's."

"You used to distract the other cats and cons while they were drinking and telling Martin about grabs they'd contracted to do."

Samantha lifted an eyebrow. "He undercut his own friends' jobs?"

"Whenever he thought he could get away with it."

"You never talked about Martin this way before," she noted.

"He got caught right when you turned eighteen, and then died three years later. I figured you had your own way of doing things, and didn't need to hear about some of the crap he pulled."

"I knew about a lot of it. But in all honesty, he pretty much taught me everything I know about being a cat."

"He taught you the mechanics. You gave yourself a conscience and some pretty high standards." He looked out the window for a long moment, then cleared his throat and turned back. "I mean, I've"—he glanced forward at their driver—"redistributed for dozens of cats. You're the only one who refused to ever hit a museum."

Samantha grimaced. "I know I wasn't that easy to work with."

"Don't you apologize, honey. I was . . ." He cleared his throat again. "I was proud of you. And as much of a pain as a security business and keeping company with a pushy billionaire is, I'm still proud of you."

For a minute Samantha struggled not to give in to tears. Since she didn't think she could talk without blubbering, she leaned over and kissed Stoney on the cheek. "Thanks," she whispered.

"Yeah, well, I'd be just as proud of you if you decided to unretire and take a couple of those European jobs I keep getting calls about."

"Ask me again in a week," Samantha returned. Free and easy in Cannes, or being tailed and jailed by the NYPD. If not for Rick, the decision wouldn't have been all that difficult.

Stoney led the way into Hannigan's. Fourteen years later it seemed smaller, cheaper, and smellier than Samantha remembered, but some of the faces, even at eleven o'clock in the morning, were familiar.

"If it ain't Stoney and Baby Jellicoe," the bartender said loudly.

A couple of patrons headed out the back door in response, but none of them was Martin. So some of her old cronies didn't want to be associated with her. It was weird, but not much of a surprise. After all, she actually had contacts now who were lawyers and cops.

"We're looking for an old friend of ours," Stoney said, plunking himself on one of the barstools.

"Who might that be?"

"He'll know if he hears, and you'd know if you saw him," Samantha put in. "And if *you* see him, give me a call." She handed over a business card with her cell phone number written on the back.

"Jellicoe Security. Damn. So is it a scam, or are you on the side of the angels now, Baby Jellicoe?"

"I haven't decided yet. But if you call me with the right information, I've got a ton of cash with your name on it."

"I bet you do. I've seen you on the news. Saw you yesterday morning, in cuffs. I laughed."

Samantha leaned over the bar. "Did you now, Louie?" she murmured. "And did you see anything that would make you think I couldn't kick your ass?" She used to live among these people, though most of them couldn't match the grabs she'd made. They weren't nice people, for the most part. Falling back into their old lookin'-out-for-number-one mentality was like putting on an old, comfortable shirt.

The bartender's last snort sounded more like a choke. "Come on, you have to admit, you don't see a Jellicoe in cuffs very often. Not since they brought in your dad."

Aha. "And that was funny, why?"

"Because he used to say he'd never get caught. Nobody was slicker than Martin. And then he ends up dying in the slam. It's funny. Ironic funny, I guess."

Okay, not *haha* funny. "Ironic. Yeah. So don't forget to call me if you see anything."

In the back of the bar where the shadows seemed to have been designed as part of the decor, a chair scooted back noisily. "Hey, Stoney, I like your camera. That your new gig now, paparazzi to famous Baby Jellicoe?"

"Willits," Stoney grunted, facing the voice. "Why don't you come over here and smile, and we'll see if your picture goes up in the post office?"

"Let's go," Sam muttered. "They don't know anything we need."

"Okay," Stoney returned, gesturing her toward the door. He'd cover her back, just in case. "I'm thinking maybe Doffler next."

With a sigh, Samantha nodded. "I hate that guy."

Chapter 9

Thursday, 12:25 p.m.

Richard stood sipping a hot cup of tea and looking out the fiftieth-story window of his New York office. Behind him a half dozen of his people argued with a half dozen of Hoshido's staff over lease transfers and property tax benefits. As he'd suspected, things weren't going as smoothly today—apparently the opposition saw the Hogarth robbery as a chink in his armor. "You know, from here Edison Towers on Forty-seventh and Broadway looks appealing," he commented. "Kyle, give their management a call and get me a conversation with the owner."

"Yes, sir." Kyle reached for one of the conference room phones.

"I beg your pardon," one of Hoshido's lawyers said, "but wouldn't it make more sense to conclude your negotiations with us before you look at another hotel? The Edison and the Manhattan are in competing locations, anyway."

Rick smiled at him. "Yes, they are. And if you keep handing me that proprietary parking bullshit, you can go home and Hoshido can compete with me at the Edison Towers."

"This is a negotiation, Mr. Addison," the attorney returned, his jaw tight. "Nothing's been set in stone."

"Mm-hm. I'm just beginning to wonder whether you have Hoshido's best interests or your own in mind, Mr. Railsmith."

"The—"

The phone at the head of the table rang on line one. "Excuse me." Rick walked over to pick it up. "Addison."

"Sir, it's Sarah," came the soft British voice at the other end. "The profit reports for Kingdom Fittings came in today, but Omninet and Afra are late. Do you want what I have, or should I wait until the other two come in?"

"You did tell them how much I want those reports," he said.

"Several times," she returned. Even over the phone he could hear her disgust. "Apparently they want to hear it from someone other than your secretary."

Yes, they would want to hear it from him. A little cajoling, a little back-patting—he was a master at getting what he wanted. Lately, though, he'd been less single-minded about business, and most of his holdings seemed to know both that and the level of his distraction. "I'll take care of it," he said. "Hold on to the Kingdom report until tomorrow. And would you phone John Stillwell at the Sunrise office again and have him call me at this number?"

"Right away, sir."

Nothing had fallen out of his control yet, but if his life with Samantha continued as it was, he was going to have to face some unpleasant facts. The major one seemed to be that as much as he liked his independence, his ability to simply appear wherever and whenever one of his companies needed a kick in the pants or some fine-tuning or plain morale-boosting, his personal life had become of paramount importance. To quote Tom Donner, he wasn't a one-man band any longer. Perhaps if he'd thought or felt that way three years ago, he would still be married to Patricia.

Patricia, though, had been a business accessory—the wife on his arm for social events and hosting parties. Through no fault of her own, Patricia hadn't spun him around, lit him on fire, or made his bones melt. For that he'd needed Samantha. And since he wasn't willing to give her up, and since he wasn't willing to simplify his holdings, he needed assistance.

His phone rang again. "Addison."

"Sir," the receptionist said, "I have a John Stillwell on the phone for you?"

"Splendid. Hold on to him for a moment while I find an empty office."

"Karen Tyson is out of the office today, sir."

"Good. Put it through in there in two minutes."

He hung up and turned to the dozen attorneys quarreling at the other end of the room. "Ladies and gentlemen, order some lunch and calm down a little. This deal will be made, and we'll all be reasonably happy about it."

Across the hallway from his own office he found personnel manager Karen Tyson's door. As he entered the room, the phone rang. "John?" he asked.

"Lord Rawley," the crisp voice returned. "I mean to say, Rick. Good afternoon."

"John, I have two overdue profit reports from companies based in London. If you can get them to me by Sunday, I intend to offer you a position as my personal assistant. And I don't mean someone to fetch me tea. Your duties would be similar to what they are now, but a bit . . . higher-profile. In addition, it would involve more travel and picking up overflow details from my personal business. Think of it as being my chief of staff."

"Sir, I don't know what to say."

"I've been paying attention to your work at Sunrise, and Matumbe speaks very highly of you there. To start with, the position pays two hundred thousand pounds per annum, plus living expenses. You do have a valid visa, do you not?"

"Yes. Yes, I do."

"If you're interested, then I hope to see you in New York on Sunday."

"Thank you, L—Rick. I will be th—"

"Just a moment, John," Richard interrupted. "Are you married?"

"No, sir."

"Seeing anyone?"

"Not at the moment."

"And do you have a problem with spending what may well amount to a majority of your time traveling on short notice?" After all, he was calling in assistance to help him manage his businesses so he could manage his private life. It would be unfair to expect someone to give up his own in exchange. And that was another revelation of thought for which he could thank Samantha. "Honestly, John. Don't say what you think I want to hear."

"I do not have a problem with traveling, sir. If I may say, this is exactly the kind of opportunity I've been hoping for in working for one of your companies."

Richard cracked a smile. "The sycophancy isn't necessary unless I specifically request it. Sarah in the London office there has all of the information you'll require."

"I'll take care of it, Rick."

"I hope so."

That was one thing taken care of. Or three, actually. Now all he needed to do was stop letting the attorneys across the way keep throwing up roadblocks so he could get to work. His stomach rumbled, and he looked at the clock on the desk. Damn. Pulling out his cell phone, he hit speed dial number one.

"*Hola*."

"How hungry are you?"

"I'm actually already eyeing a pizza place," Samantha's smooth voice came. "How long do you think you'll be?"

"Too long. I think I'm going to order in."

"Don't forget to feed your minions."

He smiled. "Yes, love. I've already told them to find some crumbs. I'll see you in a few hours." That was his Sam, professional criminal and champion to overworked office staff everywhere.

"Okay." She paused. "How's it going today?"

"Fairly well. I'm currently threatening to drop the Manhattan and buy another hotel instead."

She chuckled. "I'm never playing Monopoly with you. See you tonight."

This time he waited for a second. When she didn't continue, he tightened his jaw a little. "I love you."

"I love you, too, studmuffin."

Patience, Rick, he reminded himself. Eventually she would feel easy enough to say it first, and without prompting. Both of their lives had changed dramatically since they'd met, and they were both still figuring out how to be partners. And if he had things his way, which he intended to do, they would have a very long time together to figure everything out.

* * *

Samantha folded over her pizza crust and jammed the end of it into her mouth. Across the table from her, Stoney took dainty bites of his Italian garden salad. The two of them probably looked like the Odd Couple from Hell.

"I notice you didn't tell Addison that you punched Doffler," her former fence said after a moment.

"I'm shopping today, not chasing hoods." She glanced around the half-full pizzeria. "Besides, Doffler shouldn't have said I lost my edge."

"So what are you trying to do, then—find Martin, or keep up your rep? Because last time I checked, you were retired. That's what the guy you just talked to on the phone thinks, anyway."

"I *am* retired. But I'm designing security for people. I don't want the cats and cons thinking I'm all soft now and they can hit the places I've wired."

"Mm-hm. So it's business, not ego."

"Eat your damn salad."

"I thought so."

Ignoring the smugness in his voice, Samantha pulled out a piece of paper from her pocket. "I didn't punch Nadia Kolsky or Merrado." She'd felt like it, out of frustration if nothing else. Somebody had to know where Martin was. And from what Stoney had been telling her, not too many of Martin's old acquaintances would necessarily care to do him the favor of keeping him hidden.

"That's because Merrado's bigger than King Kong."

"Okay, what about fences?" she asked, scratching out some more notes to herself. "I know Martin used you most, but some of the stuff he snatched was just bargain basement."

"Those guys don't tend to last very long in the business.

I'll make a couple of calls after lunch and see if I can track a few of them down."

She took another bite, musing as she did so. "Can I ask you a question?"

"As long as it's not about you and Addison."

"Why did I end up so different from Martin?"

Stoney snorted. "If I knew that, honey, it would have saved me a lot of arguments. Martin liked to blame it on your mom."

Samantha stopped mid-bite. "Why?"

"She was a smart lady. He kind of conned her into marrying him. When he couldn't figure you out, I guess she was easy to blame. And he wasn't always a snatch-and-grab man."

"I know. He used to be the best second-story guy in the business. He just—"

"He got older."

Samantha froze at the low voice over to her left. Her heart actually stopped beating—or it felt that way. Stoney's dark face had taken on a gray tinge, but she still didn't want to look over at the neighboring table. Why hadn't she known? Why hadn't she sensed that he'd walked through the door and sat down beside them?

"Cat got your tongue, Sam?"

Get it together, Sam, she shouted at herself. With a deep breath she turned her head. "Hello, Martin."

He sat there, looking exactly like he had the last time she'd sat across a table from him. No, not exactly, she amended. More gray in his light brown hair, deeper lines across his forehead and around his mouth. And he was a little thinner. But the man who sat at the white plastic table was unmistakably Martin Jellicoe.

"What—" Stoney rasped shakily. "How—"

Brown eyes slid over in the fence's direction and then returned to Samantha. He smiled, the smooth, confident expression that she remembered. "Surprise."

"What the hell is going on, Martin?" Stoney managed, his voice low and rumbling with emotion.

"I'll get to you in a minute, Stoney," Martin returned. "First, what were you about to say, Sam? That Martin got too old to pull top jobs? That he became a glorified purse snatcher?" He leaned closer, lowering his voice. "I guess I'm still good enough to come back from the dead, eh?"

"I don't understand," Samantha finally whispered, her voice shaking beyond her ability to control it.

He clapped a hand on the table's surface. "I hope you're not always this slow on the uptake," he said with a chuckle. "What's important here? I'm alive. Do you really want to waste time asking me why and how?"

"Yes, I do. Apparently you've had a little longer to process your not being dead than I have." Samantha swallowed. In a sense, he was right. Under the circumstances, with him here and a missing painting, she needed to catch up, and fast. "I watched your funeral, Martin."

"You thought you did. And that's your mistake. I told you not to come anywhere near me if I ever got nabbed. You always were soft, Sam. Or I thought you were. How much do you siphon off from that Brit every month? A mil? More? I saw you'd moved in with him and I thought, 'That's my girl.' Maybe you did learn everything I tried to teach you."

"I don't want to talk about that," Samantha shot back, shock beginning to warm into anger once he brought Rick into the equation. "And if you're delivering more lessons here, then the why of you being here *is* important. You didn't die in prison, but you couldn't have gotten out on your own.

Somebody would have mentioned a jailbreak on the news, otherwise. And then there's the little problem of *where* you've been for the past three years. You couldn't even send a postcard?"

"I've been here and there. Busy. And speaking of lessons, if we had one rule you never broke, it was that we stay out of each other's business. You're stepping pretty far into mine right now."

"What the hell are you talking about?" Stoney blurted. "Do you know what you put this girl through? How the hell—"

"Lay off the Hogarth. Both of you. And quit looking for me. Your British boy hasn't lost anything. Insurance'll cover the painting."

"You set me up." Samantha stood, leaning her clenched fists on the table in front of her, every muscle longing to hit Martin over and over again—not just because he'd stolen from Rick, but because he'd been alive for the past three years and hadn't bothered to say anything to his own daughter. "I tried to set up a rendezvous with you, and you used it to set me up."

"Be glad it was me you tried to meet with. Remember to keep your flank covered, Sam. You left your golden gander totally open to attack, because you were curious. How many times have I warned you about that?"

"You reappear to give me more lessons in thieving? What about being my damned dad for a minute?" That was exactly it, she realized; Martin had always positioned himself as her superior and her instructor. Apparently a six-year absence hadn't changed that at all. Christ. Her head felt like it was spinning right off her neck. And if anyone would take advantage of that, it was smooth, the-end-justifies-the-means Martin.

He snorted. "You're just mad because I outmaneuvered you. Come on. You can't begrudge your old dad one little egg out of that nest."

"When the cops blame me for taking it, I can." And now abruptly they were having another job argument, like it had been six days and not six years since they'd last spoken. "And since they're looking at me, the insurance company won't pay off. If I get arrested again, they could even go after Rick for fraud."

"So you'll have to find a new goose. You've been with him for what, six months? You've—"

"Five," she corrected stiffly.

"Whatever. You've probably squeezed everything out of him you can. He'll notice the furniture's missing, eventually."

She didn't try to explain her relationship with Rick. Martin wouldn't get it, anyway. Whatever the hell he had going on, though, she wasn't going to take the fall for it. She knew how he played the game. Apart for six years or not, some things never changed. The one lesson he was best at, the one he'd taught her first and repeated most often, was to look out for yourself first. Which meant she had better do the same—except that in her new world, that included Rick. "Who hired you for the Hogarth?" she asked.

"That's none of your business. Just do your shopping and partying and I'll go on with my thing."

"Until you decide to reappear in the middle of my shit again? I don't think so, Martin." Forcing her muscles to relax, she sat down again. "You could have grabbed the painting from Sotheby's. You wanted to take it from *my* house, and you waited until I went out to meet you before you made your play. So you tell me what the hell's going on, Dad. You think I stepped into the middle of your shit? You just stomped all over mine. And I don't like it."

The charm left his gaze for a moment. "Watch your mouth, Sam. I don't have to explain anything to you."

"It seems like a fair question to me, Martin," Stoney put in. "She could go to jail."

"That won't happen," Martin said dismissively, reaching over to take one of Samantha's slices of pizza and Mr. In-Control again. "If you thought it would, you'd be on your way to Paris or Milan."

Not if it meant abandoning Rick—and especially when her flight would make things worse for him. "There has to be a reason," she said slowly, "that you would vanish into thin air and then decide to reappear now, when Stoney and I didn't even have a clue that you were alive, much less still in the business." Flattery worked miracles on some of her marks; she didn't see why it couldn't work on Martin.

"Let's just say some people saw that it would benefit them more to have me out of prison than to try to keep me behind bars."

He had escaped from various facilities at least twice that she knew of. Who would find it more advantageous to have him running around free instead of keeping him in tougher and thereby more expensive facilities? Someone whom he was costing money. "You're working for the government?" she whispered, unable to keep herself from glancing around the restaurant.

"Smart as ever, aren't you, Sam? It's not exactly the government, though. I've been helping Interpol." He grinned, the jaunty I'm-the-smartest-guy-in-the-room expression she used to see on him every time he successfully pulled off a tricky job.

"Excuse me," Stoney cut in again, skepticism dripping from his deep voice, "but how does stealing from Rick Addison help Interpol?"

"Remember the job at the Louvre last year?" Martin took a large bite of Samantha's pepperoni pizza.

"That wasn't you," she countered flatly. "The news said at least four guys were involved. They shot and killed a security guard."

"Right. They ticked off Interpol, and so they made me a deal. *I* found out who the Louvre guys were, and I've been working my way into the crew. I just needed to set up one last quick score worth a couple million, and ta-da, I'm part of the team."

"So you let me see you at the auction, waited for me to set up a meeting, and then went into my house while I was out, just so you could get in with a crew of hoods?"

"*Your* house?" he repeated, his grin deepening. "And they're hardly hoods. They're some talented guys—that's why Interpol needs me. Now that the crew trusts me, all I have to do is rat out their next job, and I get to settle into happy retirement under a new name in a warm country. I'm thinking Monaco, maybe as John Robie."

John Robie. Cary Grant's character from *To Catch a Thief.* Martin had always imagined himself as that guy, Samantha knew, even though she considered that his reality fell far short of the fantasy.

"I want the Hogarth back, Martin. Go make your reputation on somebody else's hide. Not mine."

"Too late. I'm not the one who took it, anyway. I just set it up."

Samantha went cold. "You let the guys who shot a security guard break into my house with Rick there?" she snapped. It was one thing thinking Martin had gone in; despicable, but at least like her, he never carried a gun. A crew of killers, though . . . "Jesus Christ, Martin."

"Keep your voice down, Sam. And just leave this alone. After Interpol grabs the crew, you'll probably get the art back."

"Like they'd hold on to it for that long," Stoney grunted. "Nobody keeps something that hot for any longer than they have to. Trust me, it's how I make some of my best deals." He glanced at Samantha. "How I used to make some of my best deals," he corrected. "I'm retired."

"It's not that long. Leave it alone, and leave me alone, and maybe I'll invite you to my retirement party. If you go after the Hogarth, they'll know I told you about it, and you can come to my next funeral, too, Sam. For real, this time."

With that he stood and left the pizzeria. For a long moment Samantha and Stoney sat there looking at each other. "What the fuck am I supposed to do now?" she ground out, slamming her fist against the table. "He just shows up, and suddenly I'm twelve and he's the grand master Jedi of cat burglars again? Has he ever done anything straight in his life?"

"Not that I know of. And I'm thinking Hong Kong, honey," Stoney returned. "On a slow boat."

She blew out her breath. "Like a rowboat."

Her cell phone sang the James Bond theme. Rick. She flipped it open, her heart beating wildly. Great. It wasn't like he could have seen her there talking with her supposedly dead father. "Hi, sweetie," she said, keeping her voice cool and steady. "Did you change your mind about lunch?"

"No. I'm pretending to be on the phone with Trump about doing a deal together. You should see Hoshido's guys. They've already given up the top eight floors of the Manhattan."

She cracked a smile. "You're so lame."

"The hell you say. How's shopping going?"

Crap. "I'm more just looking." She stopped for a moment. What could she tell him without screwing up whatever she might need to hide from him later? He would expect something. Sam Jellicoe didn't have many dull days. "You'll be happy to know that some plainclothes cops tried to follow my cab."

"Did they, now?" he returned, his voice sharper. She could picture him sitting down, leaning forward over his desk. "And?"

"I lost 'em. Changed cabs, put on a moustache."

"Samantha, I'm glad this is amusing to you, but—"

"It's not. Actually, I'm not really sure how I'm supposed to react to all this. I've never been in this situation before."

"I know. Me neither. Hey, I picked up a present for you. Something for after dinner."

"Ooh, naughty." Across the table Stoney rolled his eyes, and she stuck her tongue out at him. "Can you give me a hint?"

"No. I'll be home about six."

"I should be back by then, too."

"I love you, Yank."

"Me, too, Brit." She hung up.

"What are you going to tell him, Sam?" Stoney finally gave up on pretending that he was eating his salad and pushed it away. "Because whatever Martin's up to, throwing Addison into the middle of it can't be good."

"No shit." She took a breath. "I don't know what I'm going to tell him. 'Sorry, my dad's back in business and he wants everything of yours that's not nailed down' doesn't sound very reassuring. I have to think about it. Can you stick around for a while?"

"I'm not going anywhere, honey. But be careful where

you go with this, or by the time the smoke clears I might be the only one left."

"I know," she muttered, picking up her pizza and dumping it into the nearby trash can. "Now I have to go buy something cute so Rick doesn't think I've been up to anything evil."

"I'll see to it, Wilder," Richard said, motioning the butler away from the front door.

"Very good, sir. Vilseau says dinner should be ready in twenty minutes."

Wilder vanished back toward the kitchen, and Richard looked out the front window again. Samantha handed a few bills through the passenger window to the taxi driver, then straightened, hefted her Bloomingdale's bag, and headed for the door. Former thief, current theft suspect, she made his heart speed the same way she had when she'd dropped through his ceiling five months ago to propose a business partnership.

He pulled open the door. "Good evening."

"What did you get me?" she asked, pulling his face down with her free hand and giving him a ferocious kiss.

Still attached at the mouth, he somehow remembered to close and lock the front door. Not that locks mattered much to most of her acquaintances. He pushed her back against the door, taking the shopping bag from her hand and dropping it to the floor. Her freed hand immediately went to his belt, to be joined by the other as she undid his zipper.

"What's all this, then?" he murmured, groaning as she reached into the front of his jeans, kneading and stroking.

"I want you."

With her hand still in his pants, they stumbled into the front sitting room. Richard closed the door with one foot as they fell over the side of the sofa onto the floor. "Slow down, sweetheart," he said, as she pulled his jeans down past his thighs and then shoved him over onto his back. "I'm not going anywhere."

"I don't want to slow down."

Wriggling, she undid her own slacks and kicked them off, her cute blue panties following. With a gasping moan she sank down onto him. Lifting his head, breathing hard, Richard watched as his cock disappeared into her, inch by inch, in a hot, tight slide. Whatever the devil was going on, he wasn't going to argue.

She lifted up and down on him, hard and fast. Fighting for a tiny measure of control, Richard slid his hand up under her blouse to caress her pert breasts as she bounced. Going along for the ride, as he felt her come he lay back and pushed his hips up into her until with a growl he joined her.

Samantha fell forward across his chest, kissing him again. "That wasn't very dignified, was it?" she panted, shoving her arms around behind his back and holding herself to him tightly.

"Dignified, no. Fun, yes," he returned, hugging her back.

She wasn't much for tight embraces and being held captive, and at this second her obvious and desperate affection frightened the hell out of him. For a long moment she held on to him, her cheek against his chest. It felt as though she was actually listening to his heartbeat.

"Not that I mind this in the least," he said quietly, reluctant to give up the intimacy but worried enough that he had to ask, "but is something troubling you, Sam?"

Her breath caught, then began again. Slowly she nodded against his chest. *Christ.*

Okay, it was bad. Calculating how hard he should push and how she would react, he decided to cajole her into talking. "You're not sick, are you?"

"No," she said, her voice muffled against his shirt.

So far, so good. "I'm not sick, am I?"

"No."

"No one's died?"

"No. No one at all."

Nearly complete sentences now. That seemed like an improvement. Keeping his voice calm and quiet and the questions over the top and nonthreatening, he kept talking. "You haven't stolen anything that will force you to flee the country?"

"I haven't stolen anything."

"Stoney hasn't been arrested again?"

"No."

"Someone you know has stolen something that will force them to flee the country?"

She sat up, looking down at him through the tangle of her auburn hair. She'd been letting it grow out a little, and he found the additional few inches extremely sexy. "I have to think about some things," she said slowly.

"Can you tell me about it?"

"Not now."

"Ever?"

"That's what I'm thinking about. Don't push it, okay?"

He thought about it for a moment, difficult as that was with him still inside her. She'd just admitted that something was going on. If he agreed not to ask any questions, was he giving her some sort of permission to carry on with whatever it was? They were both in a tight bind at the moment. "Can you promise me that this thing you're thinking about isn't putting your life in immediate peril?"

Samantha nodded. "I can promise that."

"I'll give you a little time, then, Sam, but I won't back off indefinitely. Obviously with us together, what affects you, affects me. And you know you can tell me anything. Anything."

"You should probably rethink that," she returned. "There may just be some things you don't *want* to know."

Richard held her gaze for a long moment. Well as he'd come to know her, there were still times she was impossible to read. This was obviously one of them. Was there something she could say that would make him wish to distance himself from her? Considering her answers to his previous questions, he couldn't imagine what it would be. Still, she hardly lived a conventional life, even when she spent the day shopping at Bloomingdale's.

"You can still tell me anything."

"Give me a day or two."

"Deal." *And not a second longer than that.*

Slowly she leaned down and kissed him once more. "Thank you." Samantha straightened again. "So where's my present?"

He snorted, despite his worry. She definitely kept him on his toes, even when he was flat on his back. "It's on the dining room table."

She stood, and he climbed to his feet, as well. At this moment, he supposed all he could do was wait for the next blow, and arm himself with all the information and ammunition he could before it came.

Chapter 10

Thursday, 8:40 p.m.

"So who's that?" Richard asked, pointing at the plasma television screen.

"That's Rodan. We've discussed him before."

"He looks different."

"You're right; he does." Samantha sat forward. "Oh, cool. They updated him. His neck even moves now."

"You're fairly easy to please, my dear."

"No, I'm not. And stop trying to distract me. Rodan's destroying New York." She hopped on the cushion. "Oh, and look! That's the U.S. version of Godzilla they have attacking Sidney. That's totally him! The Matthew Broderick one."

"As if I could distract you. I'm resigned to playing second fiddle to Godzilla." Richard sat back on the sofa beside her, his pulse thudding as Samantha curled into his left side and pulled his arm across her shoulders. Focused as he was about touching her at every opportunity, tonight he felt like he was in heaven. She held his hand, twiddling absently with his fingers, while he did the only thing he could to calm and reassure her when she wouldn't tell him what troubled her—hold her on her terms, and let her watch Godzilla.

"Thank you again for the DVD," she said a moment later. "How did you know I'd never seen this one?"

"I asked around. It was only released a few months ago, and it's never been on American cable." The Blockbuster Video clerk had recognized him and had clearly thought him insane when he'd asked for the movie monster section, but *Godzilla—Final Wars* had clearly been the right choice.

Across the hall his office phone rang, but he ignored it. The machine would pick up the call, and he had no intention of leaving the sofa without Samantha. Not tonight; not when he'd begun to think that she might be considering taking him into her confidence.

"What if that's the hotel guy?" she asked, twisting her head to look up at him.

"Then it can wait until tomorrow."

Thirty seconds later his cell phone rang. "Maybe he needs his top eight floors back," she suggested, cracking her quicksilver grin.

"Smart ass." He shifted to grab the phone. "Addison."

"Where the hell are you?" Tom Donner's voice came.

"At the opera," Rick returned dryly.

"Crap. I'm sor— Wait a minute. I hear Godzilla. You're watching some movie with Jellicoe."

Richard shifted the phone to his right ear. "I had no idea you were a fan."

"I've got a fourteen-year-old boy, remember? Mike has all the video games. Can you talk, Rick?"

"Briefly."

"Okay. I stopped by Jellicoe's office to check on things,

like you asked. Aubrey's got everything under control. Would Jellicoe care if I tried to hire him away?"

"Good, and yes. I'll—"

"So then I kind of casually asked about Walter, since he wasn't there."

From the dramatic pause, Richard was obviously supposed to be anticipating something. "And?" he prompted.

"Barstone's not in town. Told Aubrey he was taking a long weekend, and booked a flight somewhere. And before you say I'm just gossiping or something, he took off all in a hurry about two hours after you busted Jellicoe out of jail."

Bloody hell. He'd suspected that Samantha had begun looking for the missing Hogarth. Walter's disappearance from Florida didn't constitute proof, but it was a disturbing bit of coincidence, as far as he was concerned. "That's great," he said aloud. "I'll send you the next set of demands as soon as they come in. Give Kate a snog for me."

"Donner?" Samantha asked as he flipped the phone closed.

He nodded. "He had a couple of questions about one of my e-mails."

So Walter was probably somewhere in New York, and one or the other of them had found out something. Something serious enough to have the normally independent Samantha practically climbing inside him, and still unwilling to discuss any of it. He needed some bloody answers; remaining ignorant and waiting for the shit to hit the fan simply wasn't his way of working.

Samantha sat up, carefully scooting off the edge of the bed while Rick snored softly beside her. Three o'clock in the morning. Go time, in the old days. Night owls would have gone to bed, and early birds weren't up yet. A perfect time for an enterprising cat burglar to slip in somewhere and grab the worm.

The rich brown bedroom curtains were closed against the streetlights, but about an inch of light showed along the near side. She edged up to the opening and looked out. A dozen or so cars were parked along the near side on the street within her line of sight. With no parking on the far side of the street, any surveillance would have to be either among those cars, or in one of the trees overlooking Central Park's low brick wall.

Pissed off as Gorstein had been, and with the tail she'd shaken off this morning, she fully expected someone to be watching the townhouse. If they were smart and if they had it in the budget, they'd put somebody in the alley, too.

A minute later, she spotted it—a brief, round reflection of light coming through the rear window of a Honda. Binoculars. Boy, Gorstein took this catching-the-bad-guys thing seriously.

With a faint smile she reversed course and slipped out the bedroom door. They'd replaced the panel in the hall window again, and in the dark it didn't look as though anyone had tampered with it. By leaning along the wall to one side of the window she had a pretty good view of the alley below. The two homeless guys with the cups of Starbucks coffee and the shoulder-holster bulges under their shirts looked pretty promising.

Good. For once she was glad of the surveillance. It still chilled her to the bone that Martin had sent the Louvre crew in here, knowing both that she was elsewhere and that they would kill. Maybe in her dad's mind he'd been keeping her out of danger, but Rick had been there, asleep. Wilder and Ben and Vilseau slept downstairs in the old servants' quarters, but if there'd been trouble, it would have involved Rick.

Her Rick—at least until he found out that her own father had arranged for the theft of the painting. After that, all bets were off.

The bedroom door clicked open behind her, and she turned. In the corner there by the window he'd never see her. Out of instinct she froze into the shadows before she made herself relax. "Over here," she said quietly.

He turned toward her, lowering his right hand at the same time. *Jesus.* He was carrying a pistol. She knew he owned a couple of them, but she hadn't realized he'd brought one with him to New York. Briefly she wondered whether he would have done so if she hadn't been living with him. He did know some bad guys, all on his own.

"What is it?" he asked, moving along the wall to avoid being seen from the window. He'd picked up some of her skills scary fast.

"Just checking on the cops," she returned. "We're surrounded."

"Is that a problem for you in the middle of the night?"

Great. He was mad again. "They followed me yesterday, Rick, and that is a problem. I wanted to know if they were still around. Don't you?"

He blew out his breath. "Yes. If they're here, they're not out looking for my bloody painting and whoever took it."

For once that hadn't even occurred to her. If Martin had been dead, he would have been spinning in his grave. Hell, she'd actually been happy that the cops were around, and hadn't even considered that their presence meant she was still suspect numero uno.

If she told Rick that she knew who'd stolen the painting—not names, yet, but she had a pretty good idea—he would demand that she go to Gorstein with the information. She could get around mentioning Martin, but if the NYPD was lucky enough to bring in the Louvre crew for taking one painting rather than for the big score they were planning, it could negate her dad's deal with Interpol. In addition, this crew killed. She could be putting Martin's life at risk. Complicated as her relationship with her father was, she didn't want to attend a second funeral for him.

Silently Rick swept her hair forward over her shoulder and feather-light kissed the back of her neck. "I'll make a call in the morning and see if I can convince Detective Gorstein to do his bloody job, even if that means telling him to forget this one."

"Like you'd let anybody get away with stealing from you."

"There are other ways to handle that. A private detective might be more useful, under the circumstances."

Under the circumstances meaning that the cops wouldn't stop bugging her. Great. "Rick, you don't—"

"Come back to bed, Yank," he interrupted. "It's cold there without you."

She took his proffered hand, and he pulled her close against his side. There had to be a way she could clear herself, get the painting back, not compromise Martin—and not lose this man. There had to be.

"Tell me again why we're meeting here?" Stoney asked, taking a turn around the vast, echoing entrance hall.

"I'm basking in the glory of art." Samantha glanced toward the security and information desk. Three guys guarding the entrance of the Metropolitan Museum of Art. She could get around them in a damned second. The cameras would be harder, but—

"And the real story is?"

She shook herself. There she went, casing joints again.

"Fine. My cushy townhouse is surrounded by cops. I needed to get out of there." And it had felt good to lose the tail again on her way to the museum. They might know where she slept every night, but the day was her own damned business.

"Are you sure they didn't follow you, then?" The ex-fence looked over his shoulder for what seemed like the hundredth time.

She smirked at him. "Give me a break. Let's head for the European Impressionists."

"Works for me." He fell into step beside her. "I've been thinking. If Martin's telling the truth, then Interpol *will* probably recover the Hogarth and get it back to your guy. That puts Addison back out of the picture, and you out of trouble with the cops. The end."

"Like you care about the Hogarth. You're just looking for something that'll keep me from telling Rick what's going on."

"And you're trying to convince yourself to let him in on this. Big mistake, honey. Trust me. Huge mistake."

"He can't blame me for Martin being alive. I didn't know." She wrapped her arm through Stoney's so she could lower her voice. "But if Martin's only requirement to get in with this crew was to arrange for a painting to go missing, he didn't have to pick the Hogarth. I can't help thinking that he chose it because of me. He sure didn't *not* choose it because of me. And that's what Rick'll start worrying about—that whether I'm straight or not, the piranhas are going to come around nibbling, just because I'm there. And I'm not all that sure he'd be wrong."

"I'm telling you, lie to him, Sam."

She slowed in front of one of the Monets. That should have been the logical solution—she used to lie all the time, about who she was, about what she was doing at a particular party or event. Not to Rick, though. She didn't like lying to Rick. Maybe it was guilt, or fear of being caught at it later, but she didn't think so. Rick was new; that life was new. And she didn't want to wreck it. Which brought her back to lying again. "I owe him enough that I don't think I can."

"You're happy with Addison, and if you tell him all this, he won't be happy with you. And then *I* won't be happy. Don't do it."

She shook her head. "It's a question of loyalty. And until Martin showed up again, I knew I would stand up for you, and I'd stand up for Rick. So now I'm wondering why. . . . What do I owe him? Martin, I mean?"

"He's your dad, honey. You shouldn't even be talking like that. Just because he's not a grocer or a pilot or something, he raised you with what he knew. And you're the best damned cat I've ever seen. Ever."

"Thanks, Stoney." She gripped his arm hard. "But I'm not so sure that . . . what I like about myself—what Rick likes about me—is because of Martin." She cleared her throat. "So is your advice really that I should just stand back and do nothing? Do you really think I should lie to Rick?"

"Shit," he muttered, turning away to look across the room for a long moment. "I don't know."

Man, they were both becoming a pair of saps. Who would have thought? "I'm going to tell him," she decided, realizing that she'd probably made that decision the moment Martin had appeared in the pizzeria. "I might have to move in with you back in Palm Beach, though."

"You can have the spare bedroom. Unless you think we should try living in Paris. We could make a ton of money in Paris."

Samantha shook her head, smiling. "We already have a

ton of money. And I don't think you should be talking about robberies *in the middle of an art museum.*"

"Right. My bad." He took a deep breath. "So what do you want to do with your last day of being in the spotlight?"

She suppressed a shudder. She could do without the spotlight. Just not the reason for it. "Let's go see the French Masters."

"Cool."

"Let me make something clear, Detective," Richard said, pacing to his office window and back. Anger clipped his words; Samantha said the emotion made him sound even more British, which he didn't consider to be possible, since he was already one hundred percent British. "Samantha Jellicoe did not take my painting. *I* did not take my painting. And you know that, or you would have gotten that warrant and searched my home again."

"I'm not going to tell you how my investigation is go—"

"Considering that you have absolutely no evidence other than some theory that Samantha must be involved in something underhanded because her father was a thief, I'm beginning to see a situation where I might bring charges against you for dereliction of duty."

"She doesn't have an alibi, Mr. Add—"

"And you no longer have a crime. I've already put in a call to my insurance people to drop the Hogarth from their coverage. And I'm not pressing charges. If you do enjoy wasting time, I can certainly accommodate you by suing you and your department for harassment. I don't even care if I win. What I care about is that you will spend your every waking hour defending yourself. All because you wouldn't do your job today. Think about that."

He slammed down the phone.

So he'd lost himself twelve million dollars and hopefully stopped the police from tailing Samantha, but that didn't keep *him* from wanting to do so. He had some hunches, and some clues, but he wanted facts. In business, his people presented him with facts—profit margins, overhead costs, location, economy—and he decided on a strategy and made a decision based on that information. No official crime might exist any longer, but he still wanted his bloody painting back.

What did he know for certain? Samantha was fiercely uneasy about something. Walter Barstone had left Florida on what amounted to the first flight after Samantha's release from jail. The person or persons who had stolen the Hogarth had broken in exactly the same way that Samantha had twelve hours earlier. With the abundance of other art and antiques in the townhouse, only the Hogarth had been taken. Therefore, it had been the specific target. And Samantha had tried to talk him out of buying it.

Richard slowed his pacing. He'd forgotten about the way she'd tried to cajole him into leaving the auction early. And she'd thought she'd recognized someone.

His phone intercom buzzed. "Mr. Addison? I have Sam Jellicoe in reception to see you, and Mr. Hoshido on the line."

Think of the devil. "Please send Samantha in, and put Matsuo through."

The phone clicked. "Richard? You are giving my people heart attacks," came Matsuo Hoshido's low, Japanese-accented voice.

Richard lifted the receiver as his door opened. "You're the one who keeps changing the price and the conditions," he said, motioning Samantha to come in. "I'm buying a building in an old, established neighborhood, not a tank of gas."

"Ah, but when circumstances change, prices change."

"Circumstances. Allow me to put it in perspective, then, Matsuo-san. I'm in the process of locating a missing painting. It's worth less than one percent of my net value. If you think I've been damaged or weakened by the theft, you are in error. If you think it makes me willing to pay more than what we've been negotiating, you're being foolish. And I know you're not a fool."

"Then I suppose the negotiations will continue. Have a good day."

"And you, Matsuo-san."

Richard hung up. "Hello," he said, watching Samantha as she wandered the length of the room's windows. She'd worn slim black jeans and a cute green T-shirt with a glittery heart over the bosom. New York casual—designed to fit in just about anywhere.

"Hi. That was your hotel guy, I presume?"

"Yes. Matsuo Hoshido."

"You were pretty forceful with him."

She hadn't yet met his gaze. Low tension ran through his muscles. "I suppose so. Any police adventures this morning?"

"It's hardly an adventure anymore. They give up way too easy."

"I can't really blame them. You're pretty good at what you do."

"Thanks."

He waited until she finally faced him, her long, slender fingers knotted into fists. "I'm going to tell you something."

"Is this the thing you were thinking over last evening?"

Samantha nodded. "I didn't plan for any of it, and I didn't know, but I do now. And you need to know, because . . . because it's about both of us."

Richard swallowed, his vision swimming. Quickly he reached for the chair behind him. "Are you . . . are you pregnant?" he asked, his voice shaking a little. Elation, abject terror—he did his best to hold it all back. He'd thought this conversation would be about the painting, but . . . this . . . could explain her distraction of the past few days. Facts. He wanted some bloody facts.

"What? Why—" She flushed. "No. Christ, no." Scowling, she finally emitted a small snort. "It did sound like it, didn't it?"

"Kind of, yes." The odd sensation in his heart—was it disappointment?—he would review later. "Go on, then."

"Okay. And I'm sorry in advance, since we probably won't be speaking by the time I'm finished."

That did not sound good. "As I've said before, you can tell me anything."

"Be careful what you wish for."

Walter Barstone paced in the reception area of New York's Addisco headquarters. He couldn't believe he was in the damn building in the first place.

Sam had gone through the third door down the hall on the left, and he kept his eyes on it. She was an idiot, risking a good thing over something as changeable as the truth. In her own way, though, he supposed she'd always been the honest type. She had her own code, anyway.

The muttering of distant voices grew louder. Oh, boy. Next things would start breaking, and then somebody would probably end up pitched out the window. Since they were on the fiftieth floor, that couldn't be good.

On the other side of the door, something crashed. Walter rolled his shoulders. Okay, time for an intervention. He started forward.

The receptionist stood. "I'm sorry, sir, but you need to wait here. Sir! You can't go in there!"

"It's all right; I'm family," he said, and shoved open the office door. He heard her calling for security, but ignored it as he closed the door behind him. "Wow. Nice office, Addison," he said, stepping over the platter of broken drinking glasses.

Rick spun around to face him. "Walter. I see you were included in the Jellicoe family reunion."

"I was as surprised two days ago as you are now. Nobody asked for this."

Addison's eyes were stone cold. "Apparently *I* asked for it. And now all the bloody Jellicoe family and friends have carte blanche to steal from me. You can imagine how delighted I am to finally be informed of my abject stupidity."

Precise, icy, and vicious. Sam really knew how to pick 'em.

At the far end of the room Sam stood glaring at Addison, her shoulders heaving and the expression on her face one that Walter knew as hurt fury. Great. Two volcanic eruptions—with him in the middle. "Since I wasn't in here for the party," he said, "I'll just sum up for my own sake."

"Why don't you do that somewhere else?" Addison suggested, his British at full force. "This is a private conversation."

"Nah. I think I'll stay for a minute. So you told him that Martin showed up and said he was trading for a life sentence in prison by working for Interpol, right?"

"Don't bother, Stoney," Sam finally grumbled, her attention staying on Addison. "I came clean, and Mr. Lord of the Manor flipped out. Let's get out of here."

"No," Addison broke in, before Walter could. "I'd like to know what other items Miss Take It If It's Not Nailed Down has offered to her friends."

"What friends? How can I have friends when I'm around you?"

"You—"

"Oh, give me a fucking break," Walter said loudly. "Don't you get it, Addison? If she takes the painting back, the crew figures Martin ratted them out, and he's dead. Probably Sam is, too. If she—"

The door shoved open, a pair of armed security guards moving through and fanning out on either side. "Don't move!"

Addison stepped forward. "It's all right. Just a family disagreement. Thanks, lads."

They holstered their weapons and backed out. "Okay, Mr. Addison. Sorry about that."

"You missed your big chance to have me hauled off in cuffs again, Rick," Sam taunted.

"Shut up, will you?" Addison faced Walter again. "You were saying?"

"Yeah. If Sam doesn't try to get the painting back and instead turns the story over to the cops, Interpol misses its big bust, and Martin goes back to jail. I told her not to say anything at all to you, and it would blow over. Sam's got this thing, though, where she doesn't like to lie to you."

For a minute Sam and Addison glared at each other, the unstoppable force against the immovable object. At least he'd shut them both up for a minute.

"I was already a target for thieves once," the Brit finally said in a quieter voice. "I didn't tolerate it then. If I do now, then I may as well hang out a 'Kick Me' sign. None of your other former associates will care if there were extenuating circumstances this time."

"You mean they'll associate me living with you as a

welcome sign for them," Sam put in. "After this they will, anyway. I know that."

"You install security, honey," Walter broke in.

"No, Rick's right," she countered, her voice dropping further. "I knew this would happen, as soon as I saw Martin. I'm just terrific at security." She lowered her head. "Dammit."

"Your job is not to protect my things."

"It's not to get them stolen, either."

Addison closed his eyes briefly. "Walter, will you excuse us for a moment?"

"Sam?" The reinforcements didn't leave unless the Indians had the Cowboys surrounded.

She looked up. "I'm going for a walk. You two do whatever you want." Pushing away from the wall, she headed for the door.

"Go, as long as you're coming back," Addison took a step toward the door.

"Stop bossing me around, Addison," she shot.

"Stop being so defensive, Jellicoe. I'll meet you at the café in the lobby in half an hour."

"You're buying. And invite Stoney. He's been sleeping on a couch." She stepped through the door and closed it behind her.

Richard faced the ex-fence. "What the hell are you doing in New York, exactly?"

"She called me, told me she'd seen a ghost, and wanted me to come and verify whether she was crazy or not."

"If you hadn't come, she might have confided in me. Did that ever occur to you?" Still trying to absorb the conversation of the last twenty minutes, Richard felt very tempted for a moment to beat the hell out of Barstone, just out of convenience. Christ. Of all the things he'd expected to hear from Samantha, learning that her father was alive and well and apparently still in the business hadn't been one of them.

"No, it really didn't. She called; I came. We're family."

"And what am I, then?"

Barstone grimaced. "I don't think you want me to answer that."

"Certainly I do." Walter was bulkier than he was, but they were about the same height. Considering that he was about twenty years younger and worked out, he'd give himself the advantage. "Indulge me, Walter."

"Fine. You're a rich guy hanging on to a novelty until she starts impacting your business—like now. That's why you're mad, isn't it? Because now having her around is a liability?"

"Bullshit," Richard shot back, pacing to the window. "Bull shit. I'm mad because she decided that I would just . . . throw my hands up and walk away because her past showed up at the door. She didn't even tell me; she just assumed. And you told her to leave me out of it. You told her to lie to me. This isn't my fault, as much as it's yours."

"Me? Why the hell are you putting me into the middle of this?"

"Because as long as you're around she can go back," he said flatly. "You give her somewhere to go besides forward."

"No, I give her a choice. You're pretty cool, but if she wants to stay with you there's only one way she can go. The difference between us is that I'll back her up whichever direction she chooses. If you make her happy, then I retire so she won't feel like she has to worry about me. If you back her into a corner and make her feel like she has to prove herself, then you're damn right I'm going to step in and try to keep her safe."

Richard took a deep breath, closing his jaw against the retort he wanted to make. The only thing that terrified him more than Samantha going back to her old life was her doing it alone. "Do you think she'll stay out of this?" he asked finally.

"No, I don't. You made it pretty clear that you aren't happy being used. She isn't, either." He shook his head. "You know, this is typical Martin. Vanish for three years, let his little girl think he's dead, and then reappear just so he can twist her up into one of his schemes and tell her it's a learning experience." Walter blew out his breath. "He's always got to be the teacher. I mean, some of his 'lessons' are lifesavers, but he's closer to being Fagin than Howard Cunningham."

"Apparently," Richard said slowly, approaching Barstone again, "I misjudged you. A little."

"Yeah, well, thanks."

"My main concern is Samantha's happiness and her well-being. You may not believe me, but I do love her. Very much. I don't want to lose her."

"Let's say that maybe I believe you."

"That's good enough for now." Richard offered his hand. "How about a truce, at least until we figure a way out of this?"

After a hesitation Walter's large black hand gripped his. "Truce."

Chapter 11

Friday, 12:12 p.m.

Samantha wished she'd worn jogging shoes instead of the five-hundred-dollar Ferragamo sandals she had on. The low heels were comfortable enough, but at the moment she wanted to run. And run, and run, and run.

Maybe she'd approached Rick the wrong way, apologizing in advance and offering to go away. It wasn't her fault that she was Martin's kid, and even if she had followed in his footsteps for most of her life, she wasn't doing so any longer. At least she was trying not to.

"Fu . . ." she started, amending it to ". . . dge," when a lady and what looked like her two young daughters exited the Old Navy store in front of her.

The youngest girl reminded her of Tom Donner's daughter, Olivia. Kids were interesting. She couldn't remember ever really being one herself, despite her nearly photographic memory. Mostly she remembered picking pockets, researching with endless fascination the items Martin obtained and turned over to Stoney for "redistribution."

She'd loved growing up that way—no rules, no schools except when they'd settled in one place for a couple of months, picking up knowledge and languages on the fly. Even in retrospect the thrill of her first job, the first Rembrandt, the oldest Egyptian relics, that Roman fertility statue that had been so well endowed it hadn't fit into her bag . . . She chuckled.

What the hell was she doing, hanging out with Rick Addison? Not just hanging out with him, but living with him, sharing his life, falling in love with him? On the other hand, how could she not be doing what she was doing, now that she'd experienced it?

"Sam Jellicoe."

As she heard the low voice, a hand touched the small of her back. She stiffened, tensing as she turned around.

A tall, pale man about Rick's age looked down at her, his hand now at about the level of her breasts. Pale hair, almost clear, stuck out from his head in a butch porcupine cut. His eyes were just as pale, barely blue enough to qualify as a color.

"Nicholas Veittsreig," she said, taking a slow step backward.

"You remember me," he returned, showing perfect teeth in a smile. The German in his accent was barely detectable; if she hadn't known, she might not have noticed it. Well, *she* would have, but most other people probably wouldn't.

"I always remember hacks." If he was in New York, it was either the biggest coincidence in the history of coincidences, or she'd just found some missing puzzle pieces.

"Oh, Sam, you are so cruel, always thinking you're better than the rest of us. You wound me."

"I am better than the rest of you."

"It didn't look that way when you were wearing the handcuffs. Or when you were talking with your daddy yesterday."

Great. The good guys *and* the bad guys were following her. "Did you want something, or are you just high? Martin's dead, remember?"

"Your boyfriend looked very peaceful asleep on those blue silk sheets. I was hoping you would be home, too, but Martin warned you, I suppose. Do you still want to play the who-knows-what game?"

Samantha just managed to keep from hitting him. He'd been in their freaking *bedroom*, with Rick there sleeping. "Addison does look good," she agreed, keeping her voice soft and aloof, "but I didn't know you swung that way, Nicholas. Gosh. You learn new things about people all the t—"

"Enough shit, Sam. I'm here to do you a favor."

"What kind of a favor? Because I really don't swing *your* way."

"You see? This is what I'm talking about. I know why you're angry; the cops busted you for the job I pulled. So I figure I owe you one. Martin knows B and E, but you're better at alarm systems. Why don't you come along with us on our next job?"

"I don't think so, Fritzy."

"Ah, but I think I can convince you. I know your dad talked to you. Don't you think everyone would feel safer if you were included now? I'll even give you a percentage." He looked her up and down. "Maybe afterwards we can become partners. Who knows? After all, with your boyfriend and your new job, you have access to the world's most exclusive and wealthy places."

"You think I didn't realize that when I hooked up with

him?" she ventured, feeling out the path he was taking. "But cats work alone."

"Not the smart ones. If you'd been with us in Paris last year, you'd have an extra three million American in your retirement account."

Thinking fast, Samantha gave him the same assessing look he'd favored her with a minute ago. She'd been offered partnerships before, but never by anybody on Veittsreig's par. If this had been a straight proposition with no other circumstances or strings attached, she would have told him flat out that she didn't work with guns—much less with killers. This guy, though, had Rick's painting, and if she said the wrong thing she could also be putting Martin and his cover in jeopardy.

"Are you going to tell me what you're hitting?"

"Not until I know you're in and we can trust that you won't trade the information to the police in exchange for them dropping all charges."

"I doubt anything I said to the cops would convince them of anything," she said truthfully, hoping that Gorstein and his people hadn't tracked her down again in time to see this little meeting.

"Even so, Martin went through a little initiation in Munich a couple of weeks ago—a very nice Canova sculpture worth about a million. Then he got bonus points for the Hogarth."

Samantha drew a slow breath. "So you want me to go through an initiation?" she asked. "Like I've never pulled a job before?"

"I'd like to know for certain that you're still pulling jobs, and that you'll have as much to lose as the rest of us if the cops show up. You shut down Sean O'Hannon. Some people say you got him killed."

"O'Hannon's stupidity in working with the wrong people got him killed," she countered. The whole Rick-stolen-art fiasco that had brought them together—and one of the reasons she'd decided to retire. "You're the one who approached me, Nicholas. What do you want?"

He smiled, managing to look more frightening than charming. "I want a present. Something small and sparkly, and worth at least half a million. I'll give you a break on the price since this is short notice. Otherwise you'd have to match your daddy."

"And when do you want this present?"

"Today's Friday. Saturday would be good. And I want to hear about the theft on the news. No going out and buying something just to fool me."

"Jeez. Paranoid much? How about I say no to the whole gig?"

"Not an option, Sam. Remember, I know that Martin told you things. I don't know what, but you're in now. Or you're dead. So prove that I can trust you, or I'll shoot you right here."

Fuck. "What if I accidently hit the place you're setting up for your big, invitation-only score?"

"You won't. Is it a deal?"

"Some damned deal, Fritzy." She pursed her lips, pasting a thoughtful expression on her face and trying to pretend that her brain wasn't about to implode and that her heart was having palpitations. "Can you swear to me that if this goes down right I won't have to leave Rick? He's my all-access pass, after all. There has to be an upside for me."

"If it goes down right, no one will know what hit them. I'm giving you this opportunity out of professional courtesy, and out of respect for Martin. In, or dead?"

Mentally crossing her fingers, she nodded. "It'll be fun to work with Martin again. I'm in."

Veittsreig grinned again. "I knew you weren't on the straight path. Give me a number where I can get hold of you."

She gave him her cell number. "I'm only supposed to be in New York for another week. If it's going to be longer than that, let me know so I'll have time to come up with an excuse."

"You'll be back in cozy Palm Beach right on time." He took her chin in his long fingers, tilting her face up. "Nobody else gets included, Sam. If I hear of anything, I will send photos of this little meeting to the police. And don't mistake me—any double-cross and I'll kill Martin, I'll kill your rich boyfriend, and I'll kill you. Are we clear?"

Samantha let him hold her there. "We're clear. But if you cut me out or try to leave me holding the bag on this, know that you can't go anywhere that I can't get to."

He let her go. "Good. We are in agreement. I'll see you Saturday. If you pass, I'll let you in on the details and let you know your percentage."

"As long as it's not less than ten percent, I don't think we'll have a problem."

With a nod and a sly smile, Veittsreig headed down the street. Samantha blew out her breath. And she'd thought this morning with Rick had been the worst thing she would ever go through.

Obviously, though, she was going to have to go another round with both him and Stoney. Because whatever she'd promised Veittsreig, she wasn't going into this without letting them know what they might be facing.

She walked on for another block, then made a show of

checking her watch. Nicholas wasn't much for bluffing, and she believed him when he'd said photos were being taken of their little meeting. That meant he'd had people watching. They probably still were watching.

Okay, so she knew who Martin was working with, and who Interpol was after. But Nicholas had taken one piece of art from the house. Her new question was, who was *he* working for? And who the hell was she going to rob in order to buy her way onto the crew?

What a bunch of shit she'd landed in. And the old, familiar adrenaline began pumping through her muscles. Yep, that was her—danger junkie. Whatever else happened, she'd just agreed both to a break-in that was big enough to have Interpol's attention in advance, and to a dirty little deed all of her own. And if she got caught, she had no doubt that she'd end up in Gorstein's little interrogation room on her way to prison with a "do not pass go" card. To think, a couple of days ago she'd figured that visiting New York as a semi-law-abiding citizen would be dull.

The sight in the café made Samantha pause. Toward the back of the large, open room Rick sat at right angles to Stoney. Both men had their heads bent over a piece of paper, and were either playing combat tic-tac-toe or plotting somebody's murder. Probably hers.

"Hi, boys," she said, cautiously approaching the table. Fighting with Rick wore her out, and that combined with her chat with Veittsreig had her right at the edge of civility. Everybody had better watch their crap, or else.

Rick stood, as he always did when she entered a room. "Feeling calmer?" he asked quietly, pulling out the chair opposite Stoney for her.

"Yes, and no. What are you two doing?" She nodded her chin toward the piece of paper.

"It's a twelve-step program to get you out of New York," Stoney said.

"That figures. You finally decide to like each other, and it's only so you can screw me over."

"I still don't like him," Rick countered, reaching over and brushing his fingers across the back of her hand. "We merely found a mutual cause."

"Mm-hm." Still half on an adrenaline high, at least she could be amused by their presumption. She glanced surreptitiously around the café. It was located in the lobby of Rick's office building, so most of the people there worked for him, and they'd kept a respectful distance from his table. They were all watching him, sure, but she didn't think anybody was close enough to overhear. And that was good, because nobody from Veittsreig's crew could come any closer, either, without being very conspicuous.

"The way we figure it," Rick said, motioning a passing waitress for a round of Diet Cokes, "you haven't been charged with anything."

"Not yet," she noted.

"And I don't imagine you will be—until after this big score your father mentioned, anyway. Until that time, no one can stop any or all of us from leaving the country. Once we're in England, it would be a small matter to fly to anywhere there's no extradi—"

Samantha tugged him over by the lapels and kissed him softly. "You're okay, Brit."

"I'd like to think so."

She looked him in the eye for a long moment. "There's something else you need to know, though."

The waitress appeared with their sodas, and she took a sip as Rick ordered a ham sandwich and Stoney asked for a salad. She didn't have much of an appetite herself, but she ordered some nachos.

Once the waitress left again, she gave a playful smile and sat back. "No serious looks," she said, "and no conspiratorial whispering while I'm talking. Somebody might be watching."

"Somebody like who?" Rick murmured, echoing her smile as he took her fingers again. Businessman or not, he had the soul of a thief.

"Stoney, did you ever do business with Nicholas Veittsreig?"

"A couple of times. He usually dealt directly with clients. He liked—likes—big, showy jobs."

"Guess who Martin's setting up with Interpol."

"Holy Moses."

"That's an understatement," she returned. "Keep smiling, Stoney."

"Would someone care to enlighten me?" Rick asked, lifting an eyebrow.

Stoney was sucking on his soda, so it looked like she would have to take this one. "He usually works with a crew of four or five, usually European. Like Stoney said, they like big jobs. They're the ones who hit the Louvre last year and came about thirty seconds from nabbing the *Mona Lisa*. They killed a security guard."

"And took about fifty million in other art," he said, nodding. "Interpol contacted me to ask if I'd been offered any of it. I never heard a word, though."

"It's all probably in some big Hong Kong businessman's back room right now," Samantha said cynically. "Anyway, the point is, Veittsreig's crew is in New York. And they hooked up with Martin for some help with a B and E."

"Did you see Martin again?" Stoney asked. "How do you know all this?"

"Nicholas stopped me on the street a few minutes ago." Rick started forward, and she dug her fingers into his palm. "We're planning a tea party or something, remember?"

"Yes. I remember." He eased back again. "Go on."

"Okay. He told me that he knew Martin had talked to me. As far as he's concerned, that makes me either a partner, or a liability. Because of my reputation, he offered me a place on the crew for their next job."

"And you turned him down," Rick said, very quietly, all trace of humor gone from his eyes.

"He, ah, kind of made me an offer I couldn't refuse."

Lunch arrived, and she decided that delivering bad news in public definitely had an upside—Rick, for certain, wouldn't blow up at her when the potential for paparazzi or press existed. She would have to remember that.

"What kind of offer?" Stoney asked, his own voice hard. He obviously wasn't happy, either.

"Like I said, he made it pretty clear that with what I knew, I would be involved or I would be dead. And he threatened Martin, too. So I said I would go along with them, for a fair percentage."

"Samantha, we are going to the police with this." Rick's grip on her fingers was hard enough to bruise. From the look on his face, though, he might have been discussing cricket.

"No, we're not. Interpol's already involved, and I don't have a deal with them. And it gets worse."

"Christ. How does it get worse?"

"Even with my rep, Veittsreig's not convinced I'm still working for the Dark Side. He wants a gift that'll prove I'm in."

"What kind of g—"

"I'm trying to tell you the story here," she said, a little sharply. Dammit, it was hard enough to lay all this out without Rick interrupting every sentence with a question. "He wants a diamond something worth half a mil. And he wants it to be a robbery, not a purchase. If the job doesn't end up on the news, I get a bullet. If I pull it off, then I'm in for the big score because I'll be in up to my eyeballs."

"No. Absolutely not."

"What's the big score?" Stoney asked.

Rick's attention turned to Stoney. "So now you're the fence again? Is this what you meant when you said you would support her in anything?"

"It's a legit question, Addison. We need to know the whole equation before we decide what to do. So back off."

"Happy, happy," Samantha muttered, her teeth clenched. "And I don't know what the job is. It's going to happen sometime in the next week. I gave him my cell number, and he said he'd call me for a meet on Saturday, when I'm supposed to give him his present. If he's happy, then he'll give me the details."

"You are not going to pull a job. It's one thing keeping you safe when you haven't done anything. When—"

"First of all," Samantha interrupted, "I never asked you to keep me safe. That was never a part of this . . . whatever it is. Thanks for getting me out of jail, but I could have gotten out on my own. So stop pretending your knight-in-shining-armor act isn't as much for your own benefit as for mine."

"I never said it wasn't."

That stopped her well-planned outburst of righteous anger. "Second," she said with a sniff, "I don't have much of a choice. I said yes to buy myself some time."

"Time for what, if I might ask? Do you have a mark in mind for the jewelry heist?"

"Stop trying to act like Steve McQueen." She looked past him. "Stoney, can you find out what the job is?"

The ex-fence rolled his shoulders. "Maybe. I'll check with Merrado. Most people think I'm still in the business, so they might talk."

"Okay." She frowned, covering the expression by stuffing a cheese-covered chip into her mouth. "It would have been nice if Martin had given us a little more information. Or if he'd at least mentioned how we could get back in touch with him."

For a minute the three of them sat there in silence, eating—or pretending to, anyway. Rick fumed; she was somewhat surprised that he hadn't walked away. Apparently he meant it when he said he loved her. It still bothered her a little that she couldn't figure out his angle, though more and more she'd begun to believe that he didn't have one. It was Martin who'd always said that everything and everyone had an angle, a goal that would benefit themselves.

Her father had certainly proven that to be true where he himself was concerned. The damn Hogarth had been a sideshow, just something Nicholas probably contracted for knowing he'd be in New York. Martin had provided the angle, so now *she* was in for the big score.

Which brought her back to the question of why the Hogarth, and why her. "Stoney," she began, her muscles shivering a little, "before Martin got busted he asked me to partner with him for a couple of jobs."

"I remember. You did the first one, then said you wanted to go solo."

"Yes. Martin mistimed a security sweep and nearly got

both of us caught. I told him I didn't want to work with him anymore, that he needed to retire because he was getting sloppy and desperate."

Stoney gave a low whistle. "I knew he was pissed off, but I didn't know you said that to him. Jeez, Sam."

"I was kind of freaked out at the time."

While her friend was mulling over what she'd said, Rick had already figured out the implications. "You think your father put Veittsreig up to bringing you in for this job."

"Or that he set up the Hogarth robbery to push Nicholas in that direction."

"That's thin, Sam."

She nodded at Stoney. "I know, but I can't discount it. I have to wonder if all this was just to prove to me that he's still partner material, or if he's setting me up for a fall because six months after I left he got busted."

"If either of those is true, it looks as though he's definitely trying to pull you back in." Rick took a casual glance around the room, but with practically everybody watching him anyway, picking out one suspicious person wasn't going to happen.

"Yep, me and Pacino," she said dryly. "I need to know some details, and then we need a plan." And then she would have to plan a robbery with less than twenty-eight hours to play with.

Rick took a deep breath. "And an escape route would be nice, too."

Chapter 12

Friday, 7:44 p.m.

"This is stupid," Sam muttered over her shoulder as she stepped out of the limousine. "I don't want to be here." She had a damned robbery to plan, and he wanted to socialize.

Rick disembarked after her. "It's a nice gesture. And we're already here."

She let him take her hand as they walked up the sidewalk. "It's not a gesture. He only asked us so everybody could stand around and stare at me—at us—and whisper."

"I'm used to being whispered about."

"Well, good for you. You didn't get arrested earlier this week. What would they say about you, anyway? 'Ooh, he's even better-looking in person,' or 'Hey, Marge, do you really think he's as rich as they say he is?' "

" 'Marge'?" he repeated, amusement in his voice.

"You go. Ben can take me home."

"Yes, I'll just pop out to a party while you decide who you're going to steal diamonds from."

Her heart jumped at the mention. Hearing it said out loud still freaked her out. She and Stoney had never had these conversations in the open. "I'm waiting for alternate suggestions that fulfill all of Veittsreig's requirements and don't have me forced to flee the country. Well?"

He slid his eyes at her. "I'm working on it."

"So am I."

"Then let's go back home and work on it."

"We already accepted the invitation."

Obviously he didn't understand. "Since when do you like ego-stroking parties, anyway? The jugglers probably canceled, and so he needs me here to provide the entertainment. That's why he invited us. I have my own shit to deal with tonight, thank you very much."

"Samantha," he said, sending her up the steps first, "sometimes it's not the motives that matter. Sometimes the gesture is the important thing. Would you rather have these people remember seeing you on the telly in handcuffs, or here being charming at Boyden Locke's house? They're your potential clients."

Clients. And marks again. Shit. "So it's okay if they whisper, as long as they see that I got invited to the ball."

"Exactly, Cinderella. Whatever Locke might personally think of your guilt or innocence, the fact that he's invited you to his house implies his support." Rick ran his palm up her arm to her shoulder.

She knew he was right. That didn't make the idea of being gawked at for an entire evening any more pleasant. "I'd like it better if I could be someone else," she grumbled. "Maybe a blonde. You like blondes."

"I like you."

The only reason she'd gotten in the car with him was because she'd thought that whoever had hired Nicholas and Martin might be in attendance. The odds were minuscule, but being there would be the best chance she had to look around without doing a B and E. Whoever it was, they had to be loaded. Neither cat worked cheap. And as Rick had said, the people who could afford a new Hogarth and whatever else was on the menu were the same people who could afford her services.

Richard reached around her to knock. As the door opened, a wall of light and noise swept over them with an almost physical energy. "Once more unto the breach," he murmured, stepping through the entryway with her.

"My kingdom for a really big bottle of hooch," Samantha countered, then walked forward with a warm, bright smile to greet their host. "Boyden, I thought the invitation to coffee was generous. This is lovely of you," she said, taking both of Locke's hands in hers.

"Not nearly as lovely as you are. You're a lucky man, Addison."

Richard shook Locke's hand. "I'm well aware of that."

He stood back a little and watched as Locke walked Samantha around, introducing her to some of the wealthiest and most influential citizens of Manhattan. She charmed all of them, even making a few delicate, self-deprecating jokes about her taste in art and bracelets. For a moment he wondered which one of them she would decide to rob—and what the hell he was going to do about that.

"Isn't she something?" a female voice with a cultured British accent said from just behind him.

Mentally steeling himself, he turned and looked.

"Hello, Patricia. I had a feeling you might be here tonight."

Ruby red lips smiled, and she touched her artistic coil of blonde hair. "Is that why you came?"

"That's why I almost didn't. Who's your date?"

"I'm not seeing anyone at the moment. With the exception of my first husband, my taste in men has been rather poor, I'm forced to admit."

Hm. Nothing like a murder conviction for husband number two and another one for the next steady boyfriend to give a girl a reputation. Patricia certainly didn't need to be reminded of that, however, and he had no intention of doing so in public, anyway. Instead he lifted her hand and brushed his lips across her knuckles. "You look very nice tonight."

Blue eyes widened a little in surprise. "Thank you, Richard. So do you."

As if scripted in a very bad movie, Matsuo Hoshido chose that moment to stroll up to them, an attractive, petite Japanese woman on his arm. "Ah, Richard," he said, bowing. "This is the lovely Samantha, yes?"

Patricia Addison-Wallis cleared her throat, but before she could answer, Richard shook his head. "I'm afraid this is the lovely Patricia Wallis," he said, shaking Hoshido's hand. "Samantha is—" He stopped as a bare arm slipped around his sleeve, warm and familiar. "Right here," he continued, looking over at her.

Samantha's gaze was on Patricia. "Hello, Patty. I think Boyden's looking for you."

The muscles of Patricia's jaw twitched. "Thank you. Excuse me."

Not bothering to watch Patricia's exit, Samantha offered her free hand to Hoshido, bowing as she did so. "You must be Mr. Hoshido. Rick has several times cursed your keen business sense."

Hoshido chuckled as he shook her hand. "You are as charming as Richard described. Samantha, Richard, this is my wife Miazaki. I'm afraid her English is a bit—"

"*Bonsowa-ru*," Samantha cut in, offering her hand to Mrs. Hoshido. "Good evening."

"*Bonsowa-ru*. Do you . . . speak Japanese?"

"*Hai. Wazuka*."

"Wonderful!" Mrs. Hoshido exclaimed. "I also speak English a little."

Samantha grinned. "Then we should get along quite well."

While the two women began chatting and giggling, Hoshido motioned for Richard to step aside with him. Squeezing Samantha's hand, he did so.

"Your Samantha is quite remarkable," Matsuo said, smiling fondly at his own wife.

"Yes, she is."

The hotelier eyed him. "You didn't know she spoke Japanese."

Rick chuckled. "I had no idea."

"She is also brave to come here when everyone knows of her arrest."

Wonderful. "Yes, she is. Her father's past is . . . less than pristine, and the police became a little overzealous. It was an unfortunate mistake."

"But as you admitted this morning, you were indeed robbed of a very valuable painting."

"Yes," Richard conceded, working to keep his voice relaxed. "An unfortunate mistake on the part of the thief."

"So you truly think you will recover the painting?"

"I know I will."

"Ah. A very bold statement."

"I'm a very bold chap." And he would not allow anyone to steal from him and get away with it.

"I have a suggestion."

"And what might that be?" Richard asked.

"We should go to dinner tomorrow night. No attorneys, no wives. Just us. Perhaps we will be able to come to an agreement more quickly without everyone else there to interfere."

"That is a splendid idea, Matsuo. Shall we say Daniel's on Sixty-fifth tomorrow at seven o'clock?"

"I will be there."

They returned to the ladies as another mob of the wealthy elite surrounded them. From looking at Samantha, anyone would think she'd not only been born into the club, but that she was their honorary princess. So much for any of them asking her to juggle; whether she knew how to do that or not, she was clearly a master magician.

With a slight smile he pulled out his cell phone and dialed. "Maria, see if you can get reservations for two at Daniel's tomorrow night at seven. The chef's sky box, if possible."

"Right away, Mr. Addison."

That was one hurdle jumped. At the moment, though, he was more concerned with Samantha's probable business dealings tonight.

Over the next two hours, Samantha compiled a list of a half dozen possible Hogarth buyers, and twice that many potential victims for her pending cat burglary. As for who Veittsreig's boss might be, two of these guys she knew to be in the business of obtaining "relocated" items, but one of them specialized in Egyptian antiquities, and the other tended to like modern art over British masters. That left four, none of whom she was certain about.

In a great many ways, working the crowd like that was more difficult than climbing through somebody's second-story window and making off with a box of diamonds.

Face-to-face work, sizing up a mark, scouting a location before she pulled a job—she'd done it before, on countless occasions, but not when it mattered what they thought of her. In the old days she'd been in disguise, literal or figurative, and who she'd pretended to be had depended on what she was looking to get. Tonight, she'd come in as Sam Jellicoe, significant other to Rick Addison. And she would leave the same way, and she'd be that same person tomorrow.

"Aren't you just the belle of the ball," Patricia's cool voice came from the foot of the stairs.

Samantha had seen the way Rick had greeted the Ex. Whatever her personal feelings toward Patricia, she would take her cue from him. After all, he'd been the injured party. She hadn't known him back then, except as a face on the cover of a magazine, and as a legend among cat burglars—the man who'd to that point been robbery-proof.

"Hi, Patty," she said.

"I am going to tell you one last time that I hate being called Patty," the Ex murmured, gliding closer, blonde hair perfectly coiffed, and her black and gold Donna Karan dress definitely not off the rack.

"I'm waiting for you to call a truce before I lay down my weapons," Samantha returned. "Rick said you're here by yourself tonight."

"What of it? Do you think I couldn't have found a date if I'd wan—"

"That's cool," Samantha interrupted. "The new Patricia. Walks in how she wants, and walks out how she wants. No men required."

"Yes, I suppose so."

Sam took a step closer, willing to risk having a glass of wine thrown in her face. "Just so you know, Boyden Locke has been looking at you all night. He went through a sticky divorce about seven years ago, and he didn't have a date tonight, either. Not even for his own party."

"He's a little old for me, don't you think?"

"He's forty-eight. I'm not trying to fix you up. I'm just stating a few facts."

Patricia looked at her for a long moment. "I'm not calling a truce," she said, "but I suppose this is a beginning—as long as you're not trying to rally me."

"That means kid you, right?"

"Americans," the Ex muttered. "Yes."

"Then no, I'm not rallying you." Locke definitely wasn't *her* type—pompous and flamboyant—but he was rich, which made him Patty's type.

Across the room Rick broke away from the Trump and Locke power triangle and headed in her direction. Rich as Croesus, long-tailed, old-fashioned tuxedo, black hair that caressed his collar, and those blue, blue eyes—no wonder most of the women in the room were watching him. She watched him, too, but not for those reasons. Yes, he was handsome, but he was also damn sexy, and probably the smartest person she'd ever met, and funny as hell, and he liked to barbecue.

"I'd like to state for the record," he drawled in that hot British accent of his, "that seeing the two of you together still frightens the devil out of me."

"And so it should," Samantha returned.

Patricia cleared her throat. "Excuse me," she said. "I need to see a man about a . . . man."

Rick watched her walk into the other room. "Was that a joke?" he muttered. "From Patricia?"

"Weird, huh?"

He drew an arm around her waist. "Are you ready to go?"

"Hell, yes."

He pulled his phone from his pocket and hit one of the speed dial buttons. "Ben? We're ready."

"What were you and Trump talking about?" she asked, as they headed through the thinning crowd for the front door.

"That red tie he always wears. I told him he could wear a plaid neckcloth and he'd still frighten the piss out of people."

"And?"

"And I believe he's considering expanding his tie rack." He pulled open the door for her. "What were you and Patricia chatting about?"

"That cute mole on your bottom."

"Mm-hm. Seriously."

She snorted. "I just told her that Boyden seemed to like her, and that he didn't have a date tonight."

"You're fixing up my ex-wife."

"I gave her some information. That's it, fella."

Ben pulled open the limousine door for them at the curb, and she slid in, Rick behind her. "Home, sir?" the driver asked.

"Yes."

Rick probably wanted to interrogate her about what she meant to do to satisfy Veittsreig's demand for diamonds, but after an evening of charming people and looking for secrets, mostly she just wanted to be close to him and not say much of anything for the next few minutes. Samantha sank back along his side, and he put a comfortable arm around her, kissing her hair. Good. He got it. He always did, though.

"You impressed Hoshido, you know," he finally murmured into her hair.

"I lived in Japan for a couple of months. His wife's pretty funny, which means he probably is, too."

"He is, when he's not being a hard-assed hotel owner trying to wrangle a hundred million dollars out of my pocket."

"Oh, come on," she mused, chuckling, "I probably shaved ten million off that price all by myself tonight."

"You probably did. You know, you think you know somebody, and then after five months you find out she speaks Japanese."

Sam leaned forward and slipped off her heels. Curling and flexing her toes to try to get the blood flowing again, she patted him on the knee. "Your Japanese is probably better than mine, Brit, so don't pretend you're jealous."

"How do you know I speak Japanese?"

"Nearly photographic memory, remember?" she returned, tapping her skull. "*Newsweek*, May 17, 2001. 'Business acumen not withstanding, Addison's greatest asset in dealing with the increasingly Japanese ranks of California multinational corporate heads may very well be his grasp of the language—literally.'" She cleared her throat. "Shall I continue?"

For a moment he sat in silence. "You are bloody amazing, Samantha Elizabeth Jellicoe."

"Thanks. I told you I read up on you before I went back to drop in on you that second time." That had been the night, five months ago, when she'd realized just how much trouble Richard Addison was going to be for her. And had she ever been right about that.

Wilder opened the front door for them as they topped the townhouse steps. Carrying her shoes, Samantha scooted past him and up the stairs. She wanted to call Stoney—he knew more buyers than she did, and he might have something that could corroborate her initial suspicions. Of course, it was more than likely that her suspicions were nothing more than that, just a wish that the bad guy would be present and easily accessible.

The bed was already turned down—the day maids at

work—and she pulled off her dress and sat. And felt something stiff beneath her thigh. Frowning, she stood up and ran a hand over the silk fitted sheet. Something in the shape of a small rectangle was beneath the sheet, against the mattress.

"What are you doing?" Rick asked, coming into the room and closing the door behind him.

She knelt down and pulled up the sheet. "I don't know."

It was an envelope. One that, if she'd been keeping secrets from Rick, she would have been much more cautious about discovering. She pulled it free and tucked the sheet under again.

"What the hell is that?" Rick tossed his tuxedo jacket over a chair and yanked the tie free. "And how do you know it's meant for you?"

"You think it's from one of your old girlfriends?" she retorted, covering her sudden panic as she realized who must have left it there. "It's on my side of the bed." Samantha opened it. "It's from Nicholas," she said, for the moment putting aside how dismayed she was at the thought that Veittsreig had been in her bedroom—again. And of course he knew which side of the bed was hers; he'd seen Rick sleeping there.

Dammit, she should have arranged to rewire the security system here the second they landed at the airport. Most thieves weren't as skilled as her or Martin or Nicholas, but obviously it could happen. Or rather it *had* happened, and it wouldn't happen again.

Rick grabbed the paper from her, batting her hand away when she dove after it. "'I hope you enjoyed your party tonight,'" he read, his voice ice-cold. "'You look very nice in black. I only wanted to remind you that you have work to do, and that I can get to you and your British boyfriend anytime I want.'" He looked at her. "That's fairly direct."

"What do you expect? Death and dismemberment threats are just job lingo for me."

"They used to be job lingo for you. We need to call Gorstein."

"No, no, no." For one thing, it wasn't only her death that Nicholas was threatening. If she messed up, Rick would be in very real danger, too. "You don't even know about this. You can't. I haven't told you anything, remember?" She took the note back from him. "I'm not even surprised. Look at it from his point of view."

"Please, enlighten me."

"Okay. I'm living with a rich guy, I'm in a cushy position, and he's trying to get me to do something that could cause me a lot of trouble. He has to threaten me; otherwise, what's my incentive?"

"I'm glad you can be so circumspect about this," he growled, yanking off his waistcoat and shirt.

She had to be, or he would go even more ballistic than he already was. "Nothing's changed. We stick to the plan until we find out what they want."

He sat on the bed next to her. "And what's your plan for this evening?"

"A little B and E. What do you think?"

He grabbed her near elbow. "You are not going to steal anything from anyone."

"You are not the boss of me."

"I'm fucking serious, Samantha. I told you before, you will not use my house as a sanctuary while you rob people. Not for any reason."

For a long moment she looked at him. Since she'd already run through her options a hundred times, she'd half thought this part would be a little easier than it was turning out to be. "Okay," she said quietly.

"Okay, what?"

"Okay, I won't use your home as a base of operations."

Rick closed his eyes. "Fuck," he murmured, opening them again. "You'd leave, just like that?"

"You're the one who threw in the ultimatum. What am I supposed to do? Let Martin get killed? Let *you* get killed? Not to mention me. And don't tell me I should go to the cops, because you know what would happen then. Once I have something to trade with, something besides innuendoes from a couple of guys who'd lie to their own mothers, then we can reconsider. But in order for me to get where I need to be with Nicholas and his crew, I have to jump through his hoops."

"So who did you have in mind to rob?"

"I was thinking that nice older couple with the secret cookie recipe. The Hodgeses. They live on West Sixty-sixth at Columbus. And they own a Pekingese named Puffy."

"You spent half an hour chatting with the owners of Mrs. Hodges' Famous Cookies, and now you're going to break into their house. How can you do that?"

"Because I'm a thief. And this is the best reason I've ever had to pull a job. Remember, I used to do this just for the money."

He didn't say anything, just stared at her. Since he hadn't rescinded his ultimatum, either, she pretended her muscles weren't shaking with tension and worry and instead stood up to grab the clothes resting under the nightstand. Setting them on the bed, she went to the closet and pulled out her backpack. The rumpled, innocuous-looking gray thing went with her everywhere; inside it she kept everything she needed for day-to-day living. With it in her possession, she wouldn't need anything else from the house, or from him.

As for B and E gear, for this simple a job she would find what she needed at Delroy's. Slinging the backpack over her shoulder, she picked up her clothes and headed for the bedroom door. She would change downstairs, where she wouldn't have to feel his angry, stubborn gaze on her. She had a job to do, and if she was going to be successful, she needed to concentrate.

She heard Rick stand as she pulled open the door. If she turned around, though, she would cry, and she wasn't going to let him see that. Nope. She was Sam Jellicoe, thief, dammit. And he could think whatever he wanted about her, because as far as she was concerned, what she was doing was as much to protect him as it was to protect her and Martin.

The backpack yanked backward off her shoulder with enough force to make her stagger. "Hey!" she snapped, whipping around.

Rick stood directly in front of her, his jaw tight and his blue eyes narrow and burning. The hand that clutched her pack shook a little, his knuckles white with the force of his hold. For a second he stood frozen that way. Then he hurled the bundle back into the closet.

"I'm going with you," he rasped, his voice low and furious. "And don't even . . . think about trying to talk me out of it."

Samantha weighed what she needed to do against what she wanted to have. That decision should have been even more difficult, but it wasn't. "Okay."

Chapter 13

Saturday, 1:09 a.m.

Obviously his presence on Samantha's job was causing more difficulties than he'd foreseen. Richard stood next to her at the front desk of the Manhattan Hotel and handed over one of his credit cards. "Yes, the best you've got."

"That would be the Skyline Suite on the thirty-fifth floor, at eleven hundred dollars per night," the clerk said.

Either he didn't know with whom he was speaking, or he didn't know the hotel was for sale. Richard nodded. "That's fine. We're tired, and we'd like to go up now."

"Yes, Mr. . . . Addison." The clerk's expression tightened as he read the name on the platinum card. "Oh. The, um, the kitchen is closed, but if there's anything you require, we would be very happy to—"

"We'd like to not be disturbed. No phone calls, no interruptions," Rick broke in. "And we'll carry our own bags."

"Yes. Of course." His fingers shaking a little, the clerk

handed over a pair of pass cards. "There's a complimentary Continental breakfast beginning at seven in the Park Café. The—"

"We'll read the brochure," Samantha cut in, snagging the cards and picking up her overnight bag in the same motion.

Neither of them spoke on the ride up to the thirty-fifth floor. He knew she would rather be doing this on her own, just as he knew the situation had flown completely out of his control. Accompanying her felt like the only way to at least keep some idea of what was happening.

At their suite door she slid in the key card and pushed open the door. "Keep it open," she muttered, taking his bag and tossing it with hers onto the bed. She returned to the door and took the "Do Not Disturb" sign, hanging it on the outside handle. "Let's go."

"Why keep the door open?" he asked, as they traipsed toward the service elevator.

"Because some hotels keep tabs on how many times the doors are opened in their big suites. As far as they know, we're inside."

"What about cameras?"

"Elevators only. Not the service elevator. Guests on these floors like their privacy."

"So you've done this before."

"Not with a companion," she said shortly, stepping into the elevator as it opened and punching the basement button.

Once in the basement they made their way out the service entrance and onto the street. They walked a block, then hailed a cab. All of the subterfuge might have been unnecessary if she'd gone by herself, since she would simply have climbed out the back window of their townhouse and vanished, but she'd demanded that he, at least, have a verifiable alibi. Hence the ride to the hotel. With both the police and

Veittsreig's crew probably following them there, Richard had felt like he was leading a parade.

Delroy lived off 133rd Street in an apartment building that looked like it had seen better days. As they climbed out of the cab, Richard moved in close to Samantha. As angry at this entire expedition as he was, he wouldn't allow anything to happen to her.

"Quit crowding me," she muttered, walking straight to the sixth door on the left on the ground floor. She knocked three times, waited, and knocked twice more.

The door opened, and Walter gazed out at them. "Sam, you're crazy," he grunted, stepping aside so they could enter. "You can't bring a novice on an occupied."

"What's an occupied?" Richard asked, stopping as a second, very large black man came into the small living area.

"It means a break-in when the residents are home," Samantha explained, moving past him to stand in front of the mountain. "Hey, Delroy," she said, and hugged him. "You didn't bring any of those triple-chocolate muffins home with you, I don't suppose."

The big man grinned. "If I'd a known you were coming by, baby, you know I would have."

Walter scowled. "Those things'll kill you."

"So this is your guy, huh?" Delroy continued, sending Richard an appraising glance.

Rick had the unusual sensation that he was being evaluated. He kept his expression neutral. "Rick," he said, offering his hand.

"Right. Sorry," Sam cut in. "Delroy Barstone, Rick Addison. Rick, Stoney's baby brother, Delroy."

They shook hands as Walter disappeared into a side room. He came out a moment later with two black backpacks. "I didn't know exactly what you'd need, so I put in the standards, plus what you asked for when you called."

With a nod, Samantha took the two packs, hefted them in her hands, and tossed one at Richard. He caught it, surprised at the weight. "Thanks, Stoney," she said. "We'll be back in about forty minutes, if everything goes like it should."

Walter was frowning. "Are you two fighting? Because that is not good when you're about to—"

"Stay out of it," Samantha interrupted. "We're just having a philosophical disagreement. We'll be fine."

Walter lifted his hands. "Okay. None of my business. See you in forty."

Richard followed her back into the hallway and out to the street, where she hailed another cab. "Samantha, the—"

"Don't use names," she said quietly, stepping back as he pulled open the cab's door for her. "If anybody overhears, we're—"

"Gotcha," he returned, covering his own accent as he took a seat.

"Okay."

She had the taxi drop them off two blocks from their destination. At this point he'd been awake for twenty-one hours, but as he eyed her tight, clenched profile it felt like longer. Yes, she was angry, but she wasn't the only one. He'd had a hell of a lot dumped on his lap since yesterday morning.

She would have left. She'd decided that protecting her little family was more important than being with him. The fact that he was part of that family hardly felt like any sort of consolation. As mad as he was at her for making that choice, however, he was even more furious at himself for not leaving her any alternative.

Brilliant businessman that he was, he'd made a nearly fatal mistake. Veittsreig had left Samantha with two choices—death for her and those closest to her, or cooperation. And instead of coming up with a third alternative or a livable compromise, he'd put his foot down and basically ordered her to put both him and her newly rediscovered father in peril.

"Idiot," he muttered, hefting his borrowed backpack.

"Keep your commentary to yourself," Samantha returned, lowering her baseball cap over her eyes as she looked up at the set of darkened windows on their left. They both kept walking; no doubt she meant to make an alley entrance rather than risk being seen by the traffic rolling along West 66th.

"I was talking about me," he said.

"You wanted to come. Go back to the hotel if you can't deal."

"That's not what . . ." Richard blew out his breath. He needed to collect himself, get his head in the game, before he got both of them caught or killed. "You're certain everyone thinks we're still at the Manhattan."

"Yep."

He supposed if she wanted to be all business tonight, it was probably for the best. A truce would have been easier on her, but if she hadn't been a thief to begin with, none of this would have happened.

They stopped at the entrance of the alley as though waiting for the chance to jaywalk across the street. As soon as traffic cleared, Samantha turned around and led the way into the dark alley.

"How do you know which townhouse is—"

"Shh," she returned in a low murmur. "I'm counting windows."

Of course she was. With Samantha's attention on the building, he kept his on the alley. Toward the far end he could make out a pair of figures beside a trash bin. They were either getting high, or, from the faint sounds, having sex. Whatever it was, at least they didn't seem to be paying attention to anything else around them.

"Okay." She stopped and opened her borrowed backpack. "Are you going in, or waiting here?"

"In."

"Put on your gloves." Finally she faced him, the first time in better than an hour that she'd looked directly at him. "And promise that you'll do exactly what I say."

"I have gone in with you before," he said, fighting down his annoyance at being dictated to. He pulled the gloves out of his own backpack.

"Yes, but these people are home, and they're innocent. It's a bad thing we'll—I'll—be doing." She unwound the length of rope Walter had provided and tied one end around a heavy rubber dog bone.

"Will these people get their things back when we finish with this?"

"That's my plan. But it might not be my friends' plan."

"Okay. I'll wrestle with my own conscience on my own time." For a second he watched her, wondering if she was doing the same. "Why the dog toy?"

"It's rubber, so it'll make less noise when it hits the fire escape." Samantha glanced at him again. "You can't go in halfway. You have to be committed."

"I'm committed to you."

She stepped in to give him a quick, surprising kiss on the mouth. "I'll make this right. For everybody."

Christ. There went his Sam, taking everyone else's sins onto her own shoulders. And he'd thought she'd been too quick to decide on robbery, on choosing a course of action that allowed her to do something she enjoyed. Samantha had worked it through well past that point—and he needed to catch up unless he wanted to get left behind. Permanently.

She swung the rope back and forth, then flipped it up toward the lowest landing of the fire escape. The dog chew sailed over the railing and swung up to hit the underside of the landing with a dull thud. Slowly she let out more rope until he could grab the rubber bone on the far side, free the rope, and tie it off around the wheel of another trash bin. Straightening, he gave Samantha a nod.

With a jump she grabbed the opposite end of the rope and swarmed up to the landing. The metal escape gave a few protesting creaks and groans, but the sounds blended nearly undetectably with the engines and horns on the street.

For a second she crouched where she was, motionless, before she gestured at him to join her. Sending up a quick prayer that he wouldn't embarrass himself or get the two of them caught, he started up the rope.

By the time he reached the landing he had a new appreciation both for her athletic ability and for how much she was willing to risk just by letting him come along. He was no slouch by any means, but she moved with such confidence, skill, and grace—in her world she was as unmatched as he was in his.

"Okay?" she mouthed, helping him over the railing.

Richard nodded, refusing to rub the burning muscles of his upper arms. With her in the lead, they climbed the fire escape stairs to the upper landing. To his surprise the window there was open by about two inches.

Samantha reached in, drawing the curtains sideways with her fingers. For a moment she gazed into the darkened hallway beyond, then sank back again. On her face she wore an absent half smile, and probably wasn't even aware of the expression.

He had a difficult time not grinning, himself. Despite

knowing they were in the process of robbing two innocent, elderly people, and despite the anger at Samantha for having a past which allowed her to be manipulated into doing this, he could see the attraction. He could feel the adrenaline flooding his muscles, anticipating the combat of wits and nerves and luck.

"What are you waiting for?" he breathed.

With a slight frown in his direction she gestured toward the top of the window. As he looked, he dimly made out a wooden dowel shoved diagonally between the top of the movable part of the window and the inside top of the sill.

She leaned up to his ear. "Cheap but effective," she murmured, her breath warm against his cheek. Digging into her backpack, she pulled out a glass cutter and some duct tape. Swiftly she taped a small circle bisected by the dowel, then motioned him for the suction cup he carried in his pack. "Hold on to it," she instructed. "Don't push it in, or we're screwed."

Whether she'd given him a token job to keep him from feeling left out or not, he had no intention of screwing up. Silently he attached the suction cup to the center of the circle, braced himself, and held on.

Samantha steadied herself against the wall and began to carve a hand-sized circle through the middle of the tape. Other than a dull scratching noise, the cutter made no sound. As she closed the circle, he felt the glass inside give. Keeping it from moving took more effort than he'd expected, but he clenched his jaw and held steady. Rick Addison was *not* going to be arrested on someone's fire escape.

She glanced through the curtains again, then straightened. "Pull, slow and straight."

Stifling his annoyance at being put through thief kindergarten, Richard pulled. As soon as the glass came free,

Samantha reached through the hole and grasped the dowel. With her other hand she lowered the window a fraction. The dowel came loose, and she turned her wrist and pulled it out through the opening.

"Nice."

Flashing him her quicksilver grin, she set the stick aside and pulled a jar of peanut butter from her backpack. While Richard watched, deeply curious, she scooped out a fingerful and slung it inside onto the floor. She did it five more times, peppering the hallway floor with peanut butter. Only then did she push the window up.

It seemed like they'd been on the landing forever, but when he checked his watch only three minutes had passed. When he stood to climb over the windowsill, though, she pulled him back. "Wait a minute."

On the tail of her whisper, a high-pitched jingling sounded inside. They stayed motionless, half shielded by the curtains, as a Pekingese trotted from a side room into the hallway. After a few cursory sniffs Puffy went to work on the peanut butter.

"Hi, Puffy, sweet baby baby Puffy," Samantha sang in a whisper.

The dog cocked its head and whimpered.

Rick stared at Samantha as she leaned her chin on the windowsill and continued to baby-talk the dog. Slowly she reached one gloved hand, the fingers covered in peanut butter, into the hall. "Such a good Puffy. Is that good peanut butter? Yum yum, little Puffy."

"Oh, my God," Richard whispered. He couldn't help himself.

"Shut up," she sang, sliding both arms and her chest into the house. "Puffy's mama's baby, and doggies can't bark with peanut butter stuck to the roofs of their mouths."

Half a minute later she sat on the hallway floor with the Pekingese in her lap, licking peanut butter off her gloves. Bloody amazing.

"Come in, daddy bear, and bring the jar," she said, scratching the dog's belly with her free hand. "And don't talk."

Well, her way had worked so far. Silently he climbed through the window and held out the jar. Sam shook her head, standing gracefully with the dog cradled in her arms. Before he could protest one of the world's wealthiest men being reduced to dog-sitter, she smeared peanut butter on his chin and handed over Puffy.

Samantha watched for a moment as Rick realized his role in the break-in and reconciled himself to a dog licking his chin. If he hadn't been along, she would have had to carry Puffy into the bedroom and rifle through the Hodgeses' things with one hand.

Motioning him to stay in the hallway and keep Puffy occupied, she slipped into the room from which the dog had emerged. Perry and Jean Hodges lay in their ruffle-edged king-sized bed, sleeping. They were both on one side of the bed, white-haired heads sharing the same pillow.

Dammit, focus. Mentally kicking herself in the pants, she eased her way over to the credenza. Lingering over her marks' sleeping positions, getting mushy when she considered that after forty-two years of marriage they still cuddled—this was Rick's damn influence. And it was one of the reasons she couldn't do this for a living any longer.

As she passed the walk-in closet she stole a look inside. A safe crouched in the back beside the shoes. The Hodgeses had left Boyden's party late, though, just before herself and Rick, and they'd looked tired. Hopefully too tired to lock up the gems Mrs. Hodges had been wearing, especially when they were all right in the same room. Otherwise she'd have to break the safe, and that would take more time than she wanted to spend.

She reached the low chest. Bingo. A diamond necklace, together with matching bracelet and earrings, lay beside a man's wallet and a pair of diamond-studded wedding bands. Another necklace lay close by; apparently it hadn't passed muster for tonight. Even after the look she'd had of the stuff at the party, she wasn't entirely certain of the value. It would be close, though.

Silently she palmed the jewelry. The wedding rings would put her over the top, value-wise, and she picked them up, looking at them in the dim glow of streetlights through the closed curtains. Samantha drew a slow breath, then set the rings down again. Fuck it. Nicholas wanted evidence that she was one of the bad guys more than he wanted the jewelry.

When she turned around, Rick stood in the doorway, watching her. In his arms, Puffy had his head happily buried in the jar of peanut butter. Slowly Rick smiled at her.

Great. She could only guess what he would read into her sparing the wedding rings, but she'd save her speculation for later. "Move," she mouthed, returning to the doorway.

Once they were back in the hallway she pocketed the diamonds and took Puffy back. Rick slipped out the open window to the landing, while she set down the dog and the peanut butter jar and followed him. From outside she closed the window again—no sense risking the dog climbing out after them and falling two stories.

She pulled on her backpack again and followed Rick to the lower landing and then down the rope to the alley. After he untied the rope from the trash bin, she carefully pulled it over the landing where she'd thrown it and back to the ground. Just as she finished recoiling it and stuffing it into her backpack, Rick pushed her backward against the brick wall. Before she could react, he closed his mouth over hers in a hard, hot kiss.

"What was that for?" she asked, straightening her baseball cap and pretending she hadn't nearly had an orgasm right there. An adrenaline high and Rick. *Whoo momma.*

"Because I love you," he whispered back. "So we return the equipment to D . . . your friend and then sneak back into the hotel?"

"That's the plan." She brushed his sleeve as he turned up the alley toward the street. "And I will make this right."

Rick took her hand. "And I'll be supplying all my offices with Mrs. Hodges' Famous Cookies for the next year. Let's go. I want to wash the Puffy saliva off my face."

She grinned. "You are going to get so lucky when we get back to the hotel."

"I'm counting on it."

Chapter 14

Saturday, 7:42 p.m.

Samantha had placed Mrs. Hodges's diamonds in a velvet bag, taking as much care with them as she would for any piece she'd been contracted to steal.

As the day wore on, she set both the bag and her cell phone in the center of the downstairs coffee table, leaving her free to pace. No one had set a time for the phone call or the meeting, but if the job was as close to happening as Veittsreig had implied, he would have to be contacting her soon. She had a damned present for him, and she'd spent enough time watching television today to be assured that the Hodges break-in had made the news. Several times. She was now known as the "Peanut Butter Bandit."

At least they hadn't said anything about more than one person being involved, and at least she had an alibi—taking that hotel room in the Manhattan had been a brilliant idea on Rick's part. Plus, it had the added benefit of making sense, considering that he was the guy trying to buy the place.

Thank God Rick hadn't canceled his dinner with Matsuo Hoshido. As the hours ticked along with no call from Veittsreig, he'd wanted to; he hadn't made any secret of that fact. They had to look like business as usual, though, and whether it was the good guys or the bad guys or both watching the house, the Addison-Jellicoe team couldn't afford to do anything suspicious. And besides, Nicholas was less likely to call with Rick around, anyway.

Restless, she flipped the television channel to watch another round of the news. At least the spring weather looked like it would hold for the next five days. She actually preferred doing B and E's in the rain or wind, but not when she was working with strangers in what was probably a setup—if not from them, then from Interpol.

Wilder appeared at the open sitting room door. "Vilseau is making spaghetti, as you requested, Miss Sam. Might I get you a nice cold Diet Coke?"

Rick had had all of his houses stock her beverage of choice, with a supply to be kept cold at all times. "That would be great, Wilder. Thanks."

"My pleasure."

As the butler left the room, something on the television caught her attention, and she turned around to see one of the channel's ubiquitous gorgeous reporters, this one Bill Nemoski, speaking from some residential location. ". . . third break-in within a week and the second in twenty-four hours, in what the police are frankly hoping is not the beginning of a rash of upscale residential burglaries."

Samantha sat down as they went to footage recorded

earlier. "The week's third break-in apparently took place sometime between ten a.m. and noon today, when Mr. Locke's housekeeper was out shopping for groceries." A chill ran through her as on the screen Boyden Locke's townhouse, not all that different from Rick's, sat on its quiet street—quiet, that is, except for the flashing lights of police cars and the curious herds of neighbors. Neither had been present at the party last night.

"Missing is the Picasso that Boyden Locke purchased at auction last year, for a price reported to be somewhere in the vicinity of fifteen million dollars. Police are currently pursuing several leads, but haven't yet named a suspect. As you'll recall, Rick Addison's live-in girlfriend, Samantha Jellicoe, was briefly detained by police after the Addison robbery, but when I spoke with detectives they would neither confirm nor deny that she is still a person of interest."

"Fuck, fuck, fuck, fuck, fuck," Sam hissed. Rick and Stoney's half-assed twelve-step escape plan was starting to look good. Now, instead of an isolated burglary, the Hodge job was one of three. And she had personal connections to the other two.

The house phone on the end table rang, and she jumped about a foot. It wasn't the cell; it wasn't Veittsreig—and she needed to calm the hell down. "Hello?" she said, picking up the cordless receiver.

"So I'm watching the New York news on satellite," the low Texas drawl of Tom Donner came, "and what should I see but something about an art theft crime spree and Samantha Jellicoe?"

"Well, if it isn't Yale," she exclaimed, wishing she had one of those self-defense police whistles to blow into the phone, "the world-renowned gossip and Boy Scout! Shouldn't you be taking your nap after that milk-and-cookies dinner?"

"Make jokes while you can, jailbait. Where's Rick?"

"Gosh, you mean he didn't tell you he was having dinner with Matsuo Hoshido about the hotel? Hm. Maybe you're not all that vital to his business, after all."

"He told me. I forgot in the excitement of seeing you associated with criminal activity again. You would think I'd be used to it by now, wouldn't you?"

The front bell rang, and she heard Wilder answer the door, then the unmistakable Staten Island accent of Detective Gorstein. Her mouth went dry.

"Come on, Jellicoe, cat burglar got your to—"

"Donner," she interrupted in a hard whisper, "the cops are at the front door. I'm going to leave the phone off the hook. If it gets bad, call Phil Ripton. If it gets really bad, call Rick."

"Be cool, Jellicoe," his voice returned, abruptly all business.

She dove for the velvet bag and stuffed it under one of the couch pillows just as Gorstein appeared at the door, Wilder hovering around him angrily. Taking a breath, Samantha nonchalantly set the phone upside down in its cradle and stood.

Given how deeply this mess surrounded her now, nobody was going to put her in cuffs again. "Detective," she said smoothly, "I hope you brought your friend, Mr. Warrant."

"I asked him to wait while I inquired whether you were available, Miss Sam."

"It's okay, Wilder."

"Technically this is still a crime scene," Gorstein said, shoving a toothpick between his teeth and crinkling a small paper bag he held in his other hand. "Do I need a warrant to talk to you, though?"

"I guess that depends on what you're here to talk to me about."

"It's a curious thing, Ms. J. We had another break-in today."

"Two, according to the news. Wow. I guess that's more job security for you. Way to go." As she spoke, she swore she could hear Donner on the phone yelling at her not to mouth off, but she knew guys like Gorstein; they were sharks, sniffing the water for any sign of weakness or blood. Therefore, she wouldn't show any.

"I'd really prefer to be in parking enforcement," he said sarcastically.

"I'm sure Rick could arrange that for you. So do you want something, or are you just going door-to-door being ominous?"

"How about you tell me where you were at ten o'clock this morning?"

"I was checking out of the Manhattan Hotel with Rick Addison, which I think the guy you have tailing me would know."

"Yeah, that's a little curious," he said, not bothering to deny that he had people watching her. "Why'd you stay at a hotel last night?"

She snorted. "You're kidding, right? Thanks to you, anybody who watches the news knows we're in New York. And everybody wants an interview with me or with Rick. So we skipped out for a night."

"Addison's buying the Manhattan, I hear."

"He's working on it. Why, you want a room discount?"

"Where'd you go after you checked out?" he pursued, rather than following her off on her tangent.

He was good. Every bit of her rebelled against telling a cop anything, even if it might be to her own benefit. Still, since it looked like she would be jumping into the middle of this mess, the more innocent the cops thought she was, the better. "I came here. I think I'm coming down with a cold," she said succinctly, coughing for effect.

"Any witnesses?"

"Just your guys and the billionaire and the household staff." She blew out her breath. "Like I said before, Gorstein, my dad was the thief. Not me."

"Assuming that people can verify your whereabouts today, I have another question for you."

She made a show of checking her watch. "Make it fast. *Wheel*'s on."

"Do you buy the vowels, or steal them?" Pushing away from the doorframe, he walked into the room.

Samantha backed up another step, refusing to glance in the direction of the diamonds. Fuck. Four hundred thousand or so in stolen gems resting five feet from the cop assigned to high-end burglaries. "I didn't say anything about you coming into the room. You just stop right there, Gorstein."

He stopped. "Here," he said, putting the paper bag on the arm of the couch and backing away again.

"You really think I'm going to take possession of a bag without knowing what's in it? Give me some credit."

"Christ," he muttered, approaching again. With exaggerated caution he picked up the bag, stuck his hand in, and pulled out a can of Diet Coke. Shoving the empty bag into his pocket, he set the soda down on the couch's arm again. "It's a soda."

"I can see that."

"You didn't get one before, at the station. So I'm bringing you one now. It's a fucking peace offering, okay?"

Samantha snorted. She couldn't help it. "You handcuffed

me, you fingerprinted me, and you put me in a little room with bars on the window."

"Hence the peace offering."

"*Why* the peace offering?" she asked, wondering whether Donner was crying or laughing as he listened from his quaint Palm Beach house with his quaint, perfect family, none of whom had ever been handcuffed.

"Your, ah, Addison called me yesterday morning. We'd already pretty much ruled you out by then, but he pretty . . . forcefully suggested that you might have a few ideas if I'd back off. And I called your cop in Palm Beach. He vouches for you."

She lifted an eyebrow, for the moment putting aside the thought that last night she'd proven Frank Castillo a liar. "Rick said that?"

"Well, he used more profanity, and said something about me spending the rest of my career in court."

Her hero. She wished she'd overheard that conversation. "Is it cold?"

"What?"

"The soda. Is it cold?"

"Probably not. I bought it about an hour ago. I was on my way here, but I had to stop back by Locke's for an update."

"So what do you want to know?"

"Can I sit down now?"

"No. Maybe if you'd brought me a six-pack."

He leaned sideways against the bookcase while she turned off the television and sank onto the coffee table so she could face him. Wilder reappeared, looking apologetic and carrying her chilled drink, but she waved him off. While she and Gorstein sized each other up, she reached over and picked up the house phone.

"Yale?"

"For crying out loud, Jellicoe, is that your idea of—"

"Talk to you later. 'Bye."

"Who was that?" Gorstein asked as she hung up.

"Jiminy Cricket. Go ahead, Gorstein. I have better things to do than stare at you all night." She had another phone call to take, for one thing, and she for damned sure didn't want Veittsreig calling while the cop was there. Of course, if somebody from the crew was watching the house, the shit had already hit the fan. With both the good guys and the bad guys keeping an eye on her, she was a little surprised that they hadn't tripped over on another by now. Of course, the bad guys knew the good guys were there, so she supposed that gave them an advantage.

"Mrs. Hodges lost a ton of diamond jewelry, and Boyden Locke lost a Picasso today."

"I got all that from the news."

"You did a security consultation for Locke a few days ago. And you were at his house last night."

Uh-oh. "Is this an interrogation again? If it is, I'm going to call Jiminy back." Much as she hated to admit it, she knew Donner's number. She didn't know Phil Ripton's, something she meant to remedy as soon as Gorstein left.

"Much as I'd love to drag you back down to the station, if I arrest you, I have to arrest Trump, the mayor, and half the city council, too."

"Sucks to be you. And you still haven't asked your question."

"At Locke's somebody bypassed the alarm using a copper wire and some duct tape. They pried the window open with a crowbar and walked past at least three other paintings to get to the Picasso. Why?"

"Why only the Picasso?"

"Yeah."

"My guess would be that the thief is moving fast and traveling light, and he's got a shopping list."

"Nothing random about the break-in or the theft."

"I doubt it. A narrow window of time and a daylight break-in means to me that the thief had the timing down pretty well."

"You think it's the same person who got Locke and Addison."

She shrugged. There wasn't anything she could prove for certain, not that she would tell him if she did have proof, but if she could earn a point or two with the NYPD, she'd give him a little taste. "Shutting down the window alarm and using a crowbar isn't exactly difficult. It could be completely different guys. But with both houses the thief passed other valuable stuff and took one painting."

"And that thief wasn't you."

"And the thief wasn't me," she snapped, her body and her mind beginning to remember what a very long couple of days it had been.

"Because you seem to have a pretty good understanding of this shit," he continued, as though she hadn't spoken.

"That's it, I'm calling the cricket." Wondering about the marvels of irony, she picked up the phone again. Relying on Tom Donner to save her ass. The world was turning upside down.

"I'm just saying," Gorstein interrupted as she listened for the dial tone, "your average civilian wouldn't know the things you do."

"I'm not your average civilian. Do I dial?"

"I could have you in handcuffs before you punch in the first number."

"Doubt it."

"What about the Hodges place?"

"What happened? I heard they're calling the guy the 'Peanut Butter Bandit.' Did he eat a sandwich while he was inside?"

"No, he baited the dog with the stuff. No alarm, but he cut a hole in the window and came through the fire escape, just like the other two."

She nodded. "Makes sense. Do you think it was the Picasso guy?"

"I don't know. There was other stuff in that house, too. A Remington sculpture and a pair of Georgia O'Keeffe paintings."

So the Hodgeses were western fans. That meant Perry probably had had a shotgun somewhere close by. Thank Christ for peanut butter. "If you could tell me—"

At that second, the phone by her haunch rang. The standard ring, not one of the personalized ones she'd given to friends and family. *Crap.*

"You gonna answer that?"

Sending him a glare, she picked the cell up and flipped it open. "*Hola.*"

"You have a policeman in your house, just when I'm expecting my present," Nicholas Veittsreig's voice came. "Care to explain that?"

"Hi, sweetie," she returned, pasting on a warm smile. "You'll never guess who I'm sitting here talking to right now."

"What the fu—"

"Nope. It's Detective Gorstein. He wants to know where I was this morning when Boyden Locke's Picasso was getting lifted."

"And what are you telling him, Sam? I warned you about the consequences of your not cooperating with m—"

"Let's just say I'm trying to be nice, but I'm getting a little bored. Why don't you call me back in five?"

"Why don't I come see you in five? If the cop's still there, he's dead."

"Thanks, honey. 'Bye." She hung up and set the phone aside, keeping her expression calm despite the hammering of her heart. She didn't like Gorstein, but she certainly didn't want him dead. "Anything else, Detective?"

"Not right now. If any more art or diamonds go missing, though, I'll be back. With a warrant and cuffs. Then maybe you'll answer some questions."

"The next time you want my help with something, ask before you start handing out the threats. For now, get the hell out of my house."

He pushed upright. "The rich guy's house, you mean."

No, she'd actually been feeling rather territorial about it since people had started breaking in. "We share. Good night."

Gorstein chucked his toothpick into the dead fireplace. "Stay in town, Ms. J, or I'll get suspicious again."

As soon as the front door clicked shut, Samantha locked it and ran downstairs to the kitchen. Both the butler and the cook were watching a preseason baseball game on the television there. "Guys, I need you to stay down here for a little while," she said, as Wilder stood up.

"Is something amiss?"

"Not yet. Just stay down here. Do you have a cell phone?"

The butler frowned. "No, Miss Sam. The—"

She tossed him hers. "If you hear anything like gunfire or screaming, lock yourselves in the pantry and call the cops. And lock this door now," she continued, gesturing behind her. "Don't open it until you hear me, Addison, or somebody you *know* is a cop. Got it?"

"Yes, ma'am. But—"

Shutting the door behind her, she flew up the stairs to the main part of the house again. The housekeepers would have left hours ago, and Ben was driving Rick, so the only problem would be if Rick came home early. *Home.*

Pushing away the sudden surge of domesticity, Samantha checked the hem of her shirt to make sure the copper wire she'd fed in there remained. A paperclip and a rubber band lay in one pants pocket, while a strip of duct tape curved around the inside of one pants leg. If she got grabbed, she'd have a fair chance of escaping.

If Veittsreig came after her with a gun, though . . . She eyed the various items in the front sitting room. A bronze mask of Apollo, a hunk of rock with a dinosaur tooth sticking out of it, the fire poker, and sundry other knickknacks of various sizes and values. A pretty good choice of ammo, really, if an expensive one. And on top of that, if she ended up dead, at least Rick and Stoney would know who to blame.

Footsteps padded down the stairs behind her. He'd come in through the damn window again. "In here," she called, sitting back down on the coffee table. It was pretty central, so she could move in any direction.

Veittsreig appeared in the doorway. "Since when do you talk with the police?" he asked, his German accent stronger tonight. He was irritated or edgy, then—neither of which emotion was good for her.

"Since they arrested me and still consider me a suspect," she returned. "Did you forget how to knock?"

"You seem to have cops watching the house." He shrugged his wide shoulders. "Besides, I go where I want."

"And take what you want, apparently. Why the Picasso,

and why Locke? Did you know I met with him earlier this week? You knew I was at his house for a party last night."

"Are you wearing a wire, Sam? Is that why the policeman came by?"

"Fuck you. Do you really think I wanted him in here tonight?"

Nicholas shook his head. Slowly he pulled a pistol from the small of his back, where it had been hidden beneath his light jacket. "I have to be sure, though. Stand up. Hands away from your sides."

Great. "This isn't a very good way to start a partnership," she snapped, complying. "If you get fresh, I'm gonna castrate you."

He approached, and with his left hand felt up and down her legs, around her waist, down both arms, and then down the front of her bra. Before he moved off he squeezed her left breast.

"Satisfied, Mr. Grabby?"

"I thought you were going to castrate me."

"After we make some big money. I can be patient." She was also very, very grateful that her gentleman knight hadn't been anywhere around to see that. "Why Locke?"

"Where's my present?"

With a scowl she dug up the felt bag from the couch and tossed it at his head. He caught it with his free hand. Tugging the strings open, he looked inside, then dumped the contents on one of the cushions. "Very nice. Did you choose them last night at your party?"

"Are *you* wearing a wire? Why Locke?"

"We've been around, watching, for a couple of days. My buyer needed a Picasso, and you knew Locke, who has a Picasso, so I thought, hey, the more tangled you are, the more likely you are to stick with me on this."

"Gosh, I'm flattered. Who's the buyer?"

"Like I would give you the chance to cut me out of the deal. He's my business. You stick with yours."

He. A guy, and solo. That narrowed it down—by a teeny, tiny bit. "Possessive, aren't you?"

"You don't carry a gun," he said, as he put away his own weapon.

"Guns are for hacks who can't get in and out of a place clean. And they piss people off."

He cocked his blonde head at her. "Are you pissed off?"

With him as close as he was, if she sat again her face would be at his crotch level. Not a good idea, given the way he'd been eyeing her. She stayed on her feet. "I'm wondering if you think you're being sexy, or if you actually have something I'm interested in—like a plan."

For a moment he looked her up and down again, while her flesh tried not to crawl. He was good-looking, she supposed, but Rick was in a class so far beyond this guy—beyond most guys—that even if they split up she wasn't sure she'd ever want to date again, much less sleep with anyone else.

Finally Nicholas sat on the arm of the couch. "Once I tell you, you're in one hundred percent. You even flinch, and that's it."

Samantha didn't have to fake her frown. "I thought I was in already. Hence the fucking diamond theft."

He smiled. "Well, yes, but I want to make sure you understand. In, or dead. And if it helps, given your talents and your reputation, we agreed on an even seven-way split."

"My dad agreed to a seven-way split, too?"

"Your dad, too."

Her dad rarely shared credit or profit, so he *had* to be working for the white hats. "How much, then?"

"Figuring our take after redistribution, two and a half

million each. That doesn't include the Hogarth or the Picasso or the jewelry. They're a different deal—one that doesn't include you."

The diamonds would only have netted her five figures, anyway. "Euro or U.S.?"

"Good old American dollars."

Doing some swift calculations she totaled the thieves' take, and then the likely overall total net of the job. "A hundred and seventy-five million? What are you doing, hitting the U.S. Treasury?"

"Are you in?"

"Are you guaranteeing my cut?"

Nicholas chuckled. "There are no guarantees in life, Sam. You know that. If the job's successful and nobody tries to pull anything, then you'll get your cut."

"Then I'm in." Deep inside, she wished she'd had to argue with herself over the moral and material implications before she agreed to take part in a robbery. Mostly, though, she was dying to know what the gig was, and already anticipating going in. Last night had been too damned easy, and mostly it had served to remind her of how much she missed the rush. "What's the job?"

"Let me remind you first that if the cops or Interpol or the FBI or anybody else hears about this, I'll kill your father, your boyfriend, and everyone else you know."

"Now just a damn minute," she retorted, fighting the contrary rushes of panic and adrenaline. "You said I was in or dead. I'm in. But six other people plus whoever hired you know about this job, and probably in way more detail than I do. *I* won't snitch. The rest are your problem."

Slowly he nodded. "Fair enough."

"So what's the fucking gig?"

"A Stradivarius violin, Bellini's *Madonna and Child*,

Titian's *Venus and Adonis*, El Greco's *View of Toledo*, and Leutze's *Washington Crossing the Delaware*. How's that for five minutes' work?"

Samantha went ice-cold to her bones. "You're hitting the Met."

With another grin he stood and headed for the door. "I'll contact you with the details in a couple of hours, once I can verify that these are the Hodges diamonds, and that you didn't just take advantage of somebody else's bad deed. And one correction, Sam: *We're* hitting the Metropolitan Museum of Art. On Tuesday."

Chapter 15

Saturday, 11:25 p.m.

As the limousine stopped at the front steps of the townhouse, Richard climbed out. "I'll need you at nine o'clock, Ben," he said, as the driver held the door open for him.

"I'll have the car here." Ben hesitated. "Do you . . . would you like some assistance, sir?"

Richard looked back over his shoulder. "Nine o'clock."

"Yes, sir."

As the limo pulled away, Richard tried the front door. It was locked. Since he was not going to knock at his own bloody house, he searched his pockets for a key. Finally he found one, and shoved it at the lock. He missed, and the key fell onto the brick steps with a quiet clatter.

Bending down to pick it up, he almost fell off the steps and rolled into the street. That would have looked good on the front cover of *CEO* magazine. Belatedly he glanced around, but other than a few cars going by, the street looked empty. Of course, if what Samantha said was true, police were watching the house, and burglars were watching the house. And maybe Godzilla and Santa Claus, too.

With a snort that didn't feel or sound particularly amused, he retrieved the key. This time he got it into the lock and opened the door. Inside, the house was dark and quiet. It was early still for Samantha to have gone to bed, but for all he knew she was hanging out a window somewhere miles away. How would he know? Maybe Veittsreig wanted more diamonds. Or some emeralds.

He locked the door behind him and made sure to set the perimeter alarm, though neither seemed to do much good these days. People apparently came and went at will in all of his properties. Even so, he had no intention of making things easier for anybody.

Despite an irregularity of the stair spacing that he'd never noticed before, he made it to the first floor. Or second floor, rather, since he was in America. Thankfully the bedroom door was unlocked, since he didn't have a key to that one. Or to the woman he hoped was inside.

The lights and the television were on, and Samantha sat on the bed with a spread of books and papers around her. She hadn't gone off to rob the Fudge King tonight, anyway.

"Hi," she said, smiling. "Did you buy any more floors of the hotel?"

"No. I'm almost there, though. I think. Unless something happens to make Hoshido want to raise the price again. Damn Matsuo."

"Why? I liked him."

"So do I." At dinner, though, Matsuo had talked a little about courtship traditions in Japan, and the changes his wife had insisted on making both to their engagement and their wedding. Miazaki Hoshido was clearly a special and unusual woman—even given the fact that she'd probably never stolen anything in her life.

He pulled off his suit jacket and tossed it over a chair. His tie followed. He'd been wearing the bloody things for sixteen hours straight, and he was ready to relax—except that Samantha was entangled with a crew of killers, and that last night they'd stolen diamonds from a couple who gave a percentage of their profits to some of the same charities he did. Frowning, he kicked off his shoes.

"Are you drunk?"

Richard looked over at the bed. "What I am, my dear, is pissed. That's how we say it where I come from."

She began gathering her papers and books into a pile. "At least tell me the drinking didn't start until the negotiations were finished."

He undid his belt and unzipped his trousers. "Excuse me, but are you telling me how to conduct business? Because I seem to recall your refusing that advice when I offered it to you."

"I am not going to argue with you tonight," she said coolly, climbing off the bed and setting her papers on the writing desk. "I know you're *pissed*, and I know you probably need to vent. But I'm not having any conversation with you when you probably won't even remember it."

"Why not? Does my having a few drinks change the way you lied to me about knowing who stole my Hogarth? Does it change how you decided to participate in some robbery and tell me about it over lunch? Does it change that we—*we*—stole from some nice old people who bake biscuits—cookies—for a living? Does it change how whatever I try to do to help you, you actively circumvent me so you can go off with your criminal friends who shoot people?"

For a long moment she stared at him from the far side of the bed while he tried not to wobble. Then she picked up her paperwork again and walked up to him.

"You know," she said in a low voice, "I spent the last three hours thinking how much I really wanted to talk with you tonight. I really wanted your help." She moved past him to the door.

Richard turned around, nearly tripping over his sagging trousers. "Where the devil do you think you're going?"

"I'm going to the guest room. I have some more work to do tonight, and it'll take longer than I expected, because I'll be doing it alone. Good night, Rick."

She left him standing there in his dark blue shirt, checkered boxers, and black socks. "Fuck," he said, and collapsed on the bed.

Four hours later he woke up cold, cranky, and his head aching. As soon as he could stand up, he staggered into the bathroom for aspirin, grabbed his toothbrush and toothpaste, and stepped into the shower.

Twenty minutes after that he could open both bloodshot eyes at the same time, and his brain began to creak into motion again. Samantha. She'd said she was going to the guest room, but she had a nasty habit of slipping away from him in the middle of the night.

Shrugging into his blue cotton robe, he left the bedroom and headed two doors down toward the back of the house. The door was closed, but not locked—a good sign, he hoped.

"Samantha?" he said quietly, pushing open the door.

The light on the nightstand was still on, but she wasn't reading by it. The papers and books seemed to have multiplied, and they covered the bed except for where Samantha lay sprawled across the pillows. Auburn hair straggled across her closed eyes, and she still wore her jeans and T-shirt with the open shirt over it.

If he wanted an assurance that he didn't merely claim to love her but truly did, the tremendous relief at seeing her there and the overwhelming sense of . . . tenderness, of wanting to hold her and to protect her, answered the question clearly enough for him.

Moving silently, he gathered the scattered papers together. Every take-advantage-of-the-opponent instinct in his business-hardened body wanted to read through them and see what she was up to, and he just as strongly resisted. If she wanted him to know, she would tell him. He set the things on the floor, picked up the soft throw lying across the foot of the bed, and covered her gently.

She blearily opened her eyes. "I'm cold without you," she mumbled, and closed them again.

With a faint smile he climbed crossways onto the bed along the headboard to lie down beside her. Eyes still closed, she flipped the throw so it covered him, as well.

"I love you," he whispered, sliding an arm across her shoulders.

"I love you," she murmured back, curling against him.

And abruptly the world was right again. What did he care about a bloody hotel when he had his own semi-retired cat burglar? And to think, two hundred and fifty years ago as a member of the peerage he would have been obligated to have her hanged. Thank God and the devil that this wasn't a romance of a historical bent. Because come hell or high water, if she was going to commit even grander larceny than last night, he meant to help her do it.

Richard groaned and opened his eyes as somebody nudged him hard in the shoulder. Samantha. "What?"

"It's eight o'clock," she said, shimmying off the guest room bed. "You said before that you were holding a strategy thingy at nine thirty."

She'd changed clothes, he noticed, into jeans shorts and a red tank top—her staying-around-the-house clothes. Abruptly he wanted to cancel his meeting thingy and have a naked thingy with Samantha.

"Thanks. Could I get some cof—"

"Coffee?" she broke in, handing him a steaming cup as he sat up. "And Vilseau's making some toast."

"After last night I thought you might be throwing this in my face," he said, inhaling the vanilla-nut aroma. Tea was definitely more civilized, but thank God for coffee.

"It was weird," she said, hauling up her papers and dumping them on the bed again. "It occurred to me that I'm usually the one who gets all crazy, and you logic me out of it, or you stand back so I can vent." She shrugged. "So I was the responsible one last night, and I figured you needed to vent."

"I suppose I did."

"Could I ask why?" Samantha plunked herself back, catlike, on the bed.

"No," he returned, sipping the blissfully hot coffee.

"No?"

"Because last night it made sense, and this morning you'll laugh. And I'm far too important to be laughed at."

She gave her quicksilver grin. "Then you should tell me, because *my* story's not as funny."

He drew a breath. After last night, he supposed he owed her some sort of explanation. "Fine. I own a lot of things. I employ a great many people. They do as I ask, and everything runs smoothly. One of the reasons I'm successful is because I usually know what's coming next, what the next move is going to be, so I can take the appropriate counter-step. And day before yesterday when we sat in the cafeteria and you told me that you were going to participate in some big robbery and needed to commit a smaller one just for some cove's amusement, I realized I was absolutely clueless about what to do next. And at Locke's party, I knew you were looking for marks."

"Rick, you—"

"And then I toddled off to dinner while you had to wait for a phone call and a visit from someone whom I presume to be a very dangerous man."

"Negotiating an eighty-seven-million-dollar deal is not toddling, and I didn't know what I was supposed to do with Veittsreig, either. I'm not going back to being Ma Barker full-time. I was doing the least bad thing I could think of until we—*we*—could figure something out."

"Yes, but then during dinner I started trying to imagine Miazaki Hoshido breaking into someone's house and using peanut butter to subdue their dog. And I tried to imagine Patricia doing that. They would have made a complete muck of it. Out of everyone I know in the world, you are the only one I could picture doing what you do. And I got angry at myself, because I was proud of you."

"Did you start drinking before or after you realized you were proud of me?"

"After. That's why I started drinking."

She leaned over and kissed him on the cheek. "So you do have a weakness. If it makes you feel any better, I'm not always as together as I let on, either."

Richard nearly choked on his coffee as he laughed. "On that note, what's your news? Did Veittsreig call?"

"Yes, but that's only part of my story."

He took another, more careful swallow of coffee, reminding himself that she wasn't being deliberately difficult. She was being Samantha, looking for angles and opportunities, for the best way to approach . . . anything. Everything. "And?" he finally prompted.

"Okay." She bent down to sniff his coffee. "If that tasted as good as it smelled, I wouldn't badmouth it so much. But me, I like Diet Coke. I guess that's why Detective Gorstein brought me one when he came by last night."

"He what?" The cup in his hand jumped, and he set it on the nightstand.

"Apparently they've pretty much cleared me, and somebody called him and suggested that if he would be a little more civil, I might lend him some of my tremendous insight."

"Hm." Gorstein's tunnel vision hadn't been as unalterable as he'd feared. "You talked with him, then?"

"After I hid the diamonds under a pillow. I think he'd already come to pretty much the same conclusions, but at least I could point out that I had an alibi for yesterday morning. And he asked about the hotel, so they were definitely paying attention to where I was on Friday night."

Richard stopped halfway to the edge of the bed. "Yesterday morning?"

"Boyden Locke lost a Picasso. Luckily we were checking out of the Manhattan and heading back here with cops tailing us, but we both know I could have slipped out and pulled another robbery without them knowing a thing."

Obviously her story was going to get worse. She hadn't even mentioned Veittsreig yet. Holding up a hand to stop her, he picked up the guest room phone and dialed downstairs.

"Wilder, please tell Ben I'm pushing back my schedule. I'll need him at half nine."

"Very good, sir."

"No, make that ten."

"I'll inform him."

Richard took Samantha's hand, twining his fingers with hers. "What else?"

With a sigh she leaned her head against his shoulder. "While Gorstein was here, Veittsreig called. He wanted to know why the cops were at the house. I pretended he was you and told him to call me back. Instead he told me he'd be here in five minutes, and to get rid of Gorstein or else."

"Or else." His muscles tensed, even though he'd obviously arrived far too late to be of any use. If he had arrived in time, drunk, he might have gotten one or both of them killed. *Way to save the day, Rick.*

"I got Gorstein out the door in time. But guess what the gig is?"

"Sam."

"Okay, okay. We're hitting the Met. On Tuesday. You might want to clear your schedule."

She told him what she knew, up through the second call she'd gotten two hours later detailing where they were meeting and what her role would be. By the time she finished, they were both on their stomachs lying across the bed and looking at the floor plans of the museum she'd dug up in one of his art books. She hoped Nicholas or Martin had the wiring plans, or they weren't going to get very far.

"One thing that doesn't make sense to me," Rick said, pulling over a photo of *Venus and Adonis*, "is that if this gang knows—"

"Crew," she corrected.

"If this crew knows your reputation, they also know that you don't hit museums."

"I don't think they much care about my personal preferences."

He scowled, sexy as hell in his morning beard stubble, crazy black bed hair, and the blue bathrobe he'd worn all night. "What does Walter think of all this?"

"I haven't told him yet. This affects you—us—more than it does me and Stoney. I thought you should know first."

Dark blue eyes met hers. "I apologize again for being such a bastard last night. You know I don't normally do that."

"I know." What he'd said had hurt, mostly because it had been true. "And I'm trying," she said quietly, looking down at her hands. Long-fingered thief's hands, Martin had always said, as if her fingers somehow proved that she was meant to be what she'd become. "Being good is hard."

"It's only hard if you mean it," he whispered, brushing her hair back from her face. "It would be easy if you were pretending."

She looked up, smiling at him, wondering if her expression looked as sappy as it felt. "You are a very nice man."

"No, I'm not." He pulled her arm, flipping her onto her back.

Before she could roll out he kissed her, his mouth tasting of coffee and the remnants of toothpaste. Slow and soft, his lips teased at hers, his tongue joining and then retreating from the pursuit. She moaned, slipping her arms around his shoulders as he sank down over her. His beard stubble scratched her cheeks a little, but she liked the sensation.

This was what nobody in her old circle understood. That she wasn't hanging around Rick to look for any and every opportunity to rob him when he turned his back. She liked being in his presence, sharing conversations with him, knowing that she aroused him as much as he excited her. Still kissing her softly, he slowly pushed her tank top up around her shoulders. Slipping agile fingers under her bra, he pushed it up, as well, and then slid down to brush his lips over one breast and then the other.

Samantha moaned, pulling her body up against his. His robe was easy to tug off, but he covered her hands when she started to unzip her shorts. "It's Sunday," he murmured, kissing her mouth again. "Our day of rest." Rick ran his free hand down her spine, firming his grip as he rolled, pulling her over him.

"This doesn't feel like resting," she breathed, chuckling. "And you still have a meeting." Beneath the arousal of her body, she felt relief. After his deep anger at her for deciding to break into the Hodgeses', and then what she'd read as disappointment in him last night, it felt good—and safe—to be in his arms again, to feel his desire for her.

"I imagine they'll wait for me."

She slid down, kissing his chest and nipples, feeling his hard muscles quiver beneath his skin. So he'd said he was proud of her—for being good at her chosen profession, she assumed—but she wasn't convinced. People didn't come home drunk and yelling when they were happy.

"What if it happens again?" she whispered, lifting to run her lips along his jawline.

"What if what happens again?"

"What if circumstances cause me to choose a break-in over death and dismemberment?"

"We'll make certain it doesn't happen," he rumbled, his hands grasping her bottom and sliding down her thighs.

"We can't do that."

"Not now, Sam." Before she could protest that, he pulled

her down over him and kissed her until she couldn't breathe. "You are the smartest person I know," he said finally, shifting his attention to unfastening her shorts. "You are honorable, and kind, and devastatingly beautiful, and I love you. Anything else is secondary."

She smiled as he rolled them again. "I'm kind?"

Rick sat up to scoot her shorts and her blue thongs off. He did seem to like the thongs even over the frilly panties—if she could get over the feeling of having a permanent wedgie, she'd make the switch.

"You fed Puffy peanut butter. Somehow I can't imagine some of your former confederates taking the trouble to make friends with the mark's dog."

That was true; but jeez, she didn't even like killing spiders. "He was cute," she returned, then gasped as he trailed a hand between her thighs.

He lifted his azure blue eyes to hers. "You're wet."

She jumped at the motion of his fingers. "I want you, Brit."

"I love you, Yank." Rick settled over her again, brushing her hair back to expose her throat, and licking and nipping at her sensitive skin. With his hand he caressed her again, and she groaned.

When she couldn't stand the buildup any longer, Samantha arched her hips, pulling him to her. "Please," she murmured.

"As you wish," he breathed, and slowly, deeply sank into her.

She came immediately, hard, clinging to him as he began pumping his hips. Digging the pads of her fingers into his back, Samantha threw her head back, gasping. She loved having him inside her; whatever mess they were making of their relationship, this spoke more loudly. They fit together. Their hearts fit together.

Rick looked down at her. "You amaze me, you know," he panted, kissing her again.

"I know."

With a chuckle he pushed forward, grunting, then slowly sank down on top of her. "I wish I didn't have that bloody meeting," he said when he had some breath back, "because I think I could kill the both of us with the sex today."

Laughing, still feeling him inside her, she patted him on the head. "Next time, dear."

"Come with me," he said abruptly, lifting his face to look down at her.

"I just did."

"Smart ass. I meant to my meeting." He kissed her again, even more gently this time. "I'm a bit worried about you right now."

"I can't go. I need to find a way to lose the cops and the crooks, meet up with Stoney, and go shopping. Since I didn't bring my B and E gear with me to New York, I'm going to need some things. More than Delroy has lying around."

That wasn't entirely true; she did have her lock picks and a couple of the more innocent-looking tools of the trade, but nothing that was up to the standards required by the Metropolitan Museum of Art. And she wanted to try to track down Veittsreig and his crew. Knowing where they were working from could make things easier, especially if she could use them to find out who had wanted the Hogarth and the Picasso—and probably all or most of the items currently located at the museum. And finding the two missing paintings—as well as recovering the Hodges diamonds—was of paramount importance.

"May I say that it bothers me that your father seems to want you involved in this when he's made a deal to hand Veittsreig and his crew over to Interpol? How do you fit in with that?"

"I have a hunch, but whatever happens, I still have to be able to play my part up to that point." She gave him a fast, tight hug, breathing in the familiar and still-intoxicating scent of his skin. "Get off me and go to your meeting."

Clear reluctance on his face, he moved out and off of her. "Sometimes I wish I could just keep you here with me forever, Samantha Elizabeth."

Forever was a frighteningly long time, though the idea didn't scare her quite as much as it used to, these days. "We'd get hungry," she said with a quick grin, and went to find her thongs.

Wearing them and her tank top, her bra readjusted to the proper position, she headed back to the master bedroom to find a pair of jeans. As she crossed the next door, the opening to Rick's office, a shadow moved toward her.

Shrieking, she grabbed the half-open door and yanked it closed. That was *enough*. Too many damn people were breaking into this house. "Rick!"

Whoever was on the other side had a strong grip. The knob turned in her hands, and she hauled backward with all of her weight as the door inched open. As Rick charged into the hallway behind her, she shifted her weight and shoved. Hard.

The door flew open, whoever'd been pulling on it falling backward over one of the conference table chairs. Rick on her heels, she flew after him, yanking him by one ankle down to the floor. The man squealed as she knelt across his throat.

"Who the fuck do *you* work for?" she snarled, grabbing his tie off and slipping it around his flailing hands.

"He works for me, actually," Rick said in an even tone, humor dripping from his voice. "Samantha, please get off my new assistant."

Chapter 16

Sunday, 10:18 a.m.

"This is nice work," Richard said, flipping through the three reports as the limousine rumbled toward his downtown office.

John Stillwell was still fiddling with the tie Samantha had returned to him. "Thank you, sir." He cleared his throat. "I do apologize for my actions earlier. I didn't—"

"Wilder told you to wait in the office. And you didn't take any inappropriate action." He hadn't taken *any* action, actually, but Samantha could be hard to handle under the best of circumstances. At least Stillwell hadn't wet himself, being jumped by a woman in a tank top and thong underwear.

"It wasn't the first impression I wanted to make."

Rick rattled the papers. "I'll consider these as your first impression." He glanced at the younger man seated across from him. They'd actually met on several occasions, and while they'd dealt in different areas of Addisco, he'd seen the fellow's work, and he'd never heard anything but praise from Stillwell's superiors. "When did you get in to New York, anyway?"

"The flight landed at seven this morning, sir."

"Rick, please. Did Sarah arrange a place for you to stay?"

"She wasn't certain how long you would be in town. I left my luggage with your butler until I could—"

"We'll put you in the guest room," Richard decided. "We should only be in New York for another week or so." Barring disaster, that was. "You'll have considerably more space in Palm Beach."

"If I might ask, the lady, Miss Jellicoe, is she . . . I mean to say, is there anything I need to know in order to perform my duties?"

"It is very unlikely that Samantha will tackle you again." Rick stifled a grin. "We had a break-in a few days ago, as you may have heard. We've been a bit jumpy." Technically, they'd had three break-ins, all apparently perpetrated by the same man, but that wasn't for public dissemination.

"I see, sir—Rick. Of course. I should have announced my presence, but I . . . presumed you were occupied."

Yes, in the room right next door. Rick returned to the paperwork. If Stillwell had overheard part of his conversation with Samantha, that could explain the fellow's haste in trying to exit the office, and his visible nervousness now. On the other hand, John might have heard the sex, or he could be suffering from first-day job jitters. While Richard had never been excessively paranoid, with Sam in his life it would be crazier not to be a little cautious and careful.

"I should bring you up to speed for today," he continued. He sized up opponents for a living; he would assess Stillwell in the same way. "I have a price—eighty-seven million. What I don't have is a timeline for me to take over operations, or a final agreement from the city on property tax reassessment and tax incentives."

"I read up on New York commercial property ownership on the flight over," Stillwell said.

"That's excellent," Rick returned, "because you're going to be chairing the meeting. I have another matter to see to this morning."

His new assistant blinked. "I beg your pardon, Rick, but I read *a* book. I'm more than willing to assist, but frankly I'm concerned that I may make more of a muck of it than anything else."

"American laws and British laws are for our attorneys, who will be there to advise you. Use them. Right now I want to see what you can negotiate for me. I've seen you work, and I need to know whether or not I can rely on you, John. Better to find out now than later."

"I . . . very well. I won't disappoint you, Rick."

Rick looked him in the eye. "I hope not," he said quietly.

He handed over the packet to Stillwell and gave him a few suggestions, then had Ben stop the limousine at the front entrance to the building.

"You have my mobile number if you need to contact me," he said, as John climbed out of the car. "I'll be back in an hour or two."

"Thank you for the opportunity, Rick."

As soon as Stillwell disappeared through the rotating glass doors, Richard sat back again. "Ben, what's the best place to be seen in Manhattan?"

"To be seen by whom, sir?"

"Everyone."

"Times Square."

"Good. Take me there."

It wasn't much of a plan, but he'd only had the morning to

come up with it. And it had worked once before, the first time he'd tried to track down Samantha. He hoped her father was half as smart as she was.

Ben double-parked the limousine just short of Planet Hollywood. "Sir, are you sure you want to get out here? It's pretty crowded."

"That's what I want."

"But you'll be mobbed. Do you want me to go with you?"

"No. Go back to the office." He grimaced. "But be available for a rescue mission, just in case."

"Yes, sir. Good luck."

With a deep breath, Richard climbed out of the limousine. He liked privacy. Considering how many people knew of him, he was exceedingly thankful for his high walls and top-line security. In Manhattan privacy wasn't as much of an issue—unless a celebrity appeared somewhere frequented by tourists.

In his blue Armani suit, dark burgundy shirt, and black tie, he was probably at his most recognizable. And that was what he was counting on.

It took a minute and a half. Threading his way through the streams of honking taxis, street vendors, and what felt like half a million pedestrians, he strolled in front of the ABC Television Center, figuring that would be a good place to be seen. A group of young ladies two or three years younger than Samantha, all of them dressed as cheerleaders with "Texas Tech" emblazoned across their chests, bounded up around him.

"You're Rick Addison, aren't you?" one of them chirped.

He gave his photo-op smile. "I am."

"I told you!"

"Oh, can we have our picture taken with you?"

"Certainly," he said.

"What are you doing in New York?"

"I'm looking into some real estate prop—"

"Do you know Donald Trump?"

His smile twitched, and he fixed it again as more tourists crowded to join the cheerleaders. "Yes, I do."

"Do you call him 'The Donald'?"

"N—"

"Who cares about Trump?" somebody else said. "Addison's got more money."

"He's cuter; I know that."

For ten minutes he did his least favorite things in the world—he posed for pictures and he signed autographs. The crowd continued to get larger and louder, but at least no one had picked his pocket or trampled him yet.

A police officer elbowed through the crowd. Now he was getting somewhere. "Everything okay, Mr. Addison?"

He deepened his smile, and more cameras flashed. "Yes, I'm quite well. It just occurred to me that with all the time I've spent in New York, I've never walked through Times Square."

"Right." The officer said something into the radio on his shoulder. Across Broadway two mounted police began to clop in their direction. About bloody time. And finally one of the police radio-monitoring news teams scrambled out of the studio behind him.

"Rick Addison," the reporter said, pushing her way through the crowd, "what brings you to Times Square?"

For the camera he repeated what he'd told the police.

"You had a valuable painting stolen last week. Have the police uncovered any new leads?"

"No. I have a meeting with Martin, my lawyer, at noon. I imagine he'll come to my office."

The newswoman whose name he couldn't recall eyed him for a moment, then gave her professional smile again. "What about your girlfriend, Samantha Jellicoe? Is she still considered a person of interest?"

His task accomplished, Richard let his smile cool. "To me, definitely. As for the police, you'd have to ask them."

"Will we be hearing any wedding news from you this year, then?"

Rick gazed at her. "No comment."

There. The piece should run on the eleven o'clock morning news. All he could do now was get back to the office and hope that Martin Jellicoe watched the news as diligently as Samantha did, and that Veittsreig didn't, or that he wouldn't make the connection. As for how odd he might look on the broadcast, he was British. That excused quite a bit.

"Carabiners and climbing rope, check," Stoney said, jumping back into the passenger seat of the black Jeep Cherokee he'd rented.

Samantha pulled back into traffic. "This is such a pain," she grumbled. "If I'd known I would be doing a B and E in New York, I would have brought my own gear."

"Am I mistaken, or are you revved about this?"

"Come on, the other night's big trick was peanut butter. This is my first real fix in five months. I didn't give the business up because I didn't like doing it."

Stoney folded his arms across his chest. "Why did you give it up, then? Because if I'm working in a damn office and setting up damn security appointments for no good reason, I'm going to be kind of mad."

"I gave it up because I had a really long streak of really good luck, and sooner or later it was going to run out. And because three people got killed during the course of my last job." And because on that last job she'd met someone who for the first time tempted her more than the adrenaline-laced danger of her old life.

Obviously Stoney knew that last part, too, whether she wanted to talk about it or not, because he snorted as he tossed the equipment onto the back seat. "Head over to Sixty-third. I know a guy who knows a guy, and he should be able to fix you up with an electronic splitter."

Her phone rang. Frowning, she checked the number, but all she could tell was that whoever was calling her was doing so from Manhattan. "*Hola*," she said, answering.

"Is that why you encouraged me to date Boyden Locke?" Patricia's voice came, her fury obvious in the clipped British precision of her speech. "Because you knew you were going to steal from him the next day?"

"Oh, good gravy. I had nothing to do with it, Patricia. Not everything's about you."

"Why, because it has to be about you?"

"Hey, you called *me*."

"Because I won't be pushed around again. I helped you, and this is how you repay my charity. That's even nastier of you than I've come to expect."

"The Ex?" Stoney muttered.

She nodded. One of these days she was going to have a serious discussion with Rick about what had been wrong with him to marry this woman. After all, he was the one who'd brought the Ex into their lives. She certainly wouldn't have married Patty—but then she had a lower tolerance for bullshit than Rick did. "Setting you up with Boyden was how I repaid your charity. The rest of it is probably just your usual bad luck following you around. Maybe you need an exorcism."

"Only to free me from your clutches."

Samantha snorted. "I don't want you anywhere close to my clutches. And I'm kind of busy right n—"

"Destroying my chances with two men wasn't enough, was it? You have to set me up so you can knock me down yet again!"

"You slept around on the one good guy in your life, then married a murderer, and you dated another one. Blame them for crossing me, and blame yourself for being a nutball. I didn't take anything from Boyden Locke. Goodbye." She flipped the phone closed. "Now my day is complete."

"What's she blaming you for now?" Stoney asked.

"I suggested she might like Boyden Locke, so now she thinks that because he got robbed, I'm sabotaging her again."

"That is why I never try to fix people up."

"Thanks for the support."

"Uh-huh. Make a right, if you want to miss the construction up there."

Nodding, Samantha signaled and turned right. A blue Lincoln made the same turn two cars behind her. So had a half dozen taxis, though, and when she edged into the next lane over, he didn't follow.

"You need to make a right at the next corner," Stoney pointed out.

"I will. I'm just playing tourist." She waited until they were a dozen yards from the light, then cut back into the right lane and made the turn. With a more proper signal and speed, the Lincoln turned, as well.

"What is it?" her copilot asked, his gaze on the sideview mirror.

"Me being paranoid, probably. But if it's one of Gorstein's guys, I really don't want to be seen picking up a splitter. And if it's one of Nicholas's, I don't want them to know that you're involved."

"Were they behind us at the last stop?"

"Not that I noticed."

"Then they weren't. Make another turn and see what happens."

Doing the signal and lane change in the right order this time, she made another left. So did the Lincoln, moving in directly behind her this time. Evidently this guy had been paying attention during her previous taxi dodges, and he wasn't going to let her squeak out a last-second turn. "Dammit," she muttered.

"So lose 'em."

"You rented the car. If we get into a pursuit, you'll be the one they trace to it."

"They've already run the plates by now, honey." He cracked a grin. "And do you actually think I would use my real ID?"

Samantha blew out her breath, relieved. "At least one of us hasn't lost his edge. Who has this car?"

"Antoine Washington. From Brooklyn."

"Ah, one of the old standards. Get the gear out of the back seat, will you?"

Reaching around, he retrieved the climbing equipment, black spray paint, and industrial-strength glass cutters, shoving them into the backpack she'd brought along for the occasion. Then he pulled on his seatbelt.

"Ready?" Samantha asked, pulling a cloth from her purse and wiping down the steering wheel, gearshift, and door handle before she gave it to Stoney to do the same thing on his side. She slipped on her leather gloves and gripped the wheel again.

"Ready."

"Hang on." She tapped the accelerator, putting a little distance between the Jeep and the Lincoln. Then she threw it in reverse and floored it.

The rear of the Jeep slammed into the Lincoln. With a whoosh she could hear even with the windows up, the Lincoln's air bags deployed. Jamming the Jeep into drive again, she whipped a right and then a left, nearly taking out a taxi and a hot dog stand. At the next left she slowed, cruising back into legal driving speed.

"There's a parking garage up on the right," Stoney said, checking his mirror. She'd already checked hers. Nobody followed them.

"Got it."

She turned down the ramp, took a ticket, and parked the Jeep. They took turns climbing out and closing the doors using the cloth, before she wiped down the keys and tossed them on the seat. The car would probably be gone within ten minutes, but that would be to her benefit.

"I don't think you're losing your edge, honey," Stoney said, handing her the backpack and leading the way to the stairs. "That was nice."

"Thanks. I just hope the guy in the Lincoln really was a cop." Shouldering the backpack, she followed him back up to street level. "What say we divide up the rest of the shopping list, and I'll meet you in front of Trump Tower at . . ." She looked at her watch. "At three? That gives us another couple of hours."

Stoney nodded. "I'll take the splitter and the wire strippers. You get the infrared glasses and the thermometer."

"And then we'll roast the turkey."

She let Stoney find a cab first, then walked another block before she hailed one herself. In the distance she could hear multiple sirens, but since nobody else on the street was reacting or looking around, she didn't do so, either.

As she sat on the back seat of the taxi, a Mercedes-Benz service rental drove by at just more than legal speed. She caught a glimpse of black-silver hair and Ray·Ban sunglasses. Boyden Locke. That was quite the coincidence, unless he'd been following her, too. Did *he* suspect that she'd taken his Picasso?

"Follow that Mercedes," she said, gesturing.

"Okay." The driver started off. "You a cop?" he asked in broken English.

"I'm his wife," she returned, painting a pained, affronted look on her face.

"No shoot-ups from my cab, lady."

"I just want to know where he's going. No shoot-ups."

"Okay."

Locke circled the block, then the next one over. Yep, he was looking for her. So much for implying his support by inviting her to parties—though he'd still had his Picasso then. Patty had probably ratted her out. Great. She'd be getting the phone call turning down her services any day now, then. If this theft thing got any more play in Palm Beach, Donner wouldn't be the only one calling from there, either. She needed to check in with Aubrey Pendleton, to see if anybody had canceled appointments with her because of this mess. Damn Martin, and Damn Nicholas Veittsreig. If she couldn't advise security, she didn't know what the hell she would do to keep herself from going insane.

"That's good enough," she told the driver. Instead she requested him to drive her to the nearest electronics superstore. Veittsreig and his crew probably had surplus gear, but if she was coming in as a professional she was damned well going to be equipped like one. It was a matter of pride; after all, she was Sam Jellicoe, Martin's kid. The girl who'd surpassed her dad in the business and been resented by him for that ever since.

If he resented her so much, though, why had he arranged

for her to be part of this job? Did he intend to get her picked up by Interpol, as Rick seemed to think? She honestly didn't know. Martin played her like he played everyone else, but he was, after all, her dad.

Inside the electronics store she headed past the televisions, the cell phones, the iPods, and the Xbox 360s. They only carried two brands of hunting binoculars with infrared and night-vision capabilities, but the lighter one looked like it would do the trick. She usually went with lower-tech gear herself, preferring to rely on her skills rather than a piece of engineering with tiny, breakable parts, but the Met was extremely high-tech. She would have to adapt.

Halfway back down the television aisle she heard the murmur of a familiar voice, and she stopped. Rick, his face multiplied by about twenty sets, stood in the middle of a mob, the Planet Hollywood sign over his right shoulder. Swiftly she moved to the nearest TV and turned it up.

". . . artin, my lawyer, at noon. I imagine he'll come to my office."

The reporter asked something about that Jellicoe woman and then about marriage. After Rick's "no comment," Samantha stopped listening.

"That big, sneaky bastard," she muttered, hurrying to the checkout line and paying for the glasses—no sense getting nabbed for shoplifting while collecting gear for a two-and-a-half-million-dollar job.

Outside she hailed another cab and headed for Brookstone. They would probably have digital air temperature thermometers. And then she was going to Rick's office and find out why the hell he was trying to contact her dad.

Richard paced the length of the glass-walled conference room. At the table behind him John Stillwell, using a fair share of his British patience and biting politeness, actually made some headway with the New York Building Commission. If felt odd to be on the sidelines during a negotiation, but he'd already made the decision that his life with Samantha was not going to go the same way as his marriage with Patricia Addison-Wallis-whatever it was today.

He'd been growing his business, turning wealth into an empire, and he'd been very successful. He'd also been a failure. And he did not repeat mistakes. And Sam—he refused to lose her because he was spending too much time fixating on square footage and profit percentages.

His phone buzzed. "Addison," he said, picking it up.

"Sir," Maria's voice came, "the lobby has a lawyer named Mr. Martin to see you? I don't have him list—"

"Send him up."

He'd come. From the near end of the conference room Richard could just see three of the six elevators that serviced the building. At twenty-five minutes past twelve, a man strolled out of the elevator lobby and paused on his way to reception to look around.

Richard watched him through the glass walls of the conference room.

Medium build, half a head or so shorter than himself, brown hair peppered with gray, and a nice, fairly expensive-looking gray suit and nice leather briefcase—just perfect to blend in to an upscale office, the fellow was someone that any other time, or rather previous to his acquaintance with Samantha, he would have glanced at and passed over.

That was her speciality, too, blending. She was a bloody chameleon, and only as he'd come to know her better had he found the real humorous, unflinching, and even a little soft-hearted Samantha.

Something else that his own life of reading people and

circumstances had taught him, though, was keen observation. And so he noticed the high cheekbones, the long fingers, the easy way this man had of moving. He knew that walk, and it was Sam's. And therefore, her father's. Martin Jellicoe. In the flesh.

Without a word to the group arguing behind him, he pushed open the conference room door and walked into the reception area. "Mr. Martin, I presume," he said in a low voice.

Brown eyes turned to assess him. "My client, I presume," he returned, his inflection matching Richard's.

"Indeed. Will you join me in my office?"

"Lead the way."

"Maria, hold my calls," Rick said, leading the way to his office. He didn't turn around to see whether Martin followed, though he wanted to.

Inside the office, he gestured Martin to a chair, and seated himself on the neighboring one. He could sit behind his desk, he supposed, but this was a tricky meeting. This man was the father of the woman he loved, and he was also probably the greatest threat to her continued well-being. They would begin on the same even ground.

"Perhaps I should formally introduce myself," he said after a moment. "Rick Addison."

"I know who you are. The Brit who's screwing my daughter."

"If you like." Rick inclined his head. The testing had begun. "I see it as a bit more complicated than that."

"It would have to be, if she told you that I wasn't dead."

"I hear that you're currently working with Interpol. Is that what you've been doing for the past three years?"

"You just go right for the throat, don't you? Is that how you nailed Sam?"

For the moment Rick ignored the cut. "I only ask because for at least the past five months you've known exactly where Samantha has been residing, and you never made any attempt to contact her until three days ago. And within hours of that, she was arrested. It makes one a bit suspicious."

"You think I set up my own girl?"

"If I thought that for certain, I would be shooting you right now. In case I haven't made it clear, I don't like you."

"Of course you don't. Kind of hurts your ego, doesn't it, that she's willing to throw over knocking the headboard with you to spend time with me? I guess you're not as important to her as I am."

"You're certainly more trouble for her than I am."

"Right. I'm the one who gets her on TV and her picture in the papers. Get this straight, Addison. I taught that girl everything she knows, and she's made millions doing exactly what I raised her to do. You're a long weekend."

"I'm not the one who had to make a deal with the authorities to get out of prison. I think maybe she's outgrown you."

"Fuck you, Addison."

Ah, he'd hit a sensitive spot. "Why did you decide to involve her in this, after three years of not bothering to give her a ring?"

"Involve her in what? You're one paranoid fella, Addison."

Rick gave his professional, cool smile. "If you don't know, I'm certainly not going to tell you. It does seem to me, though, given your . . . affiliation with Interpol, that any contact with Samantha can't be very good for her. Especially under questionable circumstances."

The thief leaned forward a little. "Sam thinks she knows everything. She doesn't. And educating her is my job. Not yours."

"We can agree to disagree about that. All *I* care about is whether you have Samantha's best interests in mind or not. I happen to think that you don't. And I'm wondering whether I shouldn't beat the bloody hell out of you for putting her in danger."

Jellicoe—Rick couldn't quite get comfortable with the idea of thinking of him as Martin—finally settled back into the opposite chair. "I have my reasons for getting hold of her."

"And they are?"

"If she hasn't told you, then don't ask me." He smiled. "Maybe you two really aren't as close as you think."

Richard kept his fraying temper reined in as tightly as he could. The more information he could get from this man, the better. "What purpose does Samantha serve in all this?" he persisted. "You've contacted Interpol about the goings-on, I presume, so you're essentially sending her straight into peril."

For the first time brief irritation crossed Jellicoe's serene face. "She knows exactly how much peril she's in. It's part of the job, weighing the risk versus the reward, and deciding whether to go in or not. Looks to me like she's decided she wants to work with her dad once more."

"Even though she's retired."

Her father chuckled. "Yeah. She retired like Michael Jordan retired, I guess."

Rick took a slow, steadying breath, forcing his fingers to unclench from the fist they'd made. "And you know this because you've been so close to her since she made her decision."

"I know my kid. Is that why you wanted to see me? So you could chastise me for not being more involved in her life?"

"Not when I know what kind of trouble your reappearance has made for her."

"Maybe like you said, we should agree to disagree, Addison. You say it's trouble, and I say she loves it. And she's working with me again because she knows her old dad still has a few lessons left to teach her." He stood, retrieving his briefcase. "So if that's it, I have a meeting to attend."

"When Interpol moves in to grab Veittsreig and his crew, what do you have in mind for Samantha?" Rick pursued, standing as well. "Or has that even occurred to you?"

"I know what I have in mind for me. I'll be taking a new name and a nice big house on the Mediterranean. Seems like Samantha's already got that for herself. Not the new name, but I imagine she's working on that. I don't think she needs my help in that department."

Rick let him walk to the door. "Your daughter's an incredible young woman," he said as Jellicoe pulled open the door. "And not because she's a cat burglar. And certainly not because of any influence you may or may not have had in her life."

"Right. I read the news. You two met because she was robbing your house. So you go ahead and tell yourself whatever lets you sleep at night, Addison. Like I said, I know my kid. She's just like me. Adios, Rick." With a quick smile that didn't have nearly the charm of his daughter's, Martin Jellicoe slipped out the door and headed for the elevators.

As Jellicoe vanished, Rick walked over to his window. He supposed what he'd wanted from Martin had been an assurance that someone in the crew would be looking out for Samantha, or at least be on her side. What he'd heard didn't leave him any more reassured. Just the opposite, in fact.

Whoever's side she might be working on, Interpol wouldn't have any more love for Samantha than the NYPD did. Even less, probably. And without a deal like Martin Jellicoe had, they would probably jump at the chance of putting her away for thirty or forty years. Unless their little band could come up with something else, then, they were on their own.

Even more troubling, Martin seemed to have the idea that he was teaching Samantha some sort of lesson. Considering the circumstances, that could mean several things—how to rob a museum, how to double-cross your crew and work for Interpol, or how not to trust even your father when it came to matters of money. All three of them terrified Richard.

As for her father, Martin could say that Sam was just like him, and he might even believe it. Richard, though, knew differently, because he knew Samantha Elizabeth Jellicoe. And he knew that she would do the right thing—even at the expense of her own well-being.

And her well-being was firmly and irrevocably attached to his heart.

Chapter 17

Sunday, 1:40 p.m.

Samantha saw Rick sitting in the main, glass-enclosed conference room as soon as she stepped off the elevator and onto the fiftieth floor of Addisco. Slinging her backpack onto a chair as she passed by, she kept her eyes fixed on her target.

In jeans and a tank top she was way beyond anything that passed for even casual dress, but today she was not there to blend in. In fact, she hoped that Rick took really good notice of her.

Most everyone there knew her now at least by sight, and nobody got in her way. As she reached the conference room double doors, she yanked them open. "Hello, Rick," she said in her coldest voice.

He turned around to face her, shoving to his feet in the same motion. "Samantha, what—"

"Might I have a quick word with you, sweetheart?" she

cut in, ignoring the surprised muttering of the other dozen people in the conference room.

His jaw tightened. "Of course. Would you wait for me in my office for just a moment?"

Obviously she couldn't yell at him in public. With a hard nod she turned on her heel and marched to his office. Halfway there she snagged her backpack and took it with her.

For five more minutes she fumed, stomping back and forth and tempted to start breaking things, if there had been anything in there to break. Considering his lavish homes, Rick's office gave new meaning to the word *spartan*. Finally he pushed open the door and closed it behind him. "As you may have noticed," he snapped, "I was in the middle of something."

"Fuck off. What the hell do you think you're doing, broadcasting for Martin to come and see you? You think you get to go on television and summon people?"

"It worked for you," he said, his voice low and controlled.

"So you just thought you'd try it again for Martin? You went out there specifically to get his attention."

"Yes, I did. You went out in the middle of the night to meet with him."

"He's my dad."

"Yes, he is. And I wanted to talk to him."

"Why, so you could ask his permission to court me or something? How dare you butt into my life like that without even asking me first! Not to mention the fact that Nicholas and his crew might have been watching. What the hell do you think they would make of you meeting with Martin?"

Rick stalked to the desk and back again. From the straight line of his back, he was as angry as she was. Good. She hated a one-sided argument.

"You're going to break into a museum in three days, are you not?" he asked, his cultured Devonshire accent deepening.

"Yes, I am. And I don't need your permission for that, eith—"

"Sod off. I wanted to meet the man who waltzed back into your life after three years only to throw you into the middle of God knows what," he interrupted. "I reserve the right to butt into your bloody life, because it matters to me."

"You—"

"I didn't ask your father for secrets or insights into your character, or for his permission to be with you. I asked him why he picked this job to bring you back into the fold. And I didn't get an answer I find acceptable."

"*You* find accept—"

"Have you asked him whether he has an escape plan for you after he calls in Interpol? Because I would guess that he doesn't. He doesn't, Samantha. He's not going to perform some selfless, heroic deed to see that your assistance is rewarded or that your freedom is protected."

She swung at him. Rick blocked the blow with his forearm and grabbed her wrist. "Let me go!" she yelled.

"Never," he growled back, his voice shaking.

With a shriek she yanked her arm free and threw herself at him. They went over the top of his desk and landed on the floor in front of the window. Nothing coherent would form in her head. Nothing but spitting black fury. And then abruptly she was sobbing, and Rick beneath her had his arms locked around her, holding her against his chest.

"I am not . . . having a breakdown," she sobbed.

"I know."

"I'm very angry with you."

"I know."

"Why did you talk to him?"

"Because I'm concerned about you." His grip loosened a little, and he began rocking her. Dammit, he was rocking her.

She shoved upright, sitting across his thighs. "Stop that. I'm not some stupid little kid."

He sat as well, his arms straight behind him to keep him upright. "Did I say anything of the kind?" For a moment he was silent. "When my mother and father died, Sam," he continued abruptly, "I was two thousand miles away at boarding school. It was very . . . hard. If my father suddenly reappeared and then forced me to . . . to go back to school, while I was still trying to grasp that he wasn't actually dead—I can't even imagine."

"It's not that," she said, sniffing and wiping a hand across her eyes. She hated stupid crying. She didn't do it very often. Only Rick could make her cry, apparently.

"Then what is it?"

She knitted her hands together, twisting her fingers. "I didn't want you to meet him," she finally said, her voice sounding thin and wobbly to her own ears.

Rick shifted, sweeping an arm across her shoulders. "Jesus, Sam. You're not him, if that's what you're thinking."

Looking over, she met his deep blue, concerned gaze. "But I could be. I hate hitting museums, and . . . and I am still so excited about this I can barely see straight. And I *know* how good the odds are that I'll get caught. And I keep things from you, and I sneak out at night just to . . . just to do it, and my business is starting to pick up, and every time I see one of my 'clients,' I'm thinking, *I could totally rip off everything but his underwear, and he'd never know what hit him.* And now Boyden Locke is following me, so he doesn't trust me, and the rest of my clients probably don't, either. And they're right not to. And Patty called, and she thinks I'm setting her up for another fall. I told her she needs an exorcism, but maybe I'm the one who needs it."

"You sneak out at night?"

"So I can sneak in again." She slammed her fists into her thighs. "I'm such a fucking mess. Why do you even want to be around me?"

Slowly he began looping his fingers through her hair. "Because you keep breaking back into my house," he whispered into her ear. "And because when we first met you saved my life. And because you seem to regularly risk your life to help other people."

She sighed, trying to pull herself back together. "Okay, okay. So I'm great. Fucked up, but great."

"Exactly." He kissed her on the head, then took her chin and kissed her softly on the mouth.

Samantha sank into him, and Rick closed his eyes, relieved. He was also extremely alarmed, but that would wait until he had a moment or two to think. Christ. They'd fought before, but that was the first time she'd come that close to actually hitting him. And that wasn't even what troubled him.

With a last sigh against his mouth, she stood and offered a hand to help him up. Despite the bruise he would now have on his hip, he refused the assistance and climbed to his feet on his own. "Give me a few minutes and we can get out of here," he said.

"No, I'm okay. And I have to meet Stoney to collect the rest of my gear."

"I thought you went shopping together."

"We did, until the cops caught up to us, and I had to crash their car and ditch the rental, and we split up." Her lips twitched in a shadow of the grin she wore when she thought she was being hilarious.

"At least your day wasn't a complete waste, then," he said mildly, putting an arm around her as they walked to the door.

"I suppose not. Veittsreig will probably call me before you get home. If I have to leave for the face-to-face before you get back, I'll leave a note in your nightstand."

It took a great deal of his well-honed willpower to let her walk out his office door. Trying to stop her, though, would put up a fence between them that neither of them could punch through. "For God's sake, be careful," he said, hoping that verbal cautions wouldn't be overstepping. "As you've said, these men are killers."

"I wonder what the guy who hired them is like?" she muttered darkly.

"Let's try not to find out."

Samantha faced him, putting her hands on his shoulders and leaning up to plant a soft kiss on his mouth. With a fleeting caress of his cheek she headed out for the elevators.

Richard leaned against the doorframe and tucked his disheveled shirt back in and tried to straighten his jacket. Armani was a good brand, but it wasn't made for American-style football tackles.

However he felt about it, he could understand Samantha's excitement and anticipation at pulling a B and E, even if it was one in which she'd been forced to participate. He'd gone on a few minor ones with her even before last week, all for the sake of the good guys, and it was the most exhilarating thing he'd ever experienced. The thrill, the challenge, were as big a part of the lure as the considerable money she used to make.

No, he had something else to trouble him now. As hard as he'd tried to be patient, to let her grow her business at her own pace and in her own way, he'd thought that the more successful she became, the less likely it would be that she slipped away from him and back into her old, exciting life. It had never occurred to him that she didn't like her new business in any form.

What else was there for a retired cat burglar, one still at the top of her game, to do? Sitting about and doing crossword puzzles wouldn't suffice, and she wouldn't be Samantha if she settled for that. Bodyguard? She didn't like guns, and he didn't want her away from him that much. Professional wrestler? Too much in the spotlight, and not enough intellectual challenge, though it did amuse him a little that he'd thought of it.

He closed his eyes for a moment. The two of them needed to do some thinking. Neither of them would be happy if she stayed with a job she disliked, especially if it was just to ease his mind that she was keeping occupied, or allowing her to keep at least one hand in her old business. Neither did he want her clients quitting her because her father had managed to link her to a robbery. Leaving the security job should be up to her, not to her suspicious clientele.

Clenching his jaw, Richard headed back to his meeting. The first task in all this would be to make sure that Samantha stayed free and alive past Tuesday. Which meant he couldn't get involved with contacting Interpol or the police or anyone else.

He stopped. Or did it? Turning on his heel, he went back into his office, closed the door, and sat behind his desk. Then with a deep breath he picked up the phone and dialed.

"Tom Donner."

"Hello, Tom."

"Hey, Rick. I'm at Mike's baseball game. Guess who just scored a double?"

Richard smiled. Tom adored the domesticity of his life.

For a moment he allowed himself to wonder whether he would ever sit on the bleachers and cheer on his own son or daughter. *Tuesday, Rick. Focus.* "I would say it was Mike," he returned. "Tell him I said congratulations."

"I will." Tom paused. "What's up?"

"You're on retainer, right? So anything I tell you at any time or in any location is considered privileged, yes?"

"Yes. Why, did Jellicoe get arrested again?"

"Not yet."

" 'Not yet'? That doesn't sound too promising. Hold on. Let me get over behind the snack bar so we can talk."

"Don't miss Mike's game."

"He's not out on the field again yet. Hold on. Okay. What's going on?"

"Someone's going to rob the Metropolitan Museum of Art on Tuesday."

"*What?* She *told* you? Call the damn cops, Rick."

"It's an Interpol sting. Samantha's assisting . . . a friend of hers in the setup. The problem is, she doesn't have a deal of her own with the authorities."

"Then she should pull out."

"She can't. It's complicated. They threatened to kill both of us if she doesn't cooperate."

"Interpol did? That's insane."

"Not Interpol. The other thieves. I just want to know if we can take any steps to minimize her risk."

"I'm a corporate attorney, Rick." Tom growled some very inventive profanity. "And what about your risk? She may have convinced the NYPD that she didn't take the Hogarth, but if she gets picked up at the museum, that's going to change. And you're going to get pulled right into the middle of it, either for being an accessory or for being the total idiot who let it happen right under his nose."

Richard sat very quietly for a moment, reminding himself firstly that Tom had no idea that he'd been in on the Hodges robbery, and secondly that the attorney was looking out for him and that no one had actually called anyone else an idiot. "I repeat," he said slowly, "is there anything we can do to minimize her risk?"

"Lemme think. I went to school with a couple of guys in the State Department. I'll see what I can find out. But it's Sunday, so don't expect a miracle."

"At this point, Tom, a miracle would be very welcome."

"I'll call you."

"I'll be waiting." And running through a few scenarios on his own.

Samantha paid the driver and hopped out of the cab in front of the townhouse. Stoney had found her a top-of-the-line splitter, and he'd come up with three different lightweight wire strippers so she could choose the one she liked the best. She'd thanked him and left—and she hadn't said a word about Rick's surprise public appearance or his summoning of and meeting with Martin, or even about Locke trying to track her, probably to try to get his Picasso back.

Why she hadn't said anything, she didn't know. Ever since she could remember, she'd been able to talk to Stoney about anything. He'd even been the one to go out and buy her first box of tampons, although she had gotten the feeling that that was pretty much where he drew the line.

But when Rick had told her why he'd wanted to see Martin, and when he'd told her about Martin probably not having an escape route for her—it had been so far out of her comfort zone that she didn't know how to take it. She'd always looked after herself. It shouldn't have mattered that she would have to do the same on Tuesday. If Martin had drilled one lesson into her head, it had been that *everyone* always looked out for themselves first. Even Stoney worked that way to some degree, since she'd been the one taking the risks and he'd been the one selling the items she'd obtained, and both of them making a shitload of money doing it.

Rick, though, operated differently. She'd seen him do business, and he could at a moment's notice turn into a Great White shark, filleting every opponent within reach. But he also stuck his neck way, way out for her, and he'd done so on more than one occasion. It usually turned out well for both of them, or it had so far, but that seemed to be as much a matter of luck as anything else.

A car pulled up behind her as she hefted her backpack and headed for the front steps. She didn't look around, but she shifted her grip on the heavy pack. It would make quite a dent in somebody's head, if that turned out to be necessary.

"Sam."

Even with that one syllable she recognized the voice. Veittsreig. Of course he wouldn't call to set up a meeting when he could just drive by and grab her. So much for leaving a note for Rick. Dammit.

She turned around. "Are you lost?"

He shook his head from the front passenger seat of the black Ford Explorer. "Get in."

"The cops are probably watching the house."

"So get in fast."

Putting on an annoyed expression, she complied. "That was pretty stupid, don't you think?" she said, climbing into the middle seat as the two other men there shifted to give her room.

"Maybe I want the cops to see you with us," Nicholas returned. "Just to make sure you're one hundred percent committed to the project."

"Oh, now it's a project? I thought it was a robbery. I should have brought Popsicle sticks and pipe cleaners instead of glass cutters."

"You want me to search you for wires again, Sam?"

"Nope. Who're your friends? I recognize Bono, of course."

The guy sitting next to her with the long, greasy hair, hawk nose, and sunglasses frowned. "Bono. That's good." Nicholas snorted. "He's Eric. The one by the window is Dolph. Our driver is Wulf."

"Who's missing, besides Martin? You said it would be a seven-way split."

"That's right. Two shares for me. I set this all up, after all."

"I guess I won't know until Tuesday if you're worth it or not."

Nicholas turned from the front seat to face her. "I'm not the one we'll have to worry about."

Threats again. In her business they were as common as wire cutters. "If this is the big meeting, where's Martin?"

"We're joining up with him. I decided I would save you the cab fare and having to lose all the police following you."

"Thanks, as long as they're not following *you*. You have shown up at my house four times now."

"Wulf?" Veittsreig asked.

"No one's following," the driver returned in an accent heavier than Veittsreig's.

Despite Wulf's apparent confidence, the Explorer looped up, down, and around Manhattan for the next half hour. Samantha applauded the caution, though the attention to detail didn't bode well for her or Martin. When Interpol came down on these guys, they were going to have a pretty fair idea about who'd leaked the information. If what Rick had said about his conversation with Martin was true, and she had no reason to disbelieve him, she needed to come up with an escape plan. A good one.

"Are you lost?" she finally asked. "If you're not, I'd really like to get the battle plans before Tuesday. And the wiring schematics."

"Five minutes. And hand Bono your backpack."

Bono, aka Eric, said something in German about how not funny Veittsreig was. Samantha pretended not to understand, and instead with an annoyed breath dumped her backpack onto Eric's lap.

"Don't break anything. It's all new."

Eric lifted out the splitter. "GPS," he grunted.

"It's an electronic splitter, you moron," Samantha retorted. "It's for shutting off parts of alarm systems."

"Why is it new? Don't you own one already, Jellicoe?"

"Yes, I do. It's in Palm Beach. I came to New York on vacation. You guys started all this. I'm just trying to be prepared."

Eric's next muttering in German confirmed that the rest of the stuff in her pack was legit. He shoved everything back in and returned it to her.

"Thanks. Does this mean I passed? Do I get to be in the club?"

"Yes. Go ahead to the warehouse, Wulf."

Gangs—or crews, rather—of thieves always rented warehouses. Since she generally worked alone, Samantha wasn't entirely certain why, unless they'd all gone to see the same movies and didn't want the other robbery crews making fun. To her a group of guys suddenly taking over or renting a warehouse and not bringing in a lot of stuff to store screamed suspicion, but she was a fellow lawbreaker, not an enforcer.

They pulled up in front of a nondescript storage warehouse along the river and facing New Jersey. Dolph climbed out, keyed an entry code—which she immediately memorized—into the door pad, and then pushed up the corrugated metal door. The Explorer slipped under, and Dolph pulled the door down again.

"So this is the top-secret headquarters," Samantha said, getting out of the SUV. "It's . . . spacious."

Martin rounded a stack of boxes and walked up to her. "Jellicoe and Jellicoe, back together again."

"Hi, Martin."

"So much for your short retirement, eh? I always said a true champ can't retire at the top. It's not in their blood. They have to keep fighting all the way down."

"And we know which side of that hill you're on, eh, Martin?" Veittsreig chuckled, slapping her father on the back. "Let's take a look at those blueprints, shall we?"

"Before we get started," Samantha said, dumping her backpack on another ubiquitous box and noting the UPS truck behind them, now black and with "SWAT" painted over the delivery company logo, "I have a question."

"And what might that be?"

"I assume you guys have been planning this for weeks. Why are you bringing me in three days before the job?"

"First of all," Nicholas said, tossing her a beer, "we didn't know you would be in New York at such an opportune time, but since you are, we'd be foolish not to take advantage of that fact. Second, the request for the Stradivarius came in last week, and we couldn't work out how to cover it along with everything else."

"You needed more manpower."

"Womanpower," Dolph said, gazing at the chest area of her tank top.

Great. Raging hormone guy.

"And third, some hack, as you call us," Nicholas continued, "wouldn't be able to play catch-up and be ready in three days. I'm betting that you can be."

"That makes you smart," Samantha said, favoring Veittsreig with a smile. "But are you any good at a B and E?"

Nicholas rolled out the blueprints and wiring schematics. "Take a look and see."

Chapter 18

Sunday, 10:47 p.m.

Rick pulled open the front door just as she reached it. "You didn't leave a note," he said, taking her hand, key and all, and drawing her into the house.

"I didn't have a chance," she said tiredly, dumping her backpack into the front closet and pulling on a sweatshirt hanging there. Wulf had dropped her off a few avenues away, and she'd taken a cab the last chilly mile home. "They did a drive-by and picked me up right outside here." The sweatshirt said "Oxford" across the chest, and it smelled like Rick's aftershave.

Stoney came up behind Rick. "You shouldn't leave your gear in there. If the cops bust in, that's the first place they'll look."

"I know that," she grumbled. "Can I get a damn sandwich and an aspirin before you start playing good billionaire, bad fence? Or vice versa?"

"Of course you can." Rick took her shoulders and guided her toward the kitchen.

"Good," she returned. "And no bad news from anybody on my empty stomach, got it?"

Rick's hands tightened briefly, then relaxed again. "Got it."

Partway to the kitchen she turned around to see Stoney walking behind them. "And what are you doing here? Talk about the cops being suspicious."

"Addison called me when you didn't show. I came up the fire escape and climbed in through the window."

Despite her tiredness, she snorted. "*You* did a B and E?"

"Just an E," Rick said. "I opened the window for him."

She slid an arm around Rick's waist. "You're my guys."

Rick sat her down at the small kitchen table and then went over to the pantry. He pulled out a plate and a couple of slices of bread, set them on the counter, and headed for the refrigerator.

"Where's Vilseau?"

"Under the circumstances, I thought Wilder and Vilseau might be safer elsewhere," he returned. "I gave them the next few days off. Ben, as well."

"But they sleep here."

He grinned. "Allow me to clarify. I paid for them to take the next couple of days off. Generously."

"Okay, then."

"Peanut butter, or turkey?"

"Turkey. Soft on the mayo, extra mustard."

Rick lifted an eyebrow at her. "Do I look like a cook?"

"You do until Vilseau comes back. Because anything beyond microwave pizza is your territory, sweetheart."

With a grin he began slathering mustard on one of the slices of bread. "Wonderful. So now I have to negotiate a multimillion-dollar deal *and* cook? Do you want tomatoes?"

"Hell, yes, my darlin'."

"Ahem. Innocent bystander trying not to barf over here." Stoney waved a hand at them from the doorway. "What's the gig?"

"Food first. Do you want Rick to make you a sandwich?"

"Hey," Rick protested.

"No, thanks. I ate at Delroy's." Stoney made a face. "The man makes great pastries, but he can destroy a steak like nobody's business."

"What happened to the hotel?"

"I tried to leave, but Delroy got one of those hurt, puppy-dog looks on his face. So I'm still sleeping on the damn lumpy couch and eating lumpy whatever that was he piled next to the steak."

"You're such a softy." Her sense of humor beginning to return and her headache beginning to fade a little, Samantha went over to the counter to tear off a piece of lettuce for her sandwich.

"Remind me again that you two are criminal masterminds and I'm a real estate magnate worth billions, will you?" Rick leaned sideways and kissed her.

As Samantha had requested, Richard did his damnedest to keep the mood light until she'd at least eaten. Her evening was going to get worse than even she realized—she wasn't the only one with bad news.

She went over to the refrigerator and poured herself some lemonade, then scrounged around until she found a bottle of aspirin. "Stoney, I found the tortilla chips," she said, shaking the bag over her shoulder.

"Hey, quit rattling them around," Barstone grunted, coming forward with surprising speed for so large a gentleman.

"You'll break off the corners." He took the bag and retreated to the table. "Get me some of that lemonade, would you, honey?"

"Sure. Rick?"

"I'm fine."

They made a bloody odd family, Rick reflected, but a family seemed to be exactly what they'd become. He didn't know if he'd ever like Walter Barstone, but over the past two days he'd gained a much larger measure of respect for the man. Walter genuinely cared for Samantha, clearly, though his influence over her left a great deal to be desired. Compared to Martin Jellicoe, however, the man was a saint.

"You okay?" Samantha murmured, nudging him in the back with her elbow as she crossed to the table.

He shook himself. "I was just thinking about how dinky you look in my old college jersey."

" 'Dinky'?"

"Oh. Cute." *Yanks.*

"Mm-hm."

Stacking her substantial sandwich together, he pulled a knife from the case and sliced the monstrosity in half. "Dinner is served, my lady," he said grandly, carrying the plate to the table and taking the chair beside her.

She wolfed down half the sandwich, then snatched a handful of tortilla chips from Walter. "Veittsreig's got three Germans with him, plus Martin and me."

"Do you know any of them?" Walter asked, grabbing a corner of the chip bag and carefully sliding it back into his possession.

"No, I don't. If they always crew with Nicholas, though, I probably wouldn't."

"What's the plan?"

"We go in twenty minutes before closing. I disable the

central alarms—that's the fire and safety doors and barriers and shit—" she explained, glancing at Richard, "and I do the outlying sensors—the video, and the ones that call the cops. And then I head for the Music Room to get the Stradivarius while the guys go after the paintings."

"People are going to notice you," Richard said, clenching his hands together so hard his knuckles showed white, "cameras working or not. Twenty minutes before closing is—"

"It's nuts. I think Veittsreig figures with more people there'll be more chaos, and more chance for us to get out before they get the system rerouted." She picked up the second half of the sandwich and took a bite. "If it was me planning this, I would have gone in at two a.m., with a three-man crew, and winched in from the ceiling. Not that I would hit a museum in the first place."

"They'll be armed, I presume?" Rick reached over and feathered a lock of her hair behind her left ear. From hearing her talk and knowing some of what she'd done previous to their meeting, he would have imagined her to be some kind of biceps-rippling Amazon with superpowers, not a five-foot five inch, hundred-and-twenty-pound dynamo.

"Yes. They gave Martin a Glock, even. And they were kind of pissed when I said I wouldn't carry." She frowned at her turkey and mustard extravaganza. "Since it's going to end up being four against two, maybe I should have taken a piece."

"I'm not so sure about those odds," Richard said, wishing he could be telling her in private—or mostly that he didn't have to tell her at all.

"What do you mean?" she asked.

"I made some calls this afternoon."

She slammed the remains of her sandwich down. "You called Donner, didn't you? Dammit, Rick, don't you realize how rough these guys play? If they smell anything—*anything*—they'll shoot Martin and me in the head, and then go after you."

"There's nothing for them to smell."

Her brow furrowed. "What do you m—"

"Tom knows some people in the State Department, who know some people in the FBI. He put out that I might be interested in loaning some of my pieces to the Metropolitan Museum, and with a few more arm twists, he was able to learn from one of the FBI officials about a sting happening in New York. The FBI and Interpol *are* all set for the hit—on Friday. They're even going to put undercover agents inside the museum to pose as visitors."

"On Friday," Walter echoed quietly, his dark skin going gray.

Samantha sat at the table, silent, for a long time. If it had been anyone else he would have said she was simply stunned. Numb. Not his Samantha, though. She was thinking, running scenarios through her head.

Finally she nodded. "In a way, that makes me feel better."

"Better? Because Martin's crossing Interp—"

"No, Stoney, because Martin's not setting me up to take a fall. I figured he was going to cross somebody, but I just thought it would be me. But he got me pulled into a legit job. Or his version of one, anyway."

"At a museum. And with guys carrying guns."

"Martin never had a problem with hitting museums. That was my thing—me being a snob, he used to say."

Richard looked at her. "If I might point out, you are now involved in the planning of a straight-up theft."

"One thing at a time." She started to push away from the table.

"No, this first," he countered, wrapping a fist around the back of her chair, keeping her in her seat.

"I have to go in, Rick," she said, her voice harder. "If I don't, the same penalties still apply. They're finally trusting me to the point that I'm not at a complete disadvantage. If I do or say anything the tiniest bit hinky, I'm dead."

"And if you go in, there's a whole other set of penalties. Going in to steal something in the middle of a crowd, carrying guns, is not cat burglary. It's armed robbery. Do you have any idea how many things could go wrong? And even if no one shoots anyone and you still happen to get caught, you get twenty years in prison. Life, if they dig into your past."

She smirked at him. "Have a little faith, studmuffin. And give me a few damned minutes to think without you being Dudley Do-Right, okay?"

He released the chair, and she slammed it backward. Standing, she headed for the hallway. "Dudley Do-Right is Canadian," he said succinctly.

Samantha slowed, sending him an exasperated look over her shoulder. "Sir Galahad, then. I'm going to take a shower. Stoney, go back to Delroy's. I'll call when I think of something."

After she left the room, the two men sat facing one another. "She'll find an angle," Walter said after a moment. "She always does."

"But she won't be trying to find a way to back out of the job," Rick returned. "She wants to do it."

"Just to see if she can, I think."

"It's her not knowing for certain that worries me." That and the fact that if she did flat-out steal something again, their relationship would be finished. He could justify, at least to himself, her reasons for breaking into the Hodgeses'.

This robbery was on a much grander scale, with much more serious repercussions involved. And as much as he loved her, he would not let her use his home, his life, as her base of operations or something. With a breath he stood. "Come on. I'll help you out the window."

Walter climbed to his feet, as well. "Okay, but I'm taking the tortilla chips."

Samantha had said she wanted some time to think, but Richard wanted to remind her that this was about more than just a dangerous job. This was about their future together, as well.

He helped boost Walter out the back window and watched him down the fire escape, then closed and locked the thing and trotted downstairs to set the perimeter alarm. Obviously the system wasn't worth the wood and plaster it was fastened to, but he refused to make things any easier than they already were for whomever chose to break in to his house next.

As he marched back upstairs he heard a door click closed. Samantha was already running the shower—he could hear it through the closed master bedroom door. He walked past it, and stopped at two doors down. *Shit*. "John?" he said, knocking softly.

A few seconds passed, and the door opened. "Yes, sir?"

"How are you settling in?"

"Fine, sir. I, um, with your cook gone, what's the rule for meals? For breakfast?"

"Help yourself. The cupboards are full. Or order out." He paused. "Do you need any towels or blankets or anything?"

"No, sir. Everything is fine. I'm fine. The . . . you have a lovely house."

"Thank you." He backed away a few steps. "Good night, then."

"Good night, sir."

"And remember, it's Rick."

"Yes, sir. Rick. I'll remember."

"Oh, and the perimeter alarm is set. If you open an outside door or a window, it'll go off."

"I'll keep that in mind, Rick. Thank you."

The door closed, with the same click and cadence he'd heard a few moments earlier. Where had John Stillwell been during that conversation down in the kitchen? And how in hell had he managed to forget that someone else was staying in the house? It wasn't like him at all.

Richard pushed open the master bedroom door, then closed and locked it behind him. He kicked off his shoes, sending them in the general direction of his closet, then unbuttoned the dark burgundy dress shirt he'd never changed out of. Shedding it and his trousers, he headed for the bathroom, leaving his boxers and socks in the doorway.

"I forgot to tell you something, Yank," he said, pulling open the shower door.

She faced him, soap running down her bare, wet skin in delicious rivulets. His body responded immediately, and he walked into the large shower and closed the door behind him.

"I can see that," she returned, her gaze dropping to his cock.

"We have a houseguest."

Her eyes lifted again. "Stoney can't stay here."

"No. John Stillwell."

"The guy I creamed this morning?"

"Yes. I've been a little . . . distracted, so I brought him in to help me with a few things."

"So he's here. Now."

"He's in the guest room."

"You just did that so I can't move in there again."

"Yes, I'm devious that way. I'm paying a man nearly half a million dollars a year to keep you from leaving our bed."

"Okay, so now I know. Go away. I'm still thinking." She turned away, running her face and shoulders under the steaming water.

"Think about this, too," he murmured, slipping his arms around her front and caressing her nipples. They hardened under his fingers.

"Rick, you—"

"And this," he continued, leaning down to nibble at her ear and the nape of her neck.

She tried to turn around, but he kept her facing away from him, her bottom wriggling against his cock making him ache. Putting one hand down between her legs, shifting her folds apart with his fingers, he bent her forward with the weight of his body and slowly pushed inside her.

Samantha grabbed on to the safety rail and held on as he pumped into her, hard and fast. The wet slap of their skin intoxicated him, and he moaned, shifting one hand back up to her breasts again.

This, she had to understand—that they were made for one another, that he owned her in a way that neither of them would probably ever acknowledge. In the same way that she owned him.

"God," she rasped, and her muscles tightened convulsively around him.

"I love when you come for me," he whispered, increasing his own rhythm until with a grunt he climaxed.

He held her there for a long moment, breathing hard and letting the soap and sweat and water intermingle on their bodies. Finally he pulled away from her.

"I just wanted to remind you that you have more to think

about than just a robbery," he said, opening the shower door and stepping out to grab a towel.

"Rick?"

He faced her.

A washcloth hit him full in the face, warm and sopping wet. As he pulled it away, angry, Samantha was still gazing at him. "I didn't forget about that," she said in a much milder voice than he'd expected. "Now come back in here and wash my back."

This was what he never wanted to give up. Richard dropped the towel and stepped back into the shower.

Chapter 19

Monday, 7:40 a.m.

"I don't need to go into the office," Rick said, as he adjusted his black and gray tie.

Sitting at the small table beneath the windows of the master bedroom, Samantha flipped another page of the Metropolitan Museum of Art guide she'd picked up when she'd visited with Stoney. "Yes, you do," she said, gazing at the photo of the Stradivarius violin she was supposed to steal tomorrow. "I'm not writing you a note for missing your negotiations today, bucko."

"That's why I'm employing Stillwell, so when something unexpected comes up, I'll be available."

She looked at him. "You hired him so you could be free to keep track of me. You're not my damned mother. Or my parole officer."

Rick frowned. "Fine." Moving to the bedroom door, he quietly closed it. "I think he might have heard us."

"This morning? We haven't said anything too weird."

"Not this morning. Last night."

"Last . . . Oh. Shit." She paused. "Not the shower sex, right? The talking in the kitchen."

"Precisely."

"Shit. So fire him."

"He hasn't done anything wrong. In fact, yesterday he may have saved me about half a million annually in property taxes." Rick gazed over her shoulder at the photo. "And isn't it a bit hypocritical of you to assume that he'll be trouble?"

She shot him a grin. "You weren't wrong about me being trouble."

"Just keep an eye on him until we know."

"I have to say that I don't like the idea of having a potential spy in our own house."

He drew a breath. "Neither do I. But I'll handle him." He sat beside her. "And I hired him because my life has changed over the past few months, and I'm adapting. And yes, you're the reason my life has changed." Rick picked up her glass of Diet Coke and took a swallow. "It's just not the same as coffee."

"And amen to that. Go to work. I'm going to run through the schedule and make sure I have everything I need."

He tilted her chair back to give her an upside-down kiss. "I'll call you as soon as I get a moment." Setting the chair back on all fours, he picked up his suit jacket and headed for the bedroom door.

As Samantha watched him exit the room, it abruptly occurred to her. The solution. A way to stop Veittsreig, and a way to keep Martin from reneging on his deal with Interpol, and a way to move any suspicion away from Rick. Her heart stopped, and then slammed into hyperdrive.

"Hey, Brit," she called, rising and making her way to the head of the stairs.

On the landing, Rick stopped and looked up at her. "What is it?"

"I love you."

His jaw worked for a moment. "I love you, too, Yank." He hesitated, as though contemplating climbing the stairs again.

"Call me," she said, giving him a smile. "We'll do lunch. And don't forget to take Stillwell with you."

With one of his your-ladyship bows, he grinned back at her and continued down the stairs. Samantha waited where she was until she heard the two men's voices, and then the click and lock as the front door closed. Then she bolted back into the bedroom and grabbed her cell phone off the charging cradle.

She'd memorized the number the one and only time she'd seen it, and she punched the buttons before she could change her mind.

"Gorstein," the voice at the other end came.

"Gorstein, it's Jellicoe. I'd like to have a chat with you."

For a heartbeat she didn't hear anything. She'd surprised him, then. Good. "Come down to the station."

"Nope. Meet me at the Art Café on Broadway for breakfast. Eight-thirty." That should give her time to lose whoever might be tailing her this morning.

"I already ate."

"Like I care. Are you going to be there, or not?"

"Yeah. I'll be there."

"If I see any uniforms or any handcuffs, Gorstein, I'm going to assume you won't play nice."

"You are one paranoid lady, Ms. J."

"And don't you forget it."

It probably didn't matter if the cops tailed her today, but it was the principle of the thing. Besides, she couldn't risk having Wulf or Bono or one of the other members of Veittsreig's crew tracking her to a meeting with a cop. Especially one they'd seen visiting her house before.

Grabbing her phone, purse, and the museum guidebook, she left the house and hailed a cab. For a second she considered leaving Rick a note, just in case, but if this went wrong, no couple of words on a piece of paper would be able to explain it.

Four taxis later, she stepped onto the sidewalk in front of the Art Café. She liked the place—good, inexpensive food, unpretentious, and best of all, Veittsreig and his guys probably had no idea it even existed.

"Ms. J."

She turned around as Detective Gorstein approached from the corner. He was on time, anyway. So he was the guy she was going to bare her soul to. Yep, that was her brilliant plan: Tell Gorstein everything, and hope that he would be happier at being able to nab some big-time art thieves and get in good with Interpol and the FBI than he would be to get one more crack at her and Martin. As for the Hodges job, well, she hadn't decided about that one yet. Confessing to a crime no one suspected her of—that was just wrong.

At least, unlike Frank Castillo in Palm Beach, Gorstein didn't exude copness, which made talking to him in public a little less problematic. She still didn't like him, but anybody who knew her old rep and not him would think she was meeting with a fence or an antiques dealer or something.

Her thumping heart did a flip and then crashed into her gut. Gorstein *didn't* look like a cop, yet Nicholas had identified him as such the night he'd come to collect the diamonds. And Nicholas hadn't been in town long, so how had he known what Gorstein was? Well, she could think of one reason. Gorstein was dirty. And that meant she was about to shoot herself in the head.

"Are we going in?" he asked, holding open the door.

Christ. She needed to know for sure. Subconsciously, she'd trusted the way she'd felt about him enough to make the call. If her gut was right, the plan could still work. If she was wrong, Nicholas knew exactly where she was, and was waiting to see if she was willing to sell him out to the police or not.

She went into the café. "Since I'd like to keep this low-key," she said, signaling that they needed a table for two, "do you have a first name? Besides Detective, I mean."

"Yeah. It's Sam."

Samantha blinked. "You're kidding, right?"

"Nope."

"Well, I'm not calling you that."

"I didn't think so."

Trying to buy some time while she ran all of their past conversations through her head, she ordered the pancakes with bananas and walnuts, plus a Diet Coke. He asked for a bran muffin and coffee. Cop food, not that that meant anything at this point.

"I thought you'd eaten," she noted, glancing around the room for any familiar faces. Nothing.

"I had some gum and a Tic Tac."

"You're trying to quit smoking, aren't you? That explains why you're so cranky."

"I don't smoke," he grunted. "I'm always cranky."

Other than the ubiquitous toothpick, which he wasn't chewing on this morning, he wasn't bad-looking, either. That fact made her feel disloyal, but it gave her another reason for wanting to see him besides spilling her guts—if it turned out that she needed another reason.

Once the waiter brought them their plates, Samantha leaned her elbows onto their small booth table. "Any leads on the stolen art?"

As she leaned forward, he sat back. "If I'm here so you can yank me around, then forget it. I have a lot of work to do."

It sounded like genuine frustration. To her that signified honesty, which was good—unless he was just a better actor than she was. Man, she was an idiot to go into this without backup. She only hoped she had the chance to learn and benefit from the lesson.

She offered him a slow smile. "I'm not yanking you around. But in my position I have to be cautious, you know." Okay, that was good.

"And what position is that?"

"You said you went after my dad once. Did you ever see him? I mean, how did you know it was Martin Jellicoe you were after?" Especially since it hadn't been. But if he was crooked, he'd probably seen him after—and very recently.

"No, I never saw him. Not then. That son of a— Sorry, I know he's your dad, but he was one, you know."

"I know. He never told me much about what he did for a living, but I know." No, she wasn't going to completely bare her soul. She wasn't an idiot.

"Yeah, right. Okay, I kind of liked the way you got right in my face, and your obsession with Diet Coke is kind of . . . endearing, I guess. But if you laugh, I'm gonna find a way to bust you. I swear to God I am. And I know you wrecked an undercover car yesterday, by the way."

"Not if you can't prove it. And I won't laugh. I promise." With the way her nerves were rattling around, she'd be lucky if she didn't start screaming and run away.

"I didn't have a clue who pulled that job. Not until eight months later, when the Miami PD caught him elbow-deep in a pile of Spanish doubloons at the Historical Museum of Southern Florida. The MO matched my job, and they gave me a call. I flew down to Miami to question him, and he wouldn't say a damned word. He just smiled at me. It was this 'prove-it' look, like he knew I couldn't. And I never could. Slick, slick, slick." He set down his coffee so hard that it sloshed onto the saucer. "They gave him how many years in prison?"

"One hundred and eighteen," she supplied quietly.

"One hundred and eighteen years in prison, and I couldn't prove the Warhol. I'd give my left nut, excuse my language, to have been the one to bring him down."

Samantha watched his expression, listened to his voice, to the words he used and to the obvious frustration and anger there. Even though Martin wasn't the one who'd stolen the Warhol, she couldn't believe that the man sitting opposite her would ever under any circumstances agree to work with her father, much less help him get away with an even bigger robbery.

And Martin had seen Gorstein before. He would have recognized him the night she was arrested, on the television news, and the night the detective had called on her for help. It made sense. And more importantly, it felt like it made sense.

"That Warhol was eight years ago," she said, inwardly steeling herself, ready to run if he went after her. She couldn't trust the honest cops any more than she could the crooked ones, although for completely different reasons. But this cop, she was about to bet, was an honest one. *And* one she could trust. "The statute of limitations has run out."

"It still bugs me. And the bastard's dead, so I can't get a deathbed confession out of him. I hate loose ends."

"Well, in the interest of what I hope is about to be a kind of a partnership, the Warhol went to a private collection in Amsterdam. It's still there, as far as I know."

Brown eyes narrowed. "Are you saying what I think you're saying?"

"I took it."

He started to his feet. Samantha held out a hand, her other going to the butter knife on the table. "Statute, honey. You can't arrest me for it."

"Are you here to gloat, then? To say that I wasted all that time going after the wrong Jellicoe and there's nothing I can do about it now?"

She grabbed his wrist and yanked him back into the booth. "Will you keep your damn voice down, Gorstein?" she hissed. "No, I'm not here to gloat. You brought me a soda, and you've been up front with me. Maybe I can pay you back a little for the Warhol."

"Fuck. And how are you going to do that?"

"Okay. I'm not going to play the on-the-record or off-the-record snitch. I'm going to tell you some things because basically I have two choices in front of me, and one gets me dead, while the other one loses me . . . some things I don't want to lose. You're my third choice."

"You *did* take the Hogarth and the Picasso, didn't you? I knew it, you—"

"I did not." She lowered her voice further. "I only have one ground rule, and that's that you listen until I'm finished."

Gorstein edged upright again. "And then I can arrest you."

The tips of her fingers went cold, and she flexed them. "That would be choice number four, but I'll leave it up to you."

"I'm getting a little weary of having this same conversation over and over again," Richard said, standing at the head of the conference table to emphasize his point. "If the city council would rather have a derelict thirty-five-story building in the middle of Manhattan and if they prefer to forgo my offer to supply twenty million dollars toward low-income housing, then just mention traffic congestion one more time and we're finished."

John Stillwell cleared his throat as Rick walked to the window. "I believe that Mr. Addison's point is that the amount of increased traffic would be negligible when compared with the prestige of having a five-star hotel in the middle of your downtown area. Employment will increase, as will your tax revenues. Mr. Addison has been very patient, but at some point this becomes a losing proposition, and we will move on."

"But we have to consider—"

"Oh, for God's sake." Richard strode to the conference room door. "My people, out." As his employees filed past him into the reception area and the seated council representatives looked at one another, stunned, he exited the room as well, stopping in the doorway. "Consider all you want for the next fifteen minutes." He closed the door on them.

"Rick?" Stillwell said, approaching him with some paperwork.

"No. We are not doing anything else on this project until I get an answer from the city. Go get a cup of coffee or something. I don't want them even to *see* any of us for fifteen minutes. And John?"

"Yes, sir?"

"That was a nice bit of bad cop/good cop. Well done."

Stillwell smiled briefly, glanced toward the glass walls, and stifled the expression again. "Thank you."

His team scattered. Wishing he could lock the bloody conference room doors, Richard retreated to his office. Halfway there his cell phone rang in the tri-tones he'd assigned as

Samantha's ring. He took the phone from his belt and opened it. "Hello, my dear."

"Are you in the middle of something?"

"We're on strike for the next fourteen minutes," he said, slowing at the monotone of her voice. The hairs on the back of his neck pricked. "What is it?"

"I would very much appreciate it if you could come to the Art Café on Broadway," she returned in the same quiet tone.

"Are you safe?"

"Yes. If you could not be followed, that would also be good."

Bloody hell. "Sam?"

"I'm okay. But we don't have a lot of time."

Something was seriously troubling her. "I'm on my way."

Turning around, he strode into Stillwell's new office. "John, I have an errand. If they aren't ready to move past traffic when you go back in there, adjourn for the day. Tell them the mayor can call me if he wants our discussions to continue."

"Very good."

He descended the fifty floors in the elevator, trying not to fidget and wishing he'd had an executive elevator installed. Or a bat pole. Samantha would like that.

In the first cab he headed east for three blocks, then turned right, got out, hailed another cab, and went back in the opposite direction. He bloody well hoped that someone was trying to follow him, because otherwise he would just look like an idiot. He had the second cab drive past the café, and since he didn't see any overt signs of battle he exited and took a third cab back to the front door.

Inside he saw her immediately, sitting in one of the back booths with her face to the door—and Detective Gorstein seated opposite her. The diners in his vicinity stirred as he walked past, but he ignored them. She waved, so at least she wasn't handcuffed, thank Christ.

She scooted over, and he kissed her on the cheek, sitting in the booth beside her. "Detective," he intoned, looking from one to the other.

"Ms. J. has been telling me a story," Gorstein said.

"What kind of story?"

"Oh, you know," Samantha took up. "People coming back from the dead, museums being robbed, things like that."

Rick felt the blood drain from his face. "I beg your pardon?"

"Mr. Addison?" a waiter said, approaching. "Can I get you something to drink?"

"No, thank y—"

"He'll take a cup of tea," Sam interrupted. The waiter nodded and left.

"Saman—"

"We're being social," she said in a low voice. "This is not an official meeting."

"I should hope not." Beneath the table he gripped her hand. Hard. "You just decided you wanted to have a chat with the man who arrested you?" he breathed. "And you declined to tell me where you were going?"

"This was my deal. My decision."

"You told Walter, I suppose?"

"What part of 'my decision' did you not get, Addison?" she returned, despite her clipped tone squeezing his fingers back. "I figured if I went to Gorstein it would absolve everybody else."

Richard turned his gaze to Gorstein. "And what was your opinion of this story, then, Detective?"

"That nobody would tell me that kind of craziness if it

wasn't true." The detective glanced at Samantha. "It took a lot of guts to trust me with this."

Trust. A promising word, under the circumstances. The waiter delivered the tea and a pot of hot water, and Richard nodded his thanks. "And what inspired this trust?"

"I weighed all the options, and I figured it had to be Gorstein, and it had to be me going to talk to him." Samantha shrugged. "If you want to fight about it, we can do that later. Right now we have some stuff to take care of. My . . . outing is tomorrow afternoon."

Her *outing.* The understatement of the year. And finally the setting for all this struck him. "You two actually sat here and discussed all of this."

"Mostly she talked and I sat here with my mouth hanging open."

"Rick's right, though," Samantha said. "Nobody much paid any attention to us here before. Now that you're here, though, Sir Galahad, maybe we should try to find somewhere more private."

That was a switch, he reflected, as his stunned surprise that this meeting had even taken place began to fade. *His* life, his fame, he supposed, was creating the difficulty this time. "How did you get here, Detective?" he asked.

"My car. It's in the garage around the corner."

Richard stood, drawing Samantha out of the booth with him. "Then let's go collect it."

He laid enough money on the table to cover what looked like the remains of breakfast, and rejoined Samantha to follow Gorstein to his car. It was insane, a clandestine Deep-Throat-style meeting in a parking garage, but as Samantha had said, they didn't have a great deal of time.

"I assume you've come up with some kind of plan?" he

asked, leaning against the back bumper of the late-model Taurus.

Samantha clambered onto the trunk to lean on his shoulder. "Gorstein's going to give a tip to the FBI that the timing of the robbery has changed."

"So we're back to you being in the middle of an armed robbery. I don't see much of an improvement."

"We get white hats there to make arrests and keep the artwork from leaving the museum, and Martin still gets credit for the setup."

"I'll see if I can make a deal to get some of my guys inside the museum," the detective said, standing a few feet from them. "We'll do what we can to back Jellicoe up."

"That's not good enough."

"Well, since she volunteered to jump into the middle of this little operation without first getting a deal from anybody in authority, there isn't much else I can do at this point." Gorstein looked at Samantha. "I would assume that you have some . . . things Interpol might be interested in talking to you about. Things that happened less than seven years ago and are still pursuable. You're as hot a commodity for them as this Veittsreig guy, I'd bet."

What in the world had she told him? "All the more reason that this is not an acceptable plan," Rick grunted. He couldn't stop Samantha from stepping into dangerous situations. He accepted that her craving for adventure was part of her character. This, though, entailed far too great a risk.

"My other option with Gorstein is to have him arrest me, so I can't hit the museum."

"I choose that one, then." Surprised that she'd even thought it, much less said it aloud, Rick took the hand that rested on her thigh. "I'd rather have you in jail for a day than for life."

"I choose neither," she said flatly. "The problem with that

plan is that if I get arrested, Nicholas and Martin will probably call off the job. I'll—we'll—still be on the hook when I get out, and Interpol will be pissed at Martin."

"They *should* be pissed at him. He's double-crossing them."

"Maybe he hasn't been able to get them the updated information. This job was put together pretty fast." She frowned. "Which probably means it'll get sloppy."

"You're not making me feel any better."

"I'm going in, Rick. This job has to start so it can be stopped by the cops, or we'll just get sucked into it again later, someplace else. I expect to go in on my own, and I'm not going to assume that Martin's going to look out for me. I've covered myself as best I can, but that's the way it's going to be."

"Do you two want a minute?" Gorstein asked, fishing in his jacket pocket for a toothpick and jamming it in his mouth.

Richard wanted several minutes. Pushing away from the bumper, he glared at Samantha. It had been a very long time since anyone had attempted to lay down the law to him, and he liked it even less now. He wanted to stop her. To handcuff her himself, throw her on a plane, and take her back to England where at least he had a very large fence separating his things from the rest of the world. And where a fence might not keep Samantha in, it could certainly help to keep anything or anyone who might harm her, out.

"Very well," he said stiffly, grinding the words out through clenched jaws.

"Good," the detective put in before Samantha could say anything. "Because I've got like thirty hours to get the FBI and Interpol and the NYPD together, come up with a plan, and pull it off."

Richard kept his gaze on Samantha. "And if he can't, I will take whatever steps are necessary to keep you out of that museum tomorrow. Are we clear on that?"

Green eyes narrowed. "Crystal."

"Okay," Gorstein grunted, clapping his hands together. "Get off my car. I need to get to the station."

"And you're keeping my name away from everybody else."

"Everybody but the guys I'm going to put on your ass tomorrow." He pulled out his keys and opened the driver's door. "And you be somewhere I can get hold of you, just in case. I'm gonna have to answer some tough questions."

"We'll be at home," Rick said, "making certain Samantha has an exit plan." Or several of them.

Chapter 20

Tuesday, 8:23 a.m.

"Okay, I got them," Stoney said, grunting as she helped haul him over the window frame in the upstairs hall. "And I'm getting damn tired of climbing in through the window."

"I used to do it for a living," Samantha returned, closing the window again and pushing the hall table back in place.

"You're a little more spry than I am. And about thirty years younger."

"Excuses, excuses," she murmured, leading him toward the library, which she'd commandeered to lay out her gear. "Let's see 'em."

"Say thank you, first."

"Thank you, Stoney."

"That's better. This is a little more high-tech than you like to go, though, isn't it?"

"A lot more. I hope I can figure out how to wire them."

"Especially since you'll have about five minutes total to do it. I have to say, Sam, you've done some shit that scared me half to death, but this is just plain crazy."

She flashed him a smile. "At least if it doesn't work I'll be going out with a bang."

"Don't even say that." He closed the library door behind them. "Where's the Brit?"

"Downstairs, keeping our houseguest occupied until he can send him off to work."

"Is this going to be a new thing? You two with a live-in chaperon?"

"We already live with other people," she returned, holding her hand out to take his backpack. "And Solano Dorado is a big house. Besides, Stillwell's going to be doing a lot of traveling."

"It just makes me curious about why Addison needs a helper all of a sudden."

Sam glanced at him. "He needs a helper because he wants to be able to spend more time with me."

"Keep an eye on you, you mean."

"No. Yes. Probably. I don't know. I'm trying to be open-minded about it until I see how it plays out. Because all three of us know that I am not going to end up tethered to Rick, no matter how much I like having him around." She freed a half dozen mini remote controls and receivers from the pack. "These are nice. Ramon?"

He shook his head. "Douglas. And I had to *pay* him, so you owe me four thousand bucks."

She sat at the library table, her tools spread around her, to pry the back off the first of the units. "I'm good for it." Shaking herself out of her pre-job concentration, she patted the chair beside her. "That's my fault, isn't it? That you had to pay cash."

"You made me retire, so yeah, it's your fault. All these guys are catching on that you can't barter with somebody who won't be taking in anything worth trading for."

"I'm not going to apologize. This life is safer for both of us."

He snorted. "Oh, I can see that."

Samantha frowned. "Well, it's supposed to be." She went to work with the soldering iron. "You know, this would go over better with Gorstein and everybody else if I could deliver the buyer, too."

"That's stepping way, way over the line, though. You know a lot of buyers. If they start thinking you're likely to rat them out, you can't even count the number of ways you'd be in trouble, and with a lot of rich guys."

"That's a possibility," she mused, "but those guys are mostly pretty smart. And since they are, they'll know that this guy stepped over the line first. Taking a painting out of a cat burglar's house is so uncool. It makes me look bad."

"Then get the information out of Veittsreig before you go in."

"I tried, but he thinks I might try to go around him and renegotiate."

"It just doesn't pay to be a crook anymore."

"Tell me about it. But whoever this guy is, he made me mad, and I'm not giving up."

For a minute Stoney watched her work. "Can I ask you something?"

"Mm-hm."

"Why did you decide you had to bring in the cops for this gig?"

"Because we couldn't go directly to Interpol."

"That's not what I mean."

"Then what did you mean?"

Stoney put a hand over hers, blocking her view of the remote. "I meant, Martin wrangled you into a pretty generous job. He made it kind of hard for you to turn it down, even. I mean, I know it's a museum, and that you have a thing about museums, but other than that, it's—"

"It's the kind of job that would appeal to me," Samantha finished, putting down her pair of pliers. "You mean why shouldn't I take the opportunity and dive back into my old life?"

"You're obviously loving this right now. You can't wait to go in this afternoon, can you?"

She'd spent most of last night debating those same points with herself. "It's a challenge. You know how I am about challenges."

"It's more than the challenge. You're like a junkie getting a fix after five months. You had a sip of tequila with those diamonds, and now you're dying for a nice, big bottle of Jack Daniels."

"Oh, nice. Thanks a lot."

"You know what I mean."

Yes, she did. "Why did Martin want to pull me into this, Stoney? Did you ever wonder about that?"

"You already figured that he's not trying to double-cross you. He needs your help to pull off this job."

"No, he doesn't. Two of us together can get the electronics done faster, but he doesn't *need* me to do it."

Stoney sat back in his chair. "Okay, you tell me, then. Why does Martin want you doing this job? You already know it's not to get you caught, because he put Interpol off until Friday."

She twisted to face him, drawing one foot under her bottom. "He's been keeping tabs on me for the past three years, since he supposedly died. For three years he's danced around, playing nice with Interpol, doing the least he could to keep on their good side and keep them from putting him back in the slam."

"I figured the same thing about that."

"How many other jobs do you think he's jammed them on? It's his new scam, Stoney—pretending to work for the good guys. It gives him all kinds of freedom to do small jobs on his own. He can even blame them on whoever he's setting up for the next Interpol sting."

For a few seconds he sat silently. "I can see that. Martin's always been pretty good at playing other people to suit his own purposes."

"I remember. And all the while he could say he was teaching them—or me—lessons. So what happens if he can get me to help him pull this one off? I get yanked away from Rick, because even if he could cover for me this time, he wouldn't. Martin gets the cash, stays in good with a very successful crew, and here I am with nowhere to go and a high-profile hit under my belt."

"He gets you to be his partner after you turned him down six years ago."

She picked up her Diet Coke and tipped it in his direction. "Give the man a gold ribbon."

"Is that why you called in the cops, then? So you wouldn't have to work with Martin again?"

"Give me a break. My life right now isn't perfect, but there are moments when I'm really, really happy. I'm in love. And I'm safe." She flashed a grin at his dubious expression. "Safer than I was. Today is an exception."

"How many exceptions will Addison put up with?"

Samantha had been debating that, too. "I don't know. I guess I'll find out when I hit the magic number."

"Do you want to hit the magic number?"

"Who are you, my guidance counselor?"

"I thought I was your Yoda."

"Well, this morning you're being my C-3PO, and you're annoying the shit out of me. Of course I don't want to hit the magic number. If Rick and I split, I don't want it to be because I didn't have the . . . guts to keep my face pointed in the direction I've decided to go."

Rick rapped at the door. "Everybody decent?" he asked at the same time, pushing it open.

"Is Stillwell gone?"

"Yes, I've sent him off to stall the city for today. It's only fair, since they've been waffling about for the past three days." He sat opposite her. "Should I ask how you're going to get all of this into the museum in the first place?" he asked, gesturing at her equipment.

"Let's just say we won't be using the front door. Not all of us, anyway."

"And explain the exit again to me. That's the bit that I want to make certain doesn't have any flaws."

The worry clear in those blue eyes of his made her reconsider the flip answer she'd been about to make. Anything she embarked on wasn't just about her anymore. That was probably the hardest thing to get used to; somebody else had an emotional, even physical, stake in her life.

"The exit's pretty simple. As soon as the white hats start moving in, I dump my gear, head out through the nearest exit, walk a block to where you're waiting with a cab, and we head to your office so I have an alibi. With Gorstein's guys giving me an extra couple of seconds, it should be easy."

"Yeah," Stoney muttered, "easy. Except for all the guns and the running around and the chance that somebody might try to follow you. Or that somebody might recognize you. You've been on TV, if you'll recall."

"Ah, but I thought of that," she returned, reaching into a sack beside her and pulling out a blonde wig.

"I hope that thing's bulletproof," her former fence said dourly.

She smiled at Rick. "Is it true, Mr. Addison?" she chirped, pulling on the headpiece. "Do billionaires prefer blondes?"

He snorted, reaching across the table to twist a strand of the golden blonde hair in his fingers. "You look good in any color, Yank. If being blonde will get you out of the Met safely, then yes, today I prefer blondes."

She stood, leaning over to kiss him on his sensuous mouth. "Good answer."

Letting go of her wig, he returned his attention to the electronics spread out on the table. "If you're just going to dump your gear, why are you fiddling with these things?" Rick asked, picking up one of the remotes and examining it.

"Insurance. Nicholas or Martin might check to see what I'm carrying. I have to at least look like I'm going to pull my weight on this." If she told him what they were actually for, he'd probably lock her in a closet until Doomsday. There were some things it was just better that he not know.

"And what's the exit plan according to you and your partners?"

"We've been through this."

"Go through it again, if you don't mind."

That was how he worked, she reflected, examining all aspects and angles of a situation. It was one of the ways they weren't so different. "Martin and I disable the sensors and the alarms," she said, keeping the impatience to get going out of her voice, "and while the docents and security are starting to empty the exhibit halls, we start yanking things off the walls. Panic starts, and we toss out some flares and smoke grenades, then head for the pieces we actually want and bag them."

"Like groceries."

"Just like. Still disrupting the displays, we jam out the front door and into the waiting UPS truck made up to look like a SWAT-mobile. With lights and sirens going, we head away from the museum, ditch the truck for a van, and head back to the warehouse. Then we dump off our loot and split up."

"But even if the alarms are shut down, armed security will still be on the premises."

"Hopefully they'll have their hands full with the civilians and the art we'll be scattering all over the place."

"According to Veittsreig, I presume?" Rick pressed. "He shot a security guard in Paris. He'll do it again. I hope you realize that."

"I'm not stupid, Rick," she retorted, the heady buzz of adrenaline already pulling at her. "The cops know what he's capable of. They'll be ready. That's the whole point of me telling Gorstein. Remember?" He continued to look skeptical, and so, sending him her best don't-mess-with-me look, she shoved away from the table. "I need another soda," she snapped, and stomped out of the room.

As soon as she was gone, Richard sat forward. "When do you think they'll call her in?"

"Within the next two hours, would be my guess. That way they'll have time to make last-minute adjustments with no chance of anybody getting the word out to anybody else."

"No honor among thieves?"

"Not with those guys. Man, I have a bad feeling about this."

"You're not the only one." Rick lowered his voice further. "As soon as she leaves, you and I will have a few steps of our own to take."

Walter furrowed his brow. "What kind of steps?"

"Steps to make certain our girl stays alive. Are you in?"

The ex-fence offered his hand. "Oh, yeah, I'm in. All the way."

Rick shook it. "Good."

Just as Samantha would do what she had to, so would he.

As an art collector, the thought of anyone tossing priceless artworks about for the sake of causing a distraction made him queasy. *His* feelings about the methods of Veittsreig's crew, though, didn't matter. Once the authorities began to materialize throughout the museum, her fellows would realize they'd been set up. They would turn either on Martin or on Samantha, or both. As far as he was concerned, Martin was on his own.

But no one in the FBI or Interpol would blink if any of the thieves should end up dead, and whatever Detective Gorstein might be hoping, his people were not going to be anything remotely close to in charge. Which left Walter Barstone and himself. And after what he'd overheard of the conversation between Walter and Sam a few minutes ago, nothing—*nothing*—was going to happen to Samantha if he had any say in the matter. Therefore, he would take steps to make certain that he had a say.

When Samantha returned to the library, soda in hand, Walter climbed to his feet. "If you two don't mind, I'm going to go see if I can catch the news. Make sure none of the local stations are doing 'A Day at the Met Museum' or anything."

"Chicken," Samantha said, setting down her drink and going back to work on the half dozen little gadgets Walter had brought her.

"Are you going to tell me what those are for?" Richard asked after a moment, watching her.

"They're so I can trigger an alarm on or off from a short distance away," she said, labeling them A through F with pieces of duct tape and a permanent marker. "That way I can kind of control when the rest of the museum knows that something's up." She flashed him her quicksilver grin. "Hopefully."

"My offer still stands to sweep you off to the Bahamas, you know," he commented. "You can bring the wig." He'd seen her climb walls and cut through windows, but while he'd known she had technical expertise, seeing it was something new. And fascinating.

"I know. I'll let you sweep me back to Palm Beach when this is over with. How's that?"

So she could get back to the security consultation business she didn't particularly like. "It sounds very good to me," he said anyway.

When she finished whatever she was doing with the remote controls and receivers, Richard helped her load everything she needed into her backpack. And to think, a few months ago he never would have believed that aiding a woman—his woman—in preparing for work would include packing wire cutters, a mini blowtorch, twenty yards of copper wire, an electronic splitter, and infrared binoculars, among other things.

He could see in her expression, hear in the excited tremor at the edge of her voice, how she felt about the coming job. It terrified him, but at the same time he could certainly understand it. "Do you want a peanut butter sandwich to go in there, too?" he asked, indicating the backpack.

"The other thieves would laugh at me."

"We can't have that."

Richard wanted to touch her, to haul her off to the bedroom and strip her naked, to remind her that he could arouse her just as much as a good B and E. Right before the moment of concluding a business deal, though, he would have hated the distraction, the threat to his focus. And since in her case focus could very well be all that kept her alive, he wasn't going to do anything to risk dulling hers.

"What now?" he asked.

"I pace around and get cranky until meeting time."

"How likely is Veittsreig to alter his plans at the last moment?"

"I've never worked with him before, but this whole thing is so seat-of-the-pants I'm not sure what he could change and still have it work. The basic plan will stay the same, at any rate."

"What if he—"

Her phone rang, with a theme that sounded familiar but he couldn't quite place. Richard frowned as she pulled the cell out of her pocket.

Samantha glanced up at him, grinning. "It's from *The Terminator*," she said, and flipped the phone open. "*Hola*." She listened for a minute, her face expressionless. "Will do," she finally said, and closed the phone again.

"Well?"

"It's a go. I have to leave now."

Now that the moment had come, he wanted to change his mind. His male ego and desire to possess warned him not to let her leave, to keep what was dear to him close by and safe. He took a deep breath.

"Be careful," he said, taking her hand and pulling her up against him.

She lifted up on her toes and kissed him, warm and worried and excited all at the same time. "Just be there when I make a run for it."

"I will be. Count on it."

With a wink she slung the backpack over her shoulder and headed for the stairs. "I love you, Brit."

That was twice now she'd said it without being prompted by him. And it wouldn't be the last time, either. "I love you, Yank. See you soon."

Chapter 21

Tuesday, 4:41 p.m.

While beneath a stand of trees Bono/Eric and Dolph speculated in German over whether either of them had enough money to tempt her away from Rick and into bed, Samantha, Martin, and Nicholas pretended to be tourists a few yards away. Martin spoke German, as well, but apparently the conversation about her virtue didn't bother him. "Four minutes," Veittsreig said, tapping his thigh the designated number of times for the benefit of their companions.

From Martin's expression he might have been waiting for his turn at playing chess. The Germans looked a little smug, but that was nothing new for them.

"Are you ever going to tell me who we're pulling this job for?" Samantha asked.

Nicholas shook his head. "You'll get your money. That's as close as you need to get."

"You're making me feel left out. At least tell me if he's

getting the Hogarth, the Picasso, and the jewelry on top of everything else."

Martin laughed. "He can't not get one of them."

"Martin, please. A little discretion."

"She is part of the team, Nicky."

"No. The only reason *you* know is because you helped me get the Hogarth."

The buyer couldn't not get one of them. Did that mean he already had one of them? And not the Hogarth, because Martin had helped with that one.

"Look, she's trying to figure it out."

"Shut up, Bono." Samantha blew out her breath. She had more immediate things to be concerned about right now. Only three minutes left. She'd just run out of time. "Nicholas, could I talk to Martin for a second?" she asked. "We have this thing we do before a job when we're working together."

Veittsreig took a draw on his cigarette. Unfiltered. Blech. "You're not getting nervous are you, Sam?"

"I've been out of the game for a few months," she retorted. "Let me talk to my dad, okay?"

"Sure. No talking about our buyer, Martin." With a loose grin, Veittsreig strolled over to join the other two members of the team. Wulf was already in their fake SWAT-mobile, waiting to pick them up when they exited the museum.

"Martin," Samantha began, "how are the—"

"What are you doing," he interrupted, "letting a hack like Nicky think you're nervous about a job? How many times have I told you never to let anybody see you sweat?"

"I don't care what he thinks. How are your friends today?"

She knew the answer to that; his friends, as far as he knew, were gearing up for a mission on Friday. Rick was certain Martin was playing her just like he played everybody else, but she wanted to hear it from her dad's mouth before she started her own dance.

"It always matters what the other guys think," he returned, in the low, slightly superior teacher's voice he always used to use when he lectured her about something. "We live in a small world. You don't want a reputation for nerves, especially when you're really cool as a cucumber."

"This is a last-time, onetime gig for me, Martin, and you know it. I'm giving you a hand. And I'd like to know what I should be looking for from your damned friends."

He folded his arms over his chest. "So you think you're giving me a hand. Fuck that. I'm giving you a hand. And when you get that two and a half million bucks in your pocket, you'll be grateful for it."

Dammit. Rick had been right, all the way across the board. She put a stunned look on her face, then swiftly buried it again. "Your friends aren't coming, are they?" she whispered.

"Thanks to my 'friends,'" he returned, "I've been having the best three years of my life. They set me up with Nicky, if you can believe it. After this, Interpol becomes a liability, and we part ways."

The best three years of his life. When she'd thought he was dead. "Just like that? You think they won't be interested in talking to you after you help pull a hundred and ninety-five-million-dollar job and then disappear?"

"Who cares? They hunted me for twenty-five years before they got lucky. I'll take those odds again."

For the moment she refrained from commenting that the point seemed to be that they *had* eventually caught up to him. He could be as arrogant about all of this as he wanted, but it didn't change that fact.

"What about me, then, Martin? When I pull this job do

you think Rick won't know? I got busted for art theft last week. Do you think the cops won't suspect that I'm part of this?"

"You need to start thinking about yourself first, girl. You used to know the rules of the game. I think I showed up just in time."

"You're too late. I retired."

"No, you didn't; you took a vacation. And to welcome you back, I've got a pair of tickets to Venezuela back where I'm staying. One of them's for you."

"So we're supposed to be Butch and Sundance now? That didn't end well."

"We're smarter than they were."

She'd been right. This was supposed to be her big coming-out-again party. A big, spectacular extravaganza unlike anything that had been pulled in the United States for fifty years. Yay, her.

"You're still in, right?" he asked, for the first time hesitation visible on his face.

"You and Nicholas made it kind of hard for me to refuse," she returned truthfully. "It would be nice if you didn't think you had to play me, too, though. And it would have been nice if you'd come by Stoney's house sometime over the past three years to say, 'Hello, I'm not dead.' "

"You shouldn't be bringing up your gripes one minute before a job, Sam. Suck it up, play it straight, and by tomorrow we'll be in South America."

She didn't respond to that. Sucking it up was a very good idea, though, considering that if everything had been set up as she expected, anywhere from a dozen to a hundred law enforcement officials were lurking somewhere on the premises just a hundred feet away. And most of them wouldn't look at her any differently than they would the rest of the crew.

Nicholas approached again. "Are you ready for this, Sam?" he asked. "Because if you screw it up for the rest of us, I'll shoot you first."

"Yeah, I think you've told me that before. I'm ready. Just make sure you don't fall behind."

He gestured at the other two. "Let's go shopping."

Samantha handed her backpack to Martin, keeping the wire cutters and a screwdriver in her purse, inside her sanitary pad bag. While the rest of them headed in through the garage service entrance, she walked around to the front of the building.

A pair of security guards stood at tables just inside the doors, checking bags and purses. She unzipped hers without being asked, holding it open as she stopped in front of the younger of the two men. "I'm not too late to get to the gift shop, am I?" she asked, picking up one of the floor plan maps from the table.

"No. We're closing the galleries in fifteen minutes. The store and cafeterias close at five-thirty."

She flashed him and the security camera above him a smile. "Thanks."

As of this moment she was on camera. Her wig itched a little, but she frequently wore them on jobs, and she ignored the discomfort. She also did her best to ignore all of the visitors standing around in the lobby. From her peripheral vision it looked like an unusual number of loiterers were men without families, but it might have been her imagination. At the moment, she had to fool them, too.

Not hurrying but walking with a purpose, she headed for the Met Store, walked straight through and out the back, and wound her way around to the rear wall outside the security office. Okay. For the benefit of the camera in the hallway there, she looked down at her museum map like she was lost. Beneath the cover of the paper she took her leather gloves out of her purse and pulled them on, then wandered underneath the camera out of its sight, pulled out her wire cutters, and snipped the feed line. Checking up and down the short hallway, she picked her spot along the rear wall, changed her grip on the cutters, and jabbed them into the wall at about waist height.

Bingo. The schematics were right on target, anyway. Moving quickly, she squeezed her fingers around a two-by-four crossbeam, pried open the back of the fuse box, and started randomly pulling the switches she could reach. She gave herself twenty seconds, then shoved the metal plate in place so from the front no one would be able to tell that it had been removed. That done, she circled around to the corner where she could see the front of the office again. A few seconds later three guards hurried out of the door and fanned out.

Moving in behind them, Samantha slipped into the security office before the door could click shut and lock again. One guard remained, rounding on her as she closed the door behind her. "What the hell are you doing h—"

She sprayed him with pepper spray. As he stumbled over, coughing, she lashed him to a chair with the duct tape she'd carried around her wrist, taped his mouth closed, put a paper bag over his head, and wheeled him behind the door. Straight-on confrontations. She hated them, and prided herself on her ability to slip around them. Under the circumstances, however, she figured taping the guy to the chair was better than seeing him shot. Swiftly she disabled the camera feeds, yanking all the connectors and clipping off the ends so it would at least take some effort to get them up and running again.

Then she unlocked the emergency exits and shut off the

exterior alarms. The clock on the wall read 5:07. Ha. Nearly a minute to spare.

The crew would come in through the garage's emergency exit, Martin would join her inside the security office and hand over her backpack, and then they would be off to the races.

Two minutes later, a knock came at the office door. She listened for the pattern, and then opened it. "Hi." No names, or the wrapped-up security guard would be in trouble again.

He slipped in and closed the door again. "A few of the guards are milling around like they're confused," he said, grinning, "but nobody knows for sure that anything is up yet."

"They will soon." She took her pack and pulled out the splitter so she could bypass the wall sensors on the second floor, stuffing her purse into its place.

"We'll be out before anybody can organize a shutdown."

"But you're ready to shoot people in case we're not."

He glanced up from the computer, where he was disabling the heavy fire doors that would drop from the ceiling to seal any endangered exhibits once the wall sensors were tripped. Without the doors, in theory their only obstacle would be the security guards who weren't busy trying to stem the visitors' panic. "When in Rome," he said, and went back to work.

"We're not in Rome. We're in a fucking museum."

"Get back to work. We can argue on the plane to paradise."

She took a breath. *Focus.* As she cut the phone lines she watched Martin work, noting that he was only shutting down the doors and sensors in the three main galleries they would be hitting. It made sense; every system in here had a backup somewhere else in the building, and they had a very finite amount of time before somebody realized what was going on and rerouted the systems.

"I'm set," she said a minute later. "Anybody with a mobile phone can still call the cops, but nothing will trigger automatically." Not without some help, at any rate—which was what she was counting on.

A few seconds later Martin stood, as well. "The doors are locked open, and the wall sensors are down for at least the next nine minutes." He hefted his own backpack. "Let's go."

"After you."

As Martin slipped back out the door, making sure it would still lock behind them, Samantha swiftly reached over and tapped the flashing reboot indicator on the screen where he'd been working. It would take a few minutes for the entire system to come up again, but within three minutes partial control would be restored. And that was what she wanted. She liked to take risks, but she also believed in having at least two ways out of every situation. She only hoped the one she'd just arranged would work.

Back in the main part of the museum, she and Martin made their way upstairs. Once they reached the second floor, they split up, he heading for the American art exhibit, and her supposedly for the Music Room. Samantha glanced at her watch. In about one minute, all hell was going to break loose.

Taking a deep breath, she made her way around to one of the three main entrances to the European Paintings gallery. Handily it shared a door with the American wing, which would hopefully work to her advantage. She found the circuit box and loitered there in the second-floor shop doorway, looking at an art book and waiting.

Her heart pounded. So damned many things could go to hell. And if only one of her assumptions was wrong, she would end up in jail or dead. And Rick was sitting in a cab a block away and would have no idea what was happening until Gorstein called him with the news.

At precisely 5:15 p.m. the docents and security announced that the gallery was closed, and began clearing it. As the crowd flowed out of the exhibits and into the shop, she risked a peek into the room—just in time to see Bono club a guard across the back of the head, move in, and yank a large Pompeo Batoni painting off the wall. She actually gasped at the speed of it.

Somebody close to her screamed, and then a smoke canister went off with a loud pop. Visitors began yelling and trampling past her. Samantha faced the wall, popped open the circuit box, and stripped the wiring. Luckily everything was labeled, and it only took a second to bypass the power to the circuit she wanted and splice in one of the remote receiver units.

She slammed the box closed and joined the exodus until she could cut into the next room over. Inside the gallery it was a maze of exhibits, but only three doors enclosed the entire main perimeter of the gallery. Two more boxes, and she could move on to the next gallery.

"Hey!"

A guard grabbed her shoulder as she stood wrist-deep in wiring. Whipping around, she caught him across the head with her backpack, and he dropped like a stone. People noticed her now as they fled for the nearest stairs. Fuck. She pulled out a smoke grenade and tossed it in the direction she was heading. "Get out!" she yelled, waving her arms.

It was like throwing a snake into a pit full of mice. Everybody scattered away from the grenade as she sprinted past it, holding her breath. Moving fast, she threw another grenade into the music room and used that corridor as a shortcut. At least the crowds were thinning fast—that was what she needed. Samantha only slowed long enough to dimly see that the Stradivarius remained safely behind glass. It should have been, since it was her responsibility to take it, but if one of the other crew members had done the job, it would mean her cover was blown.

At the joint doorway to the European and American wings she spliced another receiver into the circuit board, then covered the other two main American gallery entrances the same way. Maybe it wasn't necessary, maybe Interpol and the FBI and the NYPD had everything under control, but it didn't sound like it. And she wasn't willing to risk her future on the theory that they could outwit Nicholas Veittsreig and Martin Jellicoe on a few hours' notice. They were probably still arguing over who would lead the exercise.

Just as she finished with the last circuit board, Martin appeared through the smoke, a large black tube over his shoulder. He had the Leutze painting. *Washington Crossing the Delaware* was about to disappear from public view forever.

"Sam, what the hell are you doing here?" he snapped. "Get the damned Strad before—"

"FBI! Freeze!"

Great. *Now* they showed. A tall guy in a dark suit materialized around an exhibit a few feet from Martin. He held a pistol in his hands. It was aimed at her dad, but his gaze was split between Martin and her, standing just outside the gallery.

"Get over here, lady. Now!"

Okay, time was up. She took one second for a single deep breath. "You set us up, Martin," she said loudly. "Damn you!"

With that, she thumbed the remote.

A few inches in front of her the heavy, fireproof metal door crashed down from the ceiling, closing Martin and the

FBI guy inside. Refusing to acknowledge the guilt that flooded through her, she dug into her pocket and sprinted around the corner. She yanked a shrieking, confused woman out of the next doorway and triggered that door. It slammed into the floor.

"Get going, lady," she snapped, shoving the woman toward the stairs.

"Thank you, thank y—"

Samantha sprinted off again. "Four to go," she coughed, rounding into another corridor. The remotes had pretty good range, but there was a lot of metal in the museum walls, and she didn't want to risk one of the doors not closing. She could have shut them the instant she popped the circuit boxes, but all of the tourists hadn't been out and safe. Hopefully by now all but the bad guys and the white hats had made it to the stairs. If she could help it, she didn't want to provide hostages.

A pair of men, one carrying a walkie-talkie and both armed, charged into the European Paintings gallery as she went in to trigger the joint door. She ducked under a bench as they passed her. *Crap.* Rising again, she moved up behind them.

"Hey," she said.

As the closest one turned to face her, she slapped the backpack into his chest, sending him backward through the joint door and into the American wing. The second one grabbed her arm, and she twisted, slamming the flat of her foot into his knee. He stumbled into the first one as that guy lifted his gun.

"You fucking freeze right there, la—"

She flicked the remote, and the door slammed closed, separating her from them. Adrenaline flooded her muscles as she turned and ran again. That sealed at least three guns in with

Nicholas and Martin, and separated them from Bono and Dolph.

It also left her inside the European gallery with two exits still to close down. The smoke was so thick she could barely see two feet in front of her. Dodging through the Greek paintings exhibit, she nearly stepped on an El Greco, and she slowed down a little bit. Veittsreig hadn't been kidding when he'd said they were going to cause chaos.

Hopefully making the mess had slowed them down enough for her to trap them in the gallery. The *Toledo* painting wasn't there, though, so one of the Germans had wrapped it up already. Shit. They'd better still be in the gallery. If she couldn't get out before they did, she would either have to risk letting them get away, or close herself in with them.

As she reached the second gallery exit, Bono rounded the Italian exhibit door on her right. "Sam, let's go," he barked.

"Hold on. I heard a police radio out there," she improvised.

He lifted the gun he held. "No problem." Bono started through the main gallery door.

Thinking fast, Samantha grabbed his shoulder. "Wait. Let me go first. I look more innocent than you do."

"Hurry it up."

Nodding, she stepped through the door, then sent it crashing down so close behind her that it tore the backpack off her shoulder. Behind her a gun went off. Bono was pissed. She hiked up her backpack again.

That left just Dolph unaccounted for, and then she could make a run for it. She tore back through the Music Room and dodged out through the shop, heading for the final rigged door that joined the two. Right behind her the elevator opened.

"Stop right there!"

Samantha kept moving. With a deep pop a bullet hit the shop wall behind her head, obliterating a Monet poster. Yelping, she ducked, diving past twin racks of postcards. Christ. Obviously Gorstein hadn't told anybody about her. As she drew even with the last European Paintings gallery door, she hit the final remote. The door fell—and stopped two feet above the floor.

"Dammit."

She backpedaled. In the rush to escape, somebody had knocked over a bookcase and a third postcard rack. The door wheezed and groaned, slowly crushing the piles of lumber and wire and hardcover museum guides. "Close, close, close," she chanted under her breath, kicking books out of the way.

A hand reached through the narrowing gap, grabbing her ankle. Off balance, she went down.

Nicholas Veittsreig rolled under the door. A second later, with a splintering crack, the two-ton behemoth hit the floor.

Scrambling away on her bottom, Samantha tried to jerk her ankle free. *Shit.* He must have traded places with Dolph. Nicholas didn't let her go. "Bitch," he breathed, twisting onto all fours and yanking her beneath him.

Samantha doubled up her legs and then pistoned them straight up. With a grunt he tumbled sideways. She rolled, and her backpack caught on one of the postcard racks. She pulled on it. Hard.

The rack tumbled across Veittsreig's back, sending him to the floor again. Giving up on the backpack, Samantha slipped free of the last strap, stumbled back to her feet, and ran for it.

She reached the top of the stairs, armed guys behind her. She hoped a couple of them had at least stopped to nab Nicholas—if they even noticed him amid the wreckage. Halfway down the first landing, half a dozen men with "Interpol" bands on their arms climbed toward her. Speeding up and sending up a quick, wordless prayer, she launched herself into the air.

As she hit bodies, she grabbed the railing beside them, pushed off again, and flipped over the edge. She dropped to the first flight of stairs, landing hard and off balance. A dozen guys yelled into radios and mikes, and she could hear more boots charging around below as she rolled down the last few stairs to the lobby floor.

She did one more roll onto her feet and sprinted along the wall, ignoring the pain of what was probably a twisted ankle. As she took it in, time seemed to slow. For a second it looked as though she'd stumbled into the middle of the skyscraper climax scene from *The Blues Brothers.* Cops and guns and chaos, screaming tourists running for the doors, packages and brochures flying everywhere, and her in the middle.

Enough of the white hats had seen her now that she needed to be someone else. Samantha ducked behind a granite trash can and yanked off her wig and her black button shirt. She wore a red T-shirt underneath, selected because it looked touristy, and made sure it was tucked in. Dumping the excess garments into the trash and running her fingers through her tangled hair, she pasted a look of confused, tearful terror onto her face and stood.

A big guy with "FBI" on his chest approached her, a semiautomatic cradled efficiently in his arms. "Hold it, lady," he barked.

She lifted her hands, not having to fake their shaking. He could think it was fear; she knew it was adrenaline. "What's going on?" she cried. "I was in the restroom, and the lights went out, and everybody started screaming."

He lowered the gun a fraction. "There's been a robbery,"

he said. "Please move through the exit, and someone will take your statement."

"I left my purse in the res—"

"We'll get it for you later."

He moved past her, and she headed for the distant exit. "Thank y—"

Somebody hit her in the middle of the back, shoving her into a marble pedestal. Dazed, she squirmed onto her back. The muzzle of a pistol shoved into her mouth, cutting her gums. Veittsreig.

"I've got you now," he panted. "Interpol!" he shouted, flashing a phony badge as attention turned in their direction.

As he yanked her to her feet, he shoved something hard and heavy into her waistband. A fucking gun. Christ. He was going to shoot her in front of everybody. And they would see that she was armed, and it would be a righteous kill, and then he'd walk out the door, find Rick, and murder him, too.

"Where's the bomb?" he yelled, shoving her backward with the gun still in her mouth and tilting her head back. "Where's the bomb? Everybody out!"

It worked. Everybody began hauling ass for the exit as "bomb" echoed through the hazy lobby.

"Goodbye, Sam," he murmured, and pulled the trigger.

Chapter 22

Tuesday, 5:33 p.m.

Samantha flung herself sideways as Nicholas squeezed the trigger.

In that same second, a large, hazy figure swept out of the shadows and struck Veittsreig across the head with something big and heavy. *Rick.*

Fire blazed across her left cheek even with the sound of gunfire still echoing through the lobby. Samantha rolled, staggering back to her feet. The noise so close to her head made her ears ring.

Veittsreig collapsed in a heap, Rick standing over him with a Roman bronze bowl clutched in his fist. For a moment he looked like he wasn't finished with Nicholas.

"Rick?" she said, wobbling.

He faced her. For the first time she noticed that he wore a fake moustache and long sideburns. "Come on," he said, grabbing her arm and chucking the bowl into a planter.

"But—"

"Come on," he repeated. "No time for gentlemanly fisticuffs. You can't be seen here."

Half carrying her, he moved them to the exit. As soon as she remembered it was there, Sam yanked the gun from her waistband and dropped it to the floor. No guns. Ever. A guy in an NYPD uniform looked straight at them, and Samantha jerked her thumb in Veittsreig's direction. With a nod, he moved off. Gorstein had kept his word, at least.

Rick shook out a handkerchief and pressed it gently to her cheek as they squeezed through the crowded exit doors. "Move aside," he said in a fair Southern accent that only sounded British around the edges. "My wife's been cut with glass."

Trying to shake the worst of the cobwebs from her head, Samantha stood away from him a little. "You can't be here, either," she muttered.

He ran a finger over his moustache. "I'm not here. Nice, eh?"

"Who are you supposed to be, the seventies?"

Rick took hold of her arm again, and they headed with the rest of the museum refugees toward the street. The cacophony of sirens and bullhorns and police radios began to sink thuddingly into her throbbing skull. It looked like Armageddon on Fifth Avenue. With Rick still helping her to walk straight, they moved to the edge of the milling, half-panicked crowd. In the mass of people she felt a little more protected, but Rick didn't stop. Instead he pulled out his cell phone and dialed.

"Let's go," he said without preamble, and hung up again.

A SWAT truck, sirens wailing, pulled up to the curb in front of them. *Jesus.* Wulf. Ignoring her shoving backward against him, Rick pushed her up the truck's two steps. "Rick, no! You—"

"It's okay, honey."

She looked up at the truck's driver. Looking back at her sat Stoney, his grin looking a little strained.

"Get in, baby. The meter's running."

"But—"

As Rick moved past her, the truck lurched into motion. While she watched, a hand against the ceiling to keep her balance, Rick opened one of the rear doors and kicked a large lump covered in canvas out onto the street.

"That was Wulf, wasn't it?" she asked, as he pulled the door closed again.

"Was that his name? He never said."

Samantha sat heavily on the floor of the truck as they sped down the street. "What the hell is going on? Am I unconscious? Or dead?"

"Neither." Rick sat beside her. "Did you really think I would sit in a cab a block away and wait for you?"

"You agreed to."

"Of course I did." Leaning closer, he peeled the handkerchief away from her cheek. "That was too close, Samantha," he said, his voice shaking. "I almost didn't reach you in time."

She fingered her cheek. It was shallow, more a burn than anything. Damn, it hurt. "Under the circumstances, I won't complain."

"Why the hell didn't you just run for it when the robbery started?"

"I wanted to make sure they didn't get away with it. I had to trigger the gallery fire doors one at a time. Nicholas got under the last one."

"Walter, head for the nearest hospital," Rick ordered.

"Already on the way."

"No, no, no. Head toward the river, Stoney."

"Are we still fleeing?"

"That's where Veittsreig's warehouse is. We were supposed to drop the goods there. The Hogarth and the Picasso might be there now."

"After," Rick said, carefully putting the handkerchief back in place.

"Ouch. If we wait until after, one of the crew might have given up the location to the cops."

"And what's wrong with that?"

"I want to make sure everything is there, and I want to make sure there aren't any surveillance photos of me with Nicholas lying around."

And she still wanted to know who the buyer was. If trouble was coming after her, she wanted to know who was sending it.

Wincing, Richard pulled off the moustache and muttonchops. Samantha hadn't been too impressed by them, but he would guess that they'd served their purpose and no one had recognized him. "All right," he said reluctantly. "The warehouse first."

He wished he'd had more time to beat Veittsreig to a pulp; that Wulf character hadn't been much of a challenge at all. Then again, as Walter had pointed out, he'd been fairly angry at the time, and might have hit harder than he strictly needed to.

His phone rang. Automatically he opened it up to answer it. "Addison."

"Rick, it's John Stillwell."

"John. Might I call you back in an hour or so? I'm a bit—"

"Turn left, Stoney," Samantha said. "Two blocks down on the right."

"Rick, I have Matsuo Hoshido on the other line. He says if he can talk with you, he'll make the deal tonight."

"What about the city?"

"He says he has some kind of plan to deal with them."

Samantha leaned forward. "Stoney, stop."

"What is it, honey?"

Richard frowned. "I'll call you back, John."

"But—"

He flipped the phone closed and pocketed it again. "What's wrong?"

"Nothing's wrong," Samantha returned, standing and moving to the steps. "We're in a big truck made up to look like it belongs to SWAT. I'd rather not drive up to the front of the warehouse in it, whether anybody there thinks it's Nicholas coming back, or not."

"Right." With a somewhat chagrined look, Walter pulled onto a side street.

When they left the lorrie, Richard moved up beside Samantha. As he did so, he tucked a hand into his right pocket, fingering the Glock resting there. He'd never been closer to shooting someone than he had been in the lobby of the museum; the sight of Samantha backing away, off balance, from Veittsreig, a man who literally had a gun jammed into her mouth . . . If he'd thought he could have gotten a shot off before the bastard could react, he would have done it, FBI or not.

With a quick look around them, Samantha walked up to the touch pad beside the main warehouse door, flexed her fingers in their leather gloves, and keyed in some numbers. The red console button turned green. "Try and lift it," she said, stepping back.

Richard had been half expecting her to pull the cover off the touch pad and rewire it. Shaking himself, he moved in and shoved the door up. Once all three of them were through, he closed it again.

"If somebody talked, the cops could be here any minute," Samantha said, trotting over to a worktable covered in blueprints. "You guys look for the paintings. If they're here, they're probably boxed."

"There are a lot of boxes in here," Walter said, looking over at him. "Right, or left?"

"Left," Richard decided, and headed for the far side of the warehouse.

"Rick."

He faced Samantha, catching the old pair of work gloves she picked up and tossed at him. Right. Fingerprints. All he needed was something else to convince the insurance company that he *had* stolen the Hogarth himself.

Boxes lay stacked in haphazard piles across the length of the warehouse. He didn't know the size of the Picasso, but the Hogarth was fairly large. That gave him a starting point, anyway. Neither Samantha nor Walter seemed to be taking much care as they tore through the contents of the warehouse, so Richard grabbed up a screwdriver and went to work.

"I'm only seeing car and truck parts, Sam," Walter called, as he emerged from the middle of a stack and hurried to the next one. "They probably bought them as cover for the warehouse."

"I would." She'd given up on the table, and squatted to pull some cardboard boxes from underneath. "Dammit," she swore, dumping a third box upside down. "I'm not seeing anything, either. If the stuff isn't here, I'm not sure where it would be. They were living *here*. This is where everything should be."

"Unless the paintings have been sold already," Richard put in, moving to the row of cots against the wall and tilting each one over to see if anything had been attached beneath.

He wanted his painting back, but if any photographs of Samantha talking with Veittsreig existed, finding them took priority.

To one side of the cots he spied a door marked "Janitor." Obviously no janitor had set foot in the warehouse for at least a decade. In front of the door, though, he could make out footprints and scrape marks in the thin layer of dust.

He pulled down on the door handle. Locked. "I may have something here," he said. At the same moment his phone rang again. "Bloody hell," he muttered, otherwise ignoring it.

"What?" Samantha asked, leaving the piles of thief refuse to approach him.

"The d—"

Walter gave a high-pitched whistle.

"Shit. Hide," Samantha hissed, diving behind a box beside him, and dragging him down next to her.

The main warehouse door rattled and lifted. A minute later a silver Mercedes-Benz coasted inside and stopped.

"What the fuck?" Samantha breathed.

He glanced at her. Her eyes were narrowed, her expression set and grim. Obviously she knew whoever was in that car.

The car door opened, and a stocky man with dark hair going gray climbed out to pull down the metal warehouse door. Expensive suit, expensive car—and familiar-looking. "That's Boyden Locke," he whispered.

"That son of a bitch." She scooted sideways, and Richard shifted to keep an eye on both her and Locke.

He'd been her client. One day after they'd arrived in New York he'd called and wanted Samantha to give him a review of his home security system. Then he'd invited the two of them to a party. And it had been his Picasso that went missing the next day. What the hell was he doing at the warehouse of the crew who'd most likely taken his painting?

"You think he hired Veittsreig, don't you?" he murmured to Samantha.

She nodded, keeping her gaze on Locke as he crossed the warehouse, heading in their direction. "I do now. And I tried to set Patty up with him, dammit." She paused. "Move back," she breathed, shifting around the boxes to keep them between her and Locke.

Rick, a few feet farther away, could only duck lower. Obviously Locke had no idea that a cat burglar—or rather, a former cat burglar—was hidden three feet from him. If he had known, he would not have pulled out a key and unlocked the janitor's closet.

He went in, and Samantha stood up, moving silently behind the door. For a moment Richard thought she meant to close Locke in, but she stayed where she was. A minute later Locke emerged, dragging a flat, rectangular crate with him.

"Boyden," she said, and Locke started, turning around.

Samantha slugged him across the face.

Dancing backward as the crate fell over with a crash and an eruption of dirt and dust, Samantha watched Locke stagger a few steps back. He was a big guy, but she had backup. Besides, he'd played her. Practically everybody she'd met with in New York had tried to play her, it seemed like. That's what she got for trying to go straight: people taking advantage of her.

"What the hell are you doing here?" Locke spat, running the back of his hand across his bloody lip.

Did he think she was still part of the robbery? Hm. She could damned well use that to her advantage. "I'm hiding," she retorted. "That was some great plan. You set us up, didn't you?"

"It *was* a great plan, and no, I didn't set you up. Help me get these in the car."

"For two and a half million, maybe. Otherwise, we're going to have quite a disagreement."

Behind Locke, she saw Rick slowly moving closer, edging sideways to put himself between Boyden and the Mercedes. And he didn't look any happier than she felt. He didn't move in, though; Rick definitely had good instincts, and she still thought he would have made a damn fine thief.

"The money was for the museum job. Help me with these and I won't mention to the authorities that Addison suggested you might be willing to steal paintings from me for the insurance money."

He had a point; both he and Rick were in the warehouse, and if it came down to it, who would the cops be more likely to believe? The rich guy, or the richer guy whose girlfriend was suspected of doing some shady things? *Fuck.* Then she noticed what Rick had in his hand. It wasn't a gun, as she'd first thought; it was his phone. His camera phone. She stifled her sudden urge to smile.

"You had the museum theft planned before I came into town," she continued, moving toward the edge of the crate. "How did you work in the Picasso and the Hogarth?"

"Serendipity," he returned, wiping his mouth again. "I bid for the Hogarth over the phone, but Addison outbid me. That put plan B into motion. And then I thought, as long as he's going to be robbed, I may as well be, too. The insurance payout for a stolen Picasso pays the fee of Nicholas and everybody in his crew. And inviting you to the party, well, that was just smart."

"That was thinking on your feet," she admitted. "But I still don't haul paintings around for free." She jerked her thumb in Rick's direction. "For him, I might. But not for you."

Locke turned around. "What—"

Rick gave him a smile. "Say cheese," he said, and snapped a photo with the camera.

With a bellow, Locke launched at him. Rick tossed her the phone, sidestepping the charge and delivering a nice kidney punch at the same time. Apparently now was the time for gentlemanly fisticuffs. Rick knocked the staggering Locke sideways into a pile of boxes, and they both went down.

Good. Rick had been spoiling for a fight for days. From the trash-talking going on, he was in heaven.

Moving fast, Samantha ducked into the janitor's closet. Another, larger crate leaned against the wall, and three manila envelopes, clean, new, and clearly out of place, sat on a dusty shelf. She grabbed them, ripping the first, bulky one open. Bingo. The Cookie Lady's diamonds. Compared to the value of the rest of the take Nicholas had planned on they were insignificant, but the Hodgeses would be happy to see them again. She'd be happy to see them back with their owners. Carefully she set the package back down in plain sight.

In the second envelope she saw photos of her talking with Nicholas in front of Rick's building, photos of her leaving Locke's house—nothing incriminating in itself, but thrown in with some other bits of circumstantial evidence, it would have been enough.

She tucked them into her shirt and opened the third envelope. This one contained pictures of Locke meeting with Veittreig, mostly, and a couple of photos of Nicholas with Martin. Taking a deep breath, she removed one of the ones with Martin, then replaced that envelope on the shelf. If the thieves were paranoid enough to photograph themselves taking meetings, they could live with the consequences—as long as she didn't have to.

Rick's phone rang again. Frowning, she answered it as

she left the closet and whistled for Stoney. They needed to get the cops here, and then clear out. "*Hola*," she said.

"Miss . . . Sam?" Stillwell's voice came.

"Hi, John. Rick's a little busy right now," she returned, sidestepping as Locke stumbled by, Rick on his heels. "Can he call you back?"

"If he doesn't talk to Hoshido right now, the deal's off. Matsuo-san thinks Rick is toying with him, and he's getting angry."

"Okay. Hold on a minute." She covered the speaker with one hand. "Rick, it's for you."

"Take a bloody message," he growled, blood running from his lower lip, and one sleeve ripped off his shirt.

Locke grabbed at her, and she backstepped, then kneed him in the head. He dropped with a grunt.

"It's Stillwell. He says Matsuo thinks you're playing him, and if you don't take the call, you'll lose the hotel."

"I don't care."

"I do. Take the damn call." She tossed the phone back to him.

"Bloody . . ." He lifted it. "What is it, John?" he snapped, shaking out his scraped right hand.

Sitting on Locke to make sure he wasn't going anywhere, Samantha pulled her own phone out of her pocket. She dialed, lifting the phone up, then wincing as it brushed the bullet graze. "Dammit," she muttered, switching ears. This one would probably leave a scar.

"Gorstein."

"Hey. How's tricks?"

"Tricks are good. I'm a big hero. Three Germans and a world-class cat burglar, previously thought dead. The guy in the street was a little hard to explain, though. And the girl who kicked the shit out of two FBI guys. Plus one of my guys is on the way to the hospital."

"Is Interpol talking with Martin?"

"Yep. I can't get near any of 'em, but it sounds like he's taking credit for shutting the Germans in the galleries."

"Okay. Get some guys over to the warehouse at West End Avenue and West Fifty-ninth. I think they might find a couple of stolen paintings and the guy who arranged to hire the Germans."

"We're on our way. Are you going to be there?"

"Not if I have any s . . . Did you say *three* Germans?"

"Uh-huh."

Abruptly she realized that Rick had gone silent across from her, and that she hadn't heard from Stoney after she'd whistled for him. She lifted her head to see Nicholas Veittsreig standing by the warehouse door, a gun in his hand and Stoney kneeling at his feet.

"Hang up the phone, Sam," he called.

Samantha closed the phone.

Chapter 23

Tuesday, 4:55 p.m.

"You hang up, too," Veittsreig said, swinging the gun around to aim it at Richard.

"Rick? Are you there?" Stillwell asked.

"Make the deal, John," Richard said, and snapped the phone closed.

Rage pounded just beneath his skin, but he held himself in check. Back in the museum he'd been intent on pulling Samantha out of danger. Now, though, the man who'd tried to kill her had every ounce of his attention.

"The cops are on the way, Nicholas," Samantha said, her voice smooth and cool.

Beneath her, Boyden Locke groaned and tried to turn over. "Get off Mr. Locke, Sam." Veittsreig leveled the pistol in her direction. "I thought you were in a relationship with Mr. Addison, here."

She stood, and while Richard would have preferred that she move closer to him so he could at least offer her some measure of protection, instead she stepped sideways in the opposite direction. Strategically, it made sense to have more distance between them; the farther apart they all were, the more Veittsreig would have to divide his attention. As the resident Sir Galahad, however, he didn't like it one bloody bit.

Locke rolled to a sitting position. "He took pictures," he groaned, holding his forehead and gesturing at Richard with his free hand. "With his phone."

"Toss it over here, then," Veittsreig instructed. "Nice and easy."

His jaw clenched, Richard tossed over his phone. Veittsreig aimed, and with a sharp crack the phone exploded. In the same instant, Walter rolled backward under the half-open warehouse door and vanished.

"Get him back!" Locke yelled, stumbling to his feet.

"What for? We have what we need." Veittsreig looked straight at Samantha. "And what we want." He gestured with the pistol again. "Sam and Addison, put the paintings in the back seat of the Mercedes. Now."

"You heard him." Locke shoved Samantha from behind.

Moving forward, she picked up one side of the crate. "Rick?"

Shifting his attention from Locke, Richard picked up the other side. "I should have killed both of them when I had the chance," he muttered.

"Be cool, Rick," Samantha whispered at him, covering a scowl.

"He's going to kill you. Don't tell me to be fucking cool."

"He's going to try to kill both of us." With a heave they

shoved the crate onto the Mercedes' back seat. "*Try*, Rick."

"I'm armed," he breathed in her ear as they straightened. "When I signal, get behind some cover."

Veittsreig moved in closer. "Let's all go get the other one. And no chatting. I might get nervous."

Richard sensed that once he and Samantha walked into the janitor's closet, they wouldn't be walking out again. "You know, Veittsreig," he said, keeping his tone even and conversational, "you have me at a fairly steep disadvantage at the moment. If you were to make a monetary demand, I would hardly be in a position to argue with you."

"I already have twelve million dollars of yours. I'm not greedy."

"Actually, you have a portion of twelve million. No doubt you'll be taking a smaller cut than Locke, here."

"We're both happy with our agreement, Addison," Locke countered. "Get a move on."

"I wasn't talking to you. If I were, I would say that I already e-mailed the phone video of you confessing to Samantha about hiring Veittsreig." He shifted his attention to the gunman. "And since killing us now would make you the focus of a very high-profile international manhunt, you might prefer cash, instead."

"He's lying," Locke sputtered.

"Oh, now *I'm* convinced," Samantha said sarcastically. "Locke's got way more legal resources than you, Nicky. Who do you think will spend more time in the slam? Because I'd guess y—"

A siren ripped through the rest of her speech. Veittsreig grabbed for Samantha as the metal warehouse door exploded inward, followed by the SWAT truck. *Walter.*

Richard swept forward, grabbing Veittsreig's gun hand and twisting with all his weight and momentum. The pistol went flying as the three of them went down in a writhing, kicking heap. Shrieking, Veittsreig snagged Samantha by the hair as she tried to roll away. She sent a hard elbow into his chin, and he let her go.

"Don't let Locke get the gun," Richard rasped, taking a fist to his rib cage.

Samantha was already scrambling after the weapon. So was Locke. He had the weight, but she had the speed. Sam did an absurdly graceful flip, kicking Locke in the face as she grabbed the gun in her right hand, ending on her feet with the weapon pointed about an inch from his bloody nose. "Don't move," she panted.

With that resolved, Richard could concentrate on the man who'd tried to kill her. He scrambled back around to one knee just in time to block a kick aimed at his face. He grabbed Veittsreig's ankle and shoved, knocking the thief backward and swarming over him. Richard knelt hard across his chest, curled his fist, and punched.

As Veittsreig grunted, his eyes rolling back in his head, Rick pulled the Glock from his pocket. Breathing hard, he cocked it and jammed the muzzle into the thief's mouth.

"Rick!"

"You were going to kill her," he growled, his hands shaking. No one got to take Samantha away from him. No one. "Get up."

He stood, hauling Veittsreig up by the shirt, the gun still jammed between his teeth. "You blackmailed her into working with you, and then you tried to kill her when she outsmarted you."

"Rick, stop!"

Dimly he heard more sirens, official ones this time, approaching the warehouse. Walter was wrapping duct tape liberally around Locke's arms and legs. Rick returned his gaze to Veittsreig, studying the fear in his nearly colorless eyes.

"Do you know the American saying," he murmured, removing the muzzle and backing away a few inches, "how does it go? Oh, yes. Payback's a bitch."

He pulled the trigger.

Samantha screamed as Nicholas reeled backward, stumbling to the floor. *Dear God, dear God.* Then he rolled onto his hands and knees, and she could breathe again. He doubled over, clutching the side of his head.

"You shot my ear off!"

"Only part of it," Rick said dismissively, and pocketed the pistol again.

She stood gaping as Rick approached her and carefully took the other gun from her hand. For a second she'd forgotten that she held it. He ejected the magazine and the bullet waiting in the chamber, then walked over and placed everything on the hood of the Mercedes.

"I thought . . ." she muttered, and couldn't finish the sentence.

"I nearly did," he returned, his gaze still hard and set.

Samantha swept forward and threw her arms around him. In all of her nightmare scenarios, she was the one who went too far and drove Rick away. It had never been Rick who'd made the mistake. And he nearly had. Christ. He'd nearly murdered a man because that man had tried to hurt her.

His arms closed around her, hard and warm. And safe. For her, always safe.

"Are you staying for this?" he murmured into her hair. "It's not just Gorstein about to drive through the front door."

"I have to," she returned, pretending that now she wasn't shaking in her boots. Guns were one thing. Interpol and the FBI—they scared her.

"You don't have to."

"I do. Even a superhero like you couldn't have done all this single-handedly."

Stoney trotted by. "You two be the white hats, then. I'm outta here. I'll call you tonight, baby." With that he climbed over the wreckage of the door and headed toward the docks and the river.

Twenty seconds later the first police car rolled in. It wasn't Gorstein. "Hands up, everybody!" the cop yelled, more uniforms fanning out behind him.

Rick released her, spreading his arms. "We're the ones who called you," he said in his perfectly calm, ultra-charming British accent.

"Let me see your hands until we get this straightened out," the officer amended.

Two others hauled the moaning Nicholas to his feet. "He shot me!" Veittsreig gasped, trying to hold his damaged ear while the cops tried just as hard to frisk him.

Guns lifted again in Rick's direction. *Shit.* If he hadn't been disheveled, dirty, and bloody, the superior British thing probably would have worked.

"And he stole my painting!" Locke sputtered from the duct tape mess Stoney had left him in.

"Where's the gun, fella?"

Rick had enough brains not to move. "In my right front jacket pocket," he said, still cool.

They swarmed over him. For a moment Samantha realized how . . . helpless Rick must have felt when he saw her being handcuffed. He kept his gaze on her while they jostled him around, as though they were as significant as bugs and he was more concerned with willing her not to do anything stupid.

She wanted to do something stupid. With all the cops' attention on Rick, she could have grabbed a gun, hustled him into a car, and been gone. Concentrating on breathing, her own hands clenched, she stood back and watched as they pulled his hands behind his back and put on the cuffs.

"Ms. J."

At the sound of Gorstein's familiar voice, she could have fainted with relief—if she'd been the fainting type. Man, life had become screwy, if she was happy to see a cop. "Gorstein, get them off Rick, will you?"

He walked into the warehouse, a dozen FBI and Interpol officers flanking him. "Gentlemen, this is Samantha Jellicoe," he said, "the one who called to tip me off about this location."

"Jellicoe," one of the Interpol guys, a stocky Italian, said. "His daughter?"

It took all of her guts to nod. "My dad called to tell me he'd been working on a big case," she improvised, "and to say that he thought Rick Addison's painting might be here. When I heard on the news about the thing at the museum, I thought we should get here to make sure nobody got away with the Hogarth."

"I followed her here," Locke said loudly, as cops exchanged the duct tape for handcuffs. "I only wanted my Picasso back, and she and Addison tried to kill me, for God's sake."

"Let's get Mr. Addison and Mr. Locke out of those handcuffs," Gorstein said, shifting his toothpick to the other side of his mouth. "We'll take everybody down to the station and get statements."

Surprised, Samantha jabbed a finger at Locke. "He planned this whole thing!"

Gorstein edged closer to her, as Rick reached her other side. "Do you have any proof?" he muttered.

She glanced from the remains of Rick's phone to his

scratched, bloody face. He subtly shook his head. *Dammit.* The thing about e-mailing the video out had been a bluff.

"The photos," she said abruptly, remembering. "In a manila envelope in the closet there. They show him with that guy," she continued, gesturing at Nicholas. "He's the one who pulled the museum robbery. According to my dad."

Locke kept proclaiming his innocence as they led him out of the warehouse. Gorstein seemed content to let Interpol take custody of Veittsreig, but his expression wasn't all that happy as he looked at her.

"What?" she muttered. "You're a big hero, aren't you?"

"You made a hell of a mess at the museum," he grunted. "Smoke grenades, cut wiring, bullet holes, the—"

"I don't know what you're talking about, Detective," Rick interrupted, gently taking her hand in his. "We were at home until we saw the news and got the call from Samantha's father."

"Right. Okay, you two can ride with me, but we are going to the station, and I am going to get sworn statements."

"They'll be identical to what we just told you," Rick said, "but of course we're happy to cooperate."

"I can hardly wait to see how all this plays out." Gorstein pulled out his toothpick, flicked it aside, and replaced it with a fresh one from his pocket. "This should be really interesting."

Three hours later, Gorstein came back into the conference room where they'd stashed her and Rick. Apparently when Sir Galahad entered into the equation, the little room with the barred windows wasn't good enough. Phil Ripton had joined them better than an hour ago, but he'd mostly been relegated to keeping the FBI from trying to identify her as the suspect who'd roughed up several officers in the museum.

Billionaires might like blondes, but she was glad to have her regular auburn hair showing again.

"How are you holding up?" the detective asked, setting a cold can of Diet Coke in front of Samantha. It was the third one he'd provided; apparently it was his way of demonstrating gratitude.

"I'd be holding up better with a pizza," Samantha returned. However grateful he might be, *she'd* feel more comfortable once they were out of the police station. Her cheek stung, and both she and Rick needed a shower. Preferably together.

"I think we're finished." Gorstein took the seat beside Ripton. "Mr. Veittsreig's out of the hospital and on his way to the FBI office. The other three Germans and your dad are already there."

"What kind of statement did Martin give?" she asked carefully.

That had been the hardest part of all this; she'd stopped him, put him in a position where it would be to his benefit to do the right thing. She couldn't *make* him cooperate, though. He had to do that on his own. And he had to decide how much he wanted to tell the authorities about her involvement in all this.

"I don't know all that much about it," the detective returned. "The FBI's pulling rank. But I do know that he says he tried to get hold of his contact to let him know that robbery had been moved up by three days, but Veittsreig was keeping too close an eye on him. That's why he went through you."

Okay. She could live with that. Rick, though, tightened his grip on her fingers. He'd held her hand all evening. And independent as she considered herself, she was glad for the support and the contact. It had been a very long day. They both had the bruises to prove it.

"That is the extent of Samantha's involvement, yes?" he said.

"For now, yes."

"Not good enough."

"All this just landed on my lap yesterday, Mr. Addison. And excuse me, but my priority is making damn sure that the crew who tried to rob my museum in my town goes to prison for a long time. If Martin Jellicoe can get me that, then I'll do everything I can to see to it that Ms. J.'s out of it."

"I am not—"

"I'll accept that for now," Samantha interrupted. She had no intention of ever being a witness for the prosecution, but Gorstein—and Interpol—didn't need to know that.

Rick looked at her. "That is—"

"It's fine," she said firmly.

He drew a breath and slowly exhaled. "Okay."

"Is everybody happy now?" the detective asked.

"What about Boyden Locke?" Samantha pursued. He'd been nearly as instrumental as Martin in getting her tangled into this mess.

"At this moment, the DA has declined to prosecute."

Stunned, Samantha sat there gaping at him. "What?"

Gorstein frowned. "He's a well-respected citizen with some good connections."

"You have photographs of him with Nicholas Veittsreig!"

"Contextless photographs. That makes it your word against his. And you won't step up to the plate—for reasons I can understand, of course."

"Bloody hell," Rick swore.

"Look at it from the prosecutor's point of view. The two guys who owned the two missing paintings are both in the bad guys' warehouse, with the missing paintings. One guy shows up in photos with Veittsreig, and the other guy has a girlfriend whose dad worked with Veittsreig. It's kind of a toss-up."

Samantha gave a disbelieving snort. "Why am I trying so hard to be a good guy?" she asked. "Do you know how much money I could have made today?"

Gorstein cleared his throat. "Excuse me, I think I have a phone call." He stood, walking to the door and holding it open. "Beat it, Ms. J. And after what I just heard, we're even."

She stood up and walked past him, not waiting for Rick and Ripton. "You remember that, too, the next time you need my help for something. Since we're even, it'll cost you a case of soda. Adios, Sam."

He grimaced. "Goodbye, Sam."

Rick caught up to her in the corridor. "His name's Sam?" he asked, jerking a thumb back in Gorstein's direction.

"Yes." She eyed him.

He swallowed whatever it was he'd been about to say. "That's a stupid name for a bloke."

Samantha slipped an arm around his waist, leaning into him. "Take me home, sweetheart."

"By way of the hospital, I think."

"I'm fine."

"Maybe so, but I may have sprained my toe."

She laughed as he leaned down and kissed her forehead. "You are so lame."

"That's why I'm going to the hospital."

"Great. Now we're Abbott and Costello."

Phil Ripton gave them a ride to the emergency room, and then waited while Rick got five stitches in his forehead and they cleaned and bandaged her cheek. The attorney must have been on a good retainer, the cynical part of her acknowledged, though she supposed he might have gone out of his way just because Rick was a good guy.

Considering what Boyden Locke had just gotten away with, though, it was probably Rick's money that got him the ride. Money definitely talked louder than behavior. Shit. She knew Rick bent the rules sometimes. As far as she could tell, everybody with money did, at one time or another. But what Locke had done—it hadn't been just about money. He'd tried to obtain priceless artworks from a public museum. And he'd gotten off because he knew the right people.

"You okay?" Rick asked, as he helped her into the back seat of Ripton's Mercedes and then went around the other side to join her. She did kind of like that—Phil Ripton, attorney to the obscenely wealthy and chauffeur to same.

"I'm okay. I got shot again."

"It was a graze. Again."

"You're just jealous because you've only been roughed up a couple of times." She patted his thigh. "Someone will shoot you eventually. I'm sure of it."

"Mm-hm. Probably you."

"Probably."

Chapter 24

Wednesday, 12:31 a.m.

"I hope you have your key," Samantha said, hopping up to sit on the cast-ironwork railing that bordered their front steps, "because I am way too tired to pick the lock."

Richard sent a last wave at Phil Ripton as the attorney drove away. That was someone else he now owed a hefty favor. He dug into his pocket, wincing as the material scraped his raw knuckles. "I have it."

"Hurray, you," she said, yawning.

He unlocked the door. As he turned the knob, it jerked out of his hand. For half a heartbeat surprise stopped him. *Not again.* Then he shoved the door with his shoulder and charged in.

In the dark he grabbed a handful of material as it stumbled away from him. Snarling, he raised his fist.

Samantha grabbed his arm. "Whoa, cowboy," she said, her voice rich with amusement.

"Sir! Rick! It's me!"

Shaking himself, Richard set Stillwell loose. "Apologies," he said gruffly, flipping on the light.

"It's been a long day," Samantha added, closing and locking the door behind them.

"I saw you, on television. Both of you. I left several messages on your cellular, Rick."

"My cellular's out of commission," Richard returned. And currently in FBI custody, to see if they could somehow recover the digital images of Boyden Locke's confession. That would be another job for Ripton: to ensure that the image was the only thing they looked for on his phone.

"I thought perhaps you might have turned it off. But I—"

"If you don't mind, John," he cut in, "perhaps we could do this in the morning." He wanted a shower, and then he wanted Samantha.

"Of course, Rick." Stillwell backed up the stairs as Richard ascended them behind him. Downstairs he heard Samantha set the alarm and then head down the hall toward the kitchen.

"I'm making a PBJ," she called. "You want one?"

He'd passed starving several hours ago. "Yes, please." He looked back up at his assistant again. "Was there something else?"

"Yes, actually." John stumbled on the top step and kept backing. "You probably remember that I was trying to set up a phone conference between you and Matsuo Hoshido."

Hell. The hotel. It *had* been a long day. "I'll give Matsuo a call tomorrow to apologize for putting him off. The—"

"That's the thing, Rick. He had the news on, as well. The attempted theft at the Metropolitan Museum, and then you at that storage warehouse with the FBI. He . . . pardon me, but he said you have balls. He'll be calling the Building

Commission in the morning and telling them to stop stalling you."

Rick stopped. "That is outstanding, John. Well done."

Stillwell smiled. "Thank you, sir. Rick. The same to you."

It seemed a rather straightforward example of what he was always telling Samantha—that strength gravitated toward strength. He'd helped engineer the recovery of his own stolen property, and once again he became a force not to be trifled with. "We'll go over the details in the morning."

"Of course, Rick. Good night."

Richard opened the master bedroom door, then stopped as he realized that John still wasn't moving. "What is it?"

Stillwell glanced in the direction of the stairs. "I, um, I want this job, Rick."

"You have it, John."

"Yes, but I think it's only fair . . . I mean, I want to be completely honest with you."

Richard stifled a yawn. "Unbelt, Stillwell."

"All right. I . . . overheard you and Miss Sam and that Stoney fellow the other night."

"I thought you might have."

"Why didn't you say anything?"

"Why didn't you?"

"Because I wanted to talk to you first. Going to the authorities behind your back and without my knowing all the facts, it's not the way I work."

And thank God for that. "I appreciate your candor. And I'll be up front with you. My household is unusual. If you remain in my employ, you will hear and see some things that are, how shall I say, out of the ordinary. And there will be things I won't tell you about them, whether you ask me or not."

Stillwell cleared his throat. "Will these . . . things have a similar outcome to what happened at the museum today?"

"More than likely."

"If that's the case, Rick, then I foresee no difficulties with our relationship." He gave a small smile. "Though I can't promise not to ask questions on occasion."

"Then welcome to the team." Richard offered his hand. Without hesitation, Stillwell shook it. "And in light of this, I have another task for you."

"Anything."

Rick stifled a smile. Youthful enthusiasm. "I would like a list of businesses owned by Boyden Locke. Mr. Locke is not to know about it."

"I'll look into it tomorrow."

"There will be more, later. For now, I'm going to bed."

"Yes, sir. Good night."

Finally Stillwell backed into his own room and closed the door. The lad did seem very honest, which could turn out to be a bit bothersome. Still, given that Samantha tended to break into the house at fairly regular intervals, he'd rather have honesty and a few questions than someone who might attempt blackmail.

Rick turned back to his own room—and stopped as he spotted Samantha standing at the top of the stairs, a napkin-wrapped sandwich in either hand and a bottle of water tucked under one arm, her gaze on him. Even after the day they'd just had, she still moved like a shadow.

"Hi," he said.

"Hi. Are you going to destroy Boyden Locke?"

"Yes."

"Cool." She handed him a sandwich, then slipped through the door in front of him.

Cool. That would probably be all she said about it. She had her way of doing things, and he had his. They made a bloody good team.

He closed and locked their door, and bit into his sandwich. Marmalade. She hated marmalade, so she'd obviously made two different sandwiches. "You are a goddess," he said.

She sat on the bed and pulled off her shoes. "That's me, Larcenius, goddess of thievery."

"I meant for the sandwich. Do you want the shower first?"

"We can share."

"Samantha, you could have gotten away from the museum with everything on the list today, couldn't you?"

Samantha eyed him. "Yes," she finally answered. "With a few extra days to plan, I probably could have doubled the take. If I were still a thief. And if I'd ever hit museums."

He didn't doubt any of what she said. Single-handedly she'd taken out three thieves, one of them her own father. And that had been with the FBI, Interpol, and NYPD all over the premises and expecting trouble. If she'd been concentrating on pulling a job rather than preventing one from occurring, nobody would have been able to stop her. "You do frighten me sometimes."

She flashed her quicksilver grin. "Good." Pulling off her top, she flopped backward on the bed. "Can I ask you something?"

He sat beside her. "Mm-hm."

"Did you mean to shoot Veittsreig in the ear, or did you miss?"

For a moment he considered what he wanted to tell her. "Did you ever see the movie *The Princess Bride*?"

"Yes. I always wanted to be the Dread Pirate Roberts."

Rick snorted. "Remember the fight at the end? Or the non-fight, I should say. Prince Humperdinck wants a fight to the death, but Westley wants a fight to the pain. He describes how badly he wants Humperdinck to suffer for what he's done to Buttercup. If I'd had more time, I would have taken off more than Veittsreig's ear, my love. And yes, I would have killed him. Eventually."

Samantha sat up beside him. Tangling her fingers into his hair, she leaned in and kissed him. "And I thought I was the only movie geek around here," she murmured, kissing him again, so thoroughly he could taste the strawberry jam from her own sandwich on her soft mouth.

"I'm trying to fit in," he returned, sinking backward with her in his arms. "Why didn't you tell me that you don't like doing security consultations?"

She stiffened a little, then relaxed again as he shifted his attention to removing her bra. "I don't hate it. Not all of it. I mean . . . Ah, that feels good."

"You mean what?" He glanced up at her, then went back to licking and nibbling at her breasts.

"Is this your version of . . . oh . . . of a truth serum or something?"

"Don't change the subject, Jellicoe."

She arched her back as he slid a hand down the front of her jeans. "Fine. It's my fault." Samantha twisted to unfasten his trousers. As he half closed his eyes, she reached in to wrap her fingers around his cock. "My previous . . . Christ, Rick . . . life was based on excitement."

"And you're not excited now?" He shifted aside her panties and slipped a finger up inside her.

"Sex now. Talk later," she rasped, shoving his trousers down to his thighs.

The power of speech was beginning to leave him, but he

made a last effort as he pulled off her jeans and panties and tossed them on the floor. "We will talk later. Promise?"

"Promise. Come on, Rick. I want you inside me."

Hooking one of her legs over his shoulder, he drew her up against him, pushing deep inside her. Samantha lolled back on the bed, gasping as he filled her. He moved slowly, savoring the sensation of her tight heat encasing him.

Heaving against her, he shifted her legs down around his hips again, putting her flat on her back. Samantha arched her neck, throwing her arms around his shoulders and moaning in time with his thrusts.

Five months together. Five months, and he still went hard whenever she kissed him. Five months, and he still couldn't get enough of her. "Sam," he grunted, "come for me. I can feel you. Come for me."

With a shudder, she did come, clinging hard to him. Lowering his head against her shoulder, he quickened his motions, their bodies melding into one. Finally he came, holding himself hard inside her.

Samantha rested her arms around his shoulders, her fingers playing with the ends of his hair and kissing the line of his jaw. "Most people don't get excited by their jobs, do they?" she said, making it more of a statement than a question.

"Most people *have* to work. You don't."

"Yes, I do. And security consultation is . . . fine. It's as close as I can get without breaking the law."

He rolled them, leaving him underneath, and her lying limply across his body. "I don't want you to have to settle. You're not a good . . . settler."

"That shows how much you know." Almost visibly gathering herself, she leaned down and kissed his mouth. "I really need a shower now. And so do you. Come on. We should be clean heroes. Setting a good example and everything."

"This hero is sleeping in tomorrow."

Samantha sat up, putting her hands on his chest as she looked down at him. Her wild auburn hair framed her face and shadowed her green eyes. "I love you," she said.

Richard smiled. "I love you."

He only hoped that that would be enough to keep her with him. It had worked for Westley and Buttercup, but then Buttercup hadn't been a former thief with a very great need for challenges.

"Shit."

Samantha nearly choked on her Diet Coke. Grabbing up the television remote, she turned up the sound.

"Rick!"

A few seconds later Rick emerged from his office and strode into the sitting room. "What's wr—"

"Look," she said, pointing at the television.

He sat beside her, emitting a rumbling sound that might have been either cursing or laughter. "You look very deadly," he said after a moment.

There on the news, large as life, she ran through a gallery in the Metropolitan Museum of Art. Seconds later, in increasingly shaky and smoke-filled footage, she yanked a woman out of the way and hit a remote to send one of the fire doors crashing down. "Damn tourists," she muttered, glaring at the "amateur video" disclaimer across the bottom of the screen.

At least she'd been wearing the wig. The news team could only speculate about the mystery woman, and of course comment about the involvement of billionaire Rick Addison and his live-in companion, Samantha Jellicoe, in the recovery of the two stolen paintings and the diamonds. Hopefully no one would equate "museum mystery woman" with her.

"The FBI's going to know that's me, especially when they can't track down the chick with blonde hair. And why am I always 'his live-in companion'?"

He lifted an eyebrow, then winced and touched the bandage that covered his stitches. "You're complaining about your billing?"

"No. It's just . . . Oh, what the hell do I care? I'm on damn television. Again." She tossed down the remote. "They can get pictures of me in the middle of a non-robbery, but they can't retrieve the video you took that implicated Locke."

"At least they're saying that the mysterious blonde woman aided in the capture of the thieves. They know you weren't part of the robbery attempt."

"I don't want them to be saying anything at all." Yesterday she'd thought Ripton pretty much had the white hats convinced that she wasn't good witness material. Now the news had footage of a blonde woman otherwise matching her description *inside* the museum.

Rick reached over for the phone. "I'll call Phil to give him a heads-up."

As he touched the thing, it rang. Samantha jumped, then had to laugh at herself. "Man, I need a vacation," she muttered.

He answered it. "Hello." His expression closed down, then became downright dour. "It's for you," he said, handing it over.

"Who?" she mouthed.

Rick crossed his forefingers over one another. Great. The Ex.

"Hey, Patricia," she said, scowling at him.

"I am going to assume," Rick's ex-wife said in her prim, tightly wound British accent, "that you meant to call me to say that you were wrong about Boyden Locke, and that you apologize for attempting to set me up with him."

"Okay." It sounded reasonable enough. "I meant to call you once I found out about Locke, and I'm sorry I tried to fix the two of you up." She paused. "Although Locke hasn't been implicated in anything yet, so I suppose that still puts him a notch or two above Peter and Daniel."

"That is not—" Patricia's shrill voice broke off. "He hasn't been, has he?"

Oh, good grief. "Patty, whether you ever take anything else I say seriously or not, right now I'm suggesting that you dump Locke."

"Humph. I can't wait to give you the same advice when Richard finally gets over his infatuation and relegates you to the same place he put me."

"Thanks for the words of wisdom," Samantha returned, refraining from telling Patty that Rick had hired help so he could spend more time with her.

"Yes, well, I'm extremely displeased with all of this."

"And I'm having breakfast. Goodbye, Patty."

"Patric—"

She hung up the phone and tossed it back to Rick. "Sorry if you wanted us to get along," she said.

Rick snorted. "I'll settle for the two of you staying very far apart, my love."

As he attempted to dial again, the front doorbell rang. Great. It was probably the FBI. Her heart beginning to accelerate, she bent over to retie her shoelaces. First the footage, then Patty, and now the front door. It could be a coincidence, but she wasn't willing to bet her freedom or her life on that.

"Are you going to answer the door?" Rick asked, putting his hand over the phone.

She stood. "I'm going out the back window. I'll call you from Delroy's, and you can tell me whether it's safe to come back or not."

"I'll call back," he said into the phone, and tossed it onto the couch. "Samantha, you're a good guy. Anybody who sees that couldn't think otherwise."

"Right. You may have the charter membership in my fan club, but I don't want to wear handcuffs again. Ever."

He stood, grabbing her arm as she reached the hallway. "Wait here," he said gruffly, as the bell rang again. "I'll get the door. You . . . go stand by the back window. If it's bad I'll say something about the Yankees."

For the moment she set aside the thought that if he helped her escape, he could very well be the one to end up in prison. He knew that as well as she did. So instead she gave him a swift kiss and ran into the master bedroom for the backpack she always kept close by—the one that contained everything she would need if she ever had to make a run for it.

Downstairs the front door opened, and she made out the mutter of male voices. Nobody was saying "Yankees," but she nevertheless pulled the hall table out from beneath the window and slipped the lock open.

"Samantha, could you come downstairs for a moment?" Rick called.

Okay, either it was safe, or it was very bad and he needed help. With a grimace she chucked the backpack under the hall table and headed for the stairs.

"We're in the sitting room."

Rick didn't sound worried, but then again it took more than a little trouble to bother him. Walking on the balls of her feet, still ready to move in any direction, she leaned into the doorway.

Phil Ripton sat on the couch, Rick in one of the chairs

opposite him. A third man, small and wiry and looking like he hadn't slept over the past day or so, sat beside the attorney.

Good. She could outrun these guys. "Hi, Phil," she said, stepping into plain view.

All three men stood, led of course by her Sir Galahad. "Phil's here on a bit of unofficial business," he said, gesturing her to join them.

Everybody sat again as she did. "Unofficial? What kind of unofficial?" she asked.

"Sam, this is Joseph Viscanti. Joseph, Samantha Jellicoe. Joseph is the—"

"The director of the Metropolitan Museum of Art," Samantha finished. Just great. If he wanted her to apologize for messing his building up a little, he could forget it. Officially she hadn't been there.

"Phil and I play tennis together," Viscanti said in the quiet, mild voice of a librarian. "And so I happened to know that he does some work with Addisco."

With great speed the conversation began a slide from worrisome to boring. "That's great," she said with a fake smile. "According to the news, you had quite a day yesterday, I would imagine."

"Yes, I did. Thankfully no one left the premises with anything, though we are going to have to make some repairs to the paintings that were sliced out of their frames."

"If I might ask, it seems like you have a lot of things to take care of. What are you doing here?"

Viscanti cleared his throat. If he wore glasses, she imagined he would be taking them off and cleaning them right now. "This is a bit awkward, but I'll be up front with you. Being in the business I'm in, I've heard things. I know of your reputation, Miss Jellicoe."

Rick shifted. "We all know that Samantha's father was a

cat burglar. That does not mean that she had anything to do with—"

"Oh, no, no. That's not why I'm here. I know that you're working as a security consultant, and that you've had a great deal of luck finding other people's lost artworks. I wondered whether you might be . . . interested in recovering a Renoir that was stolen eight months ago from our artifact storage area. We managed to keep it quiet, but our insurer determined that it was an inside job, and refused to pay."

For a bare moment Samantha felt as though she'd been struck by lightning. A retrieval. She'd heard of a few people who worked in the field, mostly on behalf of insurance companies. Not many, though, and not for long.

"As you said," Rick put in, his hard voice pulling her out of her reverie, "Samantha is a security consultant. She is not, and has never been, involved with breaking and entering. Not under any circum—"

"How much information do you have on the theft?" she interrupted, her voice shaking a little with anticipation she couldn't conceal. Christ. She felt like she'd just taken on a complicated B and E: the same shivers, the same deep, heavy rush of adrenaline.

"I have a two-inch-thick file I can messenger over to you if you're interested. The museum would be willing to pay eighty thousand dollars for the recovery of the painting." Viscanti's gaze shifted to Rick. "I'm not implying anything, Mr. Addison. This is merely an inquiry about whether Miss Jellicoe might be interested in assisting the museum or not."

"I'm interested."

"Saman—"

"If you could get that file to me sometime today, that would be great," she continued, rising. Rick's temperature was rising, too; she didn't have to look at him to know that. So she needed to get these guys out of here before he blew it for her.

"You'll have it this afternoon."

Both men and Rick climbed to their feet, and she led the way to the front door. "It was great to meet you, Mr. Viscanti. I'll let you know what I'll do."

"Thank you."

She closed the door behind them, then went back to sit on the couch. Retrieval. Hot damn.

"Sam."

Rick leaned against the doorframe, his dark blue gaze meeting hers. "What?"

"I don't like it."

She took a slow breath. "You don't like what, exactly?"

"You doing this job for Viscanti."

And just like that, he wanted to shoot her in the damn foot. The first cool thing that she'd found to do with herself in the legitimate world, and he'd decided after five minutes that he didn't like it. Pushing to her feet, she stalked up to him. "It's too bad it's not up to you, then, isn't—"

"Tell him no," he cut in flatly, his voice sharp and precise.

"No? Are you fucking nuts? I am not—"

"Sit down."

"I am *not* g—"

"Sit down!"

She folded her arms, glaring at him. He glared straight back at her, his expression, unlike hers probably was, unreadable. "Fine."

Stomping back to the chair, she sat. Her hands clenched into fists, and she hoped he would order her to do just one more thing.

He took the seat Viscanti had evacuated. "I'm not ordering you to do anything."

"Like I need your fucking permiss—"

"Will you shut up and let me say what I'm trying to say?"

"Sure," she returned sarcastically, sinking back in the chair. "Go ahead."

"Thank you." He took a breath, exhaling slowly. "I know you want to do this. You're practically panting at the thought of doing a burglary for a good cause."

Rick stopped, obviously waiting for her to interrupt, but she wasn't going to give him the satisfaction. He'd said he wanted to finish, and she would damn well let him. Then she would let him know *exactly* what she was thinking.

"I just want you to think about it for a minute," he finally continued. "I don't doubt that you're skilled enough and smart enough to do this, and to be successful. But if you recover the Renoir, word will get out. To other museums, to people who've been robbed, *and* to the people who did the robbing." He sat forward, touching her knee with his fingers. "You're the one who said you weren't certain how you would feel, crossing your old associates. For you, security consultation is kind of a way around that. It's—"

"It's me putting up a 'No Trespassing' sign," she agreed reluctantly. "If they cross it and get caught, it's their own fault."

He was right; going in and stealing from thieves was a much more direct confrontation. It would mean she had to decide where she stood, once and for all. And Rick had realized that, even if she'd been so excited at the thought of a B and E that she hadn't.

"Wow," she said quietly. "This is big."

"Yes, it is."

Samantha looked at his handsome, concerned face for a long moment. If she took this job, her old B and E associates would know about it. Maybe she'd be offered more of them, and maybe she wouldn't. That part wouldn't matter, though, because if she did it once, she would never be able to go back. None of her old associates would ever trust her or work with her again.

"If I did this, it could get dangerous."

Rick nodded. "Your life at the moment isn't precisely what I would call boring."

"I didn't mean just for me."

"I realize that."

"So you would be okay with it."

"It's not up to me."

"But you would be okay with it," she repeated.

"I would be worried, but yes, I would be okay with it. The question is, however, would you be okay with it?"

"Yes. I think I would."

"You 'think' you would."

She closed her eyes, waiting to feel uncertainty, or dread at the thought of being trapped into this life. It didn't come. Samantha opened her eyes again. "I know I would like to do this," she said quietly.

"That's what I wanted you to be certain of," Rick said, sliding out of his chair to kneel at her feet. "Because I think you would be a smashing white hat."

Samantha leaped forward, swept her arms around him, and gave him a very sound kiss. "You totally rock."

"Yes, I know."

Epilogue

Tuesday, 2:21 p.m.

"But we would still be in the security consultation business," Aubrey Pendleton said, sitting at the reception desk of Jellicoe Security in Palm Beach, Florida.

"That would still be the majority of our work, at least to begin with," Samantha returned, sipping at her can of Diet Coke. "Stuff with the kind of value that museums and owners would be willing to shell out big money to get back won't come around every day. Top-ticket items don't get stolen every day." She shrugged. "We may not get any other jobs like this one, at all. But I want you to be ready for them, if we do."

Aubrey smiled his charming, Southern smile. "This is quite exciting, Miss Samantha. We'd be kind of like Robin Hoods."

"Like hoods, anyway," Stoney said more skeptically from his seat in the reception lounge.

"I'm not asking for a vote." Samantha turned to face him. "But if you don't like it, don't mess around with being sarcastic. Just tell me."

"I'm just wondering what you're going to do if this *does* work out, and you get a call from some guy missing a Mayan crystal skull or something. Do you take that job?"

She knew what he meant. The crystal skull had been one of her jobs. She'd stolen it, and if she took it back from the person who'd bought it from her and Stoney, she'd pick up a shitload of enemies in addition to her generally disgruntled former associates.

"I guess we take that as it comes," she said. "A case-by-case decision."

"And Addison is backing you up on this."

"Yes, he is," Rick's polished British accent came from the doorway. He walked into the reception area, closing the door behind him. "I have the feeling it's either this or buying her a cannon to be shot out of."

She smirked at him. "And you're here because . . ."

"Tom's bringing his car around to take me to lunch. I came to invite you."

"No, thanks. Having an office across the street from Donner is bad enough. I'm not going to eat with him any more often than I have to."

"Okay." He walked over and kissed her softly on the mouth. "I'll see you later, then."

"Okay."

The office phone rang, and Aubrey picked it up. "Jellicoe Security. Good afternoon." He paused. "Just a moment." Hitting the hold button, he looked up at her. "I have a John Robie on the phone for you, Miss Samantha."

Her heart stopped beating. Stoney had lurched to his feet,

but he would recognize the code name. "Put it through to my office," she said.

"Samantha?"

Rick stood in the reception doorway, from his expression realizing that something was wrong. "Do you have a minute?" she asked.

He closed the door again and gestured for her to lead the way. "Of course."

In her office, she hit the speakerphone button. "I still think John Robie's a little obvious, Martin."

Slowly Rick sank into the seat facing her desk.

"Maybe, but it's got style," her father's voice came, echoing a little in the room. "You have me on speaker. Why? Who else is in there with you?"

"Rick."

"Pick up the phone, Sam. This is family business. Private."

"Rick's family. And you're not playing me again. What do you want?"

"You did me something of a favor, I guess," he said after a moment. "Interpol's satisfied, anyway. But the next time you try to pull one over on me, I'm not going to be very happy."

"Allow me to give you the same warning."

"That was just another lesson for you, Sam. I did teach you everything you know."

"No, you taught me everything *you* know."

He chuckled. "That's what you think. Addison, keep your eye on her. She's pretty clever."

"That's what I love about her," Rick put in coolly.

"I think you should know, Martin, that I'm going to be working with the Met Museum to recover some paintings stolen by somebody who actually got away with it." It probably wasn't wise to taunt him, but his plan might very well have gotten her killed.

"That's a damn foolish thing to do. I was going to suggest that my wasting my whole clean slate on the straight life would be a shame. We could work together again, like old times."

She felt Rick's gaze on her, but kept her own eyes on the phone. "I don't want old times, Martin. I want new ones. You just might want to avoid doing anything that could put the two of us in direct conflict."

"The only thing I can guarantee, Sam, is that you're Daddy's girl. Walking the straight and narrow might be fun for a while, but in the long run, it's not in your blood. You'll figure that out, soon enough."

The phone clicked dead.

"He's wrong, you know." Rick stood and moved to her side of the desk, squatting at her side.

She looked down at him. "I'm glad one of us is sure about that." Samantha cleared her throat. "I mean, hell, if I'd made a deal with Interpol, I could be retired with a whole new identity, and a whole new opportunity to make bad. I could be blonde, even."

"Will you stop with that? I like auburn hair. I like your hair." He paused. "And I trust you," he said more quietly. "Speaking of retirement, though, what kind of plan does this new business venture of yours offer?"

Samantha flashed him a smile. "It doesn't matter, because I have a rich guy on the hook." She slid out of the chair onto the floor and kissed him.

A rich guy, and an exciting new chapter of her life beginning. Hell, what could go wrong with hiring a former thief to recover stolen works of art?

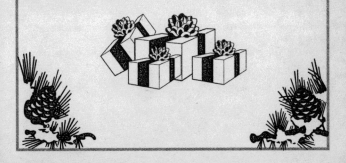

Avon presents . . .

Something Sinful

by Suzanne Enoch
(September 2006)

Lord Charlemagne "Shay" Griffin excels at everything he puts his mind to, especially when it comes to business—which is why he never expected the alluring Lady Sarala Carlisle to best him at a business transaction! Sarala sees herself as an equal to any man, and she just couldn't resist the chance to put the arrogant lord in his place. But Shay is not one to admit defeat and launches a plan of seduction against Sarala.

By the time Shay reached Carlisle House his brain had begun to sort things out rationally, and he was able to resist the urge to pound on the door and smash the pots of ferns on the front portico. The chit obviously ran wild, so he wouldn't deal with her. Business was business, and business was for men.

A large, gray-clothed man opened the door. "Yes?"

"Charlemagne Griffin, here to see Lord Hanover."

The butler blinked. Someone in the household knew him by name, at least. He stepped back, gesturing Charlemagne to follow him inside. "If you'll wait in the morning room, I shall fetch him."

The morning room was small, tasteful, and, unless he was

mistaken, smelled of cinnamon. The scent forcibly reminded him of the chit who'd bested him. And considering what she'd been doing with him in his dreams, it almost felt like a double loss on his part. And he didn't like to lose.

Before the butler could finish closing him into the room, he heard a rush of footsteps and a hurried, muttered conversation. A second later the door swung open again, and the lady herself practically skidded into the room. She wore a frilled dressing gown, one sleeve hanging to reveal a tantalizing view of smooth collarbone and shoulder. That black hair was everywhere, half up and tumbled down, caressing her cheek and sagging into an unfinished knot at the back.

The angry comment Charlemagne had been about to make vanished back into his throat, making him cough a little. Glory.

Belatedly she tugged up her sleeve. "Lord Charlemagne."

Mentally he shook himself. *Business, man. Business.* "You stole my silks."

"I did no such thing. You informed me of a potentially lucrative business opportunity, and I acted on that information."

He narrowed his eyes. "I discussed my business with you because I was under the impression that you were an admirer—not a rival."

She snorted. "Then you made two mistakes."

Charlemagne took a step closer. "Where's your father? I came to speak with him, to discuss the return of my property in a rational manner."

Lady Sarala gave what might have been a brief frown, then lifted her chin. "This is *my* affair, and you will discuss it with me, or not at all."

Good God, she had some nerve. And her sleeve had sagged again, so that he could see the pulse at her throat and the quick lift of her breast. "Then return my property," he said, returning his gaze to her soft mouth.

"It's not your property. But for a price, I will let you have every stitch."

He knew he shouldn't ask, but he couldn't stop himself. "What price, then?"

"Five thousand pounds."

His jaw fell open, then clamped shut. "*Five thousand pounds?* So you would steal from me and then overcharge me to recover my own goods?"

She looked him right in the eye. "Once again, I did not steal anything from you, or from anyone else. Make me a counter offer, or bid me good day and leave."

Incredulous, he shook his head. "This is ridiculous. Where's the liquor?"

"Over there." Lady Sarala pointed toward the cabinet beneath the window.

Her fingers shook, and he grabbed her hand, pulling her up against him. "You're not frightened of me, are you?" he murmured.

"Is that your intent? I'd heard you were a fearsome opponent, but you seem to be harping on one point of contention, which does neither of us any good. Make me a counter offer, my lord."

He lowered his head and kissed her upturned mouth. Sensation flooded through him, all the way to his cock. He didn't know how to describe what she tasted like—sunshine, warm summer breezes, heat, desire.

When she began to kiss him back, he forced himself to lift his face away again. "How was that?" he drawled.

Sarala cleared her throat, belatedly recovering her hand and backing away. "Fair. But hardly worth five thousand pounds."

Avon presents . . .

Angel In a Red Dress

by Judith Ivory
(October 2006)

As a special treat, we're re-issuing the wonderful classic, originally titled *Starlit Surrender,* with a beautiful new package and title . . . Golden-haired innocent Christina Bower is totally captivated by the Earl of Kewischesteran, a lethally charming rake whose touch alone can melt her heart.

Adrien led the way deeper into the garden, perfectly polite.

Christina felt a fool. He wasn't disapproving or making harsh judgments of her. A gentleman, she realized as she followed him. Whatever else he was, he was that. Not a sham, no deceit, genuinely upper class. Like the sound of his voice. She envied his speech. It had taken her so long, and several girls' schools, to achieve something similar.

They went around the last bend in the path, and there stood a little house made of nothing but glass. "What—" She halted.

He held the door open. "The roses are toward the back."

He motioned, then guided, putting her in front of him. His hand touched lightly at her back. She had to quell a little shiver.

The greenhouse was not particularly small, but it was

crowded with plants. Orange trees bloomed. Lemons. Pineapples. And at the rear, a wall of roses. Beautiful, peach-colored blooms. He pointed to them.

"Oh," she said. "They're lovely!"

He moved around her, brushing her shoulder as he passed. She was more aware of him—of his body, its solidness and peculiar grace—in the crowded quarters. As he bent toward her, his chest came up against her arm and breast, and he murmured an apology. As if this were perfectly excusable. He picked up some shears from the workbench.

One, two, three . . . a dozen. Methodically, he cut the flowers. When he offered them to her, she didn't know what to say. His smile, his pleasant friendliness, his sharp features were so magnetic. She damned all handsome men as she stood in a cloud of confusion. After a moment, she reached out. Then stupidly, promptly, dropped the roses onto the floor.

"Ow—" Blood oozed from the tip of her middle finger.

His hand wrapped around hers. He took her finger into his mouth.

She was stunned.

His mouth was warm. She could feel the gentle pressure, a drawing of his teeth and tongue. It took her much too long to retrieve her hand.

"Sir," she reprimanded softly. She looked away.

He bent to pick up the flowers at her feet. And the little glass house began to feel close. Where he squatted, he aligned the flowers—six, seven eight . . . Christina flattened her hands into her skirt to hold it back, to avoid stepping on his fingers. She tried to take a step back, but a low shelf caught her, pressing into her bottom. It was strange, but this was somehow alarming. She felt agitated, fidgety. She looked at her finger. It had begun to throb lightly. There was a pinprick of blood.

He stood, the bundle of roses in his hand, and reached above her—his chest against her face. The smell of him again. Soap, tobacco, leather. Was he doing this on purpose?

Christina felt suffocated by him. She held her breath rather than breathe in his warmth, his humidity. She raised her hands. Lightly against his chest. Not knowing how to push him back without touching him. Then, on his own, he moved back. As if it were nothing. As if she weren't there. She was nonplussed, a woman left in midair. She couldn't look at him. Yet, in nervous glances, couldn't stop keeping track . . .

He wrapped a piece of paper about the stems of the roses, then set the tidied parcel on the workbench and took another step back. He rested an elbow on the upper shelf and looked at her. There was a faint, ironic smile on his lips.

"I've frightened you," he said.

She was quick to shake her head. "Oh, no—"

He laughed. "Oh, yes. I'm sorry. I didn't mean to." He reached and caught her hand again.

She was half flustered, half piqued at the apology followed by the same trick. She flinched as he turned her hand over and studied it. Her hand was clammy. It shook slightly. His was steady, smooth.

He let go. She huffed a wounded breath and pressed her palm to her chest.

"It will be all right," he said. He cocked his head to the side. "The cut, I mean." As if he could have meant something else. "And I am sorry for the moment ago. Only your finger just suddenly looked—" He shrugged, smiled. "It's what I do with mine. Honestly." His smile broadened, a flash of white teeth as brilliant as a bolt of electricity through a dark sky.

Christina blushed, turned her head away. She caught sight of the door at the far end, down that corridor of plants. She really must leave, she thought.

Then she heard him laughing. "If you make a break for it, I'll drop you to the ground flat out. Wrestling team, you know, all the way through university. I'm a smash as a takedown."

Her eyes went wide to him.

His soft laughter again. "Sorry." He made a self-conscious apology with his shoulders. "Only pulling your leg. You look so bloody green." More soberly, "But I'm just a little insulted. What you must be thinking."

"I wasn't thinking anything."

"Only that I'd as soon ravish you as look at you. Which is not true. I find looking at you exceptionally pleasant." He paused. "Why did you come out here with me if I frighten you so?"

No answer. Though it remained a very good question.

Avon presents . . .

Billionaires Prefer Blondes

by Suzanne Enoch
(November 2006)

Former thief Samantha Jellicoe is enjoying her new legitimate career and her romance with billionaire Richard Addison. Then she spies someone she'd thought dead—her father, Martin Jellicoe—and she knows he's up to no good. Her worst fears come true when a new painting that Rick purchased goes missing and her father is under suspicion. Rick and Samantha's relationship will be tested like never before.

"Samantha?"

Damn. She looked back up to the head of the stairs to see him gazing toward the far window with its missing pane. He had good vision, but hell, not that good. "Yes, Rick?" she said, echoing his tone again. *Never give anything away.* That was one of the thieves' rules as quoted to her by her dad on a regular basis, until Martin had ended up in prison and then dead just over three years ago.

"There are a dozen coats and two briefcases in the entryway," Rick was saying. "How did you pass them by without realizing I was here with company?"

"I was distracted. Have fun with your minions."

"And why would you walk through the front door and up the stairs with a dress wadded up under your blouse?"

"My hands were full."

"With that missing window pane up here, by any chance?" He descended the stairs again. "You broke into the house."

"Maybe," she hedged, backing down to the first floor. "What if I just forgot my key?"

Rick joined her at the foot of the stairs. "You might have knocked at the front door. Wilder is here, and so is Vilseau," he said, tilting his head at her, his eyes growing cool.

He hated having her try to pull one on him, whatever the circumstances. Samantha blew out her breath. At least she knew when to give up. "Okay, okay. Boyden Locke talked to my boobs for forty minutes while I sold him on some security upgrades for his townhouse. And then I went shopping for the dress, and I just kept noticing . . . things."

"What things?"

"Cameras, alarm systems. Everything. It was making me crazy. Plus we're going to an art auction tonight, at Sotheby's, no less, I was just feeling a little . . . tense. So I decided to subvert my bad self by busting in somewhere. I picked a safe place."

"And I caught you again." He reached out, curling a strand of her auburn hair around his fingers. "The last time I did that, we broke a chair afterwards, as I recall."

Technically, this time he'd caught her well after the fact and only because of a huge mistake on her part, but as the raw, hungry shiver traveled down her backbone she wasn't about to contradict him. She drew her free hand around the back of his neck and leaned in to give him a deep, soft kiss. "So you want another reward, I suppose?"

He nuzzled against her ear. "Definitely," he whispered.

She was going to explode. "Why don't you get rid of your minions, then, and I'll reward you right now?"

Rick's muscles shuddered against her. "Stop tempting me."

"But I broke into your big old house. Don't you—"

He pushed her back against the mahogany bannister, nearly sending them both over it as he took her mouth in a hard, hot kiss.

Ah, this was more like it.

Avon presents . . .

Must Love Mistletoe

by Christie Ridgway
(December 2006)

When her feuding parents cause the family business, The Perfect Christmas, to flounder, self-admitted "Scrooge" Bailey Sullivan returns to resort town Coronado, California, to try and salvage something. She plans to stay from December 1 to 25—but even that seems too long when she discovers that Finn, the bad boy next door she loved a decade ago, is also home for the holidays. Still, no matter how magical her love for Finn had once felt or now feels again, Bailey's certain that no love lasts. Or can it?

The summer Bailey was fourteen she cajoled Finn to the beach with her every afternoon. His kiss one July day—her first. She hadn't known to open her mouth for his tongue, and her skin had heated like sunburn when he whispered the instruction. Then his tongue had touched the tip of hers and he'd tasted like pretzels and Pepsi and saltwater. Going dizzy, she'd clutched his bare shoulder, her fingertips grazing across gritty, golden sand sprinkled on his damp, tanned flesh.

Two years after that, the darkness of her backyard and the ghostly glow of the soccerball-sized hydrangeas. The fresh scent of night-blooming jasmine. The flinch of her stomach as his bony boy fingers touched her belly skin on their first, bold approach to her breast. The instant pebbling of her nipple beneath her neon bikini top and her naive, desperate hope he wouldn't notice.

He had.

"Something wrong?" he asked now.

He'd always paid such close attention.

She tossed her hair back and crossed her arms. "Nothing access to my car won't fix right up."

"Give me a sec."

She let herself watch him stride off, his long legs so familiar, the wide plane of his back and his heavy-muscled shoulders so not. What had he done to earn that beefcake physique? What had he done with his life? What had happened to his eye?

He'd been such a bad boy.

Her bad boy.

But the bad boy had grown into a one-eyed stranger who was already back with a hammer and who didn't appear interested in talk.

Or interested in her.

So she clamped her mouth shut, too, and watched him move away the big crate.

She then ducked into her car, turned the key, and slipped it into reverse.

Not putting voice to her questions, though, for Finn didn't make them disappear. Just as wishing her memories of him to a cobwebbed shelf in the back corner of her brain didn't immediately send them there, either.

But the fact that he didn't appear the least bit affected by her presence—or their past—should make the banishments not far off. Just, say, five minutes away.

Before that could happen, though, a knock on her driver's door window made her jump. The one-eyed pirate who was moments from being out of her mind forever was giving her another expressionless look from his one dark eye.

Bailey unrolled the window, trying to appear as if she'd already forgotten who he was and what they'd once meant to each other.

It certainly appeared as if *he* had.

"Yes?" she asked. "Did you want something?"

"Just checking."

She frowned at him. "Checking for what?"

"That you're still into skipping good-byes." And then he turned, leaving without another word.

Sinfully sensuous romantic delights from
New York Times bestselling author

SUZANNE ENOCH

Don't Look Down

0-06-059364-4/$6.99 US/$9.99 Can

When the first client of her new security business is murdered, former thief Samantha Jellicoe is determined to find the killer. If she can keep her significant other, billionaire Rick Addison from sticking his nose in her business, she just might manage to stay alive.

An Invitation To Sin

0-06-054327-2/$6.99 US/$9.99 Can

Lord Zachary Griffin believes leading Caroline Witfeld, the most spirited and least frivolous of seven marriageable sisters, to temptation would be wildly delicious. But Caroline has other plans.

Lady Rogue

0-06-087524-0/$6.99 US/$9.99 Can

Christine "Kit" Brantley is masquerading as a boy because her mission was to spy on Alexander Cale, the Earl of Everton, but it doesn't take long for him to see through her disguise. Alex is determined to discover the real reason Kit is in London.

Something Sinful

0-06-084255-5/$6.99 US/$9.99 Can

Lady Sarala Carlisle may appear naive, but too late, Shay realizes her unconventional beauty masks a razor-sharp intelligence.